H...
JOVE ...

We at Jove Books are thrilled by the enthusiastic critical acclaim that the Homespun Romances are receiving. We would like to thank you, the readers and fans of this wonderful series, for making it the success that it is. It is our pleasure to bring you the highest quality of romance writing in these breathtaking tales of love and family in the heartland of America.

And now, sit back and enjoy this delightful new Homespun Romance . . .

BLACKBERRY WINTER
by Sherrie Eddington

Blackberry Winter

Sherrie Eddington

JOVE BOOKS, NEW YORK

BLACKBERRY WINTER

A Jove Book / published by arrangement with
the author

PRINTING HISTORY
Jove edition / September 1997

The Putnam Berkley World Wide Web site address is
http://www.berkley.com

ISBN: 0-515-12146-0

A JOVE BOOK®
Jove Books are published by The Berkley Publishing Group,
200 Madison Avenue, New York, New York 10016,
a member of Penguin Putnam Inc.
JOVE and the "J" design are trademarks
belonging to Jove Publications, Inc.

PRINTED IN THE UNITED STATES OF AMERICA

10 9 8 7 6 5 4 3 2 1

Since I was thirteen, I knew I wanted to share the wonderful stories inside my head with the world. Now my dream has come true.

I want to thank my best friend of twenty-three years, Donna Smith McGuirk, who shared my dream and never stopped believing in me. I look forward to an exciting future with you as my partner.

I dedicate this first novel to my own special sheriff, my grandfather, Herbert Davidson. Grandpa, you are the smartest of us all, you read books for the story, not for the genre. Thanks for not being surprised about my success. You always have been and always will be my hero. Grandpa, this book is for you.

Thanks to my kids, Desha and Davis, who fed my dreams with their casual acceptance that their mom is a writer and would someday realize her dream. I love you both more than life itself. Never forget that if you believe in yourself enough, your dreams will come true.

I also want to thank my friend and reader, Karen Harmon, for her unstinting support, and everyone in Kennett, Missouri, who never doubted I would succeed. You know who you are.

Thanks to the wonderful man in my life, Gene Kelly; thanks for not complaining about the tap-tap of the keyboard into the wee hours while you slept, and for your confident belief in me.

Thanks to my mother, Helen Johnson, for encouraging me when I was down; and to my brothers and sisters, Pat, Debbie, Mark, Jeff, and Randy for always believing—I love you all.

A heartfelt thanks to Jean Price and Dee Pace, for their amazing patience and confidence in me, and to Jennifer Lata, a wonderful editor who opened the door and invited me in.

Special thanks to the River City Romance Writers for their enthusiasm and support, and to my Romex friends for sharing their helpful advice and listening to me, especially Rachelle Nelson, my very own "godmother."

In loving memory of my stepfather,
William Lee Brannum.
I know you are looking down from above,
watching and smiling.
We miss you.

Blackberry Winter

Prologue

CALLAWAY COUNTY
SHADOW CITY, MISSOURI
1876

LACY PLACED HER palm against the cold windowpane, marveling at how quickly the weather could change. Yesterday, it had been warm and humid, with rain showers around suppertime. Normal weather for May.

Blackberry winter, Grandpa had told her when she'd raced downstairs to breakfast in the early-morning chill. It was a time when the blackberries that thrived along the fencerow in the backyard bloomed with beautiful white flowers.

Grandma had said it would last only a few days; then warmth and sunshine would return and she could once again shuck the heavy shoes and run barefoot through the grass.

Grandma's voice drifted up the stairs. Lacy sighed and dropped her palm from the window. Just a few days. . . .

Gently, she laid the porcelain doll on the bed and covered its lumpy cloth body with a miniature patchwork quilt. She put a finger to her lips and spoke to the doll. "You sleep now, you hear? I'll be back soon as I see what Grandma wants." She raced out of the room and downstairs in search of her grandmother.

Lacy found her in the warm, fragrant kitchen preparing the evening meal. When her grandmother spotted her in the doorway, she grabbed a cloth-covered plate from the stovetop and handed it to Lacy. "Take this to Sheriff Murddock and be careful you don't spill it." She sighed and pushed a damp wisp of hair from her brow. "Don't know where your grandpa is. He's been full of himself ever since the sheriff gave him that deputy star. But I've got a pie in the oven and I can't leave it."

"I'll be careful, Grandma. Don't you worry," Lacy declared, proud that Grandma trusted her. "I'm nine years old now, you know."

Her grandmother smiled. "Yes, you are. And a beauty you're going to be, too." She reached out and smoothed a loving hand along one shiny blond braid. "Just like your mama was. Now, get along with you, but walk, don't run. The sheriff's probably hungry as a bear by now, and if your grandpa don't get here soon, he's gonna be eatin' his supper on the back porch steps."

Lacy giggled, knowing her grandmother was only teasing. Holding the plate as if it were a basket of eggs, she walked slowly from the house out into the chilly air. The jail was across the street and four buildings down, not far at all. She'd often helped Grandma, but she'd never been trusted to go alone.

Grandma was nice to cook for the sheriff every day— breakfast and supper—because he didn't have a wife to cook for him. Lacy knew he tried to pay Grandma, but she wouldn't take his money. If it weren't for Colt Murddock, Shadow City wouldn't be a town, Grandma said.

Lacy stepped around a mudhole left from the rain showers of last evening, and the plate in her hands wobbled precariously. She caught her breath, gripping the plate tighter before moving on, her thoughts on the town's history, which had been taught to her from the time she could understand.

Sheriff Murddock had started the town, made sure it was a peaceful place for decent folk to live and raise their families. He was the town hero. Nobody ever got shot in Shadow City because he didn't allow anyone to carry a gun. Why, even a fistfight warranted a night in jail.

Of course, Grandpa said that wasn't really a punishment, because anyone who got put in jail also got to eat Grandma's cooking. Lacy grinned to herself, remembering how Grandma had blushed when Grandpa had said that.

She passed the blacksmith's, then the small general store. Several of the townspeople she encountered greeted her by name. There were a few she didn't recognize, but all were wearing heavier clothing against the cold. Lacy nodded, her chin high with pride.

When she drew abreast of the telegraph office, Mr. Hyatt waved at her through the window and she paused to wiggle her fingers at him. Someone brushed her elbow and Lacy juggled the plate once again, breathing a sigh of relief when she safely recaptured it. She turned and frowned at the retreating figure.

Finally she reached her destination. Stepping onto the boardwalk in front of the jail, she carefully balanced the plate on one palm and rapped politely on the door. After several seconds she opened the door, then caught the plate securely again with both hands before going in.

"Sheriff Murddock? It's Lacy, with your supper. Grandma sent me 'cause Grandpa ain't home yet and she couldn't leave the pie." She paused to draw a breath, then added earnestly, "But don't you worry none, I didn't spill a drop."

Silence greeted her explanation. The office was dim, and Lacy frowned, looking around for the lamp. Her puzzled eyes landed on the sheriff's desk. There sat the lamp, cold as could be. Didn't he realize it was getting dark outside? Well, she'd just have to light it for him, she decided, setting the plate down. The sheriff couldn't eat his food in the dark, now could he?

Lacy found the matches in the top drawer, struck one, and held it over the wick. The flame caught and soft light chased the shadows into the far corners of the room. She sighed in satisfaction and perched her hands on her thin hips, her gaze automatically seeking the sheriff, thinking he might be taking what Grandpa called a "little shut-eye."

A large jail cell, furnished with two cots, a bucket, a small mirror, a wash pan, and a chair, took up one half of the room. Lacy moved closer to the cell, peering into the shadows where the light didn't quite reach, at the darker shadow wavering there.

"Sheriff Murddock? Is that you?" she called, beginning to feel a little frightened. Whoever it was, he wasn't answering her.

She didn't think the sheriff had any prisoners at the moment, or at least that's what Grandpa had said when he'd taken his noon break with her and Grandma. So the person moving in the cell had to be the sheriff, didn't he? He sure was tall, though, and she didn't remember Sheriff Murddock being *that* tall.

Something funny fluttered in her stomach.

She backed away until her rump met the desk. Reaching around, she fumbled for the wire handle on the lamp, grabbed it, and brought the light around in front of her. She didn't think she wanted to get closer again.

The lamplight spread swiftly into the cell, illuminating the murky interior. Lacy smothered a scream with the back of her hand.

It was the sheriff all right, and now she understood why he didn't answer.

1

CALLAWAY COUNTY
SHADOW CITY, MISSOURI
1891

*B*EN LEAPED ONTO the porch and slammed his shoulder against the door, tearing at the knob with frantic hands. Tears formed muddy rivulets on his dusty face. A fat drop gathered dirt along the way, then hovered on the edge of his chin before tracking a muddy path down his neck. It tickled, but he made no move to wipe it away.

There wasn't time.

As the door gave way, he looked over his shoulder. A moan gurgled in his throat and panic widened his eyes, giving him a stark, terrified look.

Once across the threshold, he skidded to a halt, spun around, and raced back, shutting the door against the bright afternoon sun and the man striding purposefully up the walk. For several frustrated seconds, he glared at the little-used, heavy bolt inches beyond his reach. He swallowed hard, then turned to put as much distance as possible between himself and certain death.

Gathering breath as he ran, he began to scream at the top of his lungs, "He's after me, he's after me! Don't let him get me, Lacy!"

This time, maybe the first time ever, his terror was beyond control.

Hearing his shrill cry, Lacy emerged from the kitchen just in time to catch him by the shoulders as he thundered past. "Whoa there, Ben. Slow down before you break somethin'. What's all this screamin' about?"

The sudden stop nearly sent his feet flying out from under him. He scrambled to keep from falling backward, arms flailing in the air, his boots slipping on the waxed hardwood floor. Finally, he planted his feet, gulped, and pleaded, "Hide me somewheres, Lacy. You gotta hide me!"

Lacy turned him and frowned down at his terrified face. Dark purple stains circled his mouth and mapped a path down his chin, blending with the tears and dirt. He looked like a raccoon—a very guilty raccoon.

Her eyes narrowed in sudden comprehension. "Have you been stealin' food again?" That stain on his mouth looked suspiciously like blackberry juice, and she had made a blackberry pie this morning. But she had sold that pie to Ellen, who owned Shadow City's only restaurant. . . . Lacy closed her eyes and silently counted to ten. *Thunder!* Why hadn't he taken the pie *before* she had delivered it to Ellen?

Ben sniffed and stared at his dusty boots. "Weren't stealin' nuthin'. He—he claims I did, but I weren't!" He craned his neck around her to look in the direction of the door, his face screwed into an anxious mask.

"*Wasn't.* The word is *wasn't*, Ben. And that's not the whole truth, is it?" She straightened and sighed, but kept a restraining hand on his shoulder. No matter how much she fed him, no matter how much she assured him there was always more where that came from, she couldn't seem to convince him. Most of the townsfolk understood and rarely kicked up a fuss, other than to let her know about the theft. However, they did expect payment.

They both jumped as someone pounded on the door with enough force to make the wood shudder and the hinges creak. Lacy lifted an eyebrow. Someone sounded more than a little annoyed, she thought, just before she realized Ben had said "he," instead of "she," which meant that Ellen wasn't the one. . . .

"Benjamin, just who is chasing you *this* time?" Complaints about Ben were almost an everyday occurrence, and she was at her wit's end as to how to correct the problem. She would have to do something, and soon, by the sound of it.

Ben's small frame trembled beneath her hands. "He's— he's got a *gun,* Lacy! A real six-shooter, I seen it myself!"

His tears threatened to overflow again, and Lacy stared at them, trying to recall a time when she'd seen Ben cry. She couldn't remember a single instance.

"He said he was—was going to shoot me with it," Ben finished in a strangled whisper.

Lacy felt the first stirrings of genuine alarm. Unconsciously, her fingers tightened on Ben's shoulder until he whimpered a protest. Nobody but the sheriff carried a gun, and Shadow City didn't have a gun-toting sheriff at the moment, thanks to that lying, rumor-spreading mayor of theirs. Her mouth tightened at the reminder.

The door thundered again and Lacy imagined—at least, she *hoped* it was her imagination—that she heard wood splintering. Her heart skipped a beat and she gave herself a stern mental shake—this was Shadow City, for crying out loud, and the Wild West was nothing more than Buffalo Bill Cody's traveling show in a covered wagon. Still, she supposed there were a few unsavory types out there that might not know how unpopular violence had become. Or care.

Striving to keep the uncertainty from her voice, she asked, "Are you certain he has a gun, Ben? Absolutely certain?"

Ben's head nodded vigorously. "Abs'lutely certain." He

gulped on a sob, wiping his nose against a dirty sleeve. "He showed it to me. That's when I took off runnin'." The memory set him off again. This time he buried his face in her apron and sobbed, "Don't let him shoot me, Lacy! Please don't let him shoot me. I promise to be good from now on. I'll never steal another pie, I swear it!"

Her heart constricted at the sound of his cries. Through her apron and the thick folds of her gingham dress, she felt Ben's small hands clutch at her in desperation as he sought to grab hold of the one steady anchor in his life.

Ben was depending on her to save him, to protect him.

That decided it. Whoever it was, Lacy thought with mounting anger, he should be ashamed for frightening a helpless little boy. Ashamed *and* apologetic.

"You stay put," she ordered firmly, releasing him. "Nobody's going to shoot you."

Ben obeyed, trembling and darting apprehensive glances at the shuddering door. He looked ready to bolt any second. With the pitiful sight spurring her on, Lacy marched to the fireplace mantel and removed her grandfather's shotgun from the hanger. It hadn't been used in ages, she knew, and she didn't think it was loaded, which suited her purpose just fine. She just wanted to teach the man a lesson. Maybe he'd understand what it felt like to stand in Ben's shoes when he faced the other end of this shotgun. Threatening a defenseless little boy! . . .

Hoisting the heavy gun onto her shoulder, Lacy squinted along the barrel and called, "Come in," in a voice sweet enough to charm a snake—which is what she figured he was.

Ben dived behind the sofa before the door could open, but that didn't last long. Before the moment was up, his curiosity got the better of him and he crawled to the end of the sofa until he could see both the door and Lacy. He whimpered once, then clamped his lips shut with a blackberry-stained hand.

The door swung open, slamming against the wall and sending the coatrack crashing to the floor. Lacy steadied herself, lowering the gun a fraction in order to see the man who had frightened Ben out of his mind. She refused to acknowledge that he frightened *her*. He was just a bully, nothing more, she assured herself. *But a gun-totin' bully,* a cautious voice whispered.

The man's expression registered only a flicker of surprise at the sight of Lacy holding an old shotgun that looked as if it hadn't spit a shell in twenty years. But the surprise lasted only a second—then the hard planes of his face resumed the look of a very angry, determined man.

Lacy got the uneasy feeling it wasn't the first time he'd faced a gun. Quickly, she sized him up, taking in the neatly ironed white cotton shirt tucked into tight, black corded pants, and the holstered gun at his hip. A six-shooter, as Ben had said, with a beautiful ivory inlaid handle. Be hard to forget a gun like that.

Her gaze traveled back to his face. Tiny lines fanned from his eyes, the creases white against the deep tan of his skin. But the eyes, now the eyes—she'd been right about the snake. Ice-blue, cold and angry, just like a snake's eyes got when it shed its skin. Her gaze dropped briefly to the silver belt buckle in the shape of a coiled snake, widened on the jade eyes glittering in the buckle, then jumped back to his face. There was something vaguely familiar about those snake eyes on the buckle. She shivered inwardly. No wonder Ben was frightened of this man. Where in tarnation was Grandpa when she needed him?

"Where's the boy?"

His voice rumbled through her, increasing the tremble in her hands. It was a quietly voiced question, unexpected after the violence with the door. Lacy didn't trust that calm voice anymore than she trusted his eyes. She lifted the gun higher onto her shoulder. "None of your business, mister. Now you just turn around and head back out. Bullies aren't welcome in my house."

He didn't move, other than to balance himself on the heels of his boots and tuck his fingers in his belt. "I want to talk to the boy," he stated, as if she hadn't spoken.

Lacy's fingers tightened on the gun. He was a stubborn

one, but she was too, as he'd soon find out. "Like I said, mister, I don't like bullies. So get out."

"Or what? You'll shoot me?" His eyes narrowed. "I said I just wanted to talk to him. That ain't enough reason to point a gun at me, now is it? Why don't you just put the gun down and we'll talk—"

"Like you 'talked' to Ben?" Lacy reminded him coldly. "If that's the kind of talkin' you do, mister, then we don't want to hear anything you have to say."

"Surely you don't approve of his stealin'?"

Lacy flushed over that one, but held her ground and kept the gun on her shoulder. Every instinct screamed at her not to trust him, but she supposed she owed him an explanation. If he was new in town and planning to stay, then he'd need to know about Ben. "Ben's got his problems, but we're working on them. I'll pay you for whatever he—"

"Blackberry pie," the man inserted, surprising her into silence. "He took a blackberry pie I bought at the eatin' place in town. Cost me fifty cents."

Lacy's shoulder began to ache. She glanced at Ben from the corner of her eye and noted the guilty flush on his face—as if the blackberry stains on his hands and mouth weren't enough proof. "I said I'd pay you. There wasn't any call to pull a gun on him." She lifted her chin a notch.

"I don't want your money."

Lacy frowned. "Then what—"

"I want him to work it out. Payin's too easy. He won't learn his lesson if you help him out of every scrape he gets into."

She bristled at his not-so-subtle criticism. "And you know all about child-rearing, do you?" As soon as the sarcastic question left her mouth, she flushed. The question was too personal, she realized belatedly. It was none of her business if he had a *passel* of kids. But then, it wasn't any of *his* business how she raised Ben. Still . . . nothing else had worked—

Lacy drew a horrified breath at her thoughts. How could she even consider turning Ben over to this—this snake-eyed stranger? They knew nothing about him! She must have gotten too much sun today scrubbing clothes in the backyard.

Lifting her chin another notch, she said, "Ben's not going anywhere with you, mister. You might as well take the fifty cents and leave. If there's any punishing going on, I'll be the one to do it. Besides, he promised not to do it again."

The man laughed at that. Well, it was more like a snort of disbelief, Lacy thought. Who *was* he, that he thought he could just walk into their town and commence telling people how to raise children?

He shifted, bending one knee and leaning slightly on it. "How many times has he made that promise? I could tell by the slick way he snatched that pie that he's been doing it for a while. And exactly what kind of punishment are you talkin' about? Slap his hand, maybe?" He laughed again, and this time there was no mistaking the scorn in that sound. "I bet that really turns him around."

"I don't beat on defenseless little children, mister—"

"Logan. Adam Logan."

Lacy took a deep breath and willed her temper down. "Mr. Logan. Look, you're new to Shadow City, right?"

"Right."

"Well, there are things about our town you should know, if you're planning to stay."

"I am," came his short answer.

"We're a peaceful town, and we try to teach our children to lead peaceful lives. If we show them violence, then they'll just grow up to be violent. Understand?"

Logan lifted a thick, dark brow and stared at the shotgun braced on her shoulder. "You showin' him now? By pointing a gun at me?"

Lacy's face grew hot. "No—I'm showing *you* what it feels like to be scared half to death!" But she knew that was a lie, because he didn't look frightened in the least. And blast it, he was right. She wasn't showing Ben a good example.

Looking smug, he said, "Discipline can be meted out without physical violence. I won't hurt the boy—"

"Benjamin. We call him Ben."

"Right now I call him a thief. I've got a few chores he can do to pay for the pie."

Lacy's mouth tightened. "I told you, he's not leaving this house with you. Are you hard of hearing, Mr. Logan?" Her voice rose deliberately. "And if it's the pie that you can't forget, I've got one in the kitchen still warm from the oven."

"Blackberry?"

"No. I've got apple and pecan, but I sold the last blackberry to—" She stopped abruptly, for she had been about to say "Ellen," and he'd surely put two and two together and realize they were discussing a pie *she* had baked in the first place. He probably wouldn't find that amusing.

"I had my heart set on blackberry, and we're not going to sidestep the issue here—"

Lacy wasn't listening. Her gaze had focused beyond him to the shadow slipping up with deadly intent, arms lifted high in the air.

Her expression must have mirrored her alarm, for Adam Logan tensed and spun around, his hand going to the shiny six-shooter.

He was too late. With a mighty sweep of her arms, the Indian girl slammed the thick chunk of hickory wood into the side of his head. It connected with a sickening thud.

Adam swayed for a moment. A look of pure surprise flared in his eyes before they rolled upward, then slowly closed as he sank to the floor. The girl stood over him, daring him to move. Black eyes glittered with satisfaction.

"I wish you hadn't done that, Takola," Lacy groaned. She dropped the shotgun onto the sofa and quickly knelt to check the damage. A small lump the size of a bird's egg peeped out between thick strands of dark hair. Lacy gently brushed it aside to get a better look, ignoring the tingling in her fingers as she encountered the satiny texture of his hair. She had expected it to be rough—to go with the man. Not soft, not satiny. Shaking her head at her fanciful thoughts, she examined the wound.

The skin wasn't broken, thank God. But Lacy knew

Takola's strength, a strength that defied her small frame. A blow like that could crack a skull, despite the absence of blood.

Without turning around, she said, "Ben, go fetch Dr. Martin—I think he's in his office today. If he's not there, ask around until you find him." After he scurried from the room, she looked up at Takola, who stared back at her without a flicker of regret for what she'd done. Lacy forced her anger aside, remembering the girl's gruesome drawings, her awful screams in the night. Screams that made her blood run cold and her heart go out to this defensive little Indian girl.

"Bring me a cold rag and then find Rusty. This late in the day, he's probably already at the saloon." When Takola lowered the stick to obey, Lacy added, "And please don't bite, scratch, or hit anyone along the way, no matter what they say to you."

Takola stared solemnly at Lacy, then nodded her head once to indicate she understood. It was the only thing Lacy was certain of. She understood English well.

While Takola went to fetch the rag, Lacy carefully lifted Adam's head onto her lap. She smoothed the hair away from his brow and mentally rehearsed what she would say when he regained consciousness. Ben wasn't the only one with a problem, as he would soon find out. But there had been no time to warn him, no reason to explain about Takola.

What would he do? As she recalled, he hadn't appeared to be softening toward Ben when Takola had decided to take matters into her own violent little hands.

Takola reappeared, handing the folded cloth to Lacy before leaving to find Rusty. The soft click of the door closing brought Lacy back to awareness. She was alone with Adam Logan, a man who threatened little boys and hankered for blackberry pie. . . .

He looked downright peaceful now, she thought, smoothing the cool rag over his brow and onto the bump at his temple. And he needed a haircut. She studied the thick, dark lashes and the wide mouth, relaxed now from its former rigid lines. Hesitantly, she laid the rag aside and traced the slight bumps on his nose with her fingertip. There were two of them, probably where he'd gotten his nose broken in a fight, she speculated. Rather than mar his looks, she thought the imperfection gave him character.

Lacy jerked her hand away when she realized her fingers were wandering down to his mouth. She'd been about to trace the contours of his lips! Although she was alone, she flushed. What would Adam Logan think if he awoke to find her touching his lips? Heat flooded her face again at the thought.

The door behind her opened and she jumped guiltily, twisting to greet Rusty Palmer—her grandfather. Relief limbered her spine at the reassuring sound of his voice, despite the fact that he sounded decidedly grumpy.

"What in tarnation has that girl done now?" Rusty demanded, trying to focus—without much success—on the man on the floor.

Lacy mumbled a thankful prayer that her grandfather appeared not to have noticed her flustered state. She took a deep breath. "This man—he was threatening Ben, and Takola didn't take too kindly to it. I suspect he spooked her with that fancy gun there, too." Lacy nodded at Adam's holster, then fastened her worried gaze on Rusty as she added, "I don't think any of those reasons will wash so much as a hankie with this man."

Takola slipped past Rusty and scurried up the stairs— presumably to her room. Rusty scowled at her cowardly retreat, then at Lacy. "What in tarnation are we going to tell him when he comes to? He ain't dead, is he? And what was he threatening Ben about?" He rubbed at his blurry eyes. It didn't help. "Who the hell is he, anyhow?"

Lacy mentally went down the list of questions. "I don't know what I'm going to say. No, he's not dead. Ben stole his blackberry pie, and his name is Adam Logan."

"I'll tell you who he is," Dr. Martin said from the doorway.

Behind him, Ben hovered, his expression wary although Adam had not twitched so much as an eyelid. He started to creep around the doctor, obviously intending to make his escape. Before he's gone two steps, Rusty reached out and grabbed his shirt collar, effectively holding him in place.

"Hold on there, Ben," Rusty growled. "You just wait a dad-burned minute. I got me a feelin' you're in the middle of all this."

Lacy let out a frustrated breath. "Who is he, Dr. Martin?"

"He's the new sheriff, that's who."

"What?" Rusty shouted at the doctor, glaring at him as if he'd lost his ever-loving mind. "You say *that's*"—he pointed a shaking finger at the prone figure—"the new sheriff?"

Dr. Martin nodded.

Lacy's thoughts were pretty gloomy—the foremost being what Adam Logan's reaction would be when he came to. Ben had eaten his pie, she had greeted him with a shotgun, and Takola had bashed him in the head with a stick of wood. How was she going to explain all that?

Why, she wouldn't be surprised if he threw them all in jail!

Adam groaned and twisted his head. Lacy froze, staring down at her lap as if she'd suddenly discovered she held a live rattler, instead of a man she'd been admiring only moments ago. Ben jerked free of Rusty's hold and ran in the direction of the stairs and safety. The frantic pounding of his boots echoed through the big house.

Rusty grunted and shifted closer, squinting. His mouth curved into a mutinous line Lacy knew well. "Well, he ain't gettin' my badge, no siree. I've had that star goin' on fifteen years and he can damn well get his own!"

Which explained why Adam Logan wasn't wearing a badge, Lacy thought. "Hush, Grandpa, I think he's coming around."

"Don't matter none to me, he still ain't gettin' it. And I don't care what that sneaky bas—that rat of a mayor says 'bout it, neither." With that final declaration, Rusty took himself off, mumbling beneath his breath about how excitement made a man mighty thirsty.

Dr. Martin watched the old man hitch up his pants and

head in the direction of the Whiskey Wine Saloon. "Stubborn old fool."

Lacy jumped to her grandfather's defense, a habit about as hard to break as Grandpa's increasing fondness for whiskey. "He's just hurt about losing his job, Doc. The mayor wasn't real clear on the reason, and it's eatin' at him."

Dr. Martin flushed at her defensive tone. "I'm sorry, Mrs. Ross, you misunderstood me. I was referring to his drinking. He's not a young man, you know, and all that drinking . . . I've warned him."

Lacy sighed, absently stroking Adam's brow. "I know. I've tried talking to him about it, but he just won't listen." She moved aside as Dr. Martin knelt to examine the patient, carefully lowering Adam's head to the floor. Her lap felt warm where his head had lain, and she pressed a hand there, absorbing the heat into her palm. A curious rush of pleasure shot through her. She snatched her hand back, deliberately bringing an image of David's face to mind.

It worked. Thinking of her dead husband wiped the dangerous warmth from her body, replacing it with an icy reminder.

After a quick look, Dr. Martin got to his feet, then reached out a hand to help Lacy do the same. "I'm going to bring the buggy around so we can move him to my office. He'll need looking after for a few hours."

"Do you think—is it bad?" Lacy bit her lip, thinking of Takola and what Adam might do. She couldn't forget how furious he'd been over the pie . . . what would he think of this?

Dr. Martin gave her a reassuring smile and patted her hand. "Don't worry, Mrs. Ross. I'm sure he'll be fine after he comes around. Once I explain everything, he'll understand."

"I wouldn't bet on it," Lacy mumbled morosely.

2

*A*DAM CLUTCHED HIS head against the agonizing pain. Camphor, strong and pungent, invaded his nostrils and filled his lungs. He frowned, then jerked his eyes open as full consciousness returned. A man loomed over him, his bushy blond brows drawn together to form a solid line above his eyes. Thick sideburns covered each side of his face down to the line of his pointed chin. He looked worried about something, Adam thought.

"What the hell happened? Who are you?"

Adam tried to rise, but the man gently pushed him back onto the cot. He looked around, careful not to make any sudden moves. Nothing looked familiar, so he knew he wasn't at the jailhouse. Damn, his head hurt!

"You just lie still, Sheriff," the man ordered. "I'm Dr. Martin. You've got yourself a nasty bump on the head. Might be a concussion." He probed the bump, and Adam growled a protest, which was ignored. "Don't look or feel too bad, but I wasn't expecting you to be out that long. Was gettin' kinda worried about you."

"How long?" Adam asked, trying to remember. His mind drew a blank.

Dr. Martin pulled his pocket watch out and frowned at it. "Better than half an hour. That girl's got a mighty swing."

"Girl?" Adam croaked, thinking maybe the doctor should be on the bed in his place.

Dr. Martin nodded. "Yep. Girl. *Indian* girl—belongs to the widow Ross. She hit you with a good-sized chunk of hickory right upside the head."

At the doctor's words, Adam remembered catching a glimpse of his attacker before the pain exploded in his head and everything went black.

An Indian. He remembered seeing buckskin clothes and black braids and wondering what the hell an Indian was doing in Shadow City. Everything else the doctor said remained a total puzzle.

"You . . . you said the girl belongs to Mrs. Ross. Are you saying Mrs. Ross was *married* to an Indian?"

Dr. Martin laughed as if Adam had just made the joke of the century. "Hell, no! Lacy—Mrs. Ross was never married to no Indian. Takola—that's the girl's name—just appeared one day out of the blue. Folks thought she should have been sent to a reservation, but Mrs. Ross said she'd keep her." Dr. Martin shook his head as if he didn't quite understand her reasoning. "Kicked up a mighty big fuss about it, too, did our Mrs. Ross when some folks didn't like the idea of her staying."

"I'll just bet she did," Adam mumbled dryly, leveling a measured gaze on the doctor, who didn't appear much older than himself. "So she's a widow?" Adam watched the doctor's face flush at the question, his shrewd mind storing away the information. So, the doc was sweet on "the widow Ross." But was the widow Ross sweet on the doc? Adam wondered, then wondered why the hell he was wondering. He wouldn't be staying in Shadow City long enough to attend a wedding.

Dr. Martin snapped his suspender with his thumbs, then

shoved his hands into the pockets of his baggy trousers. He looked around the room as if searching for something, then finally met Adam's half-amused gaze. "Yeah, she's a widow, been one for about five years now. Ain't been here much longer myself. Took the old doc's place after he fell from his horse into Mule Creek and drowned."

Adam was glad his head hurt, because otherwise he would have laughed over the doctor's quick change of subject. He should assure the poor man that he had no intention of competing for the widow Ross. In fact, he intended to walk a mile around her and her hellion brood if he happened to see them. Hopefully, his business in Shadow City wouldn't take too long.

Rubbing gingerly at the bump on his temple, Adam asked the burning question. "Why'd she hit me?" It galled him to know that a little girl had done this to him. What would the townsfolk think of their new sheriff when they heard? And why should he care? He wasn't here to become a hero; he was here to dig up the truth, if he was lucky enough to find anyone who remembered something that had happened fifteen years ago.

Dr. Martin walked to a long table set against the far wall of the good-sized room, turning his back to him. Adam rose slowly onto his elbows to watch as the doctor began arranging an assortment of surgical instruments that appeared to have been just fine the way they were. The ache in his head was easing, and he didn't think he had a concussion. No blurred vision, no nausea, which he knew were signs.

"I reckon she hit you because you're a white man," the doctor began slowly, without turning around. "The sight of your gun probably set her off."

Adam sensed the doctor was choosing his words with care, waiting for each reaction before continuing. Politics. "Can't hardly blame her." After a slight hesitation, he added, "And if she's heard about the Seventh Cavalry and what they did at Wounded Knee Creek up in South Dakota, that didn't help matters none."

The doctor turned around and stared at Adam, his

expression neutral, but his tone one of poorly concealed disgust. "So, you're heard about it?"

Adam shrugged, but his eyes revealed enough contempt to inform the doctor of how he really felt. "Who hasn't? What was it—three hundred Indians, women and children included—slaughtered like hogs?"

"Yes. The stories I've heard are beyond the imagination." Dr. Martin took a cloth and began dusting the vast array of medicine jars on a shelf above the table where he stood. Suddenly, he threw the rag onto the table and faced Adam again, his whiskery sideburns working along with his jaw. "There's not many who know about Takola, Sheriff Logan. What I'm about to tell you could mean her death if you should repeat this to anyone. I figure you got a right to know, you being the new sheriff and all."

Intrigued, Adam nodded. "I give you my word—as long as it's within the law." It was what the doctor would expect him to say, and he certainly wanted everyone in Shadow City to think he took his job as sheriff seriously.

Dr. Martin seemed satisfied with his answer. "Takola showed up in Shadow City this past February. Mrs. Ross found her asleep in the smokehouse, damn near frozen half to death, her feet nothin' but raw meat where she'd walked on 'em." He paused significantly and Adam realized he was holding his breath. "We believe she walked here from Wounded Knee Creek."

There was dead silence in the room. Adam remembered to breathe again, his mind trying to comprehend what the doctor was implying. "That's hundreds of miles from here! You think she was there during the massacre?" He frowned. "But they said there weren't any survivors. The cavalrymen made sure of that."

Dr. Martin nodded. "Yes, that's what they say—no one survived. We don't want them to know otherwise, either. They'd hunt her down like a rabid dog and kill her. Wouldn't be much we could do to stop it from happening."

Adam lowered himself down onto the cot. His head was beginning to pound again. If the doctor was right and the Indian girl had witnessed such a massacre, then he understood why she harbored so much hate. Hell, he even understood why she'd hit him.

And Dr. Martin was right about what the army would do to Takola if they knew.

"But Mrs. Ross would try," Dr. Martin said.

Adam sat up again, this time ignoring the flash of pain the sudden movement caused. "What?"

"I said Mrs. Ross would try to stop 'em."

"She'd get her fool self killed, too," Adam growled. He remembered how fiercely she'd protected the little thief— Ben—and knew that the doctor spoke the truth. They would take Takola over Lacy Ross's dead body, and Adam felt sure that's how it would be. Over her dead body. Without the slightest regret.

Well, it wasn't his business, and as far as he was concerned, Lacy Ross wasn't breaking the law by keeping the Indian girl. As long as she could handle Takola, and the little hellcat didn't kill anyone, then Adam felt he should stay out of it. He certainly hadn't come to Shadow City to get embroiled in the town's woes; he'd just come to pump them for information, and when he finished his investigation, he would get the hell out of town.

He had a piece of land picked out right smack-dab in the middle of Wyoming, and the sooner he got there to claim it, the better. He'd be there now, if it hadn't been for the promise he'd made to his mother before she died.

Adam swung his legs down and sat up on the cot. He discovered that if he didn't move too sharply, the pain was bearable. "How long you reckon this head's gonna hurt?" he asked, thinking of the pile of wanted posters in his desk. One of his first jobs as sheriff would be to familiarize himself with the faces of these outlaws in the off chance that any of them passed through town.

Dr. Martin shrugged. "Can't say for sure. I'd advise you to get an early night, and with luck you'll be as good as new in the morning."

"Thanks Doc. How much do I owe you?" Adam slid off the cot as he spoke, stretching carefully. Maybe he'd follow the doc's orders, and do just that. In the morning, he'd get an early start on those posters, then take a leisurely stroll around town to acquaint himself with the people. It was Thursday, and he figured by this time next week he should be able to ask a few questions without arousing too much suspicion. By then he should have a pretty good idea of who to ask.

"This one's on me, Sheriff Logan, and welcome to Shadow City."

Dr. Martin held out his hand and Adam shook it. He walked to the door, then hesitated. There was a question still burning to be asked. "About the boy, Ben—"

The doctor cut him off. "You'll have to let Mrs. Ross explain that one, Sheriff. I've told enough of her business as it is. Wouldn't want her to be mad at me." Dr. Martin looked regretful, but stubborn, and Adam realized he wouldn't get any further information out of the doc about Mrs. Ross and her family.

"Well . . . thanks for your help, Doc." As he strode out of the office into the dwindling evening light and made for the jailhouse, he thought about Lacy Ross, wondering again why he couldn't just forget it. The town was small, but if he concentrated hard, he could manage to avoid the widow and her wild youngsters for the next month or two. He needed to focus all of his energies into finishing the job he came to do, and getting the hell out. It was the end of June. He wanted to buy his land in Wyoming and build a shelter of some sort before winter set in.

He crossed the street and stepped onto the boardwalk in front of the jailhouse that would be his new home for the next few months, glad he had finally managed to get Lacy Ross out of his mind. As he passed by the building's only window, he saw light glowing inside the office. He froze with his hand on the doorknob, knowing that he hadn't left the lamp burning when he'd gone chasing the boy. Of course he hadn't, because at the time it had been broad daylight.

Slowly, he withdrew his gun and eased the door open with his boot, keeping his upper body out of sight. No one came at him as the door swung wide open, giving him a fair view of the room.

Lacy Ross stood before his desk fiddling with something in front of her, unaware of his presence. Adam walked softly into the room, grasped the door, and gave it a hard push. It slammed shut. He holstered his gun just as Lacy turned with a startled jerk. Her eyes looked enormous in a face blanched white with fear. She looked as if she'd just seen a ghost. The sight of him didn't appear to reassure her.

"You . . . I thought you might be hungry, so I brought dinner." She gestured to the plate on the desk, then let her hands drop to her sides.

Adam slanted a glance at the plate, covered with a cloth to keep away the flies, then turned his gaze back to Lacy. She was a beautiful woman, he decided, despite the drawn look about her mouth. Her hair, a dark honey color, looked thick and silky. Since their last meeting, she had wound the heavy braid into a cornet at her neck.

"Is this a peace offering?" he drawled, moving around the desk and seating himself. With a sigh he propped his feet up and closed his eyes. What a day! When a moment passed in silence, he opened one eye to peer at her, then lifted a questioning brow.

"I suppose you could call it that," she said stiffly.

Adam smiled faintly. Mrs. Ross thought he'd jump at the offering, and thought he was rude for not doing so. Maybe if his head wasn't hurting like hell, he'd have been more obliging. But right now he didn't feel very obliging. "Or you could call it a bribe." His interested gaze watched the flush break the stark whiteness of her face. Much better, he thought. Now she looked downright pretty. Mad, but pretty. No longer scared. He couldn't imagine why Lacy Ross would be afraid of him. She didn't strike him as the cowering type—like his mother had been.

Under his level stare, Lacy grew visibly taller, her chin squaring off. Her brown eyes took on a gleam Adam was already familiar with. "I don't know what you're talking about, Mr.——*Sheriff* Logan. It's customary to welcome a new town member, and this is one of the ways we do it. I don't have an ulterior motive."

She wasn't a good liar, Adam noted, enjoying himself. "I'm talking about the way you're hoping to soften me up so that I don't put the bunch of you in jail." He paused to let that sink in, knowing he was being a brute and unable to help himself. It was the headache, he supposed. "Stealing, holding the sheriff at gunpoint, attacking the sheriff—"

"I'm aware of what happened, Sheriff Logan." Adam watched her chest rise and fall with more interest than a man with such a head pain should have. "I'm sorry for all of it." She walked a few steps toward the door, then turned and walked back, avoiding his eyes. "When Ben came running into the house, looking so frightened, I lost my head." Suddenly she pinned him with an accusing look. "He said you threatened to shoot him."

"I told him thieves get shot," Adam said flatly, then added, "and where I come from, they do. Sometimes they get hanged."

The color disappeared from her face again. "He's only a *child*—"

"Who will grow up to be a man."

"But it was just a pie—"

"And next time it might be my horse," Adam inserted.

Lacy's fingers curled into her apron, a restraining gesture not lost on Adam. *So the widow Ross has a temper,* he thought.

"Would you stop interrupting me?"

When he simply sat and stared, Lacy went on. "Everyone in town knows Ben, and they all love him, despite the fact that he steals food."

"Is he your son?" Adam surprised himself by asking. His gaze dropped to her slim hips, then crawled slowly upward where they lingered speculatively on her small breasts.

Lacy's mouth fell open. She shut it with a snap, her lips pursed in a thin line of annoyance. "What's that got to do with anything?"

"Is he?" Adam wasn't certain why he wanted to know, but

he did. He dropped his boots to the floor and settled his hands on his knees, waiting for an answer.

Lacy hissed the word. "No. He's not my own flesh-and-blood child. I don't have any. But he's like my own."

Adam rose and walked around the desk, not surprised when Lacy held her ground. But he could tell by the way she tensed up that she wanted to run; the signs were there in the white line around her lips and the way she swayed back. Her sparkling anger enhanced her beauty and intrigued the male in him. But he didn't need the distraction, and instinct told him that if he didn't scare her good right now, she'd end up getting under his skin. He didn't want that. Didn't need it, either. He had two jobs to do in this town, and getting involved with a woman—especially *this* woman—wasn't in his plans.

He didn't stop walking until he was a few inches away. Her breath came faster, drawing his eyes once again to the quick rise and fall of her breasts. She had lowered her eyes, staring somewhere in the vicinity of his chin as if she were bowing to his will, but Adam wasn't a fool. "Tell me, Mrs. Ross. Do you take in every stray that happens along? Do you hold them to your breast and rock them gently until their tears dry?"

Lacy did back up a step then, and Adam followed. This time he allowed his chest to brush hers. He reached out and ran his knuckles along her clenched jaw, then down to her throat. She flinched and jerked her head away, eyes suddenly up and blazing. Adam admired the defiance he saw there, then dropped his gaze to her lips. He wondered how long it had been since Lacy's last kiss and why, after five years, she remained a widow.

"You're a bully, Mr. Logan. Just as I first thought." Her voice came out a little shaky, enticingly husky. It was filled with loathing, the vehemence of which startled Adam.

He smiled. "If I'm a bully, Mrs. Ross, then why isn't little Ben in jail right now? Or the little Indian girl, for that matter?"

And as she prepared a retort, Adam leaned in that last

inch and covered her open mouth with his own, stifling her startled gasp of shock.

The kiss ended before it really began, but Adam had planned it that way. He wasn't confident that he could handle more without wanting more. And he didn't want her screaming, just frightened enough to stay out of his way from now on. From what he'd gathered, it wouldn't take much to scare Lacy Ross.

He stepped back and braced himself, fully expecting a sharp slap to his face, which wouldn't help his aching head. Instead, Lacy covered her mouth with her hand and stared at him, her eyes wide, accusing. Finally, she swept past him to the door.

"One more thing, Mrs. Ross," Adam called, watching as she ground to a halt. She didn't turn, but held her back stiff and her head high. "Send Ben over in the morning. I've got a saddle that needs oiling. He can do that to pay for the pie."

Lacy didn't answer. The door slammed behind her and Adam grinned, then heaved a sigh of regret. But he knew he'd done the right thing. Lacy Ross would definitely be too much of a diversion, and he couldn't risk that happening. If he wasn't mistaken, she would avoid him in the future, as much as she would avoid a pile of horse manure in the road.

He wondered if his instincts were right about her. She had shown all the signs of being afraid of him, and this left him wondering what had happened to her to make her so jumpy.

The tantalizing aroma of fried chicken wafted Adam's way, drawing his attention to the food she'd brought. He dismissed his musings and moved to the desk, uncovering the plate, his appreciative gaze skimming the contents. Along with crisp fried chicken, there was a generous helping of boiled potatoes, a mound of green beans, and a thick slice of cornbread topped with creamy butter. His stomach growled with anticipation. Adam smiled. If the widow Ross cooked as good as she kissed, then he wouldn't go to bed hungry tonight.

At least, not hungry for food. He chuckled to himself and made a mental note to find out if there were any women to be bought in this town. It wasn't his normal way of scratching his itch, but he didn't have time for courting.

Lacy was mad enough to spit. She marched home, mentally flailing herself, then Sheriff Logan, in turn. What made her think she could change his mind about Ben? What made her crazy enough to bring him something to eat, hoping, just as he'd guessed, to soften things for Takola and Ben—and herself?

"Good evening, Mrs. Ross."

Lacy forced herself to smile at the blacksmith as he locked up for the night. "Good evening, Mr. Crow." She continued on as darkness slid into place around her, hoping she would find Grandpa home keeping an eye on Ben and Takola. Somebody needed to, while she made a fool of herself with Sheriff Logan.

She thought about the other reason for making the attempt to apologize to the new sheriff. For Rusty's sake, she'd hoped to get Sheriff Logan on their side before he caught wind of the rumors the mayor was spreading around town about why he had fired her grandfather. So far, she didn't think many people believed him, but with Adam Logan being a newcomer, she feared it was a matter of who talked to him first.

A groan escaped her. After what had happened today with Ben and Takola, she reckoned she was wasting her time. Sheriff Logan would never hire Rusty as a deputy now, the way Sheriff Murddock had done before his death. She loved her grandfather, but she wasn't blind to his faults. He was getting too old to be sheriff of a growing town like Shadow City, but being appointed deputy would hopefully salvage his pride and help keep him out of the saloon. Lacy picked up her skirts and crossed the road, nodding absently at the lamplighter as he passed by.

Adam Logan didn't know what it had cost her to go into that darkened office alone. The last time had been fifteen years ago, when she had found Sheriff Murddock dead. Lacy hastened her steps, a shiver racing down her spine as she recalled the awful fear she'd felt tonight as she set the plate down and lit the lamp.

Time had rolled back, and she was a little girl again. Everything looked the same: the same lamp, the same desk, the same murky, pre-dark gloom. By the time she had finished lighting the lamp, she was fully convinced that when she turned around to face the jail cell, she would find Sheriff Logan's handsome face staring at her through the bars, just as Sheriff Murddock's had done so many years ago.

She still saw that face in her dreams sometimes. David had thought she was silly for dreaming about something that had happened so long ago. Lacy only wished she could forget about it entirely. What had happened this evening only proved how futile that wish was.

If only her grandmother were still with them. Dying had been about the meanest thing the woman had ever done to her. Rusty missed her, too, and although she'd been gone for eight years, there wasn't a day that went by without Lacy thinking of her.

Ben would have twisted her around his little finger, Lacy thought, her eyes misting over. And Takola—Grandma would have ranted about the horrible things Lacy feared the girl had witnessed at the massacre. She would have cajoled Takola into talking, and figured out a way to stop Ben from stealing.

So far, Lacy had failed to do either of those things.

Pausing at the door to the two-story house, Lacy wiped her eyes with her apron before going in. For Takola and Ben's sake she made it a point to show a happy face as much as possible. And Sheriff Logan wasn't going to change that.

Ben and Takola were in the kitchen, putting the last of the supper dishes away in the cabinet. Rusty was nowheres in sight, but she saw that Takola had put a plate on the stove for him.

Lacy paused at the door, surveying the two as they worked in harmony together. Takola had taken to Ben right away, and Lacy suspected it was because the Indian girl instinctively sensed Ben's inner turmoil, his need to feel loved and protected. In a sense, he was an outcast, like herself.

They finally noticed Lacy in the doorway. Ben's face creased into a big smile and relief showed in his eyes. Takola gave her own unique greeting: a half bow and just the slightest twitch of her lips. Her black eyes revealed nothing, however. They were as impregnable as the girl inside.

Ben put his towel on a nearby chair, his smile slipping. "Is he still mad at me? Is he going to put us in jail, Lacy?"

Lacy shook her head, her own smile reassuring. "No. We're not going to jail. But—" She tried to look stern. "You have to do something for Sheriff Logan in the morning after you finish your lessons."

Immediately apprehensive, Ben moved closer to Takola. Lacy's heart jerked at the move, knowing that Ben thought she was deserting him. She hesitated, on the verge of telling him to forget it and that she would talk to the sheriff again. But then she recalled Adam's words, about how thieves got shot, and some hanged. She wasn't helping Ben by allowing him to continue stealing.

As difficult as it was for her to admit it, she knew that Sheriff Logan was right.

"Ben . . . you can't keep stealing from people. It's wrong, and Sheriff Logan means well. He believes folks ought to pay for their mistakes, so he wants you to oil his saddle to pay for the pie." There, that wasn't so bad, was it? Lacy looked silently from one child to the other, feeling as if she had just sentenced them to death. Suddenly, Takola pushed Ben gently in Lacy's direction, her meaning clear.

She was letting them know that she agreed with Sheriff Logan.

Lacy hid her surprise, waiting for Ben's reaction. It was all she could do to hold herself back, not to open her arms and forget the entire day. But she couldn't, not if she was going to help Ben become a good, honest man someday.

Ben stood in the middle of the spacious kitchen, looking forlorn, a little frightened. "You . . . you won't let him put me in jail, will you, Lacy? I just have to oil his saddle?"

Lacy spoke around the knot in her throat. "That's all, Ben, I promise. No jail." Then she took a deep breath and added, "But I don't know what Sheriff Logan will do if there's a next time." She told the truth, and it was best that Ben know it. Rusty was no longer the sheriff; that job now belonged to someone who didn't know Ben, who wasn't willing to overlook his problem.

As if to declare the matter settled, Takola picked up the scrap bucket and handed it to Ben. It was a silent reminder to feed Big Red, the hog that had managed to escape the knife four straight winters, thanks to Ben. Not even Rusty was immune when Ben begged in earnest.

Lacy breathed a sigh of relief when Ben took the bucket. He looked a little pale, and his eyes were bigger than normal, but he managed a shaky smile for her.

"Okay, Lacy. I'll do it."

"Good."

"And I'm gonna try real hard not to take any more food from folks."

"That's wonderful, Ben. I know you can stop if you try hard enough." She watched him as he went outside through the back door leading from the kitchen. When the door shut behind him, Lacy met Takola's solemn gaze and answered the question in her eyes.

"I don't think you're in trouble, Takola. Dr. Martin must have had a talk with the sheriff, but he wasn't too pleased about the bump on his head. I think if we just stay out of his way . . ." Something she fully intended to do, Lacy added silently. She touched her lips, remembering the shocking feel of his firm mouth on hers for that brief instant.

Takola nodded, then slipped past her to start the fire Lacy would need for ironing. The daily routine of cooking, washing, and ironing had become less exhausting with the arrival of the Indian girl, and Lacy never forgot to express how grateful she was for her help. Takola accepted the praise with dignity, but brushed Lacy's gratitude aside as if it embarrassed her.

Now, with Rusty no longer drawing his sheriff's pay, she would need the money she made from the washing and ironing she took in, and from baking pies and cakes for the restaurant, more than ever.

Lacy set the basket of shirts and trousers on the floor beside the ironing board, seething with resentment. Was Adam Logan aware that he had booted an old man out of a job? It just wasn't fair, the way the mayor had fired Rusty without warning a week before the arrival of the new sheriff. The decent thing to do would have been to keep Rusty on as a deputy for a while, giving him time to get used to the idea, and giving Adam Logan time to get familiar with the town.

Instead, the mayor had stomped on Rusty's pride. Lacy knew her grandfather; he wouldn't forget the slight. First, he would let it eat at him and fester, and then he'd explode. Lacy tested the iron, found it hot, and pressed it to the back of Gilbert Smith's Sunday shirt for perhaps the hundredth time. She could have ironed it with her eyes closed. Takola stood waiting, ready to take the shirt from her and fold it as Lacy had taught her to do.

"When Grandpa gets good and mad, Mr. Logan and the mayor better watch out," Lacy mumbled aloud, before she remembered her audience. She grinned sheepishly at the silent Indian girl, wishing she'd kept her mouth shut. Takola needed no encouragement when it came to vengeance, and here she was rambling about it!

Takola's eyes shimmered with something that vaguely resembled humor. Slowly, she nodded, a feral smile curving her lips.

Lacy groaned.

3

$\mathscr{A}$DAM FINISHED EVERYTHING on his plate, regretting his decision to keep Lacy Ross at a distance. She was a damned fine cook. He pushed aside the small pile of chicken bones and wiped his fingers on the cloth napkin she had covered his plate with, sighing in satisfaction. Weeks of hard biscuits, beef jerky, and beans made a man appreciate a meal like that.

He bet Lacy could bake a blackberry pie that would melt in his mouth.

Adam shook his head, amused at himself for his obsession with that damned blackberry pie—and Lacy Ross. The hankering for the pie had progressed over a period of weeks while he was traveling from Wyoming to Shadow City, Missouri. The hankering for the widow had developed in a day. Adam didn't figure there was much difference in the two. Both hankerings would pass, by either ignoring them until they went away, or indulging them.

Satisfying one wouldn't be a problem—as long as he didn't let the pie out of his sight again, once he got it; satisfying the other would be a definite problem.

Leaning back in the chair, Adam sighed again, running his hand over the hard, rigid planes of his flat stomach. Yep. He would have been poking new holes in his belt before long if he hadn't tweaked his own nose.

Somehow, his reasoning didn't make him feel any better about what he'd done. One day in Shadow City and he'd managed to insult a fine lady, albeit purposefully. He wouldn't get answers to his questions that way, he reflected ruefully, rubbing at the shadowy stubble on his chin.

With an absent curiosity, he began opening the side drawers of the battered old desk one by one. All of them turned up empty until he reached the last deep drawer. He paused to move the lamp closer, then began pulling the wanted posters out, placing them on the desk. At the very bottom of the pile, Adam came across a framed photograph. His fingers curled around the tarnished silver frame as he recognized his grandfather's rugged features.

Colt Murddock's face wasn't easy to forget. It bespoke trial and hardship, tough decisions, and regrets, but Adam also saw pride and triumph in the angle of his head. Although his eyes were a nondescript gray in the black-and-white photograph, Adam knew that in life they had been pale blue, a shade lighter than his own eyes. He stared at the tall figure of Sheriff Murddock, founder of Shadow City, ex–bounty hunter, father, and grandfather, as he stood outside the door to the newly completed jailhouse. He held a bottle of unopened whiskey high in the air.

Adam recognized the symbolic gesture signifying the grand opening of the new jail. His grandfather looked proud, and rightfully so.

The photograph was probably more than twenty years old, faded and slightly blurred, yet someone had kept it when he could have thrown it away. Adam narrowed his eyes, pondering who that person might be. Whoever it was, he must have known his grandfather well, and still respected him, even after his death and despite the ugly facts that pointed to suicide.

Adam set the picture upright on his desk in plain sight. Someone was bound to ask about it sooner or later, but right now he didn't care. Colt Murddock, Adam's maternal grandfather, was also his hero. Adam never doubted the truth: that his grandfather was not guilty of committing the ultimate sin, but rather was the victim of murder.

Until now, he had thought his mother's dying request unreasonable. After all, Colt Murddock had died fifteen years ago; memories fade. But looking at the face in the photograph, Adam discovered that he no longer found the request unreasonable or impossible.

He was going to try his damnedest to find out what had really happened the day Colt Murddock was found dead in the jail cell, supposedly by his own hand.

The keeper of this photograph would be a start; it would likely be his predecessor.

Adam was startled out of his reverie by a pounding at the door, followed by drunken, indistinguishable shouting. His hand went to the butt of his gun, then he shook his head, chiding himself. This was Shadow City, a town known for its serenity, thanks to progress and Colt Murddock.

With unhurried steps, Adam went to the door and pulled it open, unbalancing the man about to pound his fist again. He stepped back quickly as the man fell through the door, sprawling onto the floor. Adam lifted an eyebrow as he watched the older man scramble to his feet, straightening his hat in an attempt to regain his dignity. Obviously, he was about as corned as a body could get. The man smelled as if he had bathed himself in whiskey, and from the looks of his stained shirtfront, Adam didn't think he was far from wrong.

"What can I do for you, Mr.——?" Adam tucked his thumbs into his belt, his expression carefully polite. He had yet to meet the man responsible for hiring him, having done all of his dealings through the mail. For all he knew, this was the mayor. After the fiasco this afternoon with Lacy and her bunch, he didn't think anything could surprise him.

Lacy. Now, just when had he started thinking of her as "Lacy," and not "the widow Ross" or "Mrs. Ross"?

"The name's Rusty Palmer." The older man swayed on his feet as he growled the introduction, his expression mulish.

Adam decided against offering his hand. He was afraid it might throw the man off balance. Instead, he indicated the chair against the wall in front of his desk, relieved that this man wasn't the mayor. "Have a seat, Mr. Palmer, and tell me what I can do for you at this, ah, late hour."

Rusty bristled, his bloodshot eyes suddenly blazing with pent-up anger. "I'll stand, thank ye. I just came here to tell you a thing or two, *Sheriff* Logan. Whatever the mayor said about me ain't true. Now, I know you don't know me—nor anyone else in this town—but I'm here to tell ya that mayor's a snake-bellied, hog-smellin' liar."

Adam struggled to keep a straight face. He had no idea what the man was talking about, or why Rusty Palmer felt he should explain himself. "Hog-smellin' liar? Now, that's a new one on me." He hurried on when he saw the old man stiffen. "Truth is, I ain't met the mayor."

Rusty's mouth fell open. Adam drew back, blinking his eyes against the strong whiskey fumes that came rushing his way. "You ain't met the mayor?"

"That's what I said."

"You ain't spoke to him?"

Adam started to point out that he damned well couldn't speak to a man he'd never met, then thought better of it. He'd just confuse the old man. "Nope. I ain't spoke to him. Supposed to meet him for lunch at the hotel tomorrow." Though why he was telling this to a total stranger, he couldn't understand. Maybe the damage to his head was worse than both he and the doc had first thought.

Rusty removed his hat, revealing a wiry thatch of gray hair. He scratched it, his face pulled into a perplexed frown. "How'd he hire you, then, if you didn't come lookin' for the job?"

Adam thought about ignoring the question. He wasn't

accustomed to people knowing his business, but then he might as well get used to it. This was a small town, and the sheriff was a prominent figure in the minds of the people, no matter who was filling the job. Being evasive would not earn their trust.

Walking to the desk, Adam sat down and removed his gun belt, placing it within easy reach. He was tired and wanted to go to bed, but he suspected that the old man wouldn't leave until he was ready, or until Adam threw him out. Rusty Palmer had a bone to pick about something and Adam suspected he was about to find out what it was.

"Well? Think you can 'splain that to me a little better?"

Yep, Adam thought. He was right. With a weary shrug of his shoulders, he said, "Got hired through the mail." There was more, like the fact that Adam knew of the mayor through his mother and Colt, but he wasn't ready for folks to know who he was. As painful as it might turn out to be, he wanted to hear people's honest opinion about his grandfather.

Adam was unprepared for the man's reaction to that seemingly innocent piece of information.

"The mail? *The mail?*"

The longer Rusty talked, the louder he got. Adam frowned and Rusty either didn't see the warning, or didn't care. Adam suspected the latter.

"You got the job as sheriff through the *mail*? Just like that?" Although Adam remained silent, Rusty took this silence as confirmation. "Son of a bitch!" Shaking his head, he shuffled unsteadily to the desk and leaned against it with both hands.

Adam yawned and propped his feet up on the desk. He wondered if he could convince Rusty Palmer to hold the bone-picking for another time; maybe tomorrow. Or never. He didn't much care to be shouted at by a drunken old man, after the day he'd had. In fact, he was already mighty tired of it.

The sight of Adam's booted feet on the desk apparently triggered something unpleasant in the old man. With surprising strength, Rusty grabbed Adam's feet and threw them from the desk, barely catching himself before he followed.

All thoughts of sleep flew from Adam's mind. His boots hit the floor with a thud, jarring his legs. Before he could respond, Rusty stumbled around the desk and leaned over Adam, nearly intoxicating him with a blast of his whiskey-laden breath.

"You think you're fit to put your boots on this desk?" Rusty's shout stirred up Adam's almost-forgotten headache. "Why, you ain't earned it, you sneaky pup."

Sneaky pup? Adam considered shoving the old man onto his butt, and he would have, if the voice of his mother had not intruded into his consciousness. *Respect your elders.* He took a deep breath and held it, trying to avoid breathing in the fumes. He'd give the old man time to have his say; *then* he'd boot him out the door. Three minutes, not a second more.

Rusty grabbed the top of Adam's chair to steady himself. He wasn't through by a long shot. "You think being sheriff of this town's gonna be an easy job, do you? Well, you better think again. A lot of hard work went into making this town what it is today, and you"—he poked a finger at Adam's chest—"didn't have nuthin' to do with it."

Adam removed Rusty's finger from his chest and re-placed it with his arms, deliberately bringing an image of his mother's sweet, patient face to mind.

"I've been sheriff in this town for fifteen years, and before that, there was Sheriff Murddock—" Rusty stopped abruptly as his attention landed on the picture Adam had left out on top of the desk. The sight of it seemed to knock the wind from his sails. "He was a great man in his day, I can tell you. You'll never be able to fill his boots, just like I couldn't. Hell, I didn't try, 'cause I knew better."

Adam went completely still, his eyes locked on Rusty Palmer's suddenly morose expression. Remembered grief deepened the lines in the older man's face. In that instant, Adam saw a clear picture of the man Rusty Palmer had been, what he probably could be again when not in the shape he was in now.

He was also fairly certain Rusty was the man he was looking for.

Alert now, he said softly, "So you were the sheriff before me."

Rusty cursed the moisture in his eyes, blinking rapidly. He backed away from Adam as if suddenly realizing where he was and what he was doing. Squinting, he looked at Adam, his jaw thrust out. "You didn't know?"

Adam clipped a smile at Rusty's skeptical tone. "No, I didn't. All I know is what the mayor told me when I wrote him asking about employment. He said Shadow City needed a sheriff. I needed a job."

"Son of a bitch," Rusty muttered, his gaze on the photograph of Sheriff Murddock. "That mayor's a son of a bitch. You'll find out for yourself, but don't say you ain't been warned. Don't know why Colt didn't kick his ass outta town a long time ago."

"Have a seat, Mr. Palmer." Adam jerked his head toward the chair against the wall, hardly believing his luck. Hell, after the day he'd had, he felt he deserved it.

"Rusty. Folks call me Rusty, even when I was sheriff. Always have. Guess they got used to it. Hell, even my granddaughter calls me Rusty, more often than not." He sank into the chair with a grunt and a grateful sigh, as if glad to anchor himself to something solid.

Adam waited a moment, fearing that the former sheriff was about to pass out, depriving him of the information he sought. But the old man was a fighter, and full of a lion's share of pride. He remained upright, though Adam doubted he could maintain the position for long. "How did you come to be sheriff, if you don't mind my askin'?"

"Don't mind a'tall," Rusty said. "I was the deputy to Sheriff Murddock afore he died. Folks just naturally assumed I'd take over, so I did." He cast wavering eyes in the direction of the cell, frowning. "Colt, he used to sleep in there, but after he died, I built this room on back."

Adam sympathized with him, thinking he wouldn't much like sleeping in there either. He was damned glad for the extra room. As for Rusty succeeding Colt, well, that made sense too. How shocked the town must have been over their hero dying—and the nature of his death.

Or at least what they *thought* was the nature of his death.

Colt Murddock, a man Adam remembered well. His grandfather wasn't a man easily forgotten. "You were friends?" he asked quietly.

"Hell, yesh. Bes' friends." Rusty started to shake his head, then seemed to think better of it. "Knew him well enough to know he didn't kill hisself." He gave Adam a hard look, as if daring him to disagree. "Colt woulda gave his own life for just about anybody, but he wouldn't've *taken* his *own*. Hell, he was talkin' about retiring to that ranch of his up in Wyoming. Don' rightly sound like a man who weren't plannin' on livin' to me."

Adam surged forward, propping his elbows on the desk. His eyes bore into Rusty's wavering ones, silently commanding his attention. "Who found Sheriff Murddock?"

Rusty squinted, swaying in the chair. "Tarnation," he mumbled before rolling out of the chair into the floor.

Adam stood up and peered over the desk at the sprawled, unconscious figure of Rusty Palmer. "Damn."

Lacy pulled the front door shut behind her and faced the road, grateful for the oil lamps placed strategically along the road. Otherwise she wouldn't have been able to see her hand in front of her face; it was pitch-dark out, with no moon in sight. And her destination, the saloon, was situated at the far end of town, across from the train station that allowed cotton growers to send their crops by rail to St. Louis or Kansas City.

"Thunder!" Lacy muttered as she pulled her shawl more securely around her and set off at a brisk pace. Rusty knew she worried about him when he stayed out this late. The citizens of Shadow City were a peaceful lot, but it wasn't the townsfolk that worried her. Situated as it was between the larger cities of St. Louis and Kansas City, the town got its share of "hoppers," people stopping in for a week or two before setting out on the last leg of their journey. And sometimes there was trouble. Brief trouble, for Shadow City tolerated little in the way of mischief-making, as the hoppers found out soon enough.

Lately, Lacy had noticed more and more unfamiliar strangers in the town of four hundred or so people, as homesteaders scouted the area and lumber companies came in search of new timber. But the mayor owned the only lumber mill in the county, conveniently situated next to the railroad station and across from the saloon, and so far had managed to dissuade the competition from settling.

Shadow City was definitely growing, Lacy mused, and she wasn't certain she liked the idea. She passed the jailhouse on the opposite side of the road, keeping her eyes firmly ahead. But from the corner of her eye, she noticed a light glowing; she wondered if the new sheriff had bothered with the plate of food she'd painstakingly prepared for him.

She sniffed and increased her pace, chiding herself for worrying about that good-for-nothing, job-stealing bully. She didn't care if he starved to death.

As she crossed the halfway mark at the corner of Main and Oakleaf, she paused, looking down Main for signs of late-night revelers. All was quiet except for the faint sound of music coming from the Whiskey Wine Saloon. She took a deep, angry breath and hurried on, rehearsing what she would say to her grandfather when she found him. He should be ashamed, forcing her to go out this late and leave Ben and Takola alone in the house. What if Takola had one of her nightmares? What if Ben awoke and found her gone? Would he panic?

By the time Lacy reached the open doors of the saloon, she was mad enough to spit nails. The fact that she rarely lost her temper, but had done so twice today, only served to make her madder.

Both times could be traced to Adam Logan.

She shoved the swinging doors apart and marched in as if she'd been there many times, when in fact she'd never stepped foot in the establishment before tonight.

The music stopped with a crash of piano keys. The only occupants of the room other than the piano player were a couple of lumber-mill workers who looked vaguely familiar and a fancy-dressed woman leaning against the bar smoking a cigarette. Lacy saw at a glance that neither Rusty nor any of his buddies were present.

Her worry increased. It wasn't like Rusty to be this late coming home, and now it seemed he wasn't where she thought he would be, either.

"If you're lookin' for Rusty, he left about an hour ago. Said something about stopping in to talk to the new sheriff."

The deep, husky voice belonged to the Whiskey Wine Saloon's owner, June Smith. She and Lacy were only casually acquainted, but Lacy recognized her instantly from a few months back when a local farmer's house had burned to the ground during a particularly bitter cold spell. June had been one of the first to arrive with secondhand clothes for the children, bedding, and food. Obviously, the woman recognized her, too.

Lacy forced a friendly smile past the lump in her throat. Her heart tripped at the saloon owner's words. "Did he . . . did my grandfather mention what he wanted with the sheriff?" She was afraid she knew. God, please let her be wrong.

June crushed her cigarette out, her expression sympathetic. "Yep, honey, I'm afraid he did. Said something about 'tellin' him a thing or two.' He's mighty upset about the mayor hiring that young, handsome sheriff."

Lacy thanked her and hurried off to the jailhouse, praying that she wasn't too late. She had known Grandpa was working himself into a rage. She should have done something, talked to him about it. But dang it, she'd been too busy trying to get them out of hot water with the sheriff.

She picked up her skirts so that she could run faster, secure in the knowledge that there wasn't anyone out to see her indecent exposure of legs. A disturbing image of Adam Logan's face rose in her mind, adding to her rising concern. No relenting when Ben had taken the pie, no relenting when she'd tried to apologize.

Adam Logan wasn't a forgiving man, that was plain to see. After what they had already put him through, he wouldn't take kindly to Rusty throwing a conniption fit.

Grandpa could get pretty ornery, especially with a brick in his hat—and Lacy didn't doubt for a minute that that was the shape she'd find him in.

By the time Lacy reached the jailhouse, she was out of breath. She didn't bother to knock, but just pushed the door open and rushed in, bracing herself for the worst. When she saw Adam leaning over the still form of her grandfather, she didn't stop to think. She raced across the room and thumped Adam on the head with her fist.

"Get away from him, you—you bully! He's just an old man. What have you done?" Without waiting for an answer, she pushed a surprised Adam away and knelt down by her grandfather. "Rusty? Rusty, are you all right?" He looked so still . . . so *asleep*? Lacy's eyes widened as she stared at Rusty's open mouth. A snort, then a lull, then a steady stream of snores erupted from his throat.

Suddenly, she was grabbed by both arms and hauled roughly to her feet. She found herself standing nose to nose with an extremely angry sheriff. "I—I thought . . . you had . . ." She closed her eyes, praying that when she opened them, she'd be in her own bed, fast asleep. The nightmare of her marriage returned, bringing a dreaded terror with it. She prayed harder.

It was no use. That deceptively soft voice of his intruded into her wishes.

"I'm gettin' mighty damned tired of being abused, Mrs. Ross. Mighty damned tired."

What would she do if he hit her? Never mind that she had just thumped him on the head. . . . Lacy peered at him, saw the blazing eyes, and quickly lowered her own gaze again. Her stomach took a slow dive to her feet. He *looked* mighty tired. Good grief, she had hit him in the head, of all places! She licked her dry lips. "I—I'm sorry—"

"Sorry?" he ground out, still softly. "Sorry don't get it, lady." He rattled her teeth with a hard shake, as if she didn't already know he was hopping mad. "You came flying in here, jumping to conclusions. Sound familiar? Twice in one day, Mrs. Ross. *Twice.*"

Lacy felt anger returning, shoving her terror aside, yet she wasn't ready to look into those cold blue eyes. "You don't have to keep repeating yourself, Sheriff Logan. I'm not deaf."

His smile reminded her before he spoke the words. "Neither am I, and as I recall, you accused me of the same thing earlier."

Swallowing, she lifted her eyes for a brief moment, then focused on his chin. The dark shadow of his beard made him look more dangerous, if that were possible. "If you won't accept my apology . . ." She let the words hang, sincerely not knowing what else to say.

"Hmmm. That's an interesting proposition." He relaxed his grip, but didn't release her. "If I won't accept your apology, then what else do you have to offer?"

His meaning sank in by slow degrees. She should have known he would twist her words around. Stiffening, she lifted her outraged gaze to the sheriff's. His eyes no longer blazed with anger; they glittered with serious intent. Worse than anger, she thought, her stomach dropping another notch. Anger she understood, expected; this was unfamiliar territory.

The skin beneath his hands had grown warm; she felt a frightening urge to know what it would feel like for those strong arms to go around her, pull her close. Shocked at her thoughts, Lacy dropped her gaze before he read what was on her mind. Wasn't she in enough trouble?

With as much dignity as she could muster, she said, "I have nothing else to offer, Mr. Logan. *Sheriff* Logan." *Maybe reminding him of his position will remind him that he has a reputation to uphold,* was her desperate thought.

Adam laughed softly, seeing through her ploy. "That didn't work." When it appeared she wasn't going to answer, he relented and let her go. He prodded the sleeping man at their feet with his boot. "I take it you know Mr. Palmer, here?"

Lacy inched away from him and let out a slow, shaky breath. Later she would have to do some mighty hard thinking, along with giving herself a stern mental lecture about what happened to women who succumbed to their desires with men like Adam Logan. And that blasted fear of hers . . .

"Of course I know him. He's my grandfather," she announced coolly, proud to hear that the strength had returned to her voice. It gave her the courage to continue, once again attempting to explain. "He—he was a bit upset about losing his job and when he saw you, I guess it just brought it all to a head. Then he started drinking." Which wasn't the entire truth, because she knew that Rusty had been drinking before he found out about the new sheriff. Still, it was close enough to the truth. She gazed down at Rusty, her eyes softening as she studied his familiar, beloved features.

Her voice matched her expression. "He's been sheriff for fifteen years, and he's too set in his ways to realize that he's getting old. Shadow City's growing by the day and the responsibilities of sheriff are growing with it." She hesitated, glancing at Adam. "If the mayor had let him be your deputy for a while . . . it would have made things easier for him."

To her surprise, Adam nodded. "It might have at that. Now, what are we going to do with him? It's getting late. . . ."

Lacy flushed, realizing that she and her family had caused Adam Logan enough trouble for one day. *Enough to last him quite a while,* she added to herself. "I'll see if I can wake him." She knelt again and shook Rusty several times, to no avail. There wasn't even a break in his snoring.

"Just leave him. He can sleep here," Adam said. Watching her closely, he added, "I'll just put him on one of those cots in the jail cell, leave the door unlocked."

Lacy came swiftly to her feet, facing him squarely. "You can't do that! He'll be mad as a hornet in the morning if you do."

"Believe me, I don't think he knows anything right now, and I'll deal with his anger in the morning. I'm not locking him up, Mrs. Ross. Just giving him a place to sleep tonight."

She bit her lip, wanting to explain about Sheriff Murddock

and how Rusty would feel waking up in the jail cell where his best friend had died. Yet it didn't seem right, telling such things to a stranger. "I guess it will be all right. Just as long as you explain it to him in the morning." Adam folded his arms and nodded. Lacy brushed at her dress, not looking at him. "Well, good night, then."

"Good night."

With one last glance at her grandfather, Lacy headed for home. She blamed the prickly sensation of her skin on the balmy night air, scoffing at the ridiculous possibility that Adam Logan could cause such a reaction.

When she'd gone, Adam grabbed Rusty by the arms and pulled him into the room leading from the office, hoisting him onto the bed that should have been his own. He left him there to sleep it off, and with a weary sigh, settled himself in the chair and tried to get comfortable. It was going to be a long night, he thought disgustedly.

So much for following doctor's orders. Of course, he could always crawl onto one of the two cots in the jail cell.

Adam cursed beneath his breath and leaned his head back, closing his eyes. He shouldn't have lied about putting Rusty in the cell. But somehow, he couldn't resist ruffling her feathers at every turn. *Payback,* he told himself. *That's all it was.*

He smiled, realizing that he hadn't enjoyed himself so much in a long while, despite his aching head. She'd flown at him like a furious mother hen defending her chicks, big beautiful eyes all afire, her bosom heaving.

He wondered if she made love with such passion. She'd seemed mighty shocked over the stolen kiss earlier—and again tonight, over the way he had deliberately miscon-strued her words.

It made him wonder if her dead husband had bothered arousing her passion at all. Adam stirred himself long enough to turn down the lamp, reminding himself that he didn't have time to dally with the fiery widow Ross. There was serious work to do if he was going to solve the puzzle of his grandfather's death before the end of summer.

Best he avoided her as much as possible, which he'd certainly been unable to do so far. Tomorrow would be different, though. After tonight, he wouldn't have any reason to visit Lacy, nor she him.

4

*L*ACY STUFFED SEVERAL small chunks of wood into the flaming cavity of the stove beneath the hot plate, then slammed the small door, feeling mean and miserable. Behind her at the kitchen table, Rusty groaned and covered his ears. Lacy felt no sympathy for him when she heard the agonized sound. She hadn't slept a wink all night, worrying about him sleeping in that jail cell. And all for nothing, according to Rusty, who had awakened her before dawn by banging on the front door.

"Why would he do a spiteful thing like that?" she demanded, not for the first time. Maybe if she said it enough, a reasonable answer would come to her. "If he was going to put you in his bed instead of the cell in the first place, then he just told me that for pure spite!"

"I told you I don't know. Now, would you please stop makin' all that racket? My head is killin' me."

"Good. Serves you right for putting me through that." She emphasized her point by scraping the coffeepot across the grate, creating a screeching noise that she hoped increased his misery tenfold. "And why was he asking you those questions about Sheriff Murddock? Doesn't make sense, him interested in a man who's been dead for fifteen years." Swinging around, she aimed the pot at his cup, sloshing coffee over the sides in her agitation. She swiped at it with her apron and glared at her grandfather. "And how could you just leave Ben with him? There's no telling what he's doing to him." Rusty had informed her that Ben was already at the jailhouse waiting to 'serve his time' for Adam Logan. In fact, Ben was the one who had awakened him and sent him home.

Rusty lifted his gaze without lifting his head. "You was the one that agreed to send Ben to him." When she didn't hit him with the pot, Rusty stepped across the line. "Besides, he ain't so bad. He could have thrown *me* in jail, the way I acted last night. Hell, I wouldn't have blamed him. If it'd been the other way 'round, *I* would have."

Lacy ground her teeth. "Don't cuss—you know Grandma didn't allow it. I guess you think he should have put Takola and Ben in jail too? And what about me? I hit him on the head because I thought he had hurt *you*." Groaning in remembrance, she squeezed her eyes closed. "He probably thinks we're the craziest bunch of folks he's ever run across."

Rusty nodded in agreement. "Yep. Probably does. Can't blame him for that, either."

She felt the strangest urge to stomp her foot at his traitorous words. "Grandpa! How can you say that? *He's* the one that—that scared Ben half to death, and threw my apology back in my face. Then he had the livin' gall to pump you when he knew you were pickled. Next thing you'll tell me is that you don't blame him for stealing your job."

Prudently, Rusty waited until she returned to the stove and set the coffeepot down before he spoke. "Lacy, he told me he didn't know he was takin' anyone's job. He ain't even met the mayor."

She snorted in disbelief. "What? Did he think a town this

size didn't have a sheriff?" Recklessly, she dusted the table with flour before slapping a small mound of pie crust into the middle of it.

Rusty wisely covered his coffee cup and scooted back in his chair to escape the white cloud that arose from her furious movements. "Wasn't you the one that told me that I should let it go? Let bygones be bygones, you said."

Lacy rolled the dough vigorously back and forth with the heavy oak rolling pin and mentally cursed Rusty's excellent memory. A rascal he was, for reminding her. "I might have," she admitted with great reluctance. "But that was before he—" She stopped abruptly, clamped her mouth shut, and continued rolling the pie crust. She didn't have to look at her grandfather to know that he had gone still. *Thunder!*

Rusty leaned over the table until he came into her line of vision, which was stubbornly centered on the dough. His voice deepened as he demanded, "That was before he what, Lacy? What did Sheriff Logan do that's got you in such an all-fired tizzy?"

She couldn't stand it. She just couldn't stand him thinking what she knew he was thinking. "Nothing, Grandpa. He— he just kissed me, that's all." Heat seared her face. She waited tensely for his reaction. It wasn't a problem either one had dealt with before.

When her husband, David, had courted her, he'd been the perfect gentleman all the way up to the wedding. Not that he hadn't kissed her before the wedding—just never without her consent. It was not until later that she discovered David was not the man she had first believed him to be. Lacy shuddered at the memory. Not on her life would she take that chance again.

She had Grandpa, Takola, and Ben, and they kept her plenty busy. Her life was full and she had the freedom to do as she pleased, when she pleased. Marrying again anytime soon just didn't appeal to her. Twenty-four wasn't so old; she had plenty of time, if she could ever bring herself to trust again.

Strange noises interrupted her train of thought. Alarmed, Lacy jerked her head up, her eyes flying in her grandfather's direction. Her jaw dropped, then snapped shut. She pursed her lips together so hard she feared they'd remain flat.

"What's so funny?" she demanded.

It was too much. Rusty burst into laughter, alternating between holding his aching head and holding his aching middle. Finally he managed to gasp the words out. "Your grandma got that mad the first time I ever kissed her." He grabbed the edge of her apron to wipe his streaming eyes. "Can't believe I didn't catch it afore now."

Lacy jerked the apron out of his hands, feeling insulted without knowing why. "What are you jabbering about?"

"You, girl, you. I'm talking about you." He pointed a finger at her, his silly smile looking out of place in the lined wisdom of his face. "You got a hankering for the new sheriff, Lacy Lynn Ross."

It was several moments before Lacy found her voice. "That's ridiculous, Grandpa. Absolutely ridiculous." She took a deep breath. "In fact, I've never heard of anything so ridiculous in my life."

Rusty slapped his thigh and rocked back and forth, laughing, even harder. "That's exactly what your grandma said when I told her she had a hankerin' for me. Damn near word for word."

The dough hit him squarely in the face, effectively smothering his grin. Lacy harrumphed in satisfaction and left him to his insane, totally ridiculous imaginings.

And they _were_ ridiculous. Why, putting her and Adam Logan together was like trying to mix bacon fat with water. A person could shake and shake, but within no time the two would fight their way apart again.

Adam awoke with a stiff neck. Groaning, he opened his heavy eyelids and found himself looking into Ben's fearful face on the other side of the desk.

They stared at each other in silence, until Adam's groggy mind realized he wasn't dreaming. How long had the boy been standing there, watching him sleep? Uncomfortable at the thought, he turned his head toward the window, blinking his gritty eyes. A red dawn speared a bar of scarlet light through the glass panes, signifying the barest beginning of a new day.

Adam stretched, massaging the tense muscles in his neck and shoulders and vowed he would have his own bed tonight, come hell or high water.

Which reminded him. He focused on Ben again. "Palmer still here, boy?"

Ben jumped, eyes widening at his cranky tone. "Nope. He went on home." Then, daringly, he added, "And the name's Ben, sir."

Despite his foul mood, Adam felt a smile tugging at his lips. The youth had spunk, just like his—but no, she wasn't his *real* mother. Yet Adam had a feeling she was that and more to this little stick of fire. His protector, definitely. "Okay, Ben. Do you always get up this early?"

Ben scraped the floor with his boots, dropping his agitated gaze to follow the nervous movement. "Nope. Just couldn't sleep. Thought I'd get this over with before I start my lessons."

"You mean, before you go to school?"

Ben shot a quick glance at Adam through curly lashes before dropping his eyes away again. His pale skin brightened the freckles dotting his entire face. He cleared his throat. "School's out. Besides, I don't go to school, sir."

"And why is that? You look old enough to me." Adam waited curiously for the answer to his question, ignoring the chiding voice that reminded him of his decision not to get involved.

Just when he decided Ben wasn't going to talk, the boy mumbled, "I'm old enough, be ten in December. But I—I ain't so good at book learning, and the other kids poke fun at me. Lacy says it's best I learn at home until I get better at readin' and writin'. Catch up with the others."

Once again, Adam mused, Lacy had come to Ben's rescue. But in this instance, he found himself agreeing with her. In fact, he felt sorry for the boy as he imagined the humiliation he must have suffered. Low self-esteem wasn't good for a growing child. He should know. His stepfather had gone out of his way to try to make certain that young Adam retained little confidence in himself.

Pushing those sorry thoughts from his mind, Adam tapped a contemplative finger against his beard-roughened chin. Maybe he had stumbled upon the reason behind Ben's stealing. The possibility chased the last wisp of sleep from his brain.

"Ben . . . does it make you feel smart when you steal something from someone?"

Ben lifted startled eyes to stare at Adam. "Sir?"

Aha! Adam thought, homing in on his theory. "How many other boys do you know can steal a pie from the sheriff right beneath his nose?"

"But you caught me!" Ben blurted out in confusion.

"Yes, but you damn near got away with it. If I hadn't turned around when I did, I wouldn't have known what happened to that pie. How many times do you succeed? Without them catching you?" He already knew from what Lacy had said that Ben stole frequently from the townsfolk. It was just a hunch, but one worth digging into.

Frowning in thought, Ben said slowly, "Well, I don't always get *caught,* if that's what you mean." His chin came up a notch. "And I ain't never met anyone else what can steal like I can." In the blink of an eye, his expression turned gloomy. "Ain't much else I *am* good at, though. Can't hardly read or write. Most folks don't consider stealin' such a smart thing to do, neither."

Adam nodded in silent satisfaction. There was still the unresolved question of why Ben stole only food items, but Adam felt he was definitely on the right track. Maybe there was hope for the boy yet.

Tactfully changing the subject, he said, "Let's go see if anyone else is up at this hour. That saddle's gonna crack if I don't get some oil on it."

"Okay, but I warned you, I ain't much good at nothin'." Ben sounded disgusted with himself and Adam resisted the urge to squeeze the boy's shoulder. He didn't think a show of pity would be appreciated. Ben had a streak of pride in him that reminded Adam of himself, something that had gotten Adam his share of beatings.

"We'll see," was all he said in response. Standing, he reached for his hat and set it down nice and easy on his head. The swelling had gone down, he noted, but the bump was still a little tender to the touch. In rueful remembrance, he shook his head and grabbed his gun belt from the desk, buckling it in place as he strode to the door with Ben in tow.

As they made their unhurried way to the livery stable down the street, Adam looked around him with a mixture of curiosity and astonishment. The town didn't awaken gradually, with a slow filtering of folks onto the streets. It seemed to happen all at once, as if there were a silent bell that told the townspeople it was time to be up and about.

Locks clicked open, windows were thrown wide to catch the cool early air before the afternoon heat arrived. The lamplighter scurried up and down the street extinguishing the lamps with his snuffer, a long metal rod topped by a tiny, deep cup. A heavy wagon rumbled by, loaded with enormous logs destined for the lumber mill. Across the street, Adam caught the eye of several curious ladies as they made their leisurely way to the large general store on the corner of Main and Oakleaf.

They entered the cool, dim interior of the big, barnlike structure to the smell of horses, leather, and hay. As they passed between the rows of horse stalls, many of the animals nickered and thrust their heads over the doors of the stalls in greeting. Ben called a few by name and patted their noses before hurrying to catch up to Adam's long strides.

They found the stablemaster in the tack room, searching through a large bin filled with a collection of old horseshoes, broken bridles, and moldy blankets. He straightened at their approach and smiled as he recognized the new sheriff.

During the short time it had taken Adam to stable his horse and make arrangements for its upkeep, he discovered that Matt Johnson had seen his fiftieth year, had lost a wife and three children to the smallpox epidemic of eighty-two, and had recently remarried.

"Your horse settled down right nicely, Sheriff. Sometimes they kick up a fuss being someplace new, but your ol' Sandy didn't." He wiped his hands on the corner of a saddle blanket, glancing curiously at Ben, who hovered behind Adam. "Ain't that the widow Ross's boy?"

Adam reached around and grabbed Ben's shoulder, pulling him to his side. "Yeah, this is Ben. Ben, you know Matt Johnson here, don't you?" Then to the stablemaster he said, "He's gonna help work my saddle over for me." He felt Ben tense beside him, probably wondering if he planned to tell the stablemaster *why* he was helping him. Adam had no such intention. That was between him and Ben, as far as he was concerned.

If Matt was surprised by the information, he hid it well. He smiled at Ben. "Well, that sounds like a man's job, don't it? Tell you what, if you do a good job on the sheriff's saddle here, then I might pay you to do a few for me."

Ben glanced at Adam, then at Matt, as if he couldn't believe what he was hearing. "You might? Really?" Then his face creased into a familiar frown. "I ain't no good at oilin' saddles, Mr. Johnson." He studied his boots, his chin dropping onto his chest.

Adam suppressed an aggravated sigh. It was worse than he'd first thought. Ben seemed convinced that he was worthless at everything. "You ever oiled a saddle, Ben?" he asked, looking at the bend head.

"No, sir. I haven't. That's why I'm tellin' ya, I can't do it."

"Now, how can you possibly know you can't if you've never done it? I ain't never been a sheriff before, either, but I'm willing to give it a try."

"That's not the same thing," Ben argued, but he sounded less sure of himself.

Adam exchanged an understanding look with Matt. "I'm gonna leave you here with Matt and he's gonna show you how it's done. Later, we'll look it over and I'll decide if you can or you can't." Before Ben had time to protest, Adam took his leave.

He had an entire town to get to know before he could begin his investigation. But first he needed to shave and to change into some clean clothes. He wanted to look his best for the boss—the mayor—when they met for lunch. Maybe the mayor would be able to tell him who did the laundry in town. Adam made a mental note to ask him.

"The buckboard's ready," Rusty informed Lacy as he came through the back door. He took off his hat and swiped at his forehead. "Gonna be hotter'n hell today, I surely believe."

Lacy spared him a cool glance before sweeping past him with a basket of neatly laundered clothes, calling over her shoulder, "Thank you, Rusty. I'm running late, and Ellen'll be frantic if I don't get these pies to the restaurant before lunch starts. Can you help carry them out? You know what it's like on Fridays, and laundry has to be delivered and collected, too." Then, before Rusty could respond, she hurried on, "Where's Ben?"

Rusty grumbled something she didn't quite catch, then said, "He's upstairs doin' his lessons—just like you told him. Seems we're all doing just what we're told."

Surprised by his disgruntled statement, Lacy halted in the doorway and turned to face him. She supposed she had sounded a mite bossy, but she had so much to do today. . . . "I'm sorry, Grandpa. Would you please help me load the wagon? Takola's coming with the last basket of laundry, and since Ben got a late start on his lessons . . ." She followed this with a pleading look that she knew worked every time.

This time was no exception. Within minutes, everything was loaded, and she and Takola were on their way to the restaurant. Normally Ben rode along with her, but he'd returned late from helping Sheriff Logan and she needed *someone* to help. Some folks wouldn't be too pleased at the sight of Takola, but Lacy didn't see any other way around it. Rusty might load the wagon, but he drew the line at coming along with her on her delivery route.

Besides, she thought darkly, it was plain silly for folks to get upset over a little thing like Takola. She staunchly refused to think about the lump on Sheriff Logan's head, and how it got to be there. That was a fluke, a mistake that shouldn't have happened. Takola hadn't meant to hurt him; she'd just been frightened by his gun and the way he had chased Ben.

Lacy expertly guided the old mare through the narrow alley that ran alongside the three-story building that served as both hotel and restaurant. The eating area occupied most of the ground floor, along with the hotel office and the kitchen. She pulled the wagon around to the back door and set the brake. Before she could step down, Ellen came out to meet her, wiping her hands on a food-stained apron and wearing a sunny smile that never failed to make Lacy's own mouth curve upward.

"Thought you was gonna be late, and I got the new sheriff asking for another blackberry pie," Ellen said by way of greeting. She stepped up to the wagon and bent her tall frame over the side, peering hopefully around. "You did bring one, didn't you? I swear, that man must love blackberry pie. He bought the one you brought me yesterday before it had time to cool!"

Lacy's smile faltered. She exchanged a half-mused, half-dismayed look with Takola. "You . . . you didn't tell him who baked the pie, did you?"

A hint of deviltry gleamed in Ellen's gray eyes. She shrugged. "He didn't ask, so I didn't see no reason to tell 'im. Might be bad for business for folks to know I can't bake a pie worth a hoot."

"I don't think anyone would believe you, the way you cook everything else," Lacy said sincerely. It was true, too. Ellen was the best cook in the county; people came from miles around just to dig in to a plate of her chicken 'n' dumplings.

Lacy and Tokola stepped down from the wagon and began gathering up the pies. Takola took one, Ellen two, and Lacy balanced the last three on her arms. Together, they started inside to set them on the table in the kitchen. Lacy brought up the rear, and Takola, not accustomed to doors, let it slam behind her before Lacy could catch it with her foot.

The door slapped her full force. The pies began to slip

from her arms. She caught two of them against her chest; the other fell to the ground with a plop. Dismayed, she stared at the blackberry filling covering her shoes and soaking the hem of her dress.

The *only* blackberry pie she'd made. *Why* did *it* have to be the one to fall?

Apparently realizing that Lacy hadn't followed, Ellen jerked the door open and took one look at Lacy's horrified face, then at the crumbled mess at her feet. Groaning, she said, "Looks like our new sheriff won't get a blackberry pie today."

Lacy bit her lip and grimaced. "He didn't get one yesterday, either, Ellen."

"What? Of course he did . . . I ain't senile, you know. I sold it to him myself." Bending, she began scraping the pie from Lacy's shoes. "Looks to me like he would have satisfied his craving yesterday, what with a whole pie and all."

"Ellen."

"Maybe I can sweet-talk him into one of these apple—if they ain't squashed too bad." She gently pried a pie from Lacy's chest, heaving a relieved sigh to find it still in one piece. A little crushed, but edible.

"Ellen—"

"See, it ain't too bad. Put a dab of thick sweet cream on it and they'll never know the difference. Now, let's get a gander at the other one."

The pies had survived the disaster, save the one at Lacy's feet. With her hands finally free, Lacy touched Ellen's shoulder to gain her attention. "Ellen, Ben stole the pie Sheriff Logan bought yesterday."

Understanding finally dawned. Ellen's eyes went wide. "Oh. Guess he wanted this one pretty bad, then. Ain't never seen a man hanker for a pie as much as this new sheriff."

Lacy closed her eyes and swallowed hard. Didn't she know it. Suddenly, an idea came to her. She pushed Ellen inside the kitchen and waited for her to land the pies safely on the table. "Ellen, you stall him while I run home and bake him another one." Frantically, she motioned for Takola to join her at the door.

"Lacy! How in the world can I stall him that long? It'll take you nigh onto an hour to bake that pie, and he's ordered his food already."

"Does he have it? The food, I mean? Is he already eating?" Lacy held her breath for the answer.

Ellen held up a finger and went to the door, pushing it open a crack to peer into the dining area. Lacy resisted the urge to tiptoe up behind her and look too. After a few seconds, Ellen let the door close and said, "No, not yet. But like I said, he's ordered his meal."

"Stall him. Tell him you ran out and had to cook more. Anything, just take as long as you can."

With obvious reluctance, Ellen nodded. "All right, but I hope he doesn't get mad. Hate to lose a good customer, you know. Especially the sheriff. Never know when you might need him."

Tugging on Takola, Lacy backed out the door. "Thank you, Ellen. I'll make it up to you, I promise."

With a careless lift of her skirts, she jumped onto the wagon bench and waited impatiently for Takola to join her. Then she slapped the reins sharply, sending the mare into a startled trot down the narrow alley. Her mind raced ahead. She would instruct Takola on preparing the blackberry filling while she rolled the pie crust. While the pie was baking, she'd make a few laundry deliveries, then rush back to the house to get the pie.

She could do it, she *could*. With determination, speed, and a lot of luck, Sheriff Logan would get his blasted pie. Maybe then he'd be in a better frame of mind and consider taking Rusty on as his deputy. The way Rusty had talked, they'd had a nice, friendly chat instead of the falling-out Lacy was expecting.

Was she, then, thinking of asking him outright to hire Rusty? Lacy called herself a fool, but that didn't banish the idea from her mind as it should have. She loved her grandfather, and it seemed he grew more melancholy each day. He had taken such pride in his job as sheriff, and as deputy to Sheriff Murddock before that.

And while there were lots of things to do around the house, like taking care of the chickens and the hogs and making certain the buildings were in good shape, she suspected her grandfather still felt useless.

Adam's arrival had made matters worse, so in her opinion it was only right that he should help rectify the matter.

With the decision made, Lacy felt a small measure of relief. Yet the thought of asking Adam for a favor—any favor—made her knees tremble and her throat dry.

She wouldn't put it past the rascal to want something in return.

Something Lacy couldn't give.

5

*A*DAM TAPPED HIS foot beneath the table while the mayor of Shadow City, Jamis Goodrich, detailed his life story. The man was a few years younger than Rusty Palmer, as near as Adam could guess. It was the only thing the two older men had in common, but it interested him. Anyone old enough to remember Colt Murddock could be important.

But *damn,* the old man was windy.

"Havin' the only lumber mill around these parts made me rich, and I ain't ashamed to say so. The railroad comin' through was a stroke of luck," the mayor informed Adam.

The mayor didn't say how he managed to remain the only lumber mill, but Adam suspected he knew. Jamis Goodrich *kept* the competition away, probably by any means he could think of—lawful or otherwise. During the long, lonesome journey on horse back from Wyoming, Adam had traveled through miles and miles of prime lumber, most of which he encountered after crossing into Missouri. Plenty for everyone, but he didn't think Jamis Goodrich was willing to share.

But Adam didn't really give a damn about Goodrich's personal history, or, for that matter, the weak fools who allowed Goodrich to stop them from adding to the competition.

Adam's wandering gaze traveled around the large dining room, filled with twelve or so tables decorated with red-and-white checkered cloths. Absently, he nodded to Dr. Martin, seated about four tables over, near the window. With him was a thin, elderly gentleman wearing a dark gray suit. Adam didn't recognize him, but made a mental note to find out who he was. He looked older than Adam's grandfather would be.

The mayor rambled on. So far, the self-centered ass had not mentioned anything of great interest, and hadn't paused long enough for Adam to direct the conversation into more lucrative areas—like Sheriff Murddock, or Rusty Palmer.

Or Lacy Ross.

Which reminded him. He wondered how she had reacted to Ben working for Matt Johnson this morning. Ben had done such an excellent job on his saddle that Matt had asked him to stay and help him in the stables for a while longer. Adam took a chance and agreed on Ben's behalf. He figured Lacy would chew him good for making Ben late for his lessons. The thought made him smile with anticipation.

If he ever managed to leave this restaurant, Adam mused, he'd have to think of some excuse to go see her, to tell her his theory on Ben. But from the looks of it, he'd be here for supper, too.

Adam tapped his fingers on the table impatiently. They'd been waiting for their food for almost an hour. His stomach had begun to growl in earnest and he was sorely tempted to grab something from a nearby table. *Those* people had gotten their food promptly.

His restless eyes strayed to the mayor's hands, to his collection of rings: a hefty-looking gold nugget, a ruby surrounded by diamonds, more gold rings on the other hand. The man displayed his wealth almost to the point of

vulgarity. Adam felt his lips curling in disgust and stopped
the action. He couldn't afford to make an enemy of the
mayor at this early date.

Adam didn't like him much; he'd spent the last thirty
minutes trying to figure out what his mother had found to
like about a greedy, middle-aged land-hogger. Whatever it
was, it continued to elude him.

But she *had* liked him, and so had his grandfather, if his
memory served him right. Jamis Goodrich had been one of
the first settlers of Shadow City, a man obviously respected.
He had opened the lumber mill, ensuring a profitable
business for himself and steady employment for many
people.

Yet there was something about him . . . something
Adam couldn't put his finger on. Shifty? Maybe. The
mayor's eyes never stayed in one place long. It was one of
the reasons he hadn't informed the mayor of his relationship
to Colt Murddock. He didn't trust him to keep quiet.

Mercifully, the mayor finally halted his boring recitation
and craned his neck around the crowded, noisy room,
frowning. "I wonder if they've forgotten us, Sheriff Logan."

Adam swallowed a sarcastic retort. Well, at least they
agreed on something. He had a feeling it was going to be
just about the only thing they agreed on. "I've been
wondering the same thing for the last thirty minutes,
Mayor." He didn't much care that his drawling answer
implied that he hadn't been listening to the conversation.

The mayor didn't appear to catch the slight. He tossed his
handsome gray head in the direction of a tall woman
chatting with the people at a table nearby, clearing his throat
loudly to get her attention. "Ellen—where's our food?"

Adam watched the woman turn and dart a nervous glance
at him before looking at the mayor. "I'm sorry, there's been
a little problem . . . with . . . in the kitchen. She . . . it
won't be long now."

Before Ellen completed the sentence, a harried young
woman barreled through the crowd in their direction,
holding two heavy plates aloft. Without ceremony, she

nudged past Ellen and plopped the steaming food down, then disappeared into the kitchen again.

Ellen appeared even more flustered. "See, there it is. You boys enjoy your meal, you hear? And take your time."

Jamis Goodrich chuckled, digging into the plate of dumplings. "Well, Sheriff Logan. Do as she says. I think you'll find it was worth the wait."

But Adam wasn't listening. *Take their time?* He didn't like the sound of that. Hell, they'd already been here half the day! He caught Ellen by the elbow before she could step away. Forcing a polite smile, he said, "You haven't forgotten about the pie, have you—Ellen?"

Ellen looked shocked, as if he'd suggested something lewd. She pulled from his grasp and shot a nervous glance at the kitchen door before facing him again. "No, Sheriff. Of course I haven't forgotten the pie. Blackberry, wasn't it?"

Feeling slightly ridiculous for making such a big deal of something so trivial, Adam widened his smile, revealing an impressive show of white teeth. "My apologies, ma'am. I should never have doubted your efficiency."

The woman seemed to melt beneath the substantial force of his roguish smile. "That's all right, Sheriff Logan. I know what it's like to get a hankerin' for something, just to have it snatched from beneath your nose."

She was gone before Adam could recover from her startling words. He stared after her for a moment, wondering how she had known about Ben and the pie. Finally, when no answer came to him, he shook his head and picked up his fork to calm the embarrassing rumbling of his stomach.

By the time the pie arrived, delivered by Ellen, Adam and the mayor had long since finished their lunch. *Never in my life have I wasted so much time eating,* was Adam's exasperated thought as Ellen took their empty plates and replaced them with clean ones.

He took an appreciative sniff of the steaming pie, his mouth watering in anticipation. With just the barest hesitation, he offered to share with the mayor.

Jamis Goodrich patted his stomach and shook his head.

"No, sir. I couldn't handle another bite. You go right ahead. You waited long enough for it."

Adam couldn't have agreed more. He cut a large slice and slid it onto his saucer, listening to the mayor with half an ear. Carefully, he wiped his fork with his napkin, not wanting anything to interfere with the taste of the pie.

"That Ellen cooks a mean meal, doesn't she?" The mayor's compliment was followed by a satisfied sigh. "Thought about marryin' her when she lost her husband, but decided she was too old. Now, the widow Ross, she's more to my likin'."

Adam paused at the mention of Lacy, then sank the fork into the warm pie. It was none of his concern *how* many admirers the widow Ross had. First Dr. Martin, now the mayor. And that sharp little twist in his gut didn't have anything to do with jealousy, he told himself sternly.

"She can cook right fine, too. In fact, she baked that there pie you're eatin'. She bakes all the pies for Ellen, brings 'em every day just like clockwork. She's a hard worker, and a fine-lookin' woman."

The mayor's informative rambling skimmed the surface of Adam's subconscious as he forked a huge bite of blackberry pie between his lips. He closed his eyes and bit down, fully expecting a wondrous flavor to burst in his mouth.

There wasn't time to reach for his napkin.

He sprayed the salt-laden pie onto the checkered cloth and grabbed for his water. In fact, he couldn't get enough water. After draining his own glass, he slammed it down and reached for the mayor's without asking. He had never tasted anything so awful in his life!

When the mayor's glass was empty, Adam managed to croak, "Did you say Lacy Ross baked this pie?"

Maybe he hadn't heard the mayor right. But he knew better. Who else could do this to him? Now he knew why she hadn't slapped him when he had stolen that kiss; she'd been planning a different retaliation.

Concerned, the mayor leaned forward, eyeing Adam's thunderous expression. "Yeah, the widow Ross. Ellen don't like folks to know it, but she can't make 'em herself. Somethin' wrong with the pie?"

"I'm gonna kill her for this," Adam said from between clenched teeth. He could just imagine her, standing over the pot and pouring in the salt, probably wearing a great big grin.

His furious gaze landed on the innocent-looking pie. When Lacy Ross least expected it, he'd get his revenge.

The week passed uneventfully for Lacy. As usual, her daily routine kept her busy with little time to spare for standing around jawing about Adam Logan, like the rest of the townsfolk appeared to be doing.

By Thursday, she was mighty tired of hearing about the new sheriff, from Ben, Rusty, and anyone else she happened to run into. Adam Logan was a gentleman. Adam Logan was strong, and honest. Adam Logan was handsome and unmarried. Adam Logan would make a fine addition to the growing population of Shadow City. He was trustworthy and fair.

"A wolf in sheep's clothing, more likely!" Mumbling beneath her breath, Lacy lugged the butter churn outside to the backyard to enjoy the slight breeze while she churned. The wash swayed gently on the ropes Rusty had strung from tree to tree; the garden had been weeded during the cool, early hours of the morning and the chickens pecked happily at the crushed corn she'd strewn about. From the time she had risen at dawn to stoke the fire in the stove for coffee and breakfast, Takola had worked steadily at her side, seeming to anticipate Lacy's every need.

How had she managed her workload without Takola? Lacy wondered, her affectionate gaze on the small brown Indian girl standing outside Big Red's pen. She was scratching the huge hog behind the ears as he made grunting noises of pure pleasure.

Settling herself on a stool, Lacy began to rotate the wooden paddle in a circular motion. Her shoulder muscles strained in protest, sore from a hard day of washing clothes. She paused often, staring down into the sweet, creamy mixture without really seeing it, her thoughts as jumbled as the cream.

It was Ben's turn to churn the butter this week, but when she couldn't find him, Rusty had informed her that Ben had promised to help Adam build a new set of shelves to replace the old ones in his office.

Ben had forgotten his chores.

"Fiddlesticks," Lacy said aloud, blowing a damp curl out of her eyes. In the week Adam Logan had been in town, he had managed to turn everyone's head, young and old alike, man, woman, and child—with the exception of herself and Takola.

Lacy began the monotonous circular motion with the paddle again, her mouth pursed in a grim line. She might as well admit it, at least to herself, that she was a little jealous of Sheriff Logan. Rusty spent most of his time visiting Adam at the jailhouse; Ben was with him more often than not. And Grandpa didn't appear the least bit resentful anymore. He seemed content to help her with the daily chores and spend his idle time at the jailhouse talking about Lord knew what with the sheriff.

It was the same wherever she went.

The regular Tuesday night quilting bee had turned out to be a gossiping session about the new sheriff, instead of their usual exchange of recipes and dress patterns, talk of children, and discussion of what Reverend John had preached on Sunday.

Why, nobody had even mentioned the upcoming festivities in September. Every year, the townspeople planned a grand gathering to celebrate the anniversary of Shadow City's official birth; this year the town would be twenty-five years old. The celebration had grown with the town until it resembled a fair of sorts. People came from miles around to join the festivities, bringing prize cattle, crafts, and food to be entered in contests or sold from small, hastily constructed booths set up in the park.

Lacy remembered her exasperation by the end of the bee, wondering how many of the single young ladies present would make a fool of themselves like she had. She wanted to warn them, but couldn't without becoming the subject of their gossip, so she remained silent. It hadn't been easy, especially when her close friend, Carrianna Simmons, blushingly announced to the entire room of girls that she was going to bake a peach cobbler for Sheriff Logan.

Carrianna's announcement, much to Lacy's disgust, prompted others to confide their plans for welcoming Adam, ranging from a new shirt to a set of new curtains for the jailhouse window!

They'd find out that Adam Logan appreciated nothing. Not once had he mentioned to Ellen what he thought of the blackberry pie he'd wanted so desperately. *Not one nice comment!* Nor had he mentioned the meal she'd taken him that fateful day, and he hadn't returned the plate. Rusty eventually brought the dish home, without a word of thanks from Adam.

Then there was Ben. As far as Lacy knew, he hadn't stolen a single crumb of food from anyone lately. Either the townsfolk weren't telling, or he was getting even better at it than before. If Ben had finally managed to overcome his impulse to steal food, then she was glad, she really was. But it pricked her pride a little to realize that what she hadn't been able to accomplish in several years, Adam Logan had accomplished in a single day.

Of course, Lacy sniffed, he'd scared the living daylights out of Ben. But Ben wasn't afraid of him now. He talked about the sheriff enough to set her teeth on edge.

She seemed to be the only one who knew Adam Logan for the rascal he was, and this, she knew, was the problem. Was it her? Or was everyone else blind to his faults?

She couldn't decide, and since she'd managed to avoid him—or was he avoiding her?—she hadn't had the opportunity to change her mind.

That suited her just fine. Adam Logan had enough of the townsfolk falling all over themselves to please him. He didn't need her, and she didn't need him. Not by a long shot. He was too—too *rough*. Yes, that was the word she was looking for. Rough and ill-mannered. And dangerous.

As far as asking him to consider hiring Rusty as his

deputy, well, she would get around to bringing it up if and when she saw him. With a town this small, they were bound to run into each other eventually. But lately, the matter didn't seem quite so urgent, with Rusty in such a confounded cheerful mood these days.

Steeped in her puzzling thoughts, Lacy jumped when a hand touched her shoulder. She swung around to find Takola standing beside her. "Oh, you startled me, Takola. What is it?" Lacy's eyes lit on the pile of small tin crocks Takola cradled in her arm. "Oh, is it ready?"

Dazed, she looked into the heavy churn. To her amazement, she saw that the butter was indeed ready to be spooned into the containers. After that, she would take it to the general store, where she would trade the butter for flour and sugar. With the money she made from selling her pies and doing laundry, she bought coffee, tea, and any other items she needed.

This month, she planned to buy Ben a pair of new boots, and Takola could do with a dress or two with money she had saved. They never went without any of the necessities, and although Lacy wouldn't dream of mentioning it to Rusty, they were getting along just fine without his sheriff's pay.

Thank goodness she had more important things to do than to sit around thinking about Adam Logan.

"Damn, I'm out of nails." Adam turned the sack upside-down and shook it. The new shelves were nearly completed; the ancient, warped shelves lay in a broken heap in the tiny, enclosed backyard of the jailhouse.

Adam twisted around, looking for Ben. He found him searching the floor for rusty nails. "Ben, will you run to the general store and get more nails? Those old ones are weak and keep bending when I hammer them." He reached into his pocket and withdrew a handful of copper pennies. "And keep the change. Buy yourself some candy."

Ben took the pennies and carefully slid them into his left pocket. His right pocket held the money he'd made working for Matt Johnson. He'd already confided to Adam that he was saving it to buy Lacy something nice. Shyly, Ben asked,

"Mind if I get Takola a licorice whip? She likes 'em a lot."

"Go ahead, and if you have enough, bring me a peppermint stick." Adam smiled faintly as Ben shot out the door.

Seated comfortably at the desk, Rusty chuckled, but his eyes studied Adam shrewdly. "You're as bad as Sheriff Murddock, with that sweet tooth of yours. He liked his sugar. In fact," Rusty added softly, "he'd get downright ornery if he didn't get what he was cravin'. Just like you do."

Slowly, Adam put down the hammer and braced his hands on his hips, narrowing his eyes at Rusty's seemingly innocent expression. "Is that a fact," he drawled.

Rusty put his hands behind his head and closed his eyes as if preparing for a nap. He chewed slowly on a toothpick. After a moment, he opened one eye and looked at Adam. "That's a fact."

"How long have you known?" Adam asked bluntly. He should have guessed Rusty would notice the resemblance sooner or later. But he would *never* have guessed that his sweet tooth would give him away.

Sighing, Rusty shifted his feet on the desk and rearranged the splinter of wood hanging from his lips. "Well, now. Let me see. To begin with, you askin' all them questions about Colt got me to thinkin'. Secondly, I hear you been askin' the same kind of questions of a few other folks here in town, mainly older codgers, like myself. Thirdly, you and that sweet tooth, and lastly," Rusty grinned, "you're the spittin' image of Colt around the same age.

"You see, Sheriff, me and Colt was bounty hunters together. We caught our fair share of varmints, let me tell ya. Course, this was afore he met and married your grandma. She didn't much like his line of work, but Colt didn't quit right off. No, he didn't quit until we went after that woman killer, Earl Baker." Rusty's eyes slanted sideways toward Adam. He lifted his bushy eyebrows in question. "You heard this story before, son?"

Intensely interested, Adam nodded. "Yep, I have. But I wouldn't mind hearin' it again, from a different point of view." He leaned against the wall and crossed his feet, his gaze steady on Rusty. To his knowledge, his grandfather had never mentioned having a partner. Adam wondered why. The two had obviously been close friends.

"Well, we went after Earl Baker, not only for the reward money—which was five thousand dollars—but for the principle of it all. That mangy dog had killed four women, tortured them afore he killed 'em, too. Colt knew one of 'em, so I can't say it wasn't personal." Rusty paused significantly, his voice low. "You might as well know the truth, son. Colt didn't plan on taking Baker in alive."

"You knew this?"

"Yep. I knew it. You gotta understand, I saw what Baker did to that girl, too. Life was even harder back then, and a man just about had to take the law into his own hands afore justice was done. Earl had friends, and Colt—we—didn't want to take the chance of him gettin' loose again. Anyways, we chased him plumb to Mexico and then lost him again. We got a tip from someone there that he was holed up in a shack a coupla miles from the border." There was a long, heavy pause as Rusty remembered back. "We found it and Colt busted in shooting."

"And killed the wrong man," Adam concluded. He had always had mixed feelings about the story, but hearing it from Rusty, he could very well understand how it had happened.

"He was pretty torn up about it. Didn't help none that the man he thought was Baker weren't nuthin' but a young boy, at the most sixteen. After that, Colt quit bounty huntin'."

"He didn't finish the job? Go after Baker?"

"No," Rusty stated gruffly. "I did."

There was no need to ask if he had succeeded. The satisfied look on Rusty's face told the story. Adam felt the same satisfaction knowing Baker had gotten it in the end. It also explained the close bond between Rusty Palmer and Colt Murddock. Adam wondered if Lacy knew about her grandfather's past, and how she felt about it.

"Before she died, my mother said Colt had done some things in his life he regretted, but he'd more than made up for it by making this town a place where folks could sleep without fear of gettin' murdered in their beds."

"She was right. He spent his whole life trying to make up for that mistake," Rusty agreed. "Sorry to hear about your ma. I heard she was a mighty fine woman. Colt talked about her a lot, and about that fine grandson of his—which is you, right?"

"Yes."

Rusty spit the toothpick out as if it had suddenly became something nasty. "But he didn't much care for that step-father of yours. Said the only reason he didn't run him off his ranch was because he knew your ma loved him."

"She didn't," Adam said harshly, his expression pained. "She married him so that I would have a father."

"I take it he wasn't much of a pa?" Rusty guessed.

Adam thought of the beatings, of the ridicule he'd suffered over the years. He'd stayed for his mother's sake, and as soon as she was gone, he'd left without looking back. It had taken all of his willpower not to put a bullet through Rudy Wagner's black heart. Not only had the bastard abused him, but Adam suspected he had abused his mother as well. "He wasn't much of a husband, either."

"If it's none of my business, say so, but why didn't she leave? Colt would have been more than happy to have y'all. As I recollect, he only bought that ranch because your pa was so dead set on raising cattle. Now, there's a man he liked. Shame he had to die so young. Stampede, wasn't it?"

"Yeah. A bull gored his horse and he went down. He was trampled to death before anyone could get to him. Happened when I was about Ben's age." It appeared that Rusty knew a lot about his life and the thought gave him a warm feeling, knowing that his grandfather must have talked quite a bit about him and his mother.

Absently, he pushed against the shelves with his boot. "As for Ma leaving, I know why she didn't. Because of my brothers. She had two sons by Wagner, and after that, I reckon she felt she had to stay."

"Oh, yeah. I'd forgotten about them. Colt never got to meet them, did he?" When Adam shook his head, Rusty continued, unable to hide his curiosity about the grandson of a man who had been like a brother to him. "But that still don't explain why you're here, and not running that ranch. You're a fur piece from Wyoming."

Adam waited to feel the familiar bitterness, and was surprised when he felt nothing more than a mild disgust over the way things had turned out. "The ranch belongs to my stepfather, now that my mother's dead. The ranch became hers after my grandfather died, then her husband's when she died." He shrugged. "That's the way it goes."

Rusty sat up in the chair, his mouth working in anger. "I told that son of a bitch to make a will. I told him a thousand times, when he'd start bitchin' about that no account son-in-law of his."

Adam didn't take offense at Rusty's colorful description of Colt Murddock. He smiled, but his eyes were hard. "That ranch has been Wagner's so long, I'd never get the stink of him out of it anyway."

Unappeased, Rusty sputtered, "But that was your land, Adam. Colt intended for you to have it, I heard him say so many times." Rusty was taking the news hard. "In fact, I told you the other night he was talkin' about going back there before he died. Said he missed his daughter, and wanted to see his grandson. I'm tellin' you, Sheriff Murddock didn't kill himself."

"I know. That's what I'm here to find out," Adam said quietly. "I promised Ma I would, and I'd appreciate your help, and your silence about the reason I'm here." He waited tensely for Rusty's answer.

Rusty didn't disappoint him. He slapped his hand on his knee and grinned, his earlier seriousness vanishing. "It's about damned time somebody found out what happened. You're damn right I'll help."

"Good." Adam kicked the shelf hard. Frustration roughened his voice. "Because it looks like I won't get any help from anyone else." He locked eyes with Rusty, demanding the truth. "Why is it that every time I mention Sheriff Murddock's name, people clamp their lips shut?"

Rusty hedged. "Folks don't want to remember."

Adam snorted. "Tell me something I haven't already figured out. What I want to know is why. My grandfather practically built this town."

With a heavy sigh, Rusty said, "They're ashamed, Adam. I hate to say it as much as you probably hate to hear it, but that's the blamed truth of it. Colt was their hero, the man they looked up to. In their eyes he took the coward's way out when he put that rope around his neck."

"But he didn't—"

Rusty held up his hand. "I know, I know. But you've got to remember: you and me are about the only ones that believe that. The rest of the folks believe what they saw. Sheriff Murddock didn't have no enemies in this town, and there was the note."

Adam's head came up with a startled jerk. "What note?"

"The note he left on his desk. Said how sorry he was about killing that boy, and how he couldn't live with the guilt any longer."

"You believe that?"

It was Rusty's turn to snort. "Hell, no! Colt felt bad about it, real bad, but not enough to kill himself. It was a mistake anyone could have made, and it was part of the past. That's where Colt left it."

Adam strode to the door to see if Ben was in sight, saw that he wasn't, then took the seat opposite Rusty. His mind churned with questions burning to be answered, but he knew Rusty couldn't answer them all. "Did you investigate?"

"Much as I could. Didn't have any luck. Whoever did it must have put a lot of plannin' in it. Couldn't find a clue nowhere."

"Any strangers in town the day he was found?" Adam pressed.

Rusty thought hard. Fifteen years was a long time ago. Finally, he nodded. "There was. Seems someone was drivin' cattle through that day on the way to St. Louis. Bunch of rowdy cowhands roamin' the streets. I questioned a few, but they didn't even know who Sheriff Murddock was. Then there was a fire and afore I got the chance to ask any more questions, the drive moved on."

"A fire?"

"Yep. Seems someone got careless with a smoke. Probably a drunk cowpoke, is my guess. We lost a few buildings afore we could get it put out."

Adam could understand how distracting a fire in town could be, with most of the business buildings connected the way they were. He shook his head, unable to find a connection between the fire and the death of his grandfather, so he dismissed it from his mind.

"Who found my grandfather?"

Rusty hesitated, and Adam saw a flash of worry pass over his features before they were interrupted by Ben's return from the general store.

Ben's dejected expression and the way he shuffled his boots along the floor told them the errand had not gone smoothly. Fumbling in his pocket, he pulled out the small sack of nails along with the leftover pennies and handed them to Adam.

Adam exchanged a puzzled glance with Rusty, who shrugged, then turned to Ben, noting his flushed face and shiny eyes. "What's the matter, Ben? And where's your candy . . . and mine? Did you forget I told you to spend the rest?"

Ben's face turned even redder. "Naw, I didn't forget." He fell silent, obviously reluctant to continue.

"Well?" Rusty prompted with a frown.

"Miz Ida, she didn't believe me when I told her you said I could buy candy with the rest." He pointed the toe of his boot at the floor and drew a line with it. "She . . . she followed me 'round the store, too, while I got the nails, an' checked my pockets before I left." Ben blinked furiously at the unmanly tears burning his eyes.

There was silence after his words as both men thought carefully about how to handle the situation. Adam imagined Lacy's reaction. She'd stomp down to the general store and raise holy hell, probably embarrassing Ben further— innocently, of course. He met Rusty's eyes again, saw the glint of amusement there, and realized Rusty was thinking the same thing.

Rusty cleared his throat, gaining Ben's attention. "You know, Ben, when people lie a lot, others tend not to believe 'em anymore. Stealin's the same thing. Miz Ida weren't being mean, she just don't trust you. You know why, don't you?"

Ben whispered miserably, "Yes, sir. I stoled from her before, and she caught me. She thought I was gonna do it again."

Adam silently applauded Rusty's wisdom, resisting the urge to pat Ben on the back. Some lessons had to be learned the hard way, and he knew this was one of them. "Maybe if you went back and apologized to Miz Ida, and offered to work for what you took before, she'd trust you again. You know, like you did for me."

"You reckon?"

Adam smiled, a little discomfited by the hero worship he saw in Ben's eyes. "I reckon she might. You've just got to earn her trust. Right, Rusty?"

Rusty nodded his approval. "He's right, Ben. Folks'll come around when they see you've changed."

"I *have* changed," Ben said, so dramatically that Adam had to clamp his lips together to keep from smiling. He heard a gasping sound from Rusty's direction before the old man was able to smother it.

"Now, let's get back to those shelves. I want to finish them before dark so I can take that pile of dirty clothes to the laundress. If I don't, I'll be walking around this town naked."

Ben giggled at the image Adam's teasing words evoked, his embarrassment forgotten. "Nah, you won't have to do that. Lacy's purty quick with the washing, since Rusty built that washroom out back. It's got a pump where she can fill up that big tub in no time a'tall." He frowned suddenly, unaware of Adam's dismay. "Course, she did the wash today, so I don't know if she can get to it . . . Damn! I was supposed to churn the butter today!"

"Watch your tongue, boy, or Lacy'll be washing it for you with lye soap," Rusty growled. He cocked his head at Adam, trying his best to contain his laughter over Adam's expression. "What'sa matter, Adam? Didn't you know my Lacy did the washin' here in town?"

Adam scowled at the older man, who was so obviously enjoying himself. "No. I did not. Is there anything she *doesn't* do?" he asked sarcastically.

With a toothy grin, Rusty shrugged, "She likes her independence."

"Well, I hope she's better at launderin' than she is at cookin'," Adam growled, much to Rusty and Ben's mystification.

6

"*M*IGHTY FINE MEAL, Lacy," Rusty said around a mouthful of stew. He scooped another portion up with a biscuit and popped it into his mouth, winking at Ben, who copied his movements with a little less grace.

Lacy tried to look stern. "Grandpa, use your spoon. Ben needs to learn table manners."

Rusty grumbled, but picked up his spoon. "What's he need table manners fur? Maybe he'll marry some gal who don't harp all the time 'bout things that ain't important." He shot her a meaningful look.

"Or maybe he'll marry a *woman* who appreciates a gentleman," she quipped, fighting to keep from smiling. She saw Takola's lips twitch out of the corner of her eye.

Grinning impishly, Ben tapped his spoon against the side of his bowl to gain their attention. "Whoever it is, I just hope they can cook like you, Lacy."

Blushing, Lacy said, "Why, thank you, Ben. That's the

nicest thing anyone's ever said to me." It was her turn to shoot Rusty a meaningful glance. He feigned an injured look, which made her laugh.

"I don't know how come Sheriff Logan says you can't cook," Ben added innocently, reaching for another biscuit.

The laughter stuck in Lacy's throat. She put down her spoon and patted her mouth with the napkin. When she tried to speak, it came out in a hoarse whisper. "Did . . ." Taking a quick drink of her water, she finally found her voice. "Did you say that Sheriff Logan said I can't cook?" She wanted to get it right. Perfectly right. Maybe Ben had meant something else.

Rusty kicked Ben under the table and Ben let out a betraying yelp. "Hey, what'd you do that fur?" he demanded, rubbing his shin. "I was just tellin' Lacy—ouch!"

"Stop kicking Ben, Grandpa. I've already heard what he said, so it doesn't matter if he repeats it." The quiet dignity in her voice sobered the moment. "Adam Logan's entitled to his opinion."

"Ah, hell, Lacy—"

"Grandpa!"

"I mean, tarnation, Lacy, Adam didn't mean it."

"Then why would he say such a thing?" she pointed out, wishing it didn't hurt. No wonder Adam hadn't returned the plate, or mentioned anything to Ellen about the blackberry pie. She blinked at the sudden moisture in her eyes, deciding she must be more tired than she realized. Certainly she wouldn't cry over a silly thing like the sheriff not liking her cooking. As long as she pleased her family, that was all that mattered.

When Ben saw the sheen of tears in her eyes he nearly burst into tears himself. "Tarnation, Lacy," he cried, unconsciously echoing Rusty's slang. "I sure didn't mean to make you cry. Like Grandpa says, the sheriff probably didn't mean it. He was just mad because he found out that you did the lau—" This time he didn't jump or yell when Rusty kicked him. He snapped his mouth closed and continued to look miserable.

Lacy looked from Takola's angry, glittering black eyes to Ben's guilty face and felt ashamed of herself for getting worked up over something so—so—*unimportant.* She didn't give a hoot if Adam never ate another morsel of food she prepared. And she certainly couldn't care less if he'd rather eat Carrianna's peach cobbler, or Susan's special spice cake.

"I'm not crying, Ben. I—I just got a little choked on the stew." Ignoring Rusty's skeptical look, she lowered her eyes to the bowl and forced herself to continue eating. She wanted nothing more than to race up to her room and fling herself onto the bed for a good cry.

Rusty studied her bent head and chewed his food with more vigor than the tender venison warranted. After some thought, he ventured, "Me and the young'uns are goin' fishing after dinner. You want to go?"

Lacy shook her head, pushing a potato around in the bowl with her spoon. Grandpa knew she didn't like to fish, but it was nice of him to ask. She swallowed hard. He probably felt sorry for her, and that possibility made her feel even sillier. It would also reinforce his ridiculous belief that she had a hankering for Adam Logan. Well, she'd just have to do something about that fantasy. Nip it in the bud, as Grandma would say.

When she lifted her head high and smiled, she felt as if her face would crack with the effort. She knew by the expression on Rusty's face that she hadn't fooled him, but Ben had visibly brightened and Takola didn't look so—so *hostile* any longer.

"If y'all catch enough fish, we'll have a fish fry tomorrow evening. How's that?" And while they all nodded enthusiastically, she added cheerfully, "And we'll invite Dr. Martin over to share it with us. Wouldn't that be nice?"

Ben had yet to learn how to hide his emotions. His happy expression fell as if someone had taken a hand and waved it downward over his face. "But . . . how about Sheriff Logan? I bet he'd . . . like to come . . . too." He faded into silence as Rusty, Takola, and Lacy stared at him in amazement. "Well, I just thought . . . never mind."

"Go get the fishing poles," Rusty growled at him. He shook his head in exasperation as Ben pushed his chair back and gathered up his dishes to take to the sink. "Takola, you think you can rustle us up some of those wigglers out by the hog pen?"

Takola nodded eagerly. She was gone in a heartbeat, leaving Lacy and Rusty alone in the kitchen. Silence stretched, thick with tension.

Finally, Rusty laughed, but it lacked its usual heartiness. "Girl likes to fish, don't she? Catches more than the menfolks, that's for sure. And I ain't never seen anyone that could find a mess of wigglers like she can."

Lacy started to remind him that the dinner table wasn't exactly a place to talk about worms, but refrained. She didn't really want to talk at all. She'd made up the story about the stew stuck in her throat, but she felt as if *something* were.

Rusty pushed back his chair with a sigh. "Leave the dishes. Takola and Ben can do 'em when we get back. Got about two hours of good light left and I want to make the most of it."

"You go ahead, Grandpa. I'll just get an early start on my ironing." She was looking forward to the solitude.

He stopped at her chair and squeezed her shoulder affectionately. "You work too hard, girl. It ain't right that you don't get out more, do something fun once in a while." When she didn't respond, he grunted and went to find Takola and Ben.

Lacy let out a shuddering breath after he'd gone. Unshed tears still clogged her throat, but she refused to give way to them, even if she was alone. Imagine, crying over something so ridiculous. Grandpa was right; she did work too hard and sometimes forgot to relax.

She could take a leisurely bath in the spacious tub she used for rinsing clothes. The washroom was fairly isolated, and they wouldn't be back for hours. Maybe soaking would help the soreness in her muscles, she thought.

Having made the decision, Lacy put water on to heat and

went upstairs to her room to search for a few extra pins for her hair. While she was there, she retrieved a small bar of jasmine-scented soap, a bottle of bath oil, and a clean shift. She paused to look in the mirror, trying to remember the last time she had bothered to look at her reflection.

She couldn't remember.

What she saw made her blanch. There was a streak of flour across her forehead; bluish shadows beneath her eyes, and her mouth looked pinched, as if she had eaten a green persimmon. Her hair was a mess and in need of a good brushing. She had washed it yesterday, braided it, and had forgotten about it.

She looked older than her twenty-four years, she thought. Was it any wonder Adam avoided her? And her hands, why, they looked as if they belonged to someone else. They were red and roughened from the harsh soap. She should have been soaking them in cream after she finished the wash on Thursdays.

Determined to take better care of herself from now on, Lacy marched downstairs to finish preparing her bath. Later, after the ironing was done, she would soak her hands and do something with her nails. Before she went to bed, she would brush her hair a hundred times.

And she would do it for *herself*. It had absolutely nothing to do with Adam Logan and what he might think of her, nothing at all. Grandpa was crazy for having such notions. He should know better, too. She liked her life just the way it was, and had no desire to complicate it with thoughts of the new sheriff.

She'd leave that to Carrianna, Susan, and the other young, single women who thought their lives incomplete without a husband. They would discover that marriage wasn't so wonderful, just as she had.

Lacy stopped before the hall mirror, staring at her reflection again, remembering another time when she had stood before a mirror, wondering how she would explain how the purple, swelling bruises came to be on her face. Eventually, as David's rages had become more frequent, it had been a struggle to think of a believable lie.

She'd been too ashamed to tell anyone, even Carrianna.

She'd been even more ashamed over the relief she had felt when she got the news of David's death.

With a resolute squaring of her shoulders, Lacy forced herself to move on. She shoved her dark memories where they belonged: in the past. She was free now, and as long as she remained free, she would never again have to worry about how she would explain the bruises.

Adam found the painting at the bottom of the tiny closet, hidden beneath a pile of dirty laundry. Carefully, he picked it up and backed out of the closet to view it in the light. It was a remarkable depiction of the town, right down to the painted star on the outside office door of the jailhouse. Of course, the town was bigger now, and many businesses had been added to the town that weren't shown in the painting.

He smiled as he noticed that the saloon had been moved since the artist had painted the picture. According to the picture, the saloon had once been right across the street from the church on Main Street. Obviously, the townspeople had not approved.

Tucking the painting beneath his arm, he found the hammer and nails and hung it on the office wall. Standing back, he studied it, wondering why Rusty had taken the painting down in the first place. Had it belonged to his grandfather? He'd ask Rusty, and if it had, he'd take it with him when he left. The painting would make a good momento of his time spent in Shadow City.

That done, Adam knew he could no longer put off taking his laundry to Lacy. He knew why he hesitated. Ben and Rusty mentioned her often, and Adam dreamed about her every night. He didn't need to *see* her to imagine her face, that long glorious hair, and those firm breasts. Those thoughts alone had the power to heat his blood.

He couldn't get her out of his mind, no matter how hard he tried.

Many other beautiful young ladies had presented themselves to him in the week since he'd last seen Lacy, plying him with food, clothing, and even a set of flowery curtains for the jailhouse window—all in the guise of being neighborly. But his initial instincts had been right; he felt nothing for them, other than a mild amusement at their not-so-subtle flirting and a healthy appreciation for the variety of dishes they brought him.

Lacy, however, was a different story. Despite the sorry trick she'd pulled with the blackberry pie, he couldn't stop thinking about her. Every shadow that passed by the window caused him to glance up with eager eyes, hoping to catch a glimpse of her. He looked for her while making his rounds about town, and she was his last waking thought every night.

Damn, she had tasted good. She had, by far, the sweetest pair of lips he'd ever settled his own upon. That brief contact had told him what he'd already suspected, that Lacy wasn't someone he could dally with and then just forget about when he went on his way. No, the widow Ross would get under his skin if he let her.

Who was he foolin'? Hell, she already had.

He was smart enough to know it wouldn't work. Lacy loved this town—hell, he didn't blame her—but he liked the wide open spaces and had every intention of buying that land in Wyoming when he was finished here.

Aside from these facts, Lacy didn't appear to like him.

Adam stuffed his laundry into a burlap sack and slung it over his shoulder, cursing beneath his breath. He'd dump the laundry on her, then skedaddle.

Or maybe he'd talk to her about Ben. That should be a safe enough topic. Besides, Rusty would be there to keep him in line. He shouldn't have a problem keeping his hands to himself because he wouldn't want to do anything to offend Rusty. If that wasn't enough, then all he had to do was remind himself how vicious Takola could be.

Adam laughed, shaking his head in wonderment that he could do so. Hefting the burlap sack, he set off in the direction of Lacy's house.

As he strode up the walkway leading to the front porch that ran the width of the house, he was reminded of the last time he'd walked up to this door. Lacy had met him with an old shotgun. He grinned, wondering if he would get the same kind of greeting. Was she still mad at him? Adam shrugged, thinking it might be better if she was. It would be hard to get close to a porcupine, and he needed all the help he could get.

He set the sack down and knocked. After a few minutes, he knocked again, this time louder. Still no answer, and he couldn't hear any sounds coming from within. It didn't make sense, since he knew Rusty was expecting him.

Frowning, Adam tried to recall the conversation he'd had with Rusty and Ben before they had left the jailhouse to head home. He couldn't remember Rusty saying anything about going anywhere this evening. What he did remember was Ben talking about a washroom out back where Lacy did the laundry. Maybe that's where they were, he thought. If not, then he would leave the laundry there. Rusty would explain where it came from, and he wouldn't have to see Lacy at all.

Adam squashed the disappointment he felt at this simple solution and grabbed the laundry bag. As he rounded the corner of the house, he heard the clear, sweet sound of a woman singing.

It came from a small building several yards from the back door. He stopped in his tracks, his heart suddenly galloping.

Lacy. It was Lacy singing, and the sound of her voice raced through his veins like a swig of potent moonshine.

Slowly, Adam approached the building, stopping at the closed door. He lowered the sack to the ground, then reached out and pushed gently on the crudely fashioned door until it swung open a couple of inches.

His heart reversed directions, slowing until the pounding grew loud in his ears.

Lacy reclined in the tub, one leg propped on the side as she made leisurely sweeps with a sponge from toe to thigh. Back and forth, back and forth. Adam followed the movement, his mouth going dry at the delicious sight. His eyes remained riveted as she switched legs and gave the other one the same treatment. When that was accomplished, she sat up and twisted her arm behind her, soaping her back.

The movement thrust her small, firm breasts outward. Adam swallowed, staring at the rosy crests, at the way they tipped upward as if beckoning him to touch them, nibble and taste.

A blast of raw desire robbed him of breath. He had to do something, before he said to hell with it. Before he stripped naked and joined her and damn the consequences.

He needed to put distance between them, so he did it the only way he knew how; he pushed the door the rest of the way open and stepped across the threshold.

She didn't scream as Adam had expected. She just sat there, frozen, her eyes wide in shock. Damp tendrils of hair framed her face, softening her rigid expression. A thick strand had fallen from the pins and lay against her white skin, the water turning it to a dark gold.

Adam wanted to touch it, to pull it from the water and wrap the wet strand around his finger. He lowered his lids to hide his lusty expression and drawled, "I have to say I prefer this greeting to the last one."

The sound of his voice released Lacy from her paralysis. "Get out," she hissed, sinking beneath the fading bubbles and trying to cover what she could. "Get out!" How *dare* he barge in while she was taking a bath! And dear God, how long had he been watching her? A flush pinkened her pale skin at the thought. Why her? Why did he treat everyone else with respect, and insult her at every opportunity?

Adam ignored her command, looking around for a chair. He spotted one and grabbed it, plopping it down in front of the tub before straddling it. He smiled when she scooted to the far side, her hands slipping in the process. For a heart-stopping moment, a rosy nipple peeped from between her fingers.

Lacy tried to control her panicked breathing as her eyes collided with his heated gaze. Her nipples hardened against her palms and she thanked God he couldn't see her body's betrayal. She didn't understand what was going on, but she knew it wasn't something she *wanted* to go on. She'd never reacted this way when David looked at her!

Panic overrode pride. She pleaded, not bothering to hide her desperation. "Please leave, Sheriff Logan. Please."

"Adam. I think due to the . . . uh, intimacy of the situation, you should call me Adam." He draped his arms over the top of the chair and settled his chin there, getting comfortable. He inhaled the scent of jasmine, knowing that from this moment on he would associate the smell with this slim, beautiful woman with the loveliest soft brown eyes he'd ever seen.

"Why are you *doing* this?" Lacy breathed, growing angrier by the moment. She felt helpless, and she hated feeling helpless more than she hated anything.

"I'm as entitled to my revenge as you are to yours. I'd say this just about makes us even."

"Even?" Lacy repeated, completely lost. "What in the *hell* are you talking about?"

Adam waved an admonishing finger at her. "Watch your mouth. You wouldn't want me to have to go searching for that soap, would you?"

Lacy gulped. No, she would not. The soap was in the water, somewhere. . . . Oh, God. He wouldn't dare . . . would he? She wasn't about to find out. "You talk as if—as if we've been playing some kind of game. I assure you *I* haven't. I don't even know what you're talking about."

"Does blackberry pie ring a bell? You gonna deny you were behind that nasty little trick?" Adam kept his eyes steadfastly on hers. He had to, or something was bound to bust.

Lacy shook her head in genuine confusion. Unless he was referring to the long wait while she raced back home and baked the second blackberry pie, she had no idea what he was talking about! "I'm sorry you had to wait so long, but you see, I dropped the first one."

Adam clicked his tongue. "My, you must have been running mighty low on salt. Two pies, you say?"

"Salt?" Lacy frowned. "I don't use much salt, just a pinch or two."

"Oh, I think you used more than a pinch or two in the one you made especially for me. It was *full* of salt, Lacy, so quit pretending you didn't know. You got your revenge on me for stealing that little kiss, and now I have mine." He bared his teeth in a wicked grin. "Though I have to admit, my revenge tastes a lot *sweeter* than yours."

Lacy wasn't listening. She thought back to the day she'd dropped the pie. They had returned to the house, and with her instructions, Takola had put the ingredients together for the pie filling while she prepared the pie crust.

Takola. Oh, God. Takola had used salt instead of sugar. Accidentally, or purposely? Lacy closed her eyes and groaned. She couldn't tell Adam, which meant he would continue to believe she had done it for revenge.

Adam listened to the throaty, provocative sound and gripped the chair with his hands to keep from hauling her up against his hard body. God, did the woman know what she was doing to him? Her voice jarred him from his naughty thoughts.

"You'll have to take me at my word, Sheriff. It was an accident."

"Hmmm. Well, it was an accident that I walked in on your bath, too."

"Now that we've got that settled, you can leave." It galled Lacy to agree with him because she knew he lied, but she wasn't in any position to argue at the moment.

"I don't think so," Adam said. "There are a few things I've been curious about."

"The water's getting cold," Lacy gritted out between clenched teeth. It was true, and it wasn't helping her condition any. If only he would stop looking at her as if . . . as if she were a tasty morsel and he a starving man. That hungry look frightened her, made her feel things she had no business feeling.

Adam reached into the tub and flicked his fingers, testing the temperature. She jumped, smothering a squeal of surprise. "Stop it!"

"It *is* gettin cold. Guess I'll have to hurry up with the

questions, and you'll have to hurry up with the answers."
She glared at him. He grinned.

"Then *hurry up and ask them*." She felt around with her
toes and located the soap. If he tried to come closer again,
she was going to hit him in the face with it.

"I want to know how Ben came to be with you," Adam
said. "Where's his folks?"

Lacy put her foot on the soap, gathering her thoughts. She
didn't know what she had been expecting, but it hadn't been
questions about Ben. Slanting him a look filled with
suspicion, she said, "His folks are dead. He was about six
when Rusty found him wandering around in the woods in
the dead of winter." She noticed Adam had stopped smiling.
Reluctantly, she went on. "We didn't find his folks till
spring, when the pond thawed out. Ben said they'd gone
fishing and never came back. Evidently they fell through the
ice and drowned.

"When Rusty found Ben . . . he was carrying his father's rifle, trying to shoot a rabbit. He was half starved to
death, and nearly frozen. He couldn't remember how many
days it had been since he'd eaten."

"God. So that's why he steals food."

Lacy flashed her eyes at him. "What did you think? That
he did it out of meanness? Ben's a good boy—"

"I know. And I didn't know what to think because I didn't
know about his past. Has he always had trouble learning?"

Surprised, Lacy forgot for the moment that she was
sitting naked in a tub full of cold water. "You know about
that?"

"He told me. I think that's another reason he steals,
because it's something he's good at."

Lacy considered his theory and reluctantly conceded that
he might be right. She remembered his question. "He gets
his letters mixed up, and often writes them backwards. But
he tries, and we found signs at the cabin that his mother was
trying to teach him." She tilted her head. "Why are you so
interested in Ben?"

Adam shrugged. "He reminds me of someone I once
knew."

A tense silence grew between them, and when it appeared that Adam was through with his questions, she asked, "Can I get out now?"

Adam spread his arms wide, the jaunty grin back in place. "Be my guest." He didn't move.

Narrowing her eyes at him, Lacy quickly snatched the soap and brought her hand up in a threatening gesture. She slid her free arm across to cover both breasts. "Get out or I'll throw this at you!"

Laughing, Adam stood and moved the chair back to its original place. "I'm leaving, I'm leaving. My laundry's sitting beside the door." He walked to the door, then turned to look and take one last fill, knowing she'd haunt his dreams more than ever.

Lacy shuddered beneath that consuming look. He hadn't touched her physically, but she tingled all over as if he *had*.

"I'll be back for my clothes tomorrow evening."

Lacy sputtered. "I can't get them done tomorrow, I've got the pies to do, and deliveries to make—"

Adam lowered his hot gaze to her lips, wishing he could kiss her long and hard. "If you don't, then you'll get to know my body as well as I know yours because I'll be walking around naked." He left her mulling over that ominous promise, closing the door politely behind him.

There was a loud thump as the soap hit the wood, followed by a string of names, some of which he'd never heard. With a wicked smile, Adam began to whistle as he headed back to the jailhouse.

He'd be sorry later.

When the sound of his cheerful whistle had died away completely, Lacy scrambled from the tub and began to dry herself with a towel. For a moment there, she had had the silliest notion that Adam Logan wanted to kiss her. But no, it was just her imagination. He seemed to take a perverse pleasure in embarrassing her, that was all.

And he had succeeded.

Lacy raked the clean shift over her head, bemused over the full tenderness in her breasts. The soft cotton fabric felt like wool against her sensitive skin. What in thunder would have happened if he had touched her?

She took a deep, calming breath. The feelings were natural; after all, she had been a married woman. But she didn't want to be one again, so that meant she had to control her wayward desires. Staying away from Adam Logan would be a good start.

Lacy reached into the tub and pulled the rag from the drain. Thanks to Rusty's ingenious thinking, the dirty water traveled through a long series of metal pipes into a field beyond the yard. Lacy gathered the wet towel against her chest and cautiously peeped out, relieved to find the yard empty.

Adam Logan didn't seem like the marrying type anyway, she reflected, scurrying across the short expanse of ground to the back door.

She stopped just inside the kitchen as another thought struck her, a startling thought. If Adam wasn't the marrying kind, then what was she worried about? It wasn't likely that the fire would have the opportunity to get out of control—if there *was* a fire. She knew that her body had responded to the heat in his gaze, but what did she really know about men and how they felt?

She knew they could hit hard.

Would Adam be like David?

Lacy raced up the stairs, her earlier fatigue forgotten. She was a fool to think such dangerous thoughts. . . . There was her reputation to consider, and Rusty, and the children.

As long as she avoided being alone with Adam, she would be safe, she decided. She had her family, people she knew and trusted.

It was all she needed.

She was dressed and well into her ironing by the time a pleasing thought occurred to her. Adam had said he didn't like her cooking, but that was because of the pie Takola had ruined. Which meant it wasn't *her* cooking, not really. She groaned to think of what that pie must have tasted like, filled with salt instead of sugar.

She should have a stern talk with Takola. If word got

around about that blackberry pie, then it could mean the end of her pie-baking business. A reluctant smile tugged at her lips. She admired Takola's spirit, but if she was going to live among them, she would have to learn to be more civilized.

Lacy sighed. Being civilized wasn't always easy, or fun.

7

*A*DAM DIDN'T KNOW whether to laugh or cuss. He held the shirt before him and studied the penciled markings, his dark brows lifted in amazement. "She hates me, she really hates me."

"That weren't Lacy's doing, Sheriff," Ben said, hopping from foot to foot. "Takola did it. She draws all the time."

"Hmmm." Adam studied the drawing. There was no mistaking what the picture was about. The soldier's face portrayed a gruesome look of glee as he fired down at the Indian woman. A small child clung to her leg, its mouth open in a soundless scream. Adam muffled a curse. "My God, did she actually see this happen?"

Standing next to Ben, Rusty rubbed his whiskered chin and said sadly, "Reckon she must have. Don't see how she could've drawn it otherwise. I'll take the shirt back to Lacy; she'll wash it again fur ya."

Adam moved it out of his reach. "No. I want to keep it. You say she draws others? Are they all the same?"

Ben shook his head. "No, they're all different, or most of 'em anyway." He threw an uneasy glance at Rusty, and Adam caught the exchange.

"Don't worry, Ben. Dr. Martin told me about Takola. I won't be tellin' it to anyone."

Rusty and Ben sighed collectively. "There now, Ben, see? The sheriff'll keep our little secret." He seemed to forget that he had been as worried as Ben. "Don't know why they'd be concerned nohow. She don't talk, just draws. She drawed on all four walls of her room, right after she showed up."

"How did you find out her name?" Adam asked curiously.

"'Pears she can write some. She got tired of us calling her 'that girl,' and wrote her name for us. Drew a picture of a fox to show us what the name meant." Rusty chuckled as he remembered. "That fox looked so real, I kept waitin' for it to take off running."

"She's good," Adam agreed. "But why my shirt?"

Ben's face was earnest as he answered, "She likes you. If she didn't, she wouldn't've drawn you nuthin'. Ain't that right, Rusty? She gives us pictures all the time, and she likes us."

"Reckon she might have been tryin' to apologize, too."

Adam lifted a brow at Rusty. "Apologize? Oh, you mean the whack she gave my head."

"No, I mean the ornery stunt she pulled with the pie. Lacy told me about it, how she let Takola mix it up 'cause she was in an all-fired hurry to get it to ya."

"*Takola* made the pie?" Adam nearly shouted.

Too late, Rusty saw the hole yawning before him. "You didn't know? But I thought Lacy . . . I thought she told you . . . Ah, hell. Now I'm gonna be in hot water."

Adam carefully spread the shirt on the desk, his mouth grim. Why didn't Lacy just tell him the truth? What in hell did she think he would do to Takola? Beat her? Shoot her? Throw her in jail? It made him furious to think that Lacy might actually believe any of those things about him. Yes, he had teased her about throwing them in jail . . . but hell, she had known he was teasing, hadn't she?

"Ah, hell," Adam muttered aloud. It seemed he had some additional talking to do with the tempting widow Ross.

Lacy stepped carefully into the house, mindful of the half-dozen eggs cradled in her apron. She stopped short at the sight of Rusty and Ben seated at the kitchen table. Rusty was bent over his knife, paring at his fingernails. Ben sat with his chin in his hands, watching Rusty. Takola was nowhere in sight. There was nothing unusual about her absence, for she often went off by herself to draw, or sit quietly and stare at her heart-wrenching creations, yet Lacy instinctively sensed something wrong.

"Where's Takola?" she demanded.

It was Rusty who explained, or tried to. "Upstairs with Sheriff Logan. She drew him a picture on his clean shirt and—"

Lacy didn't let him finish. She dropped the eggs, leaped over the broken mess, and raced up the stairs. Oh, God, how had Takola managed to do something like this without her seeing it? Her heart pounded against her chest as she reached the landing. If he had laid a hand on Takola's sweet head she'd kill him. The poor child had suffered enough to last a lifetime, and the last thing she needed was for some cocky sheriff to be hitting her.

Oh, God. *Would* Adam hit the child? Not the Adam *she* knew, but what if there was a darker side, one she didn't know about? Her husband had been a quiet, gentle man, or so she had thought.

She slowed to a halt outside Takola's room, then edged around the corner of the doorway, praying she wasn't too late. She heard Adam's voice, speaking low and gentle, but she couldn't see him, or any sign of Takola.

"And this one? Is that Chief Sitting Bull? I thought I recognized him."

Lacy craned her head, wondering if her ears were playing tricks on her.

"And this is Chief Big Foot being killed, right?"

Lacy flinched at the sound of pure rage that followed his

question. The sound had came from Takola. She was further surprised by Adam's reaction.

"It's all right to be angry, Takola. The army let power go to their heads, and they should have been stopped. There are lots of people who don't agree with what happened at Wounded Knee Creek—lots of people. You like Lacy, Rusty, and Ben, don't you? That's because you know they had nothing to do with this tragedy, just like a lot of other innocent folks."

Relaxing a little, Lacy moved into the room, her eyes scanning the artistic drawings on the wall. She'd seen them many times before, but they always drew her eyes again and again, their powerful message pulling at her soul.

They were also the room's only decoration. There was a pallet of blankets in the corner where Takola slept, and a basket filled with her few belongings.

Other than that, the room was empty.

Lacy explained softly, "She—she wouldn't leave the furniture in here." Adam turned at the sound of her voice. Blue eyes burned into hers and a jolt of awareness flashed between them, bringing a flush of heat to her face. The last time he'd seen her, she had been stark naked; that wasn't an easy thing to forget. She wondered if *he* had. She held his penetrating gaze, trembling inside and so very glad he couldn't see it.

No, Adam had *not* forgotten, she decided.

Finally, he looked at Takola again. He smiled down at the small upturned face. "I don't blame you. Give me a sky full of stars and a warm blanket and I'm in hog heaven."

To Lacy's astonishment, Takola returned his smile. If Big Red had suddenly trotted into the room and begun to talk, she wouldn't have been more surprised. So Adam had managed the impossible. What a wonderful boost to his ego. That left only one person in all of Shadow City, and it would take more than a charming smile to win her over.

A little respect would go a long way, was her tart thought.

Suddenly, she noticed Takola held something hugged to her chest. "What's that you've got, Takola?"

Adam answered for her. "I brought paper and pencils,

hoping she'll draw more of these for me." He swept his gaze around the walls again, where every available space was taken with heart-wrenching, intense depictions of the massacre. It was gruesome, sad, yet Adam suspected it helped Takola in some way to be able to express her grief and rage.

"That could be dangerous, if anyone sees them—"

"They won't," Adam interrupted. "I'll keep them for a long, long time before I show them to anyone. She's making history, Lacy. If she truly is the only survivor of her people, then that means only one side is being told. I don't have to tell you which side will get all the blame."

Lacy bit her lip. Once again, Adam was right. Still . . . if the drawings fell into the wrong hands, it could be dangerous for Takola. "What if you get careless?" she demanded, thinking only of Takola. History be damned, if it meant Takola might die for it.

"You have a low opinion of me, don't you, Mrs. Ross?"

For an answer, Lacy kept silent.

Adam's face hardened. He clenched his jaw, remembering why he had followed Rusty and Ben home in the first place—not only to see more of the drawings, but to get something straight with Lacy Ross. She'd been afraid to tell him that Takola had sabotaged the pie, for fear of what he would do to the little Indian girl.

That damned pie. He didn't care if he never set eyes on another blackberry pie in his life. Lacy had put an end to his hankering, at least in that direction. And now she was going to discover a thing or two about the man, Adam Logan.

Recognizing the signs, Lacy edged closer to Takola. She hated the fear, hated the wobbling betrayal of her voice but could do nothing about it. "Takola, go downstairs so I can talk to the sheriff."

Takola obeyed instantly, melting away without a sound. Lacy buried her trembling hands in the material of her dress and kept her chin level. She wanted to run. She wanted to hide, but she wouldn't. Never again would she cower from a man's anger. This was Rusty's home, *her* home, and Adam wasn't her husband.

When he began walking toward her, she held herself in

place by calling on every ounce of courage she possessed. She watched his face, her own frozen with dread, drained of color.

Adam continued his advance until he stood only inches away. He could see how she trembled, and his anger reached the breaking point. With infinite tenderness, he cupped her chin in his hand. She flinched, but held steady.

"What the *hell* did that bastard do to you?"

His harsh words faded away, leaving a thundering silence echoing in her ears. Dazed, she stared into his eyes, saw compassion and pity mingled there and drew in a sharp breath.

He knew. Somehow, Adam Logan knew her terrible, humiliating secret. How—? A hot wave of shame slammed into her like a physical blow, nearly buckling her knees.

"Wh-who?" Maybe if she pretended she didn't know what he was talking about, he'd leave her alone.

She should have known better.

"You *know* who." Adam took a deep breath, softening his words. She was scared to death—of him—and the knowledge twisted his gut. "That bastard you were married to."

Lacy tried to drop her chin, but he wouldn't let her. She dropped her eyes instead. His grip remained gentle, but firm. "I—I don't want to talk about it. Let me go."

But Adam wouldn't, couldn't. "You thought I was going to hit you, didn't you?" His voice echoed with disbelief. "And you lied about the pie because you were afraid of what I'd do to Takola. Right?" His grip tightened for a brief instant, but still didn't hurt. He could never hurt a woman. He could never hurt Lacy. "Am I right, Lacy?" A lock of hair fell over his forehead and he shoved it back with impatient fingers.

Lacy didn't believe him. She couldn't let herself believe what she saw in his eyes. To do so would be giving up her freedom, and that was something she could never do. Adam Logan was lying, and she would prove it.

She knocked his hand away, then drew her arm back and slapped him hard. His head rocked backward; her hand stung, but he didn't raise a hand to hit her back. Not that she had ever hit David. No, his rages had always been unprovoked, out of the blue. Shaking, she waited for his reaction, never doubting there would be one. But she never would have guessed what that reaction would be.

Adam smiled.

Lacy caught her breath at the beauty of that smile.

"It didn't work," Adam said softly, pulling her close. He nuzzled her nose with his own as if they were old lovers, as if he didn't have a red handprint burning his face. Lacy was too shocked to be outraged by the intimacy. She'd been so sure that he would strike back.

Their mouths met, parted; his in breathless anticipation, hers in disbelief that it was happening. Adam kissed her, slowly, thoroughly. She was everything he thought she would be, right down to the soft little sounds of surprised pleasure gurgling in her throat. She tasted of honey, and sweet creamy butter.

Lacy felt her bones turn to water. She was weightless, floating in a sea of pleasure. He tasted of peppermint, and with a curious little sigh, she pressed fully against his hard length. For just a moment, she would enjoy this piece of heaven, pretend it was real.

Adam pulled away slowly, reluctantly. Damn, he didn't want to, but this wasn't the place. There would never be a time or place for them, because in the end he would leave and she would stay. He tipped her head back and stared down into her face, soft and dazed with passion.

"Now you know what to expect when you make me mad, Mrs. Ross," he said huskily. He saw the moment she pulled herself together, the very instant when the fog of passion cleared from her eyes.

"Then I'll know not to make you mad, won't I?" She had meant to be flippant, to ease the exquisite tension between them, but her voice betrayed her; it was husky, as his had been. She stepped back and it was like stepping into the shade after warm sunshine. Lacy turned away so that he wouldn't see how much she preferred the sunshine.

On Saturday, Adam was on his way to the saloon when Rusty caught up with him. It was a few minutes past noon, and June had sent a cowpoke to the jailhouse to fetch the sheriff. Something about a fight over a bet.

"She say who it was?" Rusty asked when Adam told him what he knew. He lengthened his strides to match the taller man's, but ended up taking two steps to Adam's one.

"Nope. But I hope it's good. I was about to sink my teeth into a piece of Mary Ann's spice cake."

"You mean Susan's spice cake," Rusty corrected, beginning to huff and puff as he hurried to keep up.

Adam slanted Rusty a careless smile without slowing his ground-eating strides. He shrugged. "Whatever."

"Well, if you want to keep gettin' those vittles, you'd better get it straight. Women put a lot of stock in their cookin' around here. Mary Ann makes fried apple pies, Susan's the spice cake, and Carrianna's the peach cobbler."

Adam thought the whole conversation was a bit ridiculous. "Okay." He shrugged to keep a straight face.

"And Lacy makes apple pie, pecan, blackberry, strawberry . . . and the best jerky 'round these parts. Hell, she cooks better'n all of 'em put together, 'cept maybe Ellen."

Thank God they had reached the saloon, Adam thought, wondering what had gotten into Rusty. He was singing Lacy's praises as if . . . as if he were matchmaking.

Adam slammed into the doors of the saloon without pause, hoping like hell he was wrong. He'd hate to have to hurt the old man's feelings. But hell, Rusty knew he wasn't planning on staying in Shadow City. In fact, he was the *only* one that knew.

The two men that June had filed the complaint on were still fighting, and from the looks of things, had already done a lot of damage to the saloon. By unspoken agreement, Adam and Rusty waded in, Adam grabbing one swinging man while Rusty grabbed the other. The two young men struggled to break loose, panting and cursing at each other.

"What's this about?" Adam demanded, twisting the man's arm behind his back to hold him in place. Blood streaked from a cut above his eye. The other man didn't look much better. Glass crunched beneath their boots and Adam suspected that more than fists had been used—like a whiskey bottle or two. The air was heavy with the powerful smell of cheap whiskey.

Despite his age, Rusty held his captive with ease as he introduced the men to Adam. "This is Ed Thomas, and that one's Brian Bishop. They work for Clyde Olsen, big rancher west of Shadow City."

"Well, boys? What's this about?" Adam repeated, looking from one sullen face to the other. He could hear the saloon owner, June, behind him, setting chairs upright around the tables. A cluster of dusty-looking cowhands at the bar watched them curiously.

Ed spoke first, spitting a mixture of blood and saliva at Brian's feet. "We had a bet on who'd get here first, and I won. Now he won't pay."

Brian glared at him. "That's because you cheated, you miserable, lying dog! You loosened that shoe on my horse, didn't you? I'd have beat you if you hadn't pulled such a low-down trick. You nearly ruined a good horse."

Ed struggled to get loose from Rusty's expert grip, snarling names and kicking out with his feet. Prudently, Adam moved Brian back a few more steps.

Rusty clucked his tongue at both of them. "When you boys gonna learn?" He looked at Adam. "Last time, I believe it was Brain who pulled the 'low-down trick.' Happens most every Saturday, these two start fightin' and end up sharing the same jail cell."

"And they don't kill each other?" Adam asked.

"Nope. By that time they've lost their steam. Takes a while for them to clean the place up. Plumb tuckers them out."

Adam looked around him at the mess they'd made. He could see why they lacked the energy for fighting afterward. "Well, get started, boys, and then come on down to the jailhouse. We've got a cell waitin' on you." He was a little surprised when neither man protested. They still glared at one another, but when Adam and Rusty released them— slowly—they didn't try to go at each other again.

June appeared by his side. Her admiring eyes traveled the length of him, pausing on the broad width of his shoulders.

"I'll take it from here, Sheriff Logan. Thanks for coming."

Adam tipped his hat, amused at the invitation in her voice and the heavy-lidded eyes. "You're mighty welcome, ma'am."

Rusty followed him out of the saloon, into the warm bright sunshine. Adam paused to adjust his hat lower, staring down the road at the bustling town. It looked so peaceful, and he couldn't say he blamed the townsfolk for moving the saloon. He glanced at Rusty. "I've got a stop to make, then I'll meet you at the jail. We've got business to discuss."

"What kinda business?" Rusty demanded.

Adam grinned at his older friend. "You'll see. Where's Ben?"

"Doing his chores. He'll be down later, I reckon. Can't keep the boy away."

Behind them in the saloon, they heard a muffled curse, then all was quiet again except for the swish of a broom and the tinkling of broken glass. A whistle sounded in the distance, signaling the arrival of the noon train. At the lumber mill across the road, men scurried to and fro as they readied shipments of raw lumber to load onto the incoming train, which was bound for St. Louis. Adam knew that later in the day another train would approach from the east, heading to Kansas City.

Jamis Goodrich did a brisk business of supplying the larger cities with prime lumber. He couldn't have picked a better location than Shadow City.

When the train whistle ceased its raucous warning, Adam asked casually, "How was the fish fry?"

"How'd you—"

"Ben told me."

"Oh."

Adam scowled at the laughter in that single syllable. "Just wondering," he growled. "Meet you at the jail."

Rusty's knowing chuckle followed him as he stalked away.

A half hour later, Adam entered his office wearing a brand new, shiny silver star that said SHERIFF. He had two more in his pocket, one smaller than the other.

Rusty was sitting in the chair at the desk. He scrambled to his feet, whistling low. "That's a mighty fine star, Adam. Mighty fine."

Smiling at the envious note in Rusty's voice, Adam fished in his pocket and brought out the other stars the blacksmith had fashioned out of a bag of silver dollars Adam had given him. He tossed one to Rusty. "I need a couple of deputies so I'll have more time to do what I came to do."

"I can't take it, Adam," Rusty said regretfully, pitching the star onto the desk. It landed in Adam's unfinished spice cake.

"Why not?"

"Because the mayor won't stand for it. He fired me, remember?"

Adam's mouth thinned stubbornly. "I believe I can hire whoever I want as my deputy. And I choose you. You already know the town, the people, and how to handle things." When Rusty started to shake his head, Adam demanded, "What the hell did he fire you for, anyway?"

Slowly, with a heavy sigh, Rusty sat back down in the chair. He motioned for Adam to take the other seat. When Adam obliged, he said bluntly, "He's tellin' folks I was drinkin' on the job."

"And were you?" Adam asked just as bluntly. He hadn't forgotten the condition Rusty had been in when they had first met.

"Hell, yeah! Doc Martin had to carve my tooth outta my head. I had to have something for the pain."

Adam looked incredulous. "He fired you for that?"

"Hell, no!" Rusty's expression darkened, and Adam saw the man he used to be, perhaps a dangerous one when crossed. He suspected he could be again with the right prodding. "There was a fellow came through here a few months back—man by the name of Salvage—wantin' to open a lumber mill. I told Goodrich there was plenty of lumber, more than enough for two, but he wouldn't listen. Greedy son of a bitch. He got mad 'cause I wouldn't stand by him, and was waitin' for the chance to run me down. He got it."

Adam believed this without hesitation. He'd gotten the same impression of the mayor, too. Greedy. Back in his grandfather's day, Jamis Goodrich might have been a decent man, but greed had changed him. "What happened to Salvage?"

"He got his building about half set up, and one night it caught on fire, burned plumb to the ground." Rusty didn't have to tell him who had been responsible for the fire.

"Weren't nothing I could do," Rusty continued. "Townfolks don't know that side of him, and wouldn't believe me if I told 'em. Besides, I didn't have no proof."

There would be no point in getting involved, Adam reminded himself. He'd be leaving. Besides, what Rusty spoke of was over and done with. "I want you to take the job, Rusty. I'll handle the mayor."

Rusty hesitated, then finally nodded his acceptance. He reached in his pocket and pulled out a battered old tin badge, setting it on the desk. He stared at it for a long moment before letting go of it. "I shoulda gave you that to begin with, I reckon. But it was Murddock's, and I couldn't bring myself to do it." He pointed to the painting of Shadow City that Adam had found and replaced on the wall. "Just like that there picture. Colt mentioned a time or two that he oughta send it to you and your ma since y'all couldn't get this way too often. I knew that's what he would've wanted me to do with it after he died, but I kep' it. I'm sorry, son."

Adam felt a mild irritation at Rusty's confession. How excited he would have been over that badge, and the picture would have thrilled his mother. But one look at Rusty's sorrowful expression washed the irritation away. He scooped up the legendary star and slid it into his pocket, then plucked the new deputy star out of the spice cake and pushed it in Rusty's direction. A trail of cake icing followed his movement and the smell of cinnamon, nutmeg, and cloves permeated the air between them.

"Reckon we can skip the swearin' in, since you've been sheriff of this town for fifteen years." He followed this with a disgusted snort. "Hell, the mayor didn't even swear *me* in.

You'd think he'd be more careful about who he hires to run this town."

Rusty pinned the badge on. His face brightened at the sight of the shiny new star with the word DEPUTY written in big black letters, but he shot Adam a warning look from beneath his bushy brows. "Don't underestimate him, Adam. Goodrich probably knows more about you than you think. He wants a sheriff that'll do his biddin', and not ask any questions."

Adam refrained from reminding Rusty that he wouldn't be here long enough to worry about the mayor corrupting him. He wisely changed the subject. "So, what do you say we make a deputy outta Ben?"

Rusty's mouth dropped open and Adam saw a gaping hole in his left bottom row of teeth. Adam winced, thinking how painful the removal must have been. Then Rusty grinned, rubbing at his whiskers. "Well, I'll be damned. That might be what the little feller needs."

"I was thinkin' the same thing, Deputy Palmer."

"I can't wait to see Ben's face, Sheriff Logan."

"I can't wait to see the *mayor's* face," Adam said, grinning like a fool.

"I can't wait to see *Lacy's* face." Rusty burst out laughing as Adam's grin vanished.

Ben arrived, flushed from running the entire way. After much pleading, a little pouting, and several hours of putting on his saddest face, he'd finally persuaded Lacy to let him go. Now he slid to a halt in the doorway, his adoring eyes first on Adam, then on Rusty.

"What are we gonna do today, Sheriff Logan? I noticed that fence out back could use some mending. Fixin' it would make it mighty hard for someone to break in through the back way, if'n they were thinkin' 'bout bustin' someone outta jail."

The men chuckled at his exuberance and his vivid imagination, then Adam beckoned him closer. When Ben stood before him, Adam placed the badge in the boy's palm and closed his fingers around it before Ben could see what it was. "Now, Ben, do you swear to uphold the law in Shadow City?"

Ben's eyes grew round. He nodded.

"Do you swear not to steal, kill, or lie?"

Again Ben nodded, squirming with curiosity.

"Do you swear to finish each and every chore Lacy tells you to do, without grumbling?"

"Yes, sir."

"Do you—"

It was too much. Ben wrenched his hand free and opened his fingers. His jaw dropped onto his chest. He stared at the deputy star for several seconds before slowly lifting his head. "This—this is *mine?* I'm gonna be a real deputy?" Suddenly, he noticed the new star on Adam's vest, then the one on Rusty's shirt. "This is the greatest moment of my life!" he declared, fighting unmanly tears of joy. "I'm gonna run home and show Lacy and Takola, and Big Red—" He ran to the door, his new boots clanging on the wooden floor. Stopping on the threshold, he swung back around. "You mean it, Sheriff Logan?"

Adam crossed his arms. "I mean it, Ben. It don't pay much, maybe a dollar a week?" It was becoming extremely difficult to keep from smiling as Ben's eyes grew bigger and bigger until they seemed to cover his entire face. "Of course, Lacy has to approve."

Ben's face crumpled, then straightened. Squaring his shoulders, he said, "I'll talk her into it. And you won't regret it, Sheriff Logan. I swear."

"Good. Now, hurry back. After we get the prisoners settled, we'll celebrate at Ellen's, with pie and coffee. My treat."

"Prisoners?" Ben breathed in awe. Then he realized who Adam must be talking about. "Oh, you mean Ed and Brian. They ain't no trouble. And I don't drink cof—I mean, coffee's fine, Sheriff Logan. I'll be right back." He was gone in a flurry of flying boots, his excited yelp drifting back to them.

Rusty let out a gusty sigh of contentment. "You shoulda had a passel of young'uns, the way you got a knack for 'em.

Never thought Takola would take to you the way she did, and Ben, he thinks the sun rises and shines on that noggin of yours."

"I've never had a hankering to get married," Adam drawled. He'd spent most of his life working on the ranch and looking after his mother. There had been a few women along the way, but nothing serious. He was thirty-five. There was plenty of time, if he got the notion. And town life just wasn't for him.

"Maybe you just ain't had a hankerin' for the right woman."

Adam's reply was noncommittal. "Maybe. Who's Big Red?"

"You had to ask," Rusty said sourly. "He's the biggest, fattest hog in the county, that's who he is. But this winter Ben ain't gonna talk me out of it." He made a slicing motion across his neck. "Nope, this is Big Red's last year."

8

*H*ANDS ON HER hips, Lacy stood by the bed, nibbling thoughtfully on the inside of her jaw as she studied the dress spread out on the quilt.

No. It just wouldn't do this year, she decided. She'd have to find the extra money to make herself a new one before September. Carrianna wore a new dress every year to the celebration, and she had overheard Susan, Mary Ann, and a few of the others planning their new outfits.

Why should she have to wear the same dress for three years running? Nobody would think she was selfish if she bought new material and made another, would they? Lacy reached out and smoothed the worn yellow fabric, telling herself that she wasn't thinking this way because of Adam Logan, and knowing she was lying.

Adam.

Oh, God. Just thinking his name made her feel giddy, as if she'd stood up too fast. The way he'd kissed her . . . she'd never known a kiss could feel so—so *perfect*.

Standing in the circle of his arms, she'd felt like a queen, like a woman cherished and wanted. Like one of those limber licorice sticks that Takola liked so well. Boneless.

"Now you know what to expect when you make me mad, Mrs. Ross." Lacy turned and sat down on the bed. She tilted her head back and closed her eyes as she recalled those words, spoken in such a thrilling, husky voice. Could she believe him? That kissing her when she made him mad would be the only reaction he'd ever have if . . . if they were to marry?

Oh, good gracious! Was she actually thinking of Adam in that light? He wasn't the marrying kind . . . was he? Certainly, he was good with Ben, and had even managed the impossible—he'd won Takola's respect. And it was obvious that Rusty admired and liked him.

But that didn't necessarily mean that he wanted a ready-made family, Lacy told herself sternly. And not just any family, but *her* family, which she was honest enough to admit wasn't your average, everyday family.

Had she really thought his eyes were cold? At the beginning, but not now. After yesterday, she could never think of Adam Logan as cold. He had allowed her to strike him, and had done nothing.

Oh, but he had. He'd kissed her, long and hard, as if he couldn't get enough. And she had let him. Wanted him to continue. Touch her in places where she had never craved to be touched by David.

Lacy put a hand to her mouth, stunned by her outrageous thoughts. How did she know Adam wouldn't pinch and poke in a way so painful she would dread to be touched again by him? How did she know he wouldn't just . . . She covered her hot face with trembling hands and forced herself to continue. How did she know he wouldn't just thrust into her body, into that place that didn't seem to welcome such an intrusion?

It was shameful, painful, and humiliating. How could she actually want to try again, even with Adam? If she were to marry him, then discover it wasn't any different, she would be trapped forever, forced to repeat the act, to lie there and pray it would soon be over.

No! She wouldn't. Not again, not ever again.

Lacy jumped from the bed and snatched the dress up. With determination stiffening her spine, she carefully hung the dress on a wooden hanger and hooked it over the bar braced in the corner of the room. She would wear it again, and again next year. She would not fancy herself up to catch Adam Logan's eye, or any other man's eye. One lesson was enough for her; she wasn't brainless.

Let Carrianna go after the handsome sheriff, with her dimply smile and bright personality. Or Susan, with her curvaceous figure and cloud of black hair. For that matter, Adam might choose Mary Ann. She was a petite blond with a helpless air that seemed to appeal to men.

They were all wonderful wife candidates, Lacy thought with a sigh. If Adam was thinking of settling down, any of the marriageable young ladies in Shadow City, or from the surrounding ranches, would be delighted to accept.

Except Lacy Ross, who was much too smart to make the same mistake twice.

What did she need a man for? She took care of herself just fine. In fact, she took care of the entire family. She had Rusty, Ben, and Takola for company, and Rusty was handy with fixing things. Money wasn't a *big* problem, and she didn't miss the intimacy between a husband and wife.

So, there was nothing to miss.

Then why, she wondered a little desperately, did she feel as if something was missing all of a sudden? No, not all of a sudden, exactly.

Since Adam Logan had come to town.

"Oh, thunder," she mumbled, exasperated by her fickle thoughts. She tidied her room and was about to go downstairs to check on the ham baking in the oven when she heard the front door open, followed by an ear-splitting bellow.

Ben. She smiled, a rush of love swelling her chest for the little boy who had captured her heart.

"Lacy! Lacy, where are you? I've got sumpin' to show you! You're not going to believe it!"

"I'm up here, Ben," she called, his excitement arousing her curiosity. She went to the door of her bedroom to greet him.

Ben skipped up the stairs, his face flushed beet-red, his eyes fairly popping out of his head. He barreled into her, squeezing her hard. "You'll never believe what I got, Lacy. Never, ever in a hundred years!"

Laughing, Lacy pried him loose. "What is it, Ben? A turtle? A grass snake?" She tried to guess and each time he shook his head so hard his mop of red hair flew back and forth. "Okay, I give up."

He thrust his hand out and uncurled his sweaty fingers, holding his breath as he waited for her reaction.

Lacy blinked, then looked again. Yes, it was a deputy star. Her eyes had not deceived her. "Where did you get this?"

"Sheriff Logan! And he made Rusty a deputy too. His star's bigger, but I don't mind and we're gonna lock Brian and Ed up and watch 'em really good tonight and fix that broken fence behind the jailhouse so no varmints can get through there and bust them out!" He paused and took a deep breath. "Please say it's okay if I'm a deputy, Lacy, please?"

Lacy couldn't find her tongue. Was it dangerous? Should she allow it? How could she say no?

Ben saw her hesitation. His eyes filled to the brim and his bottom lip began to tremble, no matter how hard he tried to keep it still. "P-please, Lacy?"

Lacy's resistance melted. "Okay, but—"

"I know, I know," Ben interrupted excitedly. "I gotta do my chores without grumbling, and I can't lie, steal, or kill—"

"Kill?" Lacy squeaked out. "What in heaven's name are you talking about?"

"That's what Sheriff Logan said. I can't kill. Anyways, I had to swear to uphold the law. That means I can't steal no more."

"Anymore."

"That's what I said, Lacy. No more. I gotta go, they're waitin' on me." His chest puffed with pride. "We're goin' to Ellen's for *coffee*." Before Lacy could think of speaking, he reached up and pulled her face down, planting a wet kiss on her cheek. "Don't tell nobody I did that, okay?"

Torn between laughter and chagrin, Lacy nodded. "Okay, I won't. I won't tell *anybody*."

Her grammar correction sailed over his head. "That's what I said, don't tell nobody. I love you, bye."

"Will you be home for supper?" Lacy called after him as he flew down the stairs at breakneck sped. She held her breath as he sailed over the last three bottom steps and landed nimbly on his feet.

Ben looked up at her where she stood on the landing, his expression dead serious. "I reckon we will, and Rusty too. Us men got keep our strength up, you know. Deputyin's hard work."

"Of course," Lacy agreed with a wide-eyed, innocent look.

She jumped as Ben tore back up the stairs, his energy endless. "Here, pin this on me, would ya?" He panted, hopping from foot to foot.

Lacy chased him for a moment with the badge, then finally gave up. "Ben, you'll have to stand still if you want me to do this."

"Okay, but hurry! Brian and Ed should be showin' up any minute and Sheriff Logan might want me to lock 'em up."

Lacy refrained from pointing out that Brian and Ed knew how to lock themselves up. They did it often enough, nearly every Saturday night, in fact. Good thing she'd thought to put a ham in the oven, as she knew both cowhands possessed voracious appetites.

Ben managed to hold still long enough for Lacy to latch the star onto the strap of his overalls. "Don't you want to see how it looks?" she asked as Ben started to dart away.

"Oh. Yeah, guess I do." He followed her into the bedroom to stand before the full-length mirror. For a long moment he stared at the star; then his eyes met Lacy's in the mirror.

"D-E-P-U-T-Y. That says *deputy,* don't it? They weren't foolin' me!"

"No, Ben. They weren't foolin' you." She looked at the shiny star, then at Ben as something suddenly occurred to her. "Ben, how in the world did you read what that says, in the mirror? It's backwards."

Ben shrugged. "I don't know. It looks right to me."

When he pulled loose from her grasp and skipped to the door, Lacy didn't stop him. She was too busy thinking about what he'd said.

It had been easier for him to read the letters while facing the mirror. How strange. . . .

Thoughtful, she descended the stairs. When Ben settled down over this deputy business, she'd have to expand on her idea. It was crazy, but definitely worth a try.

Once in the kitchen, Lacy set her mind to other things, like what she would fix to go along with the ham. Maybe Brian and Ed would enjoy a few new potatoes, seasoned with butter and fresh cream. She would take a little extra with her when she took the prisoners their meal.

Adam would be welcome to the extras, of course. After all, he'd restored Rusty's pride by making him his deputy, and made Ben the happiest boy in Shadow City.

And for the last hour or so, Takola had been perched on a stool in the backyard, busy drawing picture after picture with the supplies Adam had brought her. She looked more relaxed and happy than Lacy had ever seen her.

Lacy checked on the ham, then fed more wood into the fire of the stove. As she straightened from the chore, her eyes strayed to the window overlooking the backyard. Takola sat, head bent, fingers moving swiftly over the paper. Big Red wallowed happily in a huge hole he'd dug; the chickens clucked and chased each other, fighting over every speck in the dirt that might indicate food. Beyond the hog pen and the chicken house, the woods pressed at the fence Rusty had put up many years ago.

Blackberries thrived along that fencerow, so many of them that Lacy could scarcely keep them picked.

In fact, she thought with a mischievous smile, they needed picking right now.

She knew just what to do with them, too.

"That boy's prouder'n a rooster in a new henhouse," Rusty said with a chuckle.

Adam smiled, watching Ben through the restaurant window. He stood proud and tall as three boys of various ages gathered around him, gawking and exclaiming over the deputy star pinned to the strap of his overalls. Adam couldn't hear what they were saying, but he gathered from Ben's pleased expression that the news was good.

Maybe Ben would have some friends now, Adam thought. He transferred his gaze to his other new deputy, seated to his left. "When you gonna tell me who found Colt?"

Rusty's eyes flew wide. He sat straighter in his chair and decided his coffee needed attention. Deliberately ignoring the question, he poured several spoonfuls of sugar into the black brew. Then he took up the spoon and began stirring. He stirred until coffee swirled over the sides and pooled into the saucer. Finally, when he had no choice, he met Adam's narrowed gaze.

"When are *you* gonna tell Lacy you ain't stayin', and why?" He set his jaw in a way that told Adam he wouldn't be pushed.

"She don't need to know."

"Course she does," Rusty stated. "She's gonna be madder'n a wet hornet when she finds out you're Colt's grandson, and that you ain't plannin' on stayin'."

"Why would she be mad?" Adam folded his arms across his chest and waited. He was curious, very curious, to hear Rusty's answer. More curious than he should be.

"Well, for starters, she's gonna feel like you lied to her. Lacy don't like to be lied to."

When he paused, Adam prompted softly, "And?"

"Well, the other thing is, you takin' this job as sheriff an' all, lettin' folks believe you're gonna stay, then plannin' on just up and leavin'." Rusty stared at Adam hard. "Other folks besides Lacy ain't gonna like that too much."

Adam lifted a brow.

"Well, it ain't right, leadin' folks astray."

"I thought you were on my side," Adam drawled. "I thought you wanted to find out what happened to Colt."

"I *am* on your side." Rusty slammed his spoon onto his saucer, scowling. "Tarnation, Adam. I'm tellin' ya you should at least let Lacy know what's going on."

"Why?"

With a growl, Rusty said, "Because she's gonna figure it out when you start asking her questions, and then she's gonna be mad that you didn't tell her yourself."

Adam straightened from his slouched position, forgetting he was in a public restaurant, forgetting to keep his voice low. "Why am I going to be asking Lacy questions?" he demanded, deciding Rusty needed a good thrashing. The man beat around the bush worse than anyone he'd ever talked to.

"Keep your voice down, dammit!" After satisfying himself that no one was listening to their conversation, Rusty leaned closer. "Because Lacy's the one who found Colt hangin' from that rope," he announced.

Adam was stunned by the news. All this time he'd been asking Rusty, and Rusty had managed to avoid answering. It had been Lacy all along. Why, she must have been—he voiced the thought. "She was just a child!"

Rusty nodded sagely. "Yep. Tore her up pretty bad. Still has nightmares, I reckon. Sometimes she wakes up screamin' in her sleep."

Adam suspected that more than Colt Murddock invaded Lacy's dreams. The thought darkened his face. "Why didn't you want to tell me?"

"'Cause she don't like to talk about it, even now, after all these years." Rusty took a sip of his cooling coffee, rubbed his chin, then glanced out the window. He didn't like the way the conversation was going, but he had started it. "After she found him an' came runnin' back to the house to tell us, she wouldn't talk about it again."

"And you never pressed her," Adam finished softly. A part of him could understand Rusty not wanting to question a child about such a trauma, but the other part of him wished Rusty had. Lacy had had fifteen years to forget something she desperately wanted to forget. The chances were slim that she would remember much of anything now.

Rusty looked defensive. "Nope, I didn't. Ma wouldn't let me, anyways. She said the girl had been through enough, and I reckon I agreed with her."

Adam tipped his chair back and cupped the back of his head with his hands, watching Rusty from beneath lowered lids. "You don't think she'll talk to me about it, do you?"

"Nope. I don't. If she wouldn't talk to me about it, what makes you think she'll talk to you? You two are like a cat and a dog in a barrel," Rusty declared with faint disgust.

"You don't have much confidence in me, do you?"

A sly smile curved Rusty's mouth. "That snake charm of yours might work on most women, but not my Lacy."

Adam let the chair fall forward, leaning his elbows on the table. "Is that a challenge, Deputy Palmer?"

Rusty grinned. "Might be. Might be at that."

Adam stood up and stretched. He reached into his pocket, withdrew a fifty-cent piece, and tossed it onto the table to pay for their refreshments. "I need to walk that pie off. You comin'?"

With a nod, Rusty wiped his mouth and pushed out of the chair. Once outside, they stopped to see if Ben wanted to come along before they made their way down the street. Without hesitation, Ben took his place on the other side of Adam, looking back and waving at the envious boys.

Lacy hefted the heavy basket into the crook of her arm and closed the door behind her. She'd left Takola to look after the bread in the oven while she took Brian and Ed their dinner.

Nestled on top of the slices of baked ham and new potatoes smothered in cream sauce was a freshly baked blackberry pie.

Humming to herself, she set off down the street. She hadn't gone more than a few yards when she spotted Carrianna, Susan, and Mary Ann heading her way. The girls twirled lacy parasols above their heads, their full skirts swishing daintily as they walked.

Lacy thought of her own practical cotton gown, faded from many washings. Thunder, she had even forgotten to remove her apron! At least she had remembered to brush and rebraid her hair before leaving. She had also looked in the mirror to see if her face was clean.

"Yoo-hoo! Lacy!"

Lacy stifled a groan at the sound of Carrianna's bright call. She didn't want to linger and chat with her friends. The food would get cold, and Carrianna would scold her for coming out without her parasol. With a resigned sigh, she realized there wasn't any way of avoiding them. What was wrong with her? These were her friends, and she was normally delighted to see them.

They met in front of Lacy's neighbors' house. Lacy waved at the small, elderly couple as they enjoyed the evening sitting on the front porch. The Tidwells owned a milk cow, and Lacy regularly traded fresh eggs for milk. The arrangement was convenient and worked out quite nicely, except for the times when her chickens got contrary and refused to lay for days on end. When that happened, Lacy would bake extra bread, or a pie for Mr. Tidwell's sweet tooth.

"Carrianna, Mary Ann, Susan. How have y'all been?" Lacy set the heavy basket gently on the ground and rubbed at the mark on the inside of her arm where the handle had pressed into the skin.

Mary Ann, the granddaughter of Shadow City's attorney, twirled her parasol and giggled. "We've been fine, Lacy Lynn. Where have you been hiding yourself? You haven't been out with us in ages. Why, you haven't even stepped foot inside the new dress shop that opened next to Grand-dad's office, have you?"

"All you do is work, work, work," Susan complained.

Carrianna came to Lacy's defense. "Girls, not everyone lies about all day dreamin' about store-bought dresses and Adam Logan! Lacy's got a good head on her shoulders, and a family to take care of." Carrianna pointed the tip of her parasol at Mary Ann. "Mary Ann, tell Lacy your news."

Mary Ann preened, smiling like a well-fed cat. "Oh, it's nothing. Grandfather invited Adam Logan to dinner on Wednesday, and he accepted."

Lacy felt as if someone had booted her in the behind. She didn't care, she really didn't. Adam Logan could court every woman in Shadow City and it would not concern her in the least. He was a handsome man, and it shouldn't come as a shock that women liked him. Nor should it come as a shock that he liked *women*. If anyone should know that, she should.

Forcing a smile, Lacy said, "You must be very excited, Mary Ann."

"That's not all." Carrianna lifted her eyebrows in Susan's direction. "Susan, tell Lacy what Adam Logan said about your spice cake."

Susan blushed a becoming shade of peach. "Well, he said it was the best spice cake he'd ever tasted."

Lacy was afraid her smile was going to slip right off her face. She hated feeling envious, especially of her friends, but that's exactly what she was feeling. Adam Logan had said nothing complimentary about her cooking. In fact, just the opposite.

He had kissed her, but she couldn't tell them that. She also couldn't tell them that Adam had seen her in the altogether. Carrianna would faint dead away, and Susan wouldn't be able to resist telling someone else. Mary Ann would simply cry over her lost virtue.

"Aren't you the least bit interested in our new sheriff, Lacy?" Mary Ann fairly chirped at her. "Granddad says he's loaded. Owns a big ranch in Wyoming. Oh, but don't tell anyone, because that's supposed to be confidential." She giggled, then sighed. "If I were to marry Adam, I'd make him sell that old ranch so I'd know he wouldn't ever change his mind and want to move back there."

"So would I," Susan added. They all turned to look at Carrianna to get her opinion. Lacy noticed they didn't expect *her* to *have* an opinion. She suddenly felt very old—like a spinster.

Carrianna shrugged, casting a mysterious glance in Lacy's direction. "The Bible says you're supposed to go where your husband goes, I believe." Her father was the pastor of the Methodist church on Main Street, and she was a devout Christian. There wasn't black spot on her soul anywhere, Lacy knew.

As the girls began to debate the biblical issue, Lacy took the opportunity to grab her basket and slip away, calling good-byes over her shoulder.

"Don't forget, we're supposed to get together tomorrow after church, Lacy!" Carrianna reminded her with a wave.

"Wouldn't miss it for the world." Lacy's smile fell from her face the moment her back was turned from the threesome. Carrianna would not have appreciated her thoughts at the moment, Lacy mused. She wasn't looking forward to tomorrow, because she knew the conversation would center on Adam Logan. By golly, how was a girl supposed to forget about someone if she was constantly reminded of him?

Maybe she could make an excuse, plead a headache. But no, Carrianna knew her too well and would see through her lie. She'd be hurt, and she'd want to know why Lacy didn't want to be around them.

As Lacy skirted the hitching post in front of the jailhouse and stepped onto the boardwalk, an idea came to her. If she invited Dr. Martin for Sunday dinner, then that would give her an excellent excuse not to join the girls for a stroll in the park. She'd be far too busy cooking the meal, wouldn't she? And Dr. Martin would take her mind off Adam Logan.

She squashed the surge of guilt she felt over using Dr. Martin this way. He liked her, she knew, but having him over for dinner was a simple courtesy, she told herself. He was a bachelor, and bachelors got tired of eating at the restaurant all the time, even if Ellen was an excellent cook.

She'd make sure she emphasized her reason for inviting him, and that should take care of any notions Dr. Martin might get.

With that decided, Lacy pasted a welcoming smile on her face and stepped into Adam's office.

He wasn't there, she saw immediately, but Brian and Ed lounged on the cots in the locked jail cell. When they saw her, they sprang to their feet, their expression unmistakably eager.

"Well, if it ain't Miz Ross comin' to bring us our supper," Brian said, grinning at her. His eyes glowed with adoration, as did Ed's.

"Hello, boys. Been at it again?" Lacy set the basket on the desk and reached into her dress pocket for the key to the jail cell.

It had been her grandmother's key, given to her grand-mother by Sheriff Murddock so that she could feed and tend the prisoners when he wasn't in the office. Lacy never knew how it came to be her grandmother's job, she just knew that she had always done it.

After her grandmother's death, it had seemed natural for Lacy to continue the tradition. Lacy didn't mind, as long as she never had to enter the office when it was empty, as she'd had to do last week.

She unlocked the door, then slipped the key back in her pocket. Then she studied the young faces through the bars of the cell to determine the damage they had done to each other. They returned her gaze with a sheepish ducking of their heads.

"What are we going to do with you two?" she sighed, biting back a smile.

"You could marry me," Brian said predictably. He turned beet-red when Lacy laughed, determined not to take him seriously.

"She ain't marryin' you, you stinkin' cowpoke!" Ed snarled with sudden viciousness. "She's gonna marry me, ain't you Miz Ross?" His voice trailed off on a hopeful note.

Lacy turned away, shaking her head and laughing. They said the same things every Saturday, and she made the same replies. "I ain't the marryin' kind," she told them. *Not amymore.* Ignoring their grumbling, she went out back to the pump to bring in water so that she could bathe their wounds. Adam ought to be glad he didn't have to worry about patching and feeding the prisoners, she reflected as she filled a wash pan with water.

She brought the pan inside and set it down on the floor by the cell, then moved to the desk to unpack the food. Feeling stingy and silly didn't stop her from searching for a place to set the blackberry pie so that the two hungry boys watching her would not see it. Finally, she set it in Adam's chair, then pushed the chair up to the desk. She wanted Adam to have the whole pie, and if he decided to share it with Brian and Ed, then he could.

She breathed a sigh of relief when that was done. This pie had been made it, safe and sound, and free of all but the slightest pinch of salt.

Hopefully, nothing would stop Adam from enjoying this pie.

9

"*Y*OU SURE YOU won't come in?" Adam asked as they paused to lean against the hitching post outside the jailhouse. Ben started to climb up beside him, but Rusty grabbed his collar and hauled him back to the ground.

"No, thankye, Adam. We'd best get on home or Lacy'll have our hide."

"But—"

Rusty clamped a hard hand on Ben's shoulder, successfully halting his protest. "Besides, we have to check on Big Red. He likes a lot of water on warm days like this. He don't get it, he's liable to break out and head for the pond again."

"But Rusty, Big Red—"

"Shut up, Ben. And come on. Lacy's waitin' supper on us. If she's a smart woman, she'll have a bath waitin' on you."

Ben snapped his mouth shut at the threat of a bath and went along peacefully.

With an amused smile twitching at his lips, Adam waved at Ben and stepped onto the sidewalk. As he reached the office door, he heard voices from within. He hesitated outside his office, frowning down the road at Rusty and Ben as they headed in the direction of home. Had the old codger known someone was inside when he'd made his excuses not to come in?

A woman's voice, speaking in soft, soothing tones, jerked his attention back to the door. His heart rate accelerated as he recognized the voice.

Lacy.

Lacy was inside talking to . . . whom? Adam eased the door open and halted again, shamelessly eavesdropping.

"There now, it doesn't hurt that bad, does it?" Lacy crooned.

Adam chewed his bottom lip in concentration. She sounded as if she were talking to a child! And she couldn't be, for he'd already figured out she must be visiting the two cowpokes.

Perhaps this was something else Rusty had refrained from mentioning. Maybe Lacy was sweet on one of the boys they had rounded up at the saloon.

The sharp jab of jealousy hit Adam with surprising force. Damn! He couldn't be jealous, not of Lacy Ross. She was off-limits.

So, who was the lucky man? Brian Bishop, or Ed Thomas? *Just shut up,* he growled silently.

"Here, open your shirt and let me take a look at what you got on your chest."

Her suggestive statement pounded through Adam, sending a rush of hot blood to his face. He shoved the door open and stalked inside, his brows drawn tightly together. This didn't have anything to do with jealousy, he told himself. He was the sheriff, and he wouldn't stand for such goings-on in his jail cell! Lacy could find her own love nest, and take that mangy cowboy with her.

Adam came to an abrupt halt in front of the cell, freezing at the sight that met his eyes. Lacy, Brian, and Ed turned to stare at him in open-mouthed astonishment. He saw at a glance that Brian did indeed have his shirt open, but Adam realized he had been mistaken in what he assumed was going on.

Lacy held a damp cloth in her upraised hand, aiming at the nasty gash on Brian's chest. It looked wicked, and Adam guessed that the broken end of a whiskey bottle was to blame. That, and Ed.

He felt like a durn fool. He worked the stiffness out of his jaw by moving it back and forth, covering the movement by rubbing his jaw with a rough swipe of his hand. A flush crept up his neck and into the deep tan of his face. He hoped like hell nobody noticed it. And thank God he hadn't blurted out what he'd been thinking.

"Lacy." Adam nodded his head at her. "You fixin' these boys up?" Both "boys" glared at him for the slight. Adam ignored them, belatedly noticing the plates of food balanced on their laps. "And feedin' them, too?"

Lacy searched for her tongue. For a moment there, when she had first turned around at the sound of his footsteps, he'd looked furious enough to start swinging those powerful fists of his. But for the life of her, she could find no reason for him to be angry. She was only doing what her grandmother had done for years, what she'd been doing for years. Feeding and tending the prisoners. It was a joke, really, to call Brian and Ed "prisoners." They were like brothers to her, despite their silly declarations of undying love.

Finally, she managed to speak, offering him a tentative smile. "Why, yes. I'm doing just that. Somebody had to fix these fellers up."

Adam wasn't in the mood to be polite. "What about Dr. Martin?" He returned her smile with a sarcastic one of his own, knowing he was being an ass but helpless to stop it. Something about the sight of Lacy perched on the cot beside a man with his shirt hanging open just didn't sit right with him. He didn't like her being so familiar with these men, however innocent her motives. "Ain't that what Dr. Martin's trained to do?" he continued in a nasty tone.

Lacy stiffened, slowly lowering the rag to her lap. Her jaw squared off. "Of course that's what Dr. Martin's trained to do," she stated calmly. "But my grandmother always took care of the prisoners, unless they needed the doctor. He's got other patients to tend to."

Adam stepped forward and gripped the bars, frowning between them. "What if they were dangerous?" he asked softly. He flicked a glance from Brian to Ed, then back to Lacy. "What if they decided they wanted more than tendin' to? And food?"

Lacy drew in a sharp, insulted breath. "You're out of line, Sheriff. These boys would never think such a thing!"

"Wouldn't they?" Adam doubted it, but Lacy needed to know that not all men were of the same mold. She *should* know, he recalled suddenly. She should know better than most. He started to remind her, then thought better of the idea. No, he didn't want to go there, not yet. "Are you finished?" he demanded instead.

Lacy shook her head, turning her nose up at him. She picked up the cloth and began cleansing the jagged gash across Brian's chest as if Adam weren't breathing down her neck waiting for her to finish. The cowboy winced, becoming a shade paler than he had been.

"Sorry, Brian. I'll try to be gentle." She set her mouth in a straight line and finished the task. Then she dipped the rag in a solution of alcohol and muttered, "Here we go," before pressing it to the cut.

Brian was thinking about screaming; Lacy saw it on his face, the urge to let loose with a howl of pain, as he normally would. But then the cowboy's eyes met the cold, hard, derisive eyes of the sheriff and he clamped his mouth shut.

Lacy watched the exchange with rising anger. Adam was being unreasonable—totally, ridiculously, unreasonable. These boys were harmless, and had done nothing more than fight among themselves. They weren't bank robbers, for goodness' sake!

Gathering her rag and the pan of dirty water, Lacy stood up. She forced a smile to her stiff lips and said sweetly, "You boys enjoy your meal, you hear? Maybe next Saturday I'll fix you something extra special."

Brian forgot about his pain—and Sheriff Logan. Puppy

love softened the manly lines of his face. "Thank you, Miz Ross. Everything you fix is extra special, and me an' Ed, we appreciate it." He scowled at Ed. "Right, Ed?"

Ed's Adam's apple made a quick trip to the top of his throat as he gulped. When Lacy turned her smiling face in his direction, he scrambled hastily for a reply. "Yes, ma'am. We love your cookin'." He tilted his hat, his manner respectful, but adoring. "You're a fine lady, ma'am, for helping us this way every Saturday, bringin' us food, tendin' our wounds—"

"Shut up, Ed!" Brian hissed, kicking out at him.

Adam snorted his disgust. *Every Saturday,* Ed had said. Well, he wasn't a fool and he realized what the two cowpokes were up to, even if Rusty and Lacy did not. *How long?* he wondered, not bothering to deny his jealousy this time. How long had Lacy been cleaning their bare chests and swiping dirt from their innocent-looking faces? Why, no wonder they didn't mind spending the day and night in jail! If she brought them vittles like—Adam quickly identified the food items on the plate—ham and potatoes every time they landed here, he didn't blame them!

What red-blooded male wouldn't jump at the opportunity to have a fine woman like Lacy Ross crooning over his cuts and scrapes, feeding him as if he were a king? With a frustrated grunt, he looked around the office, spying more food on his desk. His mouth watered at the smell of smoked ham and brown-sugar glaze, and he realized it had been a long time since lunch.

He brushed his hunger aside for the time being, trying to decide what he would do about the sly cowboys in his jail cell. He wasn't as softhearted as Rusty and he wasn't going to stand for this type of nonsense.

He didn't have time for it.

Besides, he wasn't Lacy's grandfather, he was her— Adam bit off an oath and shoved himself away from the bars.

Lacy shot him a questioning look as she strolled from the cell, casually shutting it behind her. Bracing the wash pan on her hip, she withdrew the key and clicked the look into place.

Adam grabbed her arm before she could step away, squinting down at the key in her hand. "Where did you get that key?" he asked softly.

Lacy shivered at the sound of that dangerous tone. She knew that tone, knew what it meant when Adam used it. He was furious and trying to hide it. She tossed her head, secure in the knowledge that he would not hit her in front of Brian and Ed. Fact was, she didn't believe he would at all, but she wasn't absolutely certain.

Not yet.

"Sheriff Murddock gave it to my grandmother. He wasn't always here, and she had to tend the prisoners." Her flashing brown eyes dared him to argue, or challenge her right to have the key. This time, she noticed, she felt no fear. Just a curious elation . . . and anticipation.

Adam was spoiling for a fight. She was the cause of this gut-clenching jealousy he was feeling, and the nasty way he was acting. And deeper down, he knew he looked forward to the opportunity of kissing her into silence.

I'm no different than Brian or Ed, was his ironic thought. They had started a fight with the intention of landing in jail where the sweet widow Ross would fawn and croon over them, and feed them delicious home-cooked meals they didn't get on the ranch.

Adam wanted to start a fight so that he could taste her sweetness, too.

"I need to talk to you," he said, holding onto her arm.

Lacy forced herself to meet the heat of his intense blue eyes. They had darkened with something she wasn't quite sure of. It made her edgy, though she couldn't for the life of her pinpoint why. Maybe, she thought uneasily, it had something to do with the tingling of her skin beneath his strong fingers and the way her body tightened just being near him.

Or maybe, just maybe, it had something to do with the memory of that kiss.

Her gaze fell on the full bottom curve of his lips. The

sight made her want to lick her own. She slowly pulled her arm away from his disturbing grip, keeping a tight rein on her emotions.

"So talk," she said, shifting her gaze to a point right below his open collar.

Wrong choice, she discovered, fascinated by the tuft of dark hair peeping out of his shirt. Water sloshed over the sides of the wash basin she was holding and she muttered a sharp, "Oh!"

Adam smiled, a smile that sent warning shivers down her spine. "Not here." He jerked his head. "In there."

Lacy followed his movement, realizing with a jolt of shock that he meant the room Rusty had built onto the jailhouse.

His bedroom.

"I don't think that would be a good idea," she quavered. Taking a deep breath, she lifted her eyes once again to stare directly into his face. "What is it that you want to talk about, Sheriff Logan?"

That did it. Adam took the wash basin from her nerveless fingers and set it on the floor. He jerked the rag from her and threw it behind him without a thought to where it might land. Grabbing her elbow, he pulled her into the bedroom and shut the door on the astounded faces of Brian and Ed, who had been following the exchange with great interest.

Lacy jerked loose, glaring at him. "What do you think you're doing? I've got a reputation in this town, mister—"

"Adam!" he shouted. "My name is Adam. Not 'Sheriff Logan,' not 'mister,' but Adam!"

"Fine!" Lacy shouted back. "Adam! Adam, Adam, Adam!"

The sudden silence that followed their outburst was deafening.

Lacy had her back to the closed door. Adam loomed in front of her, too close, way too close. She felt trapped, excited, agitated. Thunder, she wasn't sure how she felt. She just knew that his broad shoulders blocked the evening sunlight, and she couldn't keep her eyes from straying to that patch of hair peeping out of his shirt opening. Fiddlesticks. Doctoring Brain had not aroused any interest—why did Adam Logan?

She wet her lips with her tongue, for they had suddenly gone dry. Just how far did that hair go? Lacy pressed herself more tightly against the door.

Adam moved closer.

"Do you have any idea what those boys are up to?" Adam demanded, wishing he hadn't suggested that they talk in here. He couldn't get the thought of that bed out of his mind. It was right behind him, with the softest feather mattress he'd ever slept on. He imagined Lacy stretched out on the bed, her liquid brown eyes beckoning him. . . .

Lacy swallowed hard. Her stomach felt as if a couple of hummingbirds had become trapped inside. "I—don't know what you mean." She moistened her lips, refusing to lift her eyes no matter how much the sight of that patch of hair made her hands itch. She wouldn't touch him. . . . She wouldn't see if it was as soft as she knew his hair to be. She wouldn't.

"You don't know what I mean," Adam mocked softly. He trailed a finger down the curve of her jaw, down, down to the slight swell of her breast. She drew in a sharp breath and held it as he said, "Those boys are gettin' themselves in jail on purpose, you little fool."

Lacy let out her breath on a hiss of rage. "How dare you call me a fool. Those boys are harmless, and you act as if they're wanted for murder. They can't hurt you, Sheriff Logan." She hadn't meant to taunt, she really hadn't. But she saw by the darkening of his eyes that it was too late.

Adam shifted his lower body closer, letting her feel how much she affected him. Her gasp of shock fed the fire steadily raging within him. He rocked gently against her. "They can't hurt me, Lacy. But they can hurt you." He lowered his mouth onto hers and kissed her, nudging her lips open. His tongue slipped inside her warm, sweet mouth.

Lacy felt her bones began to melt. She couldn't keep her eyelids apart. The hard length of his body urged her to press forward, strain for contact, get closer and closer still. With a moan of surrender, she lifted her arms around his neck and slid her fingers into his hair. Such soft, silky hair . . . Oh, God, why did he make her feel this way? It confused her, made her long for something she knew would be disastrous to have.

Somewhere in the conscious part of his brain, Adam realized he had underestimated his willpower to control himself with Lacy. But just when he thought of what he *should* be doing, instead of what he *wanted* to do, she moaned and mimicked his movements.

Oh, God, she was so sweet.

He couldn't stop. He didn't want to stop. Lacy Ross had filled his waking thoughts, as well as his sleeping ones, for the past week and a half. She was harder to shake loose than a bur in a horse's mane, and he didn't much feel like trying.

He ground against her, slowly moving his hands up to cup her small, firm breasts. When he reached his destination, she jumped in surprise, then pressed into his hands.

Adam sighed into her mouth, then slid his lips along her jaw to the delicate area around her ear, down her neck, then onto the swell of her chest.

Lacy tried to fight the fierce urgency his touch brought, and when his hot breath seared through the cotton fabric of her dress to fan the swollen flesh of her breast, she jerked back.

There wasn't anywhere to go.

The door was behind her. She panicked, bringing her hands between them to press firmly against his chest. Her fingers became tangled in short, silky hair. Her breath came out in jerky, painful bursts. Her voice was nothing more than a husky whisper, no matter how strong she intended for it to be.

"Adam—I—Don't, please."

Adam trailed his hot tongue along her neck, back to her lips, where he proceeded to kiss her into silence again. His hands fell to her waist and pulled her body tightly against his own. Roughly, he growled into her mouth, "You don't want me to stop. Say you don't want me to stop what I'm doing."

"I—" Lacy tore her mouth free and turned her head to the

left, biting into her bottom lip until she tasted blood. Squeezing her eyes tightly closed, she forced the words past her lips. "Yes. I *do* want you to stop. Brian—Ed—"

Adam slowly loosened his hold. With a deep, regretful sigh, he moved away enough to break all contact with her body. Heat shimmered between them, heat they'd created together. It was just as well, he thought ruefully. They shouldn't make love with lies between them, and he was guilty of that.

He and Lacy needed to talk.

Adam walked to the single window of the bedroom and stood looking out. He couldn't see much, mainly the narrow alley and the side of the telegraph office. But it was somewhere safe to plant his sights when all he wanted to do was stare at Lacy. Running his hand through his shaggy hair, he said, "I don't want you goin' into the jail cell with any prisoners you don't know." *Or with Brian and Ed, because I'm jealous.*

Lacy stirred against the door, wondering if her body would stop tingling and aching for more of his gentle, fevered touch. There was a slight, betraying catch in her voice when she replied, "Adam, we don't have strangers in jail very often, and when we do, I don't go near them. If—if I have to tend them, Grandpa is always with me." She wasn't brainless. Or was she? If she wasn't, then why wasn't she running while she had the opportunity? She was in Adam Logan's bedroom, for goodness' sake! And Brian and Ed knew it; they might talk.

"Are you aware that Brian and Ed do this on purpose?" Adam asked softly, keeping his eyes on the safe view of the building next door.

Lacy shrugged, then realized he couldn't see her. "I'm not naïve, Adam. I suspected their motives a long time ago, but I decided they were harmless, and in need of a little mothering."

Adam laughed unpleasantly. "I don't think they see you as a mother figure. You're not a mother, and they're not little boys."

"Maybe not to you," Lacy retorted, her tone revealing a

slight exasperation. She thought Adam was making a big deal over nothing. Rusty had not reacted this way over Brian and Ed, so she couldn't understand why it bothered Adam so much.

Unless . . . unless he was *jealous*?

Lacy scoffed at the ridiculous thought, calling herself a fool. Where in the world had she gotten such a conceited idea? Imagine, Adam Logan, jealous of Brian and Ed because of her! Why, the girls would bust a corset laughing if she voiced such a possibility. Still, the only other logical reason would be that Adam thought of *her* as a child, and himself as a father figure.

Shaking her head in confusion, Lacy said, "Don't worry about me, Sheriff Logan. I'm perfectly capable of taking care of myself." She stepped away from the door, intending to open it and escape his disturbing presence while she possessed the fortitude to do so. She hesitated, her eyes straying to the bed. What would it be like to share a bed with Adam? So far, his every touch, his every action, met with her body's approval. And her mind—her mind didn't skitter away from him, either.

Adam turned from the window just in time to catch the flash of yearning in her eyes. She was staring at the bed, her expression so still that she looked like a statue—a warm, desirable statue. He commanded his feet to be still, to stay away from temptation, yet they moved in her direction regardless. "Lacy," he murmured as he reached her. "Lacy, there's something I have to tell you."

Lacy jerked her head around, her eyes glazed from her wanton thoughts. "Oh. What? I didn't hear you." She hadn't known he'd approached her. She'd been too busy thinking of them together, on that bed.

Her face grew hot. They both stood, not touching, both struggling against the powerful, almost overwhelming attraction between them. It was like standing near a keg of dynamite. The slightest move might set it off.

Lacy hardly dared to breathe. Something was on the verge of happening, and she was both excited and frightened by the possibility.

Adam put his hands behind his back and linked them together. It was the only way he could stop himself from grabbing her and kissing those trembling, sweet lips.

His movement pulled the material of his shirt apart, exposing a large expanse of his upper chest. Helplessly, Lacy stared at the dark whorls of hair, the deep tan of his skin. She imagined him standing in the sun, his bare chest glistening with sweat, his muscles rippling, hard. She thought of slicking her hands over his back, sliding them around his waist, pressing her lips to the salty taste of his skin.

"Lacy?" Adam's gruff, commanding voice shattered her fantasy. He growled low in his throat and clenched his jaw. Damn, she'd better stop looking at him like that or he wouldn't be responsible for his actions!

Lacy blinked. Her chest felt tight, as if she needed a breath of fresh air and there weren't any to be had in the room. "I—I'm sorry, Adam," she whispered, feeling strange and light-headed. "I don't know what's wrong with me."

Her honest confession merely fed the fire. Adam swallowed and forced himself to step back. "I know what you mean. Believe me, I know. Just don't move, and stop looking at me as if—" He broke off with a nasty oath, one that made her eyes go wide. And then Adam knew what he had to do. Lacy Ross wasn't the kind of woman to be trifled with, then tossed aside. He'd never be able to live with that on his conscience.

Neither would she be easy to forget.

"Lacy, I won't be staying in Shadow City permanently."

It took a moment for his words to penetrate the fog in her mind, and when they finally did, Lacy thought she had not heard him right. Her shaky laugh bubbled out, followed by a rush of breathless words. "I thought you said you wouldn't be staying, which is ridiculous because why else would you take the job as sheriff if you weren't planning on staying?" She searched his tense features, and when they didn't change, a flash of pain hit the region of her chest.

"I'm here to find out what happened to Sheriff Murddock,"

Adam announced gently. He let it soak in for a few seconds, then mentally braced himself. "He was my grandfather."

Lacy was slow in reacting. Disbelief, followed by bewilderment, chased across her features. "You—you're Sheriff Murddock's *grandson*?" she repeated faintly. Adam nodded. "But why didn't you tell me? Does—does Rusty know?" Again Adam nodded. Lacy took a deep breath, suddenly finding it easier to breathe because the sexual tension was slowly being replaced by stupefied anger.

"I don't want everyone to know yet," Adam explained, watching her carefully. He knew how unpredictable she could be around him. "I want their honest opinion of what they believe happened that day." He waited, tensing for her comment. What did Lacy think? Did she believe Colt had killed himself? Adam hadn't asked Rusty, because he wanted to see her face when she told him. It was important, although he knew it shouldn't be.

Her eyes took on a telltale glitter as the full impact of his words sank in. "You've been duping the townsfolk, asking them questions about Sheriff Murddock?"

Adam frowned at the razor sharpness of her tone. "Don't worry, it hasn't done a damn bit of good so far," he said dryly. "Every time I ask a question, they change the subject."

"They believe you're an honest man, *Sheriff* Logan. All this time they've been singing your praises, and here you've been sneaking around—"

Adam cut into her angry spate of words. "I don't see what harm—"

Lacy didn't let him finish, because *she* wasn't finished. "You don't see what harm it's done?" She looked incredulous. " When they find out who you really are, don't you think they'll feel foolish? People don't like to be made into fools, Adam." Her voice dropped an octave, thickened with contempt. "And I'm one of those people." Tears of anger and hurt burned her eyes, but she determinedly held them back. Adam wasn't staying, had never intended to stay in Shadow City. He was here with one purpose in mind, oblivious to the feelings of those he encountered.

And what about Ben? Ben worshipped him, and when the sheriff finally just up and left, he'd be devastated. Adam apparently didn't care about Ben or anyone else in this town.

"A wolf in sheep's clothing," Lacy hissed. She jerked the door open, knowing she had to get away from him before he saw how much it hurt. She didn't want him to have that knowledge to gloat over. "I said when you first got here that you were a wolf in sheep's clothing, Adam. It seems I was right."

She didn't bother shutting the door. She marched straight through the office and out the front door without so much as a hi or bye to the wide-eyed cowboys in the jail cell.

Adam cursed long and loud before stomping into the office. He glared at Brian and Ed, who froze in the act of eating. "You're both barred from this town for a month. If I see you or hear you before then, I'll make you regret you were ever born. Is that understood?" They frowned, but nodded, neither brave enough to argue with this big, furious sheriff. "Good," Adam growled. "Now finish eating and get out!"

With that said, Adam marched around to his desk and yanked out his chair. The sight of food no longer tempted him, especially since he knew that Lacy had prepared it for someone else.

It was time to put distractions aside and get down to the business of what had happened to his grandfather, knowing he'd be lucky if the news wasn't all over town by morning. She had been mighty angry with him.

"Dammit!" he grated out, ignoring the watching men. He'd warned himself time and time again that Lacy Ross was trouble. There should be a lesson to be learned from what had just occurred. Women—one in particular—would only distract him.

Now it was time to get to work.

He needed to make a list of people he had met so far, people who might be able to provide a few answers to his questions. With Rusty along, maybe they would loosen up, trust him.

He wouldn't think about how hurt Lacy had looked. He couldn't let that get in the way of keeping his promise to his mother. There wasn't any reason, as far as he was concerned, for her to be so cotton-pickin' mad. He was just asking a few simple questions about a man who had died a long time ago. A man, he grumbled to himself, who had been his grandfather. She should understand.

Adam reached for the side drawer of his desk to retrieve pencil and paper, sitting down in the chair as he did so.

He froze with his hand on the handle of the drawer as something squished beneath him. Something soft and warm. And wet. Slowly, he stood up and frowned down into the seat of his chair.

The remains of a blackberry pie oozed in a messy glob onto the worn leather, dripped lazily from the sides, and plopped to the hard planked floor. A blackberry pie. Squashed. Ruined.

Adam knew where the rest of the pie was. He could feel its warm wetness seeping through the seat of his jeans.

10

"How are you liking our little town, Sheriff Logan?" Mary Ann's voice was soft and fluttery. She held her little finger pointed outward when she lifted her glass of wine to take a sip, licking her lower lip as she set the glass down on the table.

Adam remained unmoved by the pretty picture she made seated opposite him at the dinner table. Mary Ann Silverstone was a charming dinner companion, but he had not accepted the invitation with courting in mind.

With a sincere, but distant smile, he replied, "The town is like yourself, Miss Silverstone. Charming." To his relief, Mary Ann accepted his compliment and began eating again, giving him a brief respite from her endless questions. He smothered an impatient sigh and shot a quick, assessing glance at Graham Silverstone, who sat at the head of the table. At the moment, the distinguished elderly man was occupied with slicing the meat from the superbly cooked stuffed pheasant on his plate.

The meal was delicious, but for once Adam had no interest in food. He couldn't wait to get down to the business of questioning Graham about his grandfather, but the damned meal seemed as endless as Mary Ann's questions.

To occupy his thoughts, Adam recalled his first formal introduction to Graham Silverstone. Several days ago, during a leisurely round about town, Rusty had introduced him to the aging attorney outside the man's office. Adam recognized Graham Silverstone from the restaurant the day he had met the mayor for lunch. Graham was dining with Dr. Martin at the time and Adam had wondered about the elderly gentleman then.

By the time he and Adam had finished their friendly conversation in the middle of the busy boardwalk, Graham Silverstone had issued Adam an invitation to dinner the next Wednesday. And Adam had accepted, hiding his triumph beneath a gracious smile.

It wasn't until later that Rusty casually mentioned that Graham Silverstone was Mary Ann's grandfather, and that the young woman lived with him. Adam knew then that the situation would have to be handled in a delicate manner or he'd find himself linked hand-in-hand with Mary Ann, and while she was both pretty and gracious, it was the last thing he needed.

He solved the problem by pretending to be surprised to discover the two were related, therefore dispatching from Mary Ann's head the notion that he might have anticipated seeing her.

The disappointment in her eyes confirmed Adam's suspicions. Thank God for his foresight. . . .

Dessert arrived, a delicious combination of strawberries smothered in sweet cream and spiced with warm rum. After another twenty minutes of pointless conversation, Graham finally pushed his chair back and smiled at his granddaughter. "Excuse us, Mary Ann. We'll take brandy in my study. Adam?"

Adam tried not to appear too eager, at the risk of rubbing salt into the wound. Feeling generous now, he flashed a brilliant smile at Mary Ann. "Miss Silverstone, both the meal and company were outstanding."

Mary Ann blushed. "Thank you, Sheriff Logan." She hesitated, patting her mouth with a napkin, then delicately cleared her throat. "Will—will you join us again some-time?"

Adam lifted a brow at her bold question, understanding what she was asking. "I can't say, Miss Silverstone, but seeing you has been a pleasure." *Keep it light and promise nothing,* Adam thought ruefully, following Graham down a short hall and into a room that smelled of tobacco and leather.

Worn, leather-bound volumes lined a bookshelf from ceiling to floor. A large mahogany desk on the left took up a goodly portion of the room, and a long set of bay windows led out into a small garden. Adam saw fireflies blinking in and out as they darted through the shadowy shapes of flowers and bushes.

Graham's wealth was subtle, unlike the mayor's blatant flaunting, and Adam found himself admiring the man's style.

He turned his attention back to the man standing at a monstrous sideboard, watching as he poured brandy into two glasses. The man was as thin as a stick, tall, with a slim face and a long nose. He had the look of a wealthy blueblood, and Adam wondered why the affluent man had decided to settle in Shadow City.

"So, Adam Logan. What brings you to our quaint little town?"

Adam started as Graham echoed his own thoughts. "A job," he said with a casual shrug. He took the brandy from his host and settled into a comfortable leather chair near the open window, trying to decide how much he should tell the attorney.

Graham sat across from him in an identical chair and crossed his long legs, his expression one of polite interest.

Lacy had accused him of being sneaky, Adam recalled. Was that the only gripe she had? Or did she dislike him because of *who* he was? If that was the case, what if he told

Graham Silverstone about his relationship to Colt Murddock, and Graham reacted the same way? Sins of the father, or in this case, sins of the grandfather.

The possibility made Adam mad. He was not ashamed of who he was, and to hell with the people who believed his grandfather was a coward. With a challenging tilt to his eyes, he balanced the glass on his knee and asked bluntly, "How well did you know Colt Murddock?"

Graham looked surprised, as if it were the last thing he had expected Adam to say. He uncrossed his legs and sat forward, a frown adding to the wrinkles in his wide forehead. "Why would you ask about a man who's been dead for fifteen years?"

Adam's fingers tightened around his glass. *Hell.* "Why does everyone avoid my simple question?" he countered.

"Because—well, because it's not something most people care to remember."

Adam took the arrow without flinching. He had wanted to hear the truth, and he was hearing it. And he wasn't liking it, but Rusty had warned him. "People don't want to remember Colt Murddock? Or people don't want to remember what happened the day he died? . . ."

"He committed suicide, Sheriff Logan," Graham stated quietly, lifting his shoulders. "Everyone knows that. And no, nobody likes to remember that their hero took the coward's way out. He was a giant among men, someone I was proud to say I knew—"

"Before he died," Adam cut in. "Now everyone's ashamed to even speak his name." He paused, his eyes a cold ice-blue as he added softly, "Including yourself."

Graham cleared his throat, staring at Adam suspiciously. "Just exactly what is your interest in Colt Murddock, anyway?" He took a hefty drink of his brandy, clearly uncomfortable with the conversation.

Adam left his drink untouched. He stated baldly, "I'm his grandson."

Graham choked on the brandy. He wheezed and coughed for several minutes, until Adam began to think he would have to pound the man on the back.

"My God!" he rasped, his fine, aristocratic nose quivering as he looked Adam over through watery eyes. "I don't know why I didn't notice the resemblance before now. You really *are* Colt's grandson."

Adam smiled without a trace of warmth. "Yes, I am."

"Well, I'll be damned. I'll be *damned*!" Graham recovered from the shock slowly, his eyes remaining round. "I remember Colt talking about you and your ma. How is your ma?"

"She died over a month ago."

"I'm sorry to hear that, son." He shook his head in disbelief, then marveled again. "Colt's grandson. He sure set a lot of store by you."

"Did he?" Adam relaxed a little and took a drink of his brandy. Although Graham appeared to have changed his tune in a hurry, maybe he would get somewhere now. He had been mistaken in assuming that people would be more inclined to discuss his grandfather if they didn't know who he was. It seemed to be the opposite.

Graham shot him a quizzical look. "Yes, he did. Left you that ranch in Wyoming, didn't he?"

Adam froze in the chair, shuttering his eyelids to hide his expression. "As a matter of fact, he didn't. There was no will, so it went to my mother. Now it belongs to her husband."

If Graham had looked shocked before, he was doubly shocked now. "But there *was* a will! I don't know what it said, exactly, but Colt talked about it often enough. I know for a fact he wouldn't have left that land for his son-in-law to get his hands on. He hated that man."

There was a will. The words buzzed inside his head until he felt as if a bee had made a home there. Surely Graham was mistaken. "What do you mean, there was a will and you didn't know what was in it?" It made no sense, if Graham had acted as Colt's attorney, for him to sound so vague about a legal matter.

Graham stood and went to pour himself another brandy, so deep in concentration that he forgot to ask Adam if he wanted more. "Colt didn't like to take on airs, didn't want people to know how much of this town he owned—which was a lot of it, at first.

"Eventually people paid their loans and owned their own businesses, but there were a few things Colt kept a hand in." He leveled a serious gaze on Adam. "Colt was a smart man, and he knew what he needed to keep control of, for the good of this town." As if he realized he had gotten off the subject, he said, "Anyway, Colt came to me about a week before he died and gave me an envelope—sealed—and said he wanted the contents sent to his ranch in care of his daughter if anything ever happened to him."

"A week before his death," Adam murmured. "Almost as if he knew . . ."

Graham heard him, nodding. "Yes. Almost as if he was thinking about . . . dying."

Adam stiffened, realizing they were traveling in completely opposite directions. He bit his tongue and remained silent and Graham went on.

"I told him he should keep a copy somewhere safe, and he assured me he had already taken care of it."

Every muscle in Adam's body felt ready to burst from the strain of holding himself still. "After he died, you sent this envelope to my mother?"

"No. You see, we had a fire that day, too." There was profound regret in his eyes. "I'm sorry, Adam. I lost everything, including a lot of important deeds."

The fire Rusty had told him about, Adam thought. A timely fire that both distracted and destroyed. And for it to happen on the same day as the death of Colt Murddock, well, that was too coincidental for Adam. "And you say you never knew what was in that envelope Colt gave you?"

"No. Colt didn't want me knowing, and I'm a man of honor. Not wanting me to know what was in it wasn't a matter of not trusting his own attorney, Sheriff Logan. Colt was a private man; he was more concerned with someone else snooping into his business."

"But you said he had a copy of whatever was in that envelope."

"That's what *he* said," Graham corrected.

"Yet nothing was ever found." If it *had* been, then Rudy Wagner wouldn't own the ranch right now, if Graham could be believed. Graham *and* Rusty, he silently corrected. They were both adamant about Colt's intentions of leaving the ranch to his grandson.

Graham was shaking his head, frowning down into his liquor glass. "No. Only the . . . suicide note."

"Colt's handwriting?" If anyone should know, Graham Silverstone would, Adam thought.

"Without a doubt," Graham said regretfully, destroying the last of Adam's hopes. Yet the ranch didn't matter all that much, except for the pleasure it would have given him to run Rudy Wagner off his land. When he had told Rusty it didn't matter, that he would never get the stink of Rudy Wagner from the ranch, he had meant it.

Restlessly, Adam stood and began pacing the room, his brow furrowed in thought. "So they found a suicide note, but not a will. On the day of his death, there was a mysterious fire in your office that destroyed the only other copy." Suddenly, he stopped and pinned Graham with a hard, incredulous look. "And you still believe he killed himself?"

Graham looked away, staring out the window. "Colt didn't have any enemies in this town, and we couldn't imagine anyone forcing him to write that note and then forcing him to put a rope around his neck. It all seemed cut and dried, son."

Colt may not have had enemies in town, but Adam could think of one he had out of town. "Did you tell anyone about the will?" Adam asked tersely.

"I didn't see the point, and besides, things were kind of crazy for the next day or two. I had other clients—and, Adam—" Graham took a step in Adam's direction as if pleading for understanding. "I'm not even certain that envelope contained a will."

"It did." Adam had never been so sure of anything in his life. His mother was right; Colt Murddock did not commit suicide. He was murdered, and now Adam suspected that he knew who was behind it all. It didn't matter that it had happened so many years ago. It was never too late for justice.

But he needed proof. A witness, someone who might have seen something the day his grandfather died. Adam finally tipped back the brandy and downed the contents. There was one person who might hold the key to unlocking this mystery.

Lacy Ross.

"Bucket. The word's bucket, ain't it Lacy?" Ben crowed excitedly. He continued to stare at the paper Lacy held in front of the hand mirror as if he couldn't believe what he was seeing. The entire family had gathered at the kitchen table to test Lacy's theory. Night had fallen, and a moth found its way through the open window, attracted by the bright glow of the oil lamp in the center of the table.

Lacy beamed at him. "Yes, it says 'bucket.' Let me do another one." She lowered the paper and quickly printed out another word, then held it up to the mirror. Rusty and Takola leaned forward to peer over her shoulder as she demonstrated her amazing discovery.

Ben screwed his face together, concentrating on sounding out the letters. "S-c-h-o-o-l. School!"

With a squeal of triumph, Lacy clapped her hands. "Yes! Oh, Ben, you *can* read, just not in the same way everyone else does. For some reason, you're seeing the letters backwards, and holding them up to the mirror allows you to see them the right way—er, the right way for *you,* that is."

"Why, that's the silliest thing I ever heard," Rusty blurted.

Lacy twisted in her seat and glared at him. "It may be silly, Grandpa, but if it helps Ben learn to read, then we don't care how silly it is, do we?" With a sniff she turned back to the paper and began writing a short sentence, her head bent as she worked. "If he can learn the alphabet this way, then he can also learn to recognize the letters even when they *look* backwards to him. All he has to do is turn them around in his head. Picture that letter backwards."

Ben pulled on her sleeve. "Does that mean I'll have to take a mirror to school with me?" He didn't sound happy about the prospect and Lacy didn't blame him. Other children could be so cruel.

She paused with pencil in hand, winking at him. "No. I think in a few weeks you'll be ready to do without the mirror. Meanwhile, I'll continue helping you with your lessons at home until you feel like you're ready. How's that?"

Looking relieved, Ben nodded.

"Maybe Takola can help you, too. She has such a pretty penmanship. They must have had a teacher on the reservation." Lacy turned to confirm this with Takola, but Takola had vanished. "Now where did she get off to? She was here just a moment ago."

"She was letting me in," came Adam's drawling response as he appeared in the kitchen doorway. Takola hovered behind him, staring at Adam with something that suspiciously resembled hero-worship.

"Oh." Lacy's heart leaped in her chest at the sight of him, then settled into a faster than normal thumping. She lowered her lashes before he saw how glad she was to see him. She looked him over, noting the snug fit of his jeans and the way he had left his shirt open at the throat. *He could at least button one more,* Lacy thought crossly, swallowing hard. "I didn't hear anyone knock."

"I didn't either," Ben added, smiling a welcome.

"Then I guess it's a good thing Takola has excellent hearing." Adam shifted the burlap sack on his shoulder to a more comfortable position and stepped forward to ruffle Ben's hair. Still smiling, he transferred his gaze to Lacy's upturned face. "I guess you forgot to pick up my laundry when you delivered the clean stuff," he chided in a tone that clearly indicated he didn't believe it for a moment.

The guilty flush that stained her cheeks could not be stopped. Lacy felt its warmth creep into her face and knew by his lifted brow that he saw it. She hadn't noticed the sack on his shoulder because she was too busy looking at *him,* and yes, she had deliberately "forgotten" to pick up his laundry.

She didn't want to go into his bedroom again because she

was trying to forget what had almost happened there. What she had *wanted* to happen. Crazy, that's what she was. And so was Adam Logan.

Not to mention a sneak and a liar. She thanked her memory for reminding her, knowing that she needed all the help she could get to keep distance between them. "Fridays are rather hectic for me," she demurred, refusing to look away despite the betraying flush.

"I'll bet they are." He reached out and rubbed gently at the pencil mark on her chin.

Lacy pulled back, but not fast enough. She felt the heat of his touch warm her skin and cursed him with her eyes. Desperately, she searched for something to cool the air between them. "Had any luck pulling the wool over people's eyes?" she questioned nastily.

Adam refused to take the bait, which confused Lacy to no end. Normally he pounced on the opportunity to spar with her, as if he thoroughly enjoyed it. Now all he said was, "Not much," before his eyes fell on the mirror, then on the paper beneath Lacy's hand. "What's with the mirror?"

Grudgingly, Lacy explained about Ben. When she finished, Adam was staring at her strangely. She squirmed, wishing he would move away. Thunder, but it was really starting to heat up in the kitchen! Breathlessly, she added, "I figured it out when Ben came to show me the deputy star you gave him. He read the word 'deputy' in the mirror without any trouble at all."

Ben jumped in place, his blue eyes sparkling. "Lacy says I can go to school in a few weeks, when I don't need the mirror no more."

"Anymore," Lacy corrected automatically.

"That's what I said, no more."

Lacy gave up, meeting Adam's amused gaze over Ben's tousled head. She kept her own quivering smile out of sight. He thought he could just walk in here and charm her into forgetting how he had lied, deliberately not telling her he had no intention of staying . . .

No. It wouldn't work. Adam Logan couldn't be trusted, hadn't he proven it? Soon enough, the enamored citizens of

Shadow City would discover his duplicity. Lacy hadn't told anyone what she knew, but if Adam's didn't soon, she would.

She knew where her loyalties lay, even if Rusty had forgotten. But after a hot argument, she had promised Rusty to give Adam a month, and he'd used up the better portion of that already. She was keeping silent for Rusty, not for Adam Logan. At least, that's what she kept repeating to herself.

Adam ruffled Ben's thick mop of hair again and smiled down at him. "Why don't you take this to the wash shed for me?" When Ben grabbed the sack and skipped out the back door, Adam turned to the silent girl in the doorway. "Have you finished any new pictures for me, Takola?"

Lacy stewed silently as she watched Adam effortlessly charm her family. Takola fairly flew out of the room, apparently to retrieve the drawings she had so painstakingly created for Adam. Rusty offered Adam a seat at the table and Lacy tried to think of a genuine excuse to leave the room as Adam took a chair opposite her. Her mind was blank. It was Saturday evening, and most of the chores were done. Dinner was out of the way, the hog was fed, and the dishes were washed, dried and put away. She could plead a headache and retire to her room, but Rusty would know she was lying. Adam probably would too, and he'd give her one of those amused, challenging looks.

Thunder.

Ben returned, unknowingly saving her from herself. "Would you write out some more words for me to study, Lacy? I can't wait to go to school like the other boys." His chest swelled visibly. "They're jealous of my deputy star."

Lacy leaped on the request, taking her time as she penciled out several words for Ben. Finally she could dally no longer. She handed Ben the paper, the pencil, and the mirror. "If you have any trouble, just write the letters beneath them, as you think they should look. I think you'll have to rely on your memory, Ben, but you shouldn't have a problem with that."

"Thanks, Lacy." He raced from the room, nearly bumping into Takola as she entered laden with a stack of papers.

Shyly, Takola approached Adam and set the drawings before him, looking anxious for the first time that Lacy could recall. Adam studied each picture with great care and Lacy felt her heart soften. Adam Logan may have his faults, she thought, but he sure knew how to boost a child's confidence.

"My," he whistled, gaining a smile from Takola. "These are unbelievable."

Lacy laughed at Takola's hurt expression. "No, Takola. He doesn't really mean that he doesn't believe them. He means they're wonderful." When Takola's face cleared in understanding, Lacy added, "Our people don't always say what they mean."

Adam glanced at her sharply, eyes narrowing in warning. Lacy shot him a sweet, innocent smile that she suspected he wasn't buying. He pushed his sweat-soaked hat back and drawled, "That's true, Takola. And some people deny what they're feelin', too."

Lacy gasped.

Adam grinned, a grin of pure deviltry as he added, "But I'm tellin' you the truth. I've never seen anything like your drawings before."

This seem to satisfy Takola, although she still looked confused. With a nod in Adam's direction, she left the three adults to talk.

But Lacy didn't want to talk with Adam Logan. She wanted to escape. The room was growing warmer by the minute and it was all she could do to keep from fanning herself. *Adam would make something of that!* was her irritable thought. And just what had he meant by "some people deny their feelings"? She didn't deny anything. She just wasn't going to allow reckless passion to ruin her life.

Reckless passion. Lacy nearly groaned out loud. Where on earth was she getting these insane notions? What she felt for Adam wasn't passion . . . it was . . . it was a *physical* thing. Ordinary, when a body thought about it. A normal reaction from a woman who had experienced what happens between a man and a woman.

Which was a bald-faced lie and she knew it. It was one thing to lie to someone else, but quite another to lie to herself. Nothing she and David had experienced together had been pleasant, but just the slightest lazy look from this good-for-nothing sheriff and her heart was acting strange, her palms got sweaty, and her knees felt like jelly.

Ridiculous.

"I'm going for a walk," she said abruptly, rising from the chair. Please God, let her legs be stronger than they felt, she prayed silently.

Adam was up before she could finish rising. "I'll go with you, Mrs. Ross. Don't want to walk these streets alone at night."

Lacy froze, her jaw falling open in dismay. She'd never dreamed he'd be so bold. But she should have known. She should have blasted known. "I—I don't need protection, Sheriff Logan. And if I did, I've got Deputy Palmer here." She smiled at her grandfather, silently pleading for his help.

But Rusty showed her just how stubborn he could be. "Nope, think I'll turn in early." He feigned a huge yawn and Lacy wished she had something handy to shove down his throat when he added, "Adam, much obliged."

Lacy watched him go, speechless that he would leave her at Adam's mercy. Of all the miserable, low-down things to do. . . . *Traitor!* Oh, she would get him for this—

She jumped as a strong hand landed on her arm. "Shall we?" Adam said in her ear.

Jerking her arm free, she whirled on him, eyes blazing, throat working with the effort to slow the words enough so that he wouldn't miss a single one. "I do not want to go walking with you, Sheriff Logan. Folks might see us—"

Before she could finish, Adam closed the short distance separating them and hauled her against his hard form. Nose-to-nose, he ground out, "You ashamed of me, Mrs. Ross? Is that what you're saying? You don't want to walk with the grandson of a coward?"

Lacy stared into his furious eyes, wondering how she had

gotten herself into this mess. Only moments ago, he had been teasing her, taunting her in the usual way. *The usual way?* Was she, then, so familiar with his ways?

"I'm not ashamed to be seen with you, Adam." Her breath hitched in a little sigh of relief when he eased his hold. "I wasn't talking about who you are, I was talking about the gossip it would start." She licked her lips, watching his eyes as they immediately dropped to watch the movement as if it fascinated him. *Did he look at Mary Ann this way?* she wondered, and found the possibility painful to even think about. Was it deliberate, this seduction, or was it a natural, impulsive response? Lacy discovered that she wanted to know the answer, and in the next breath decided she had completely lost her mind.

Besides, she didn't know how to go about finding out if Adam's actions were sincere or contrived.

Adam slid his hand up her arm, raising goose bumps along the way. He used his other hand to cup her hip and pull her slowly closer, until she felt the hard muscles of his thighs flex against her softness. With his handsome face only inches away again, he said softly, "My apologies, Lacy. I'm afraid my temper's a little short today and you made me mad." He eased his mouth closer to her waiting lips. Lacy caught her breath and held it, not wanting anything to startle the moment because she had missed him, could not wipe the memory of their last kiss from her mind. Try as she might, she could not forget Adam Logan or how he made her feel.

Alive. Yes, alive and . . . quivering for something she couldn't name, something she was certain he could give her and something she was certain would trap her.

"And you know what happens when you make me mad, don't you, Lacy?" he prompted, so close that Lacy fancied she could see her reflection in his eyes.

His warm breath wafted over her face in a gentle caress. She inhaled the faint scent of mint and coffee, felt the heat of his body seep into hers. Her eyes grew heavy and her breasts strained as if they had a will of their own. She couldn't speak, didn't want to jeopardize the fragile joy of being held close against the heartbeat of another. Not just any other, but Adam, a man who turned her world upside down with just a smile and a kiss.

He chuckled in a lazy way, but Lacy could feel the tension in his body and knew that he wasn't unmoved. "Guess I'll have to show you."

Yes, Lacy thought, closing her eyes. This is what I want, what I've been waiting for since the last time. No matter how much she had tried to thrust it from her mind, it always came back to this. She and Adam, locked in an embrace. Tentatively, she lifted her arms and circled his neck.

There wasn't anything remotely innocent about his kiss, Lacy thought, parting her lips and surrendering without a fight. He didn't hesitate, nor ask her permission. He just took what he wanted, confident that she wanted the same thing.

He was right. Lacy arched against him, not caring what Adam might think of the movement or who might walk in and see them. She felt as if she had starved for his kiss this past week. What a fool she had been, telling herself she didn't care, congratulating Mary Ann for "drawing first blood," as Susan and Carrianna had laughingly called it.

What a durn fool.

The rough sound of someone clearing his throat brought Lacy floating back to the ground. Adam slowly lifted his head from her lips, staring at her heavy-lidded eyes for a long moment before looking over her shoulder. Lacy turned to follow his line of vision, warm and fluid. It was hard to snap out of the daze she was in, but she gave her head a little shake and focused on Rusty standing in the doorway.

The moment her gaze settled on him, Rusty wiped the sappy grin from his face—but not before she saw it. She frowned and moved from the circle of Adam's arms, waiting for Rusty to speak.

"Didn't mean to interrupt, but there's some men at the door, asking to speak to the sheriff." He lifted his bushy brows and grinned at Adam. "I believe that's you." He didn't seem to mind not being able to claim the job any longer, which immediately aroused Lacy's suspicions.

"What kind of men, Grandpa?" she asked sharply.

Rusty pointed to Adam with a strange smile. "They want to see the new sheriff. It's that Salvage man. He's back and he's got the money to start building a new lumber mill again."

To Lacy's shock, Adam cursed long and hard.

11

ℬY THE TIME Adam had finished cursing a blue streak, Rusty had sobered. Lacy glanced from one to the other, finally settling her accusing eyes on Adam.

"Don't tell me you're on the side of that sneaky, snake-bellied mayor!" Lacy didn't want to believe it, but why else would Adam be so angry that Mr. Salvage had come back to take another stand? And Rusty—she pinned him with a glare—Rusty had allowed the mayor to run Mr. Salvage off the last time, claiming he didn't have any proof.

Well, she silently conceded, maybe that part was the truth, but she hated the fact that the mayor had gotten away with what he had. Surely Adam wouldn't allow it? He was the sheriff . . . and he had Rusty to help. They weren't quite so alone this time.

Crossing her arms before her, she began tapping her foot, waiting on Adam's answer. It seemed he would choose his own place and time.

"Rusty, would you go tell them I'll be out in a minute? I

want to have a talk with Lacy." When Rusty had gone, Adam set his jaw and faced her. "You are the worst woman I've ever met for jumping to conclusions, Mrs. Ross."

"Stop calling me that!" Lacy burst out. The moment the words were out of her mouth, she could have bitten her tongue off. Thunder, but he had a way of bringing out her worst.

Adam hooked his fingers into his belt loops and shuttered his eyes. Lacy hated it when he did that. She couldn't tell what he was thinking, or how he was feeling—which she was certain was his intention in the first place.

"Isn't that your name? Mrs. Ross?"

Making an attempt to retrieve her dignity, Lacy said, "Yes. It is. It's just that it sounds so . . . so—"

"Impersonal?" Adam drawled. His eyes roamed down her taut figure, then settled onto her face again. "You admit we're over the impersonal stage?" His upraised brow demanded an honest answer.

Lacy shivered beneath the warmth of his blue, blue gaze, mentally cursing his talent for unnerving her. Just one look . . . Were her lips swollen from his kisses?

She choose to ignore the question, suspecting he was merely trying to sidetrack her. With a challenging glint in her eyes, she said, "You've got people waiting outside for you. What are you going to tell them?"

"What do you think I'm going to tell them?" Adam countered roughly. "That they can't do business in this town? That there aren't enough trees? That I'm afraid of the mayor?"

Lacy bristled. "Rusty wasn't afraid of the mayor! He did what he could, but he was just one man—"

"Shut up," Adam said softly. "I wasn't putting Rusty down. Why don't you come outside with me and see for yourself what I'm going to do? Since you're so determined to stick your pretty little nose in the sheriff's business . . ."

Lacy sucked in a sharp breath. "Oh!"

Adam smiled at her affronted expression. "Yes, oh. You had it comin' and you know it." To Lacy's flustered surprise, he reached out and gently tweaked her nose. "God, you're beautiful."

Air rushed into her open mouth. Lacy closed it with a snap. Her face grew warm at the unexpected compliment— until she remembered how good Adam was at distracting her from the issue. Oh, he was *very* good at it. But this time she wasn't falling for his tricks. "Then why did you curse—"

"Because I didn't come here to start a war and play general," Adam said with a heavy sigh.

"No. You came here to weasel your way into people's hearts so you could find out what happened to Sheriff Murddock." Lacy waited for him to deny it, wanted him to say he'd changed his mind and was going to stay, but knew she was hoping in vain. The determined glint in his eyes confirmed it more than any words could. But there was something else there . . . something that looked like regret. Lacy ruthlessly stifled the flash of hope that flared in her chest.

"Yes," he said harshly, "I did. I made a promise to my mother, and if that makes me the bad guy in your eyes, then I guess I'm the bad guy."

Lacy couldn't think of a thing to say. She hadn't known about his mother, or about any promise.

When he saw that she didn't appear to have a ready answer to that one, he adjusted his hat, then bowed mockingly. "I'd love to stay and chat, but I've got a job to do." He started to walk past her, then stopped, leaning close to add, "And we *will* continue this discussion another time, *Lacy*. If you're going to make judgments about me, then I think you at least owe me a chance to explain."

After he had disappeared through the kitchen doorway, Lacy took a moment to round up her busy thoughts before grabbing the lantern from the table and following him outside.

She felt small and mean. Maybe she had been wrong to jump to conclusions about Adam. Maybe she *did* owe it to him to listen to what he had to say.

Maybe she *was* being too judgmental. And she knew why

she searched eagerly for his faults. As long as she kept him at a distance, she wasn't in danger of losing her head—and her heart.

Adam hated to admit that Lacy's opinion mattered to him, but it did. He couldn't deny it any longer. Why in the hell did she have to be so stubborn? She acted as if she wanted to believe the worst about him. At every turn he found that he had to defend himself.

Yanking the front door open, he marched out onto the porch and stood beside Rusty. A lantern hung on a pole by the porch railing, casting a soft yellow glow over the yard. Adam counted four men on horseback. As he watched, one of the horsemen urged his mount forward.

"You the new sheriff?" a gruff voice asked.

Adam couldn't see his face; it was shadowed by the brim of his hat. He didn't like talking to a man whose eyes he couldn't see. Neither did he care to defend a man who didn't deserve to be defended, and as long as he couldn't see his face, he couldn't see what kind of man Salvage was. He'd already decided that he and Rusty couldn't do it alone, and if the man before him didn't have the guts to tough it out, then he wasn't about to waste his time. He wouldn't be around to protect Salvage forever.

He heard Lacy's soft footsteps behind him and resisted the urge to turn his head and look at her. God, it had been only moments since he'd had his lips and hands on her! he thought in self-disgust.

To the man before him, he said, "I'm the new sheriff, Adam Logan. Why don't y'all get down and rest a spell." He lifted a hand and indicated the rough wooden chairs along the porch, as if he had every right to act as host. "Lacy'll get you and your crew a drink of water while we talk." Glancing behind him, he encountered Lacy's feisty gaze and smiled at her. She softened and went inside to get a pitcher of water, the gentle swing of her hips drawing his attention.

The man gestured for his men to dismount and stretched his legs before climbing the steps to the porch. He held out his hand and Adam took it, automatically registering the rough feel of a working man's hand.

"Name's Lester Salvage, Sheriff." He nodded at Rusty, casting a puzzled glance at the deputy star on his shirt. "I already know Mr. Palmer here." With introductions behind them, he took one of the chairs Adam offered. The other three men settled their dusty behinds on the porch steps among stifled groans and moans, attesting to a long, hard ride. Adam took the seat alongside Lester Salvage.

Rusty rested against the porch post and chewed on a toothpick. After a moment, he said, "Guess you're wondering what happened." Lester Salvage shrugged, but his eyes strayed once again to Rusty's deputy star. Rusty volunteered the information. "Mayor fired me because I wouldn't run you out of town."

Lester, a short, stocky man with a round, youthful-looking face partially hidden by a week's growth of beard, didn't look surprised by the news. Bitterness mingled with impotent anger as he replied, "Ended up, he didn't need your help, Deputy."

Rusty nodded his grizzly head. "Yep. Right sorry about that. We both know he done it, but there weren't no proof."

"Question is, will it happen again?" Lester directed the question Adam's way, his hands propped expectantly on his knees, shoulders forward. "I lost a lot of money building that lumber shed, just to have it burnt to the ground. Now, I'm willing to try it again, if I know I got the sheriff"—he glanced at Rusty, then back at Adam—"and the deputy on my side."

Adam studied the man, deciding he had an honest face. Dammit. How much simpler it would have been if he had discovered Lester Salvage to be as ruthless and greedy as the mayor. Then he could have allowed the two men to fight it out on their own.

But he had taken the job as sheriff, and it was his duty to see that justice prevailed.

As Adam weighed his words with care, Lacy came out of the house with a pitcher of cool water and several tin cups balanced on a serving tray. Adam felt his lips twitch with amusement as he realized that she didn't trust the clumsy men with her glasses. Sensing his gaze, she glanced around and caught him watching her.

For a heated moment it was as if they were alone; tension crackled between them and pulses raced with excitement. Finally, she gave her head a little shake, then turned her attention to serving the cool water to the waiting men.

Restlessly, Adam stood and walked to the end of the porch, then back again. He leaned against the railing and cocked his hip before meeting Lester's earnest eyes. "We won't stop you from building, but you'll have to post your own guards. Shadow City can't afford to hire extra deputies."

"He's right, Mr. Salvage," Rusty said.

Lester stood up, his hat in his hand. "And if the mayor tries to burn me out again?"

Thinking of Jamis Goodrich, Adam smiled the kind of smile that he reserved for his enemies. "Well, we'll just have to cross that bridge when we get to it. This time you'll be ready for him, right?" Lester hesitated, then nodded. Adam grunted in response. "If he does try anything, we'll have a witness this time. If he tries to fire *me*, we'll go to the town council and demand a hearing. I don't think Goodrich would like that too much."

Rusty chuckled at the evil sound of Adam's voice. "He wouldn't. Never did like his laundry where anybody could see it. Reckon he wouldn't like his business where anybody could hear it, neither." He grinned at Lester. "And I know plenty of his business."

Adam held out his hand, wondering if he would wind up regretting his decision to go against the mayor, the man who had hired him for this job. With a rueful shake of his head, he gripped Lester Salvage's callused hand and looked into his grateful eyes.

Yes, he had done the right thing.

"Come on down to my office tomorrow and I'll give you a few pointers on how to catch rustlers."

Lester looked blank; then he realized Adam wasn't talking about cattle rustlers. "Yes, sir," he said, pumping

Adam's hand. He let it go and grabbed Rusty's, pumping just as furiously. "Yes, sir. I sure will."

The men replaced their cups on the tray Lacy held out for them, politely tipping their hats to her in silent thanks. After they departed, Lacy, Adam, and Rusty stood on the porch watching the dark shadows move wearily down the road leading from town. Apparently, Salvage wasn't ready for the mayor to know he was back.

Softly, Lacy said, "You did the right thing, Adam. You too, Grandpa. It's time we pulled the mayor down a peg or two. It's getting to where he thinks he owns this town and can do anything he wants." There was a proud, satisfied gleam in the look she directed at Adam. With a clank of tin cups, she went back into the house.

Rusty and Adam exchanged rueful looks. Adam spoke first. "Women. They don't know what trouble means."

Spitting his toothpick across the rail, Rusty growled, "Course they don't. That's because they *are* trouble. Hope you know what you're gettin' into, son."

Adam grunted. "Didn't see any other way around it."

"You mean, without disappointing Lacy?"

Scowling at Rusty, Adam pushed away from the railing and stepped down from the porch. "She and I are gonna have a long talk one of these days."

He turned his back on Rusty's cackling laughter as he headed for the office and the big empty bed where he knew he would lie awake half the night thinking of Lacy.

Lacy, with her hungry eyes and full, moist lips begging to be kissed. Damp, sexy tendrils of hair clinging to her temples. Her long, thick braid just waiting to be unraveled . . .

Adam doubted that she knew how much the hunger showed. He doubted that she knew how much his body wanted to sink into her, to show her what loving was all about. He suspected she didn't know the first thing about what a man and woman could do to each other.

Damn. He'd sure like to show her.

Yet that wasn't all he wanted from Lacy Ross. He also wanted her respect and approval.

What the hell was wrong with him?

* * *

Lacy paused outside the new dress shop the girls were in such a tither about, her eye caught by a beautiful dress draping a wooden dummy in the window. Takola waited patiently by her side, ignoring the curious stares of the people passing by on the boardwalk. With her hair in braids, dressed in a long, straight leather tunic decorated with feathers and beads, Takola was an object of interest to the straitlaced citizens of Shadow City, and regrettably, the recipient of several hostile glares.

Lacy knew they stared, but she was so weary of leaving Takola at the house alone. With Ben and Rusty gone most of the day now, she had taken to bringing Takola shopping with her. Too much solitude couldn't be good for the girl.

Besides, they were here to buy material to make Takola a new outfit or two. That is, if the new establishment carried suede or leather. Takola refused to wear anything but what was customary of her people, and Lacy refused to force her. It was her heritage, the only thing she had left.

Lacy wouldn't dream of taking that from her.

"Isn't it lovely, Takola?" Lacy said of the dress in the window. She wasn't expecting a response; she knew Takola most likely wouldn't find the dress lovely at all. But Takola surprised her. She pointed to the dress, then to Lacy, and nodded emphatically.

Covering her astonishment, Lacy grinned, turning her envious gaze to the dress again. The silk-and-lace concoction was lavender in color, with the tiniest edging of black lace along the round collar and off-the-shoulder sleeves. Just below knee level, a slant of ruffles edged in the same black lace flowed in layers to the ground.

Lacy sighed wistfully. It was the first store-bought dress she'd ever seen, with the exception of a picture in a magazine, and now she wished she hadn't. A dress like that would take weeks to make—if the delicate material could be found at all.

With a resolute squaring of her shoulders, Lacy grabbed Takola's hand and entered the store. She didn't need a new dress. Adam wasn't staying in Shadow City, might not even

be here for the September celebration, so there was no
need—

Oh, fiddlesticks. There she went again, thinking about
Adam. He probably never thought about her. Over a week
had passed since that wicked kiss in the kitchen when she
hadn't offered the slightest protest. She'd heard nothing
from him.

Sure, he was busy helping Lester Salvage break the
ground for the new lumber mill—that much she knew from
Rusty and Ben—but couldn't he find a moment to stop in
and say hello? Lacy hated the hurtful feelings he caused,
hated the fact that it mattered. It meant that she cared, and
that was dangerous, as she well knew.

But what about that talk he said they would have? If he
was so all-fired set on explaining to her, then why didn't he?

A hand at her waist jarred Lacy from her thoughts. She
whirled, a mock scowl on her face, thinking it had to be
Adam. He was the only one bold enough to try such a move
in a public place.

She was wrong. Her face froze. She tore the mayor's hand
from her waist and dropped it aside as if it were a dead
rattler. "Mayor Goodrich. You mind keepin' your hands to
yourself?" She flashed a warning at Takola, who had crept
up behind the mayor with a bolt of material lifted in a
threatening gesture. Takola stopped, but didn't back off. Her
black eyes glinted with savage fury as she waited to see
what the mayor would do.

Lacy knew if she didn't make haste in getting rid of the
mayor, there would be a scene the townspeople wouldn't
soon forget. A bloody scene.

Jamis Goodrich thought he was handsome. His rich silver
hair, combined with his expensive clothes and flashy
jewelry, gave him a false impression of himself.

Lacy saw him as a fat old man with greed in his eyes and
a stone for a heart. Once, a long time ago, he had been
handsome. He had even been sort of likable. But not now.
He was a pest, and more than once Lacy had had to
disentangle herself from an ugly situation such as the one
she faced now.

When he spoke, Lacy inhaled the strong, repulsive scent of garlic and whiskey. Adam always smelled of peppermint.

"It's hard to keep my hands to myself when I get this close to that delightful figure of yours," the mayor said with suggestiveness in his voice.

Lacy stiffened, but tried to keep her revulsion from showing on her face. It wouldn't take much for Takola to disregard her wishes and clobber the foppish mayor with her weapon. Maybe if she refused to talk to him, he would go away.

"When are you going to stop yearning for fine things and marry me? I'll give you all you could ever want."

But at what price? Lacy clenched her hands at her sides. Her stomach lurched at the thought of lying in bed with this man night after night . . . smelling his pungent, awful perfume . . . suffering his pudgy, bejeweled fingers on her. He couldn't know that she would rather die.

Coldly, she said, "I have no plans to remarry, Mayor Goodrich. And I have all I need, thank you. Now if you'll excuse me—" she stepped to the side with the intention of passing him, and he countered the move. Over his fat shoulder, Lacy saw Takola lift the bolt of material again and closed her eyes. She didn't want to watch.

"Mayor Goodrich. Heard you were lookin' for me."

The sound of Adam's rumbling voice popped her eyes open. He had taken the bolt of material from Takola, she saw with relief. Takola didn't look happy, but she made no threatening move to take it back, as Lacy suspected she would have done if it had been anyone but Adam.

Quickly, while Adam had the mayor's attention, she skirted around his bulky body and went to stand beside Takola, placing a hand on her shoulder—more to stay her than for comfort.

When the mayor pivoted and caught sight of Adam, his expression turned downright ugly. He appeared to forget about Lacy altogether. "Yes, I've been looking for you. There's a matter I believe we need to discuss. We'll talk in your office."

Seemingly unperturbed, Adam handed Lacy the material,

his eyes roving hungrily over her upturned face. When he winked at her, Lacy found herself returning the wink, surprised at her boldness. Adam did that to her, made her feel bold and reckless. She wondered if Takola felt her shaking, then decided she didn't care. She had missed him. He looked tanned and rugged, and incredibly . . . Lacy stifled a laugh over her wicked imagination, watching the two men as they made their exit from the dress shop.

Adam was about to have hell to pay for supporting—and helping—Lester Salvage. The thought sobered Lacy. She hoped Grandpa had warned Adam how ruthless Jamis Goodrich could be when he wanted something.

Or how deadly he could be when he didn't get it.

Adam propped his feet up on his desk and leaned back in his chair, knowing that his easy posture further infuriated the man pacing the floor in front of him. The mayor's face had turned a deep purple.

"You let Salvage start building again," the mayor bellowed.

"Yes."

"You didn't come to me and ask, you just took it upon yourself."

Adam nodded. "That's right. Salvage bought the land. He can build whatever he wants."

The mayor stomped up to the desk and leaned over. "You realize that any new business has to be approved by the town council?"

"I believe it was approved months ago, Mayor Goodrich," Adam stated coldly. "You were the only one who disagreed with the vote."

"I'm the mayor!" Goodrich shouted.

"And I'm the sheriff. The law's the law. That's what you pay me to do, uphold the law. The town doesn't mind Salvage settin' up his business, so why should you?"

Mayor Goodrich trembled with his fury. "You know damned well why I don't want him here."

Adam shook his head. "There's plenty of timber for two

mills," he pointed out. "With the railroad running through, you won't lose a nickel."

"I won't stand for it!"

Adam narrowed his eyes at the mayor, slowly dropping his feet. He leaned forward and said, with a distinct warning in his voice, "If you try to burn Salvage out again, I'll throw you in jail."

The mayor gasped, choked, then sputtered, "You can't throw me in jail, you—you young pup! I'm the mayor."

"So you've said. Several times already. Don't matter. You break the law, I'll throw you in jail just like I would anyone who breaks the law."

"I'll fire you," Goodrich threatened.

Adam smiled. "And I'll go to the town council with the story. They'll have to know how you burned Salvage out the last time he tried to build, of course."

"You don't have any proof. You can't say that, it would be slander."

"So sue me," Adam shot back. "You fired Rusty, and if you fire me, don't you think the citizens of Shadow City will wonder? Especially after I tell them about the fire a few months back, and how some folks think you were behind it."

The mayor's face purpled to an alarming shade and Adam began to wonder if the old man would solve the problem by keeling over dead. Shiny drops of spittle gleamed in the corners of his mouth. His eyes bulged. "I hired you to avoid interference of this nature."

"I suspected as much when I heard the real reason you fired Deputy Palmer."

"That's another thing. How dare you go behind my back and hire that drunken son—" He clamped his mouth shut as Adam rose from his chair and took a menacing step in his direction. The mayor began to stutter. "N-now, just a minute—"

Softly, Adam said, "I suggest you leave Rusty out of this. It clearly stated in the letter of acceptance that I could hire a deputy of my own choosing. I've still got the letter, if you'd like to see it and refresh your memory."

"I'll make you regret this, Logan. I swear it."

Disgusted with the whole ordeal, Adam let his secret slip. "I don't know how my grandfather stood you."

The air became still between them. Adam mentally kicked himself and his loose tongue. He hadn't wanted the mayor to have that juicy bit of information just yet, dammit, and here he was, blurting it out.

"So, you're Murddock's grandson," the mayor guessed. A feral gleam appeared in his shifty eyes. "Following in his footsteps?"

Adam jerked. "Is that a threat?"

"I don't know what you mean," the mayor cooed. A full smile stretched his fleshy lips from corner to corner. "You think you're pretty smart, sneaking into town, laying low about who you are. What's this all about, Logan? Lookin' for a ghost?" Cruelty twisted his lips as he added, "I assure you, there are none. Colt Murddock went straight to hell."

Adam gripped the edge of his desk to deep from smashing his fist into the mayor's smiling face. "I'm not looking for a ghost; I'm looking for a murderer." He regained some of his control when the color drained from the mayor's face. "I wonder," he mused softly, "how much you had to gain from my grandfather's death?"

The mayor swallowed hard. For the first time, he spoke without anger. "You're being ridiculous, Logan. Everyone knows Murddock killed himself."

Adam's eyes burned into the mayor's. "Well, now. Not everyone. I don't think he killed himself at all. Neither does Rusty Palmer, who was his best friend. Looks like he oughta know, if anyone did."

"There was a note—"

"He could have been forced to write it."

"The rope—"

"Someone else could have put it around his neck."

The mayor began to recover, gathering his vices around him like a child with his toys. He didn't hesitate to use blackmail. "Looks like a standoff, Logan. You go to the town council blustering about me burning Salvage out, and

I go with the story of who you are. They'll run you out of town *after* they tar and feather you."

Adam forced a laugh, knowing it was important the he bluff his way through. "Are you sure about that? Colt Murddock was a long time ago and memories fade. Hell, most of the people in Shadow City don't remember him at all, except for the stories they've heard. But you and your little bully ways of keeping all the prime timber to yourself, now that's a guarantee." He slapped his hands on the desk and the mayor jumped. Adam's smile was without humor. "If there's one thing I've discovered about this town it's that they don't like violence. Now, wouldn't you call settin' fire to a building an act of violence?"

The mayor made a choking sound. His hands curled into fists and his face reddened again. "You'll regret this, Logan. I swear it." He lurched around and headed for the door.

"Much obliged for the warning, Mayor," Adam taunted to his retreating back. The door slammed with a bang and Adam slumped into his chair. Good God, he'd had no idea what Rusty had been up against. He wondered whether Colt had gone through the same dance with the mayor, when he was alive.

Adam settled his chin on his hands, a frown pulling hard at his brows. Should he add the mayor to his list of suspects, which would bring the total to two? He couldn't discount the expression on the mayor's face when he had mentioned he was looking for a murderer.

It had been guilt, plain and simple.

He had to talk to Lacy. He had a gut feeling about how much she knew, whether she was conscious of it or not. The reason he'd waited as long as he had was because he dreaded asking her, knowing she would think he had been leading up to the moment. As suspicious as she was, she'd be convinced that every move he had made, the kissing and holding, had been a trick to lure her into softening toward him so that he could question her about the day his grandfather died.

Adam buried his face in his hands and laughed at the

irony of his situation. His laughter turned to a groan of frustration.

Hell, he almost wished she was right, because the truth was, he was going to miss her, and Rusty, and Ben—even Takola. He hadn't realized how empty his life had been until the day he bought that damned blackberry pie from the restaurant.

Chuckling, he wondered if Lacy had pondered that stain on the seat of his pants when she had laundered his clothes. After Brian and Ed had left, he'd taken his pants out back to the pump and scrubbed and scrubbed, then hung them on the fence, but when they had dried, there had still been a dark stain.

His chuckles turned into belly-rolling laughter as he imagined the look on her face.

12

"*I* DON'T KNOW, Adam," Rusty said, shaking his head. He frowned at the hot sun overhead and accepted the tin cup of cool water from Adam. "The mayor's a snake—and a greedy son of a bitch—but I don't know 'bout murder."

Adam glanced through the open door, confirming that Ben was busy sweeping the jail cells. He'd motioned Rusty out back with the pretense of needing a drink so that he could get his opinion on Jamis Goodrich. "You didn't see his face when I told him I was looking for a murderer." He took the empty cup from Rusty and filled it from the pump again, downing the contents in one drink.

"Don't necessarily mean he's guilty. Maybe guilty of *something*—he's always guilty of *something*." Rusty shook his head again. "But murder . . ."

"Money can change people, cause them to do things they wouldn't ordinarily do," Adam said quietly.

"You're right. You're right, at that." This time Rusty sounded less doubtful. "Could be you're right about the other, too. If you are, then you need to be looking over your shoulder, son. The mayor ain't gonna stand by and let someone accuse him of murder."

Adam wasn't worried. If something happened to him, folks would know that Jamis Goodrich had had something to do with it. Telling Rusty about his suspicions was his insurance. With a shrug he said, "Let him try. He'll prove my point."

"Won't do you any good if you're dead!" Rusty nearly yelled. "And I ain't too sure the townsfolk would believe me over the mayor, Adam, if that's what you're countin' on." Angry now, he jerked the cup away from Adam and began pumping furiously. Water rushed up the pump and drowned the cup, soaking the sun-baked earth at their feet. "I didn't think you came here to get dead, you ornery cuss. If I'd have known that, I wouldn't be helping you."

Adam brushed his worries aside with a careless shrug. "Nobody's going to kill me, you old fart. Now stop pumping that handle—you're flooding the yard." Rusty quit, standing back with his hands on his hips, glaring at him. Adam sighed. "I need to talk to Lacy, find out what she remembers. If she saw the mayor anywhere near that office the day she found Colt . . ."

"Then you'd better hurry," Rusty growled at him. "She's ridin' out to the old Henderson farm west of town to welcome the new family. Salvage bought it, and his wife and kids came in on the train yesterday. She's takin' them some vittles."

"She goin' alone?"

"Always does. Never know when folks might take a dislike to Takola, and Ben's busy here. Farm's about seven miles west, give you plenty of time to have that long talk you threatened to have with her."

Adam smiled. "I did, didn't I?"

Rusty forgot his anger. He grinned back. "You did. Might want to stop at the pond on the way back and rest a spell. Plenty of shade, won't be nobody around 'cause it's too hot to fish."

"Much obliged," Adam said. He peered through the open

doorway and bellowed, "Ben! Run and saddle Sandy for me, would ya?" He started inside, but Rusty held him back with a firm grip on his shoulder. Surprised, Adam turned to the older man.

"You remember that old shotgun Lacy pulled on you the first day you was in town?" Rusty inquired with innocent, unblinking eyes.

Adam nodded. "How could I forget? Hard to believe that was only a month ago."

"Well . . . that old shotgun still works, if you get my meaning, son."

Adam did, and it was all he could do to keep from laughing. But the serious expression on Rusty's face stilled his mirth. Gravely, he said, "I would never hurt Lacy. You should know that."

Rusty gave his shoulder a hard squeeze. "That's what I was hopin' you'd say." Apparently satisfied his warning had been taken, Rusty clapped him on the back. "Now, you sweet-talk her first, you hear? Talk about anythin' and everythin', and then lead up to Sheriff Murddock. . . ."

Adam bent his head to listen. Rusty knew Lacy better than anyone, and Adam wasn't about to let a little thing like male pride stand in his way.

Lacy tucked the large basket of eggs in the far corner of the wagon. The straw would keep them from breaking, and she had also prepared a barrel of coarse salt and unslacked lime so Mrs. Salvage could preserve the eggs. The mixture could keep the eggs for several years, if need be.

Chickens squawked in a cage—five of her best laying hens—along with a rooster. Preserves of peaches and blackberries, a smoked ham, a slab of cured bacon, a bolt of calico for making curtains, several crocks of butter, a round of cheese, and five loaves of bread filled the wagon.

Lacy nodded in satisfaction. Some of the supplies had been donated by the other townsfolk, gathered by Carrianna, Susan, and Mary Ann. And this morning, as Lacy gathered the items together, Takola had presented her with two cornhusk dolls to give to the little girls, and a rattle made from a dried gourd, painted and decorated with bright feathers and beads.

They had learned from Mr. Salvage that Mrs. Salvage was expecting a third child. Lacy was touched by Takola's thoughtfulness, and hopeful that this was a sign that she was beginning to realize not all white people were bad.

Tying her bonnet beneath her chin, Lacy climbed onto the wagon seat and flicked the reins. She needed to make good time or the butter would melt, despite the heavy layer of straw shielding it from the hot sun.

"Come on, Grasshopper, let's get goin' so we can make it back before dark."

Before the mare could respond to her familiar urging, a horse and rider came trotting around the corner of the house. Startled by their unexpected appearance, Grasshopper jerked her head and whinnied a protest.

Lacy gaped at Adam, then at the huge buff-colored stallion he rode. It was several hands taller than her little mare, and Lacy didn't blame Grasshopper for being nervous. "You scared Grasshopper," she chided as Adam nudged the stallion alongside the wagon. Prudently, she scooted away from the blowing horse, but her eyes fixed on Adam's damp shirt and the shadow of the hair beneath. Her mouth went dry.

Adam grinned and shoved his hat back on his head. "Grasshopper? What kind of name is that for a horse?"

Lacy felt an answering smile twitch her lips. It *was* a silly name, but there was a reason. "What else would you name a horse that eats grasshoppers?"

"What?" Adam laughed his disbelief. "That's a first for me."

A silence fell between them: an awkward, tense silence. Lacy wanted to stare and stare, drink her fill of him. Amusement danced in his blue eyes and he looked so strong and handsome astride the big blond stallion. She sighed inwardly, feeling curiously sad. "Well . . . I'd best get going. Butter's gonna melt under this hot sun."

Adam didn't move. "Rusty said you were going out to the Salvage place to welcome the family." When she nodded, he said, "Thought I might ride along with you. Sandy needs exercise."

Lacy braced herself against the thrill of pleasure his words evoked. She'd like nothing more than for him to ride along, yet the strong part of her—the self-preservation part of her—knew that the smart thing to do would be to run. She feared her heart was already in for an ache when he left Shadow City. Spending time with him would only make things worse.

"I can't stop you, can I?"

"Do you want to?"

Heat sizzled, and it had nothing to do with the sun overhead. Both were remembering the last time she had asked him to stop, and both knew she hadn't wanted him to.

She didn't now, either. Lacy tore her gaze away from his, from the promise of passion she saw there. With a feigned, careless shrug, she ignored his deep question. "It's a free country."

Adam chuckled knowingly as he dismounted and tied the stallion's reins to the back of the wagon. Lacy gave considerable thought to sending Grasshopper into a gallop, leaving Adam behind to eat her dust.

But she didn't. Instead, she slid over on the bench and handed him the reins, hoping he wouldn't take the action as a sign of passivity. She wasn't handing him control, just the reins, she assured herself.

The wagon lurched as Adam flicked the straps lightly onto Grasshopper's back. The mare moved docilely forward and soon they were on the road leading west out of town. The big stallion trotted behind them, snorting his displeasure. Thick forestry crowded both sides of the dirt road, shading them from the bright sun; a light, warm breeze ruffled the flaps of her bonnet, giving some relief from the heat.

Lacy tried to relax. It wasn't easy with Adam's hard, muscular thighs only inches from her own. The wagon bounced along, often throwing her perilously close to touching him. She wondered how he'd gotten his shirt wet, and why he didn't button those top buttons, for goodness' sake.

Finally, she ventured, "You know the way?" She glanced at his profile, at the slight bumps on his nose she'd noticed the first time she had seen him. He had been a stranger then; now she felt as if she had known him forever.

Without looking at her, he asked, "Old Henderson farm?"

"Yes."

"Then I know the way. Rusty told me."

Silence fell again. Lacy fidgeted on the seat. He didn't seem inclined to talk, but she had a million questions burning in her mind. Besides, he owed her an explanation, had promised her one. Maybe he didn't care what she thought anymore. The possibility panicked her, though she knew she was being foolish.

Adam Logan would leave when his work was done. She needed to accept this fact, and not hope for something that wasn't going to happen.

With this depressing thought in mind, she asked, "Are you going back to your ranch in Wyoming when you're . . . finished here?"

Adam jerked his head sideways to look at her, his eyes sharp with suspicion. "*My* ranch? What makes you think that ranch is mine?"

Bewildered, Lacy said, "Because Mary Ann said you owned a ranch in Wyoming, so naturally I assumed—"

"Something you're good at," Adam cut in, but this time he was smiling. "Snake River Ranch isn't mine. It belongs to my stepfather." Lacy watched his jaw harden and automatically tensed. His smile had disappeared. "Mr. Silverstone *assumed* the ranch had gone to me, since it belonged to Colt—Sheriff Murddock. But a will wasn't found."

"Oh," Lacy mumbled in sympathy. He didn't appear bitter about the settlement, but she sensed he wasn't pleased, either. "I'm sure if Sheriff Murddock had known, he would have made a will."

"Oh, he made a will, all right." His eyes met hers briefly

before he turned his attention back to the road. "I said a will wasn't found."

Lacy sat in confused silence, waiting for him to explain. A deer darted across their path, crashing into the woods on the other side, white tail flashing. Grasshopper twitched her ears at the disturbance, but continued on at a steady pace. Occasionally, the mare swung her head around and rolled her eyes at the stallion trailing behind the wagon.

Finally, Adam spoke, his voice soft with an underlying tension. "Lacy, do you believe my grandfather killed himself?"

Lacy stiffened on the bench, gripping the sides as she fought the memories that haunted her to this very day. She didn't want to think about it, not on such a beautiful day. Not with Adam. She kept her eyes straight ahead. "I don't really know, Adam. I was young." *But not so young that I can't remember, unfortunately.*

"I'm going to prove that he was murdered."

Surprised, Lacy turned to him. "Murdered? But who would want to kill such a gentle, kind man?" Too late, she realized her slip.

Adam narrowed his eyes at her. "So, you *do* remember. As for who might want him dead, my stepfather for one. Without a will, the ranch would naturally revert to my mother, and on her death, to him. He got what he wanted. Question is, did he murder my grandfather to get it? And if he did, did he also destroy the will?

"There was a fire the same day—at Graham Silverstone's place of business—that destroyed the envelope Colt had given him for safekeeping. Graham swears Colt had another copy hidden somewhere."

Lacy scrambled to put the pieces together. What Adams said made sense, but she couldn't see a way to prove any of it. Fifteen years was a long time. "If you could find the will, you might have a chance to prove that your stepfather killed Colt, but if not . . . I don't see how you could."

Adam was silent for a moment, as if he were weighing his words with care. Staring at his profile, Lacy felt a nervous fluttering in her stomach, a premonition of unpleasant things to come. She had an idea of what he was going to say, and she didn't want to hear it.

"Lacy . . . I know that you're the one who found my grandfather."

"So?" She tried to sound casual, but knew she had failed when he slanted a hard glance her way. She swallowed. "I was nine years old, Adam. You have no idea how awful that was for me."

"And do you have any idea how awful it was for me and Ma to hear he'd killed himself? We knew it was a lie, but we could do nothing about it. My stepfather wouldn't let her leave the ranch, and I didn't dare leave *her*."

"And now she's gone," Lacy concluded quietly. She heard the underlying grief in his voice, and saw the strain on his face. "I don't know what you want from me, Adam. I was just a child, and memories fade." Heat rushed into her face at the lie, and she turned away so he wouldn't see the telltale sign. Why did he have to dredge it all up again? Why didn't he just let it be? Colt Murddock was dead, had been dead for fifteen years.

As if he read her thoughts, Adam said, "What if it were Rusty we were discussing? What if everyone believed he had killed himself, but you knew he hadn't? Wouldn't you want to clear his name, prove that he wasn't a coward?"

When Lacy remained turned away from him, he pulled the wagon to a stop and grabbed her shoulders, twisting her around. A curious light burned brightly in his eyes. Lacy recognized the emotion: it was determination.

He wouldn't give up until he had what he wanted.

"What? What, Adam?" She struggled to break from his strong grip, but he held tight. Fighting panic, Lacy hissed in his face, "Tell me what you want from me, and if I can, I'll give it to you. Just don't expect miracles."

Adam kissed her then, fed from her mouth like a starving man. He raked his lips over hers and thrust his tongue inside her warm, willing mouth. Lacy opened for him without hesitation, melting against him. His arms closed around her, holding her tight. She lifted her own and circled his neck, pulling him tighter, tighter still, until she felt the fierce beating of his heart against her own.

Finally, breathless and aching, she pulled away. Her voice was nothing more than a shaky whisper. "I think you misunderstood me, Adam."

Adam chuckled, a deep, bone-melting chuckle that made her want to throw herself back into his arms. It felt so right to be there. Right, and safe, and exciting.

"No, I didn't misunderstand—I just couldn't resist. When you're that close to me, it's like my mouth has a mind of its own, darlin'."

"You shouldn't call me—"

"Why are you so confounded worried about what I call you? First, you don't want me to call you Mrs. Ross because it's too impersonal. Now you're tellin' me not to call you darlin'?"

Lacy blushed. "Well, it's not proper—"

"Woman!" Adam roared, startling both the mare and the stallion. "Make up your mind."

"Lacy. Just call me Lacy." Primly, Lacy faced forward on the wagon seat, praying she had succeeded in distracting him from the issue of Colt Murddock.

"It didn't work, Lacy," Adam drawled, turning her chin with his fingers. He met her apprehensive gaze, held it. "I've got to find out what really happened that day, and you're my only clue."

Lacy caught a sigh in her throat, wishing it were otherwise. She wished it weren't so important to Adam, that his reasons for coming to Shadow City had been because he planned to settle. "I told you, I'll do what I can to help you. That's all I can promise." He set a brief kiss on her lips before releasing her and taking up the reins again. This time, Lacy let go of the sigh. She couldn't seem to think straight when Adam was close to her.

She became downright brainless when he kissed her.

The wagon lurched forward. Spots of sunlight danced along Grasshopper's back as they found their way through the heavy foliage overhead. Somewhere in the distance, a woodpecker knocked a rapid rhythm.

They had traveled a mile or so in silence, both of them lost in their own thoughts, before Adam spoke again. "I appreciate your help, Lacy. You don't know how much."

Enough to stay? Lacy wanted to ask. But she didn't, because she feared his answer. "Don't thank me yet, Adam. I may not be any help at all." She watched a squirrel leap from limb to limb, chattering a mile a minute. Her throat felt tight, and her chest ached. *Thunder.* She would not start crying, surely?

Adam seemed to sense her inner turmoil. With a muffled curse, he said, "Lacy, you make a man think about settling down. Make him stop and take stock of his life, what he has and what he don't have."

Lacy heard the *but* in his confession. She swallowed a ball of tears and managed a careless smile. Just for Adam. "I'm not the marryin' kind, anyway, Adam Logan. So I guess it's best you don't have serious notions. I'd hate to have to break your heart." She added a laugh that sounded remarkably carefree, considering how miserable she really felt inside.

Adam shot her a disgruntled look. "Make no mistake, Lacy Lynn Ross. If I wanted you to, you'd marry me."

"Ha!" Lacy tossed her bonnet-clad head. "You think so? I've managed to avoid marriage for five years—what makes you so confident that *you* could change my mind?" Her mood had began to lighten until she caught the determined gleam in his eyes. She swallowed and started to slide as far away as she could get.

Adam's arm shot out, catching her waist. He hauled her to his side and clamped his hungry mouth on hers, kissing her until she didn't have a rigid bone in her body. When he finally released her, she let her head fall onto his shoulder. They were both breathing heavily.

The rumble of his voice vibrated beneath her cheek. "Don't ever challenge me, Lacy, unless you're ready for the consequences."

Lacy lifted her head to look at the hard angle of his chin. "What do you want me to do?" Adam knew what she meant. At least she *hoped* he did.

His arm inched up, settling in a most disturbing place just beneath her breast. Lacy caught her breath as a jolt of desire swept through her. She wanted to lean into him, but she managed to hold herself still. This wasn't the place to let her desires rage out of control.

With Adam, there wouldn't *be* a place.

"Do you think it would help if you tried to recreate that day?" Adam asked after a thoughtful moment. The wagon wheel hit a bump and his hand jumped up, closing over a firm, sweet breast. He cursed low, bit his lip, and moved his hand back to her waist.

Lacy heard his curse and knew the reason. She had stopped breathing when he touched her, and shamelessly, hadn't wanted him to stop. She ached all over and wondered if he felt the same. Pressed against him as she was, she could feel the tension in his body. It radiated through hers, thrumming like a siren's sweet call.

She had never imagined love could be so all-consuming. *Love?* Oh, dear God, yes. She loved Adam Logan.

And he would leave after he discovered what had happened to his grandfather.

They rounded a bend in the road and the Henderson farm came into sight. It was a weathered frame house, flanked by a rickety barn and a corral that needed mending. Lacy sat straighter on the bench, adjusting her bonnet and flicking imaginary wrinkles out of her calico dress. Adam dropped his hand from her waist and guided Grasshopper along the lane leading to the farmhouse.

As they approached, a skinny bird dog ran to greet them, followed by two girls who looked to be around six and seven. Lacy smiled, thinking of the cornhusk dolls from Takola. They would be perfect.

Adam pulled the wagon to a stop in front of the porch as Lester Salvage and his tiny, very pregnant wife stepped out to greet them.

"Hello!" Lester called cheerfully. "Wasn't expecting you, Sheriff, but you're mighty welcome." Lester Salvage jumped forward to help Lacy dismount, smiling at her flushed face. "Miz Ross. A pleasure to see you again."

"And you, Mr. Salvage. Is this your wife?" She peered around Lester's bulky frame to the woman waiting beneath the shade of the porch. From the size of her protruding stomach, Lacy guessed she wasn't far away from having her third child. And such a tiny thing, she thought in wonder. She hardly looked capable of bearing *one* child, much less three!

Lester led Lacy up the wobbly steps to introduce her to his wife. "Victoria, this here's Lacy Ross, Sheriff—er—Deputy Palmer's granddaughter."

"Please to meet you." Black eyes regarded her with gentle curiosity. Raven-black hair hung in two braids on either side of her face, and her skin was a light almond color. She wore a roomy, homespun dress of faded calico instead of the traditional Indian dress of leather tunic and knee-high moccasins.

Lacy thought Takola would look much the same when she reached womanhood. With a sincere smile, Lacy said, "Nice to meet you, Victoria. Welcome to Callaway County." She was surprised to discover that Lester was married to an Indian, and further surprised by her name, but she hid it well. Going to one knee, she focused on the two girls who had come to stand beside their mother. Both girls resembled Victoria, with their dark brown eyes and black hair. "And who have we here?"

"I'm Jesse," the older girl whispered shyly, hiding her face in the folds of her mother's dress.

But the younger girl obviously didn't know the meaning of the word *stranger*. She stepped forward and said, "I'm Tory. My name's almost like Ma's." She pointed a pudgy finger at Adam, who stood behind her. "Is that your husband?"

Victoria scolded her and Lester smothered a laugh. Lacy looked at Adam, her face heating. He lifted an eyebrow and grinned. "No, he's not my husband. I wouldn't have the mangy varmint." She softened her words with a smile, tugging on Tory's braid. "Actually, he's all right—he's just not my type. Too bossy. That's Adam Logan, the sheriff." She could feel Adam's gaze on her, and knew retribution was on his mind.

Tory giggled, picking up on the mischief in Lacy's eyes. "I guess he has to be bossy, since he's the sheriff. Pa says he's a right decent man, braver than—"

Wisely, Victoria covered Tory's mouth with her hand as she said, "Let's go inside and have something to drink."

"Oh, but we've got butter—"

"We'll unload the wagon, Lacy," Adam called out, interrupting her.

So Lacy followed Victoria inside the small but neat house and left the men to bring in the supplies. Obviously, Lester had worked hard to get the farmhouse in shape for his wife, she thought, for surely Victoria had not had time to do all this in the short time she'd been here. Lacy had been expecting a mess, and had fully intended to pitch in and do what she could. She knew the farm had been vacant for nearly a year.

But everything seemed to be in its place, the bare wood floor swept and scrubbed clean. Brightly colored rugs scattered here and there gave the room a much-needed splash of color. A squat potbellied stove stood in the center of the living room, used both for heating and cooking. The table Victoria led them to had been carved from raw oak, then sanded and varnished to a high shine; Lacy could almost see her reflection in it.

As Victoria squeezed lemons into tall glasses of cold well water, Adam and Lester unloaded the wagon, setting the perishable goods on the table. The girls had followed the women inside and now stood by Lacy's chair, watching her with fathomless dark eyes.

When Adam handed her the basket she had carried on the wagon seat beside her, Lacy reached inside and brought out the cornhusk dolls, dressed in leather tunics decorated with colorful beads. Jesse and Tory took the gifts from her outstretched hand, their eyes round with pleasure.

"Oh, they're beautiful! Thank you," Jesse said, suddenly losing her shyness.

"Yes, she's lovely," Tory added. She leaned forward and kissed Lacy's cheek. Jesse followed suit.

"Takola made these for you. Sometime I'll bring her out

to meet you. Would you like that?" Both girls nodded
eagerly, then skipped off to play with their new dolls.

"That was a very nice thing to do, Miz Ross," Victoria
said, setting a glass of lemonade on the table in front of her.

Lacy took a long swallow of the delicious concoction,
easing her parched throat. "Please, call me Lacy. And
Takola made the dolls, so I can't take any of the credit."
Suddenly, she remembered the baby rattle. "Oh, and she
made this for the new baby." She lifted the rattle out of the
basket and handed it to Victoria.

Victoria studied the rattle for a long moment, her expression somber. "She is Dakota, is she not?" When Lacy
hesitated, then nodded, Victoria continued, her voice hushed,
almost revered. "She must have done something very brave
when she was but a baby, to earn the name Takola. It is a name
given to male children of the tribe."

Lacy hadn't known this. "She drew us a picture—we
know it means 'fox.'"

Victoria nodded. "Yes. The fox is a brave, wily animal,
much admired by the Dakota." Suddenly, she shook her
head and smiled at Lacy. "Sometime, you must bring her to
visit."

"Yes. I will. Maybe she'll talk to you . . . she hasn't
spoken since . . . since she came to us."

Again, Victoria nodded, as if she understood. "She will
come around. Give her time, be patient." Victoria eased
herself awkwardly down onto a chair, massaging her lower
back. "This baby, he will be a boy. He gives me lots of
trouble, this one does."

"Your English is very good."

"Lester taught me much. The rest I learned from the
teacher on the reservation and from listening. You learn
much from listening." She began to examine the supplies on
the table, showing her appreciation with soft murmurings
and gasps. "So much—you bring all this?"

"Not all. The townspeople helped." Carefully, Lacy
added, "We do this for all the new settlers, to welcome them
to the town." She knew how fragile pride was, and didn't
want the Indian woman to be offended by the gifts.

But she needn't have worried. Victoria seemed pleased and excited by the many items. "You are kind, as Lester said. You will make a good wife."

"I don't want to be a wife," Lacy blurted out. The moment she said the words, she wanted to cover her flaming face. To say such a thing to Carrianna, her close friend, was one thing; to say it to a total stranger was quite another! What in the world had gotten into her? She met Victoria's shrewd eyes, wishing she could sneak quietly away.

"You have been a wife, to know you don't want to be a wife?"

Lacy thought about lying, thought about changing the subject, but decided Victoria's feelings would be hurt, and she didn't want that. "Yes, I have, and no, I don't want to be again." She lowered her eyes to her lap, studying her chipped nails, her rough hands. The cream had helped, but her hands still looked a fright. She jumped as Victoria covered her rough hands with small brown ones.

"You have had a bad time, huh? My mother was married to a white man who was mean to her—my father—and she prayed for him to die. Each night, in my bed in the loft above her room, I would hear her praying for his death. I added my prayers to hers." When Lacy's horrified eyes flew to Victoria's, the Indian woman nodded and squeezed Lacy's hands. "God answered our prayers."

"I—I don't—"

"It is not always the same, Lacy Ross. Lester is a good man, a good husband, and a good father. He does not beat me. Adam Logan would not beat you."

Lacy was floored. Her mouth gaped open, then closed. "But, how did you—"

"I know these things. If you watch and listen, you can know these things." Victoria gave her a sly look. "He makes you want to have his babies, right?" When Lacy gasped in shock, Victoria threw her into further shock by giggling. "You white women, you are all so silly!"

"Victoria!" Lacy exclaimed, covering her flaming cheeks with her hands. Then she found herself laughing along with her. When the laughter finally subsided, Lacy glanced at the

open doorway, then leaned forward, whispering, "Do you—
do you actually *like* sleeping with your husband?" This time
she ignored her hot cheeks, desperate for reassurance.

Victoria sobered at the look of terror, mixed with hope, on
Lacy's face. "Yes. It is enjoyable, very much so." She
pointed to her bulging stomach. "Why do you think I'm this
way? Because I hate it? No, it is because I *like* it."

"Oh." Lacy sighed, her mind whirling with questions she
was too embarrassed to ask. She could hardly believe she
was talking about such private things with someone she hardly
knew! But Victoria was open, wise in the ways of the world,
whereas Carrianna, Susan, and Mary Ann were innocents.
Lacy had had no one who was mature, like Victoria, to talk
about her fears.

So when Victoria said, "You will stay for dinner, you and
Adam Logan," Lacy didn't object. She wasn't afraid to
travel home in the dark, with Adam by her side.

In fact, she looked forward to it.

13

*C*HE SUN HUNG low in the sky by the time dinner was over and good-byes had been said. "I'll be back soon, and I'll bring Ben and Takola with me," Lacy promised, hugging her new friend.

Victoria returned the hug with genuine affection. "Good. I'm anxious to meet this Ben of yours, and Takola." She looked around Lacy, winking at Adam. "And bring this handsome sheriff back with you, okay?"

Lacy blushed, but didn't answer. She allowed Adam to help her into the wagon, waving at Jesse and Tory, who stood on the porch clutching their dolls. They started down the road, the stallion once again trailing behind the wagon. Soon, the girls became a blur, their tiny figures waving cheerfully.

"Sweet girls," Lacy commented with a sigh of pleasure, dropping her arm and facing the deep-shadowed road ahead. Behind them, Sandy snorted and butted his head against the back of the wagon, clearly displeased with his position.

Adam nodded. "Yes. Nice family. Salvage seems like an honest man."

Lacy had left her bonnet hanging down her back, since the sun was behind them. Earlier this morning, she had braided her hair in a single golden plait, but the breeze and the humidity had curled the shorter hairs around her face. With an impatient hand, she pulled the clinging strands away from her eyes as she said, "Mr. Salvage will give the mayor a run for his money."

Adam laughed at the hopeful note in her prediction. "Let's just hope Salvage can handle it. Goodrich isn't taking the news too well."

Snorting, Lacy said, "Who cares? He's monopolized the lumber business long enough." And not only the lumber business, but everyone else's business as well, she added silently.

"I agree."

"A new lumber mill means more work. People will have a *choice*, and the mayor will have to compete with Mr. Salvage's wages, if he wants to keep his workers. He pays them dirt."

"Somehow, that doesn't surprise me," Adam said.

They traveled in silence for a while. Behind them, the sky filled with crimson colors, casting a beautiful red haze on the road ahead. Now and then Adam slid her a musing glance. Lacy felt his penetrating eyes on her, but kept her gaze on the road. She felt charged and jittery . . . and expectant. Much the same way she'd felt that day in Adam's bedroom.

When Adam steered Grasshopper off the road and onto the overgrown path leading to the pond, Lacy didn't object or ask why. At the moment, she didn't care. She was with Adam. And she loved him. She hugged the new discovery to herself, both elated and frightened. It was a useless feeling, she told herself sternly. Loving Adam should be the last thing on her mind. He might want her physically, but he had no intention of staying in Shadow City and settling down.

Reminding herself of the facts made no difference; she continued to feel glorious anyway.

Adam drew the wagon to a halt beneath the overhanging shadow of a maple tree and set the brake. A few feet away, the pond sparkled, shimmering with a rainbow of colors reflected by the setting sun. There was a splash as a fish jumped from the water in pursuit of a dragonfly just out of its reach, and the raspy croaking of a bullfrog followed by the eerie hooting of a night owl getting an early start.

As if the owl suddenly realized it was premature in its nightly singing, it fell abruptly silent.

Without preamble, Adam turned and pulled her into his arms and locked onto her luminous gaze. Slowly, deliberately, he lowered his mouth to hers. Lacy felt the power in his kiss, sensed that he wasn't as much in control as he wanted her to think. Anticipation tingled along her spine. Yes, she had been waiting for this, craving it.

When he finally lifted his head, he murmured thickly, "So, you think I'm too bossy, huh? A mangy varmint, you called me." His mouth hovered inches from her own, a gentle threat. He pushed his fingers through the damp curls around her face, lingering on her soft skin as his eyes dropped to her mouth. He rubbed his thumb across her parted lips, seemingly mesmerized by the sight.

Lacy smiled, curiously—triumphantly—unafraid. "Yes. Bossy."

Adam caught the twinkle of mischief in her eyes. A lazy smile curved his own mouth. "You little vixen." He slid his hands down along her neck, onto her shoulders, and then wrapped her in his embrace. He drew her even closer for another long, leisurely kiss.

This time when Adam pulled away, his breathing had changed. Lacy herself had to draw in a fortifying breath, staring at him with soft, dazed eyes. She wondered if he knew. She wondered if he could see, *feel* how much she loved him. At that moment, she would have agreed to go anywhere with him, do anything his heart desired.

"I've a mind to haul you into the back of this wagon— right there on that sweet-smellin' hay—and have my way with you," he growled softly. He moved one hand from her shoulder, and homing in on her aroused peak, rubbed a lazy circle around the hardened center. "I've got a hankerin' for you, Lacy Ross."

At his words and his masterful touch, Lacy felt faint, breathless. The world seemed to go still around her. Her eyelids dropped of their own accord and she drew in quick gasps of air between her parted lips. He was touching her, and she loved it. Wanted more, ached for more, was willing to ask for more—

Adam wasn't David. Adam was kind and gentle, virile and passionate. With this knowledge came a strange urgency to explore her newfound freedom. Layers of inhibition and fear began to fall away and Lacy could feel an almost physical lightening of the burden she'd carried for so long.

A strange fervor, a reckless need arose in Lacy blocking out all thought and reason. In a bold move that inwardly shocked her, she reached up and guided Adam's hand to the top button of her dress. Then she began to finish exposing the tempting whorls of his chest hair to her eager view by unbuttoning the last three buttons of his shirt. She heard him gasp, saw the quick rise and fall of his chest at her touch and her desire reached a new peak.

She wanted Adam Logan to show her what he'd been promising. She wanted to discover for herself if it would be as wonderful as his eyes and hands and lips promised. They weren't married; she wasn't beholden to him. She wasn't a virgin. There was nothing left to be afraid of. . . . He wasn't her husband so he couldn't demand anything of her that she didn't want to give.

The only fear left was the fear of discovery. But she needn't worry, for dusk enclosed them in its comforting blanket, shielding them from the world. And beneath the darkening shade of the maple tree, they were isolated from the road.

But these considerations were only fleeting thoughts in Lacy's mind; she doubted it would have mattered if dark had been hours away, as long as she was in Adam's arms.

Once she had set him to his task, Adam worked quickly at the tiny pearl buttons, bending to drink from her mouth and placing hot kisses along her neck as he moved down her dress, revealing the white cotton shift and the creamy mounds of her firm breasts.

When he reached her waist, he stopped, smiling as she protested. He kissed her silent and whispered in a voice husky with desire, "Not here, darlin'. On the hay." With a reluctant moan, he left her and jumped from the wagon bench, swinging around to grab her and bring her with him. Gently, he lowered her over the side of the wagon, then quickly joined her in the soft bed of hay.

When Adam rose over her, Lacy gazed at the stars twinkling overhead, then focused her shimmering eyes on the dark silhouette of the man she loved. The words hovered on her lips, but she swallowed them instead. Adam wouldn't want to hear her confession because he'd be leaving. She didn't want his guilt or his pity, she wanted his love. If she couldn't have it, she would take this time with him and cherish it forever.

"Lacy," Adam breathed, kissing her more urgently. He tugged at the chemise, pulling it away from her straining, flushed breasts with impatient hands. When she lay exposed to his hungry gaze, he moaned and dipped his head to taste a sweet, taut peak. "God, you're delicious."

"Oh," Lacy gasped at the feel of his warm mouth closing around her. She strained forward, clutching his head, her eyes wide and surprised by the strong rush of feeling his lips evoked. Her hands splayed over his broad back, moving back and forth, clutching, then stroking, then clutching again as she felt his teeth rake her lightly. She'd suspected—no—she had *known* she would ignite at his touch. Deep in her heart, she had instinctively sensed that Adam could make her feel reckless and wild. Wonderful, passionate.

"Adam? . . ." She tugged at his head, only to gasp as he merely switched from one aching peak to the other. She buried her fingers in his thick, silky hair and closed her eyes at the sheer pleasure.

By the time he lifted his head, Lacy forgot what she'd been about to say. She stared at him wordlessly. He cupped her face and slowly lowered his mouth to hers, pressing his body into her soft, willing flesh. Lacy discovered the evidence of his desire, could feel him against her, throbbing with need.

She felt the same way—a deep, thrumming ache for a more fulfilling closeness. When she opened her mouth, his tongue was there, teasing and tantalizing. The kiss grew deeper, more desperate, as if he couldn't get enough. He eased his mouth away and returned it to her desire-tender breasts, his lips and tongue and teeth driving her to a frenzy of need. Something began to build, something foreign and almost frightening. Lacy sensed it—like an approaching storm.

His hands seemed to be everywhere, stroking and loving, pleasuring her as she'd never been pleasured before. Lacy squirmed and gasped, strained closer to his mouth and his hands, his hard body. She didn't want the clothes, they kept her from *feeling* him, from touching his hard, muscled flesh.

And suddenly, as if this night were magical and every wish her command, she was naked. Poised above her, Adam's penetrating gaze held her still. For a long, beautiful moment, he simply stared at her flushed face in the twilight. Moonlight reflected a light sheen of sweat on his bare shoulders and Lacy reached up with a trembling hand and felt his naked skin, stroking down his chest and onto the hard planes of his stomach.

She continued downward, her fingers tingling against muscle and sinew. Adam was naked, too. All over. The wonder of it made her bold. Her hand closed around him.

Adam sucked in a sharp gasp and swooped down to her mouth, suckling her bottom lip as he began to claim her with loving care.

Lacy froze, a tremor of unwanted fear snaking its ugly way into the fog of desire surrounding her. She opened her eyes to find Adam staring at her tenderly.

"No, darlin'. Don't be afraid, I won't hurt you. I'd never hurt you."

His whispered promise succeeded in chasing her fear back to the corners of her mind. With a long sigh of surrender, Lacy accepted him. They moved together, surrounded by the sweet smell of hay and the symphony of croaking frogs. Above her, the stars began to glow with fevered brilliance, expanding, exploding in a great white flash of pleasure such as she had never known.

Adam cried her name, and she answered the call with a husky cry of her own. They trembled, clasped together in the aftermath of loving.

Lacy's heartbeat slowed gradually. The night breeze, cool and welcoming, caressed her hot skin. She stirred slightly against the hard wall of Adam's chest as he held her tight. He made her feel so cherished and worthy. She could never thank him enough for showing her what making love was *really* like. Nervously, she rubbed her palm along the sheen of sweat on his chest. Damp curls tickled her skin. She wanted to share her thoughts with him. Heck, she wanted to share *everything* with him. "My husband, David . . . he said I was a cold woman, that I had no feeling." Beneath her stilled palm, she felt the rumblings of a chuckle. It stunned her—she expected anger.

"Darlin', that man must have been kicked in the head when he was a babe."

He closed his arms around her, pressing her face into his damp chest. Silly, emotional tears spring to her eyes. She blinked and sniffed, mildly embarrassed by his praise. "So, you don't think? . . ."

"Are you fishing for compliments?" he teased softly.

Lacy sighed as his warm breath fanned her scalp. "No. It's just that—I believed it was *me*, and I never imagined—"

"You want to know what I think? What I really think?"

She nodded, snuggling deeper into the welcoming crook of his arm. He smelled good—of loving and hard work—and peppermint. Always peppermint.

"I think your husband tried to pin his shortcomings on *you* because he didn't have the guts to admit he didn't know beans about pleasing a woman."

Lacy smiled, and she didn't have to see his face to know he smiled too. "Such confidence," she teased.

He shrugged, amusement husking his voice. "Well, a man can tell when a woman's pleased . . . Ouch!" Laughing, he grabbed her flailing hand and brought it to his lips.

She shuddered as he began to kiss each finger. "Adam, I don't regret what we've done."

"Neither do I, darlin'. Neither do I."

He drew each digit into his mouth and sucked gently. Lacy tried to tug her hand away, frightened by how easily he could arouse her. If he didn't stop, she'd be begging him to make love to her again; and, while she didn't regret it this first time, she knew it shouldn't happen again. "I don't think I realized how long I've been afraid." When he released her hand, she began to trail her fingers along his chest and stomach, grinning when he growled a warning. "You've helped me overcome those fears."

"I'm glad."

There was a roughness to his voice. With a jolt of pleased surprise, Lacy realized she was the cause. Prudently, she curled her hand beneath her chin. "Adam . . . this doesn't mean—I mean, you don't have to—" Tongue-tied, Lacy fell silent, hoping he would know what she couldn't seem to say. At the end of their makeshift bed, the restless stallion shook his head and snorted.

Adam's grip tightened for an instant; then he released her, withdrawing his arms and leaving her chilled in the abrupt absence of his warmth. He placed a lingering kiss on her mouth before he sat up and began to hunt for their clothes in the hay. Lacy watched him in the moonlight, wishing she could see his expression. Love swelled in her chest until she ached with the fullness of it.

He slipped his shirt on and carelessly buttoned the bottom buttons. Then he turned his head to look at her. "You mean, I don't have to marry you?" He uttered a short, dry laugh totally devoid of his early joviality. "Why am I not surprised that you would say the total opposite of what other women say?"

Pain pierced her heart at his words. Other women. . . . Of course, Adam would have had other women.

He rummaged in the hay until he came up with her

chemise and drawers, which he tossed onto her stomach before slipping on his pants. "I have nothing to offer a woman, Lacy. Nothing." A bitter note crept into his voice. "My stepfather took everything that should have been mine, and made my mother's life a living hell. Of course, you know all about hell, don't you? That's why you're so worried I'll want to marry you, because you *don't* want to marry me. To think I swallowed that nonsense about how I've helped you overcome your distrust of men."

"That's not true—it *wasn't* nonsense," Lacy said, frowning as she struggled into her clothes. She tried to catch his eye, but he wouldn't look at her. "I know you're not like David—"

"What *was* David like?" he cut in, jerking on his boots. "See? I don't even know the man whose ghost is constantly between us, other than he didn't know beans about pleasing you, and that he hit you."

Lacy gasped, then grabbed his arm. "He is *not* between us! How could you say that after—after what just happened? Believe me, David was not here." How could he think so? What he made her feel was so different from what she had suffered with David—she couldn't imagine him not knowing it. She thought he *did* know!

Reaching out, she grabbed his arm and held on until he looked at her. "David was violent, as you've guessed." Adam's muscles tensed beneath her fingertips; even in the moonlight, she could see the skin tighten over his cheekbones as he struggled to control his anger—anger directed at a dead man. "But that was a long time ago, Adam. I made a vow that I would never put myself in that position again, of being helpless against a man who thought it was his husbandly right to hit me."

Quietly, Adam said, "And you still think I would be the same way, don't you?" Lacy started to shake her head, but Adam carried on, convinced that he was right. "You think eventually I'd lose my temper and mar that pretty face of yours." He reached out and cupped her chin, a bitter smile twisting his lips when she instinctively jerked at his touch.

"See? You can't forget, can you, Lacy? You can't trust, can you?"

"I *do* trust you, Adam! I do!" Lacy heard the desperation in her voice and knew it damned her. "I wouldn't have made love with you, if I didn't trust you."

Adam shrugged, the gesture hurt Lacy more than any words could have. "It's just as well, since I have nothing to offer you anyway."

Slowly, Lacy dropped her hand. Her eyes burned, but she forced the tears back. "I told you I didn't expect marriage. I wanted to make love with you."

"To see if I was different," Adam concluded softly. "And what if there's a child from our coupling? What then? Would you let your fear stand in the way of making that child legitimate?"

The breath froze in Lacy's lungs. Oh, dear God, she had not given one single thought to the possibility of conceiving. How reckless, how irresponsible could she be? Gulping, she said, "If there's a child, then we'll have to get married, of course."

Adam stood up and jumped from the wagon bed, buckling his gun belt around his waist. And this time, Lacy could see his expression. It was one of cynical amusement. "I believe that was *my* line, Lacy."

Standing, Lacy slipped into her dress, then swiftly buttoned the front. When that was finished, she began picking hay out of her hair, her movements jerky, angry. How could he be so flippant? How could *she* have been so thoughtless? And how could he tarnish what they'd shared together by making jokes? Somehow, things had gotten turned around. If she didn't know better, she'd think that Adam was hurt because she *wasn't* begging him to marry her.

Humph! He was right—she wasn't like other women. She didn't feel an all-consuming desire to shackle herself to another nightmare. Surely he understood? Surely he didn't really want to marry her? He'd said he was leaving soon, and he should know that she had no intentions of leaving Shadow City. She had Ben and Takola to think of. And Rusty . . .

Thunder. Why did he have to go and spoil a perfect evening.

By the time Lacy had finished dressing and climbed onto the wagon bench without Adam's help, she was furious.

Male pride, she decided. Stubborn, male pride. If she *had* hinted that he should marry her, he'd be running in the opposite direction!

Maybe he sensed that she wasn't being entirely truthful. Maybe he knew that deep down she wished he would insist she marry him—take the choice from her because she was a coward. Lacy tossed her head and arranged her skirts. Finding a stray piece of hay in the folds, she picked it off and flung it from her as Adam set the wagon in motion.

Never again would she be able to look at this wagon without thinking of Adam and the wonderful, dreamlike time they had shared. Her future yawned before her, a big empty hole she knew she would never be able to fill completely. For that, it would take Adam. Before, she had only sensed that she was missing something from her life; and, until Adam came along, she had always managed to bury the infrequent twinges.

Now she would *know* without a doubt what she was missing.

Lacy sighed, wishing she could feel regret for losing her head. But she didn't. Couldn't. Even now, the thought of Adam's lovemaking made her skin flush hot and her bones turn to mush. She suspected it would be a long, long while before he wasn't in her thoughts and dreams.

Loving Adam Logan would take a lifetime to get over.

The shot came out of the blue, ricocheting off the short space of wagon bench between them. Splinters flew and Lacy cried out, grabbing her arm as a long splinter of wood buried itself in the skin above her elbow. The mare reared and the trailing stallion danced sideways as far as his lead rein would go. Adam fought for control of the frightened horse while drawing his gun as his eyes searched the dark road ahead.

"Are you hit?" he demanded in a low, tense voice. He

urged the skittish mare to the side of the road before setting the brake, his movements swift and silent.

"No—I've got a splinter in my arm," Lacy whispered, trying to see where the shot had come from. Who could it be? And why would he be shooting at them?

"Get down," Adam ordered softly, pushing her down on the bench even as he spoke. "And don't raise up until I tell you to." When he was satisfied that she was out of danger, he eased down from the wagon and crouched along the side. The moonlight didn't penetrate the dark shadows beneath the trees, but Adam listened and watched, waiting for a sound—any sound—that would give him an idea of where the assailant might be hiding.

Lacy wasn't sure how long she remained hunkered down on the bench, but it felt like hours. The night seemed unnaturally still, as if the creatures of the forest surrounding them were listening too. She could hear Adam's faint breathing and the uneven sound of her own.

Finally, a horse broke loose from the trees opposite them, crashing onto the road. Firing wildly into the air, the rider kicked his horse into a frantic gallop and pounded down the road, disappearing around a bend. The echoing gunshots died slowly, as did the furious pounding of the horse's hooves.

Within minutes, the forest was once more silent. Lacy shook her head, wondering if she had dreamed the apparition. It had all happened so fast!

Adam straightened and cursed in a low, vicious voice. He climbed onto the bench and helped Lacy to her feet. Lacy held still as he probed her arm, biting her bottom lip to keep from crying out as he removed the splinter. "You'll need to disinfect that as soon as you get home," he told her.

Lacy couldn't stop herself from shaking. "You mean, *if* we make it home. Who do you think it was, Adam? Why would he be shooting at us?"

"I think he was shooting at *me*," he said, removing a handkerchief from his pocket and pressing it against the wound. "Hold this against it, okay?"

"But . . . why?" she persisted, automatically following his instructions. Her arm hurt, but she was far too distracted to care. "Why would anyone want to kill you?"

Adam took up the reins, his voice grim. "I can think of a few reasons why someone might want me to disappear."

Lacy drew in a long, trembling breath. "You're talking about the mayor, aren't you? You think maybe he—"

"I think that's a good possibility."

"But, he'd know that *you* would know—"

"He wasn't counting on me being alive to tell it," Adam said. "I underestimated him, it seems. Rusty tried to warn me."

Lacy digested this in silence, her mind boggled by what had nearly happened. Yet, she wasn't convinced that the assailant *hadn't* been aiming at her. After all, the shot had landed closer to her than to Adam. She voiced her suspicions, trying to sound brave and failing miserably. "He could have been shooting at me, Adam."

"I don't think so." He sounded very sure, she noted. "Whoever it was, and whatever reason he had for shooting, he missed. When I get through with the mayor, he'll wish he'd never seen my face."

The underlying steel in his quietly spoken promise made Lacy shiver inside. It was hard to believe this was the same man that had caressed her so tenderly less than half an hour ago. As if he sensed her unease, he pulled her to him and kept his arm around her as they traveled the last few miles into town.

Adam remained alert, his eyes constantly scanning their surroundings. He didn't think the gunman would return, but if he did, Adam wanted to be ready this time.

His mouth tightened when he thought about how close the man had come to shooting Lacy. Raw fear curled in his belly as he imagined her lying in a pool of blood, the victim of a bullet meant for him. With a muttered oath, he shook the terrifying image from his mind and concentrated on calming the mare, who remained skittish, and Lacy, whom he suspected was more shaken than she'd like for him to believe. He could feel her trembling against him periodically.

The mayor would pay for this, he vowed silently.

Once they were safely home, Adam insisted on examining the small puncture himself, ignoring Lacy's vigorous protests. Rusty, Ben, and Takola gathered around the table, demanding to know what had happened. Adam explained it all to them while he washed Lacy's wound and dabbed it with alcohol. When Lacy winced at the sting, he bent close and blew gently on her arm.

Lacy held her breath, her pain forgotten as she met his tender gaze. Her heart seemed to leap into her throat. "Thank you," she whispered.

Adam stared at her a moment longer, noticing how pale she looked. Then he smiled. "You're welcome. It's the least I can do, since I got you into this mess."

"You don't know that for sure," she countered softly.

Adam's smile faded and a hard light appeared in his eyes. Lacy was glad it wasn't for her. "You have any other suggestions?" When Lacy shook her head, he said, "Come on, I'll walk you to your room. You need to rest."

"Oh—you don't have to—"

"Nevertheless, I will," Adam said, his tone matching the hard light in his eyes. He glanced at Rusty, who stood by her chair, his aged face creased with worry. "Don't worry, Rusty. I'm going to make sure this doesn't happen again."

Ben, who had remained unusually quiet through the whole explanation, nudged Adam aside as Lacy came to her feet. He fell upon her and buried his face in the folds of her dress. His words were nearly incoherent, "Don't know what I'd do if somethin' happened to you, Lacy."

Touched, Lacy smoothed his unruly hair. "Nothing's going to happen to me, Ben. Now, you go on up to bed, okay? I'm all right."

Ben lifted his face to look at her, his eyes round with fear. "You promise?"

"I promise." Lacy forced herself to smile at him. "Now

go." She watched Ben walk from the room. For the first time, he was walking, not running.

"We were right worried about you when it got dark and you hadn't made it home," Rusty said in a scolding tone. "If I hadn't've known Adam was with you, I'd have come lookin' for ya. Guess I should have anyway. Might have run into that varmint myself."

Lacy was appalled at the image his words brought to her mind. "No, Grandpa! You could have been shot." And he might have stumbled upon them in the wagon. . . . Hot color rose to her face. She prayed he would put it down to excitement. "I'm glad you didn't. As you said, Adam was with me."

Rusty stroked his whiskered chin, looking to Adam. "I'm goin' with you when you talk to the mayor. This has gone too far already."

Adam shook his head. "No. Somebody needs to ride out and warn Lester there might be trouble. I know he's got men watching the lumber mill, but after tonight, I think he need's to stay on his toes at his place, too. I'm not going to talk to the mayor until mornin' anyway."

"You don't need to go alone—" Rusty began to argue, only to be cut off.

"He's not stupid, Rusty. He wouldn't try to kill me in his own house. Besides, he won't get the chance."

"Don't be a hero, Adam," Lacy interrupted, her eyes pleading with him.

Adam looked as if he had a ready reply to that one, but changed his mind. Instead, he gently gripped her uninjured arm and led her to the door. "Come on. I want to make certain you go straight to bed and rest. Good night, Rusty. I can count on you to ride out and warn Salvage in the morning?"

"First thing," Rusty agreed.

Lacy murmured good night to Rusty and the silent Takola and allowed Adam to lead her up the stairs.

Once they reached the door to her room, Lacy turned to Adam, suddenly nervous. "Well, good night." It was difficult to look at him and not immediately remember the way he'd looked, all naked and beautiful in the moonlight. A shudder rippled gently through her.

Adam smiled and tilted her head, kissing her with a possessive thoroughness that left Lacy breathless. Leaning against the doorjamb, he studied her face as if he were memorizing it. "Good night, Lacy. I have to say there's never a dull moment when you're around."

Lacy grinned, despite her jittery nerves. "And I dare say you could do without that kind of excitement."

In a low, suggestive voice, Adam asked, "And which excitement are you referring to?"

Lacy swallowed. "Well, I was referring to the shooting, of course."

"Of course," he mocked. Reaching out, he hooked her waist and jerked her against him, all pretense gone. "It's not over, Lacy."

"What . . . what are *you* referring to?" She forced herself to meet his bold gaze, jolted by the sudden seriousness in his expression. That infernal weakness hit her knees and she buckled. Adam kept her from falling.

"You know what I'm talking about. You. Me. Us. We've got some talkin' to do."

"There's no need—"

"Yes, there is. You think we can just pretend this never happened?" he demanded. To emphasize his point, he cupped her bottom and drove her tight against him. "I won't let you forget." With one last, possessive kiss, he released her and left.

Lacy held onto the doorjamb for dear life, breathing unsteadily. She felt weak from head to toe and feared it had nothing to do with the incident with the assailant. No, Adam made her feel this way.

Adam.

God, how she loved him. And he was right, she could never pretend it hadn't happened, didn't *want* to pretend it never happened. She would cherish each and every moment, but she must not repeat it.

Her heart wasn't strong enough.

14

$\mathcal{T}$HE MAYOR'S HOUSE was impressive—an old restored plantation house set on a hill just outside of town. Stately pine trees surrounded the property in a curious, symmetrical design that reminded Adam of sentries standing guard.

He probably likened himself to a king overlooking his kingdom, Adam thought derisively as he studied the rich landscaping and the bleached white columns of the porch.

Sandy snorted and fought for his head, but Adam held him at a brisk walk as they climbed the winding, steep road leading to the house. It was barely seven o'clock; but having slept little himself, he didn't care if the mayor was still abed or not. It would give him great pleasure to yank him out of it.

Dismounting, Adam tethered Sandy to the porch rail and trotted up the steps to knock on the door. A middle-aged woman answered almost immediately, as if she had been watching his approach. Adam stared at her suspiciously. She returned his look without blinking an eyelash, her apron as blindingly white as the massive columns. Finally, he drawled, "I'm here to see the mayor."

"Is he expecting you?" she inquired courteously, her eyes darting to the star on his shirt. They widened respectfully, but she didn't budge.

Adam laughed. "I doubt it. In fact, I'd say he'll be real surprised to see me." He pushed past her and strode through the polished hall as if he knew exactly where he was going.

He didn't, but that didn't stop him. To the left he spotted a dining room, but after a quick inspection he saw that it was empty, so he continued on. The harsh clicking of his boots drowned out the housekeeper's softer steps, but Adam sensed her behind him.

He ignored her.

So the mayor still slept, he deduced, when he found the other downstairs rooms empty. He took the stairs two at a time and traversed down the opulent hall, opening doors left and right until he came upon the last door at the far end.

This had to be it, he thought. He reached for the knob just as the out-of-breath housekeeper topped the landing and caught sight of him. Her shrill voice screeched down the hall. "You can't go in there! Hey!" She stretched an arm in his direction as if she could span the distance and stop him.

Adam nodded in satisfaction. He'd found the mayor's room.

Jamis Goodrich came awake as his bedroom door crashed open. Adam smiled at his bleary-eyed expression and stalked into the room, kicking the door shut. The mayor's eyes grew wider and wider, until he resembled a bewildered owl. His nightcap hung askew, with tufts of gray hair poking out from beneath, adding to the ridiculous picture he presented. The rich purple nightshirt he wore did not surprise Adam in the least.

Finally, the mayor found his voice. "What the *hell* do you think you're doing?" he thundered, but there was an underlying thread of fear in his voice. "Who let you in?"

In contrast, Adam's voice was soft and pleasant. "Why, Mayor Goodrich. You look as if you've seen a ghost." Adam's smile was wicked, but deadly. "Don't tell me—

you're surprised to see me?" He *tsk-tsked.* "Whoever you
hired wasn't a very good shot." Moving closer to the bed,
Adam continued, his tone growing more menacing by the
second. "I never took you for a stupid man, Goodrich—
until now."

"What . . . what do you mean?" the mayor asked in a
strangled whisper. He scrambled upright, scooting his fat
bulk against the velvet-lined headboard as far as he could
go.

Adam reached the bed and leaned over, grabbing the
mayor by the front of his garish silk nightshirt. He brought
the man's face within inches of his own so there would be
no mistake about how furious he was. "I mean, Mr. Mayor,
that you failed to kill me, and in the process nearly killed an
innocent woman."

The mayor's eyes bulged in what appeared to be genuine
bewilderment. Adam wasn't ready to believe it.

"Kill you? I didn't try to kill you. I don't have any idea
what you're talking about, you idiot! What woman?"

Adam growled a curse that clearly indicated his disbelief.
The mayor's face drained of color. "I'd watch my mouth, if
I were you. And don't think I'm swallowing your innocent
act. You're the only one in this town who would like to see
me dead."

The mayor struggled to free himself from Adam's death
grip, but Adam wasn't finished. Not quite. "When I get
through with you, you'll wish you'd hired a better shot."

"You're crazy!"

Adam drew back his fist and prepared to slam it into the
mayor's lying face. The mayor uttered a high-pitched
screech, then began to babble, "No—wait! I didn't do
anything, I swear! You must be wrong—you must have
enemies you don't know about because *I swear I didn't have
anything to do with it!*"

"Hell," Adam said, just before he broke the mayor's nose.
Blood spurted and Adam released his grip on the mayor and
stepped calmly out of the way. He'd just put on a clean shirt.
"I should kill you—before you get the opportunity to kill
me. But hear this—you'd better make certain they don't

miss next time, if you're stupid enough to try it again." He flexed his fingers, watching without a hint of remorse as the mayor tried to stem the flow of blood with the bedsheet. "And leave Salvage alone. If you don't, I'll throw your powdered ass in jail—along with all of your henchmen."

Adam was halfway down the hall before the mayor found the courage to shout after him, "I'll get you for this, Logan! I'll get you!"

The pain-filled nasal sound made Adam smile with grim satisfaction.

"So you don't think it was him," Rusty said, handing Adam another log. They were in Rusty's backyard, away from listening ears. A rooster crowed, and almost immediately, the loud clucking of dozens of hens celebrated the laying of an egg. This event occurred every half hour or so throughout the day.

Adam wiped the sweat from his brow with his forearm before taking the log. He balanced it on the chopping block, drew back the ax, and split the log with a resounding thud. With barely a pause, he divided the log four ways, then promptly took another from Rusty's outstretched hand, grateful Rusty hadn't protested when he offered to take over the chore. The physical labor gave him an outlet for his anger and Rusty a much-needed break.

"My guess would be, no. Unless he's a better actor than I give him credit for, he didn't know what the hell I was talking about." Adam paused again, squinting at the sun. It was only midmorning and already the day was unnaturally hot. He glanced to the west, then to the east, wondering if a storm was brewing. Damned humidity made the air seem thick, hard to breathe. He unbuttoned his sweat-soaked shirt and pitched it aside.

Rusty began to stack the split logs into a neat pile. "Well, if you're right, then we got us a bigger problem."

Their eyes met. Adam nodded. "Better the devil you know, than the devil you don't?" he guessed accurately. It wasn't difficult, since Rusty often spoke in broken mismatched clichés.

"Something like that," Rusty muttered sourly. "So what do we do?"

The ax fell and the log split, sending splinters flying in every direction. They reminded Adam of the splinter he'd pulled out of Lacy's arm. He set the log upright and hit it again, hard enough to embed the ax into the chopping block. There was nothing he hated worse than not knowing something—especially when it involved his hide, or that of someone he cared about.

"We watch our backs and keep investigating. Could be something to do with all this snooping I been doing about Murddock. And if the mayor's not behind this . . ."

Rusty looked startled. He rubbed his chin, then removed his hat and scratched his head. Finally, he nodded. "You could be right, son. Hadn't thought of that." His frown deepened. Hesitantly, he said, "If you're right, then that means—"

"—that someone in town is watching us," Adam concluded somberly. "Aside from the mayor."

"Need to find out who, before they get too antsy."

Adam halted the ax in midswing, casting Rusty a dry glance. "You mean, before they get antsier? Seems we've already got them a mite worried."

"Got any idears in that wooden head of yours?"

"Maybe. But it'll be dangerous."

Rusty grunted. "And it ain't dangerous now?"

"You know, for an old fart, you're pretty smart." Adam dodged Rusty's swinging fist with ease, laughing at the sour look on his face.

The sound of Adam's rich laughter reached Lacy inside the house. With a thudding heart she raced to the kitchen window overlooking the backyard.

The sight that met her eyes nearly buckled her knees.

Adam stood like some magnificent Greek god, bare-chested as he could be. Sweat glistened on his broad shoulders. The hair on his chest had darkened and clung damply to his skin. She watched, her mouth slack as he lifted the ax in the air. The muscles in his back tightened, bulged, gleamed. . . . She closed her mouth and swallowed hard as thrill after thrill shot through her body.

She was shameless, wanton, to feel such wild hunger just looking at him. But it was a sight that held her frozen at the window, for she had imagined him like this, his body slick with sweat, his chest and shoulders bare for her hands to slide across and around.

He turned as he bent his head close to Rusty's, and her eyes dropped to the ridges along his hard stomach, remembering the feel of each one as her fingers had explored his tightly drawn flesh. Then they followed the thinning line of hair and muscle down . . . down to—

Lacy swallowed, trying to bring moisture back to her suddenly dry mouth. He was beautiful, she thought with a sigh. She smiled to herself as she imagined what he'd say to that feminine description.

But as she turned away form the window, her smile faded and tears blurred her vision. God, she would miss him. If only she had the courage to try to win his love. Ha! Not that she believed she could. Adam had said nothing about staying, but everything about leaving. After last evening's close call, she couldn't blame him. She was proud that he had stood up to the mayor, but now she wasn't certain it was the smart thing for him to do.

And she—she had encouraged him. That made her indirectly responsible for anything that happened to him. Lacy brushed a stray tear from her cheek and set about finishing her pies. But as she turned a pie pan upside down and cut a circle in the dough around it, her thoughts strayed once again to Adam. Could she bring herself to try to persuade him to leave before he got himself killed?

She would, she told herself firmly. She loved him, but she couldn't love a dead man. They'd been foolish to think they could fight the mayor and win. Jamis Goodrich didn't fight in the open; he hired his henchmen to do the work. Someone would sneak up on Adam one dark night and slip a knife between his ribs. Lacy lifted a trembling hand to her throat. Or they'd find him hanging by the neck in the jail cell.

Quickly, she thrust the horrible thoughts away and slipped

the last pie in the oven, then began setting out a lunch of cold chicken and potato salad for the men. They'd be hungry after all that chopping, she thought. And yes, she was eager to see Adam again. She had lain awake most of the night, thinking about that magical time she'd spent in his arms. Try as she might, she could not find an ounce of regret.

And if she had conceived . . . then she would bear his child. Victoria had been right; Adam made her want to have his babies. Lacy held a trembling hand to her flushed cheek at the thought of holding a baby in her arms. Adam's baby. When she was married to David, she had longed for a child, but after two years she'd given up hope. Then Ben had come along, easing the emptiness inside of her. And Takola. Takola had helped fill that empty spot, too.

Yet . . . yet now she ached again. Felt empty again.

Yes, Victoria was wise, but unfortunately the Indian woman didn't know all of the facts. Lacy didn't want Adam to stay unless he wanted to. Certainly she didn't want him staying, and marrying her because of a baby.

She straightened her shoulders and brought her chin up. The best thing for all would be for Adam to finish his business and leave. Get out of town before someone succeeded in killing him, or before fate could interfere and hold him there against his will.

She didn't want him to spend the rest of his life looking over his shoulder, and she didn't want to spend the rest of *her* life wondering if he loved her, or stayed with her because of the baby.

With a choking sound that was a cross between a laugh and a cry, Lacy sat down in a chair and covered her face in her hands. How silly she was, worrying about something that probably wouldn't happen anyway. She hadn't conceived in the years she was married to David, so it wasn't likely she would after one night with Adam.

Was she hoping? she wondered, and then wondered if she'd lost her mind. Well, if it was something she wished for, she needed to get a grip on her sanity and set herself to the task of helping Adam solve the puzzle of Sheriff Murddock's death.

And she knew what she had to do.

It was evening. They stood on the porch and watched the sun sink slowly behind a low-lying blanket of storm clouds still some miles away. In her hand, Lacy held a heavy china plate covered with a cloth napkin.

The plate was empty, but her mind was not.

"It was blackberry winter," Lacy began softly. She frowned at the clouds blotting out the dying sun. They were out of place. It should be clear and cool, just as it had been on that awful day she'd found Sheriff Murddock.

"Blackberry winter?" Adam queried, watching her intently. Her eyes looked dazed, as if she were in another place and time.

Lacy's gaze remained fixed on the far horizon. "Yes. It's a time in May when the blackberries blossom. For several days it stays cold, then summer resumes. I remember hating it because I had to wear shoes." A nostalgic smile tugged at her lips, then faded as uglier memories intruded. "Grandma usually took Sheriff Murddock his dinner, but on this particular day she asked me to. I thought I was so grown-up, taking that plate to the sheriff." A sudden breeze rustled her skirts and Lacy lifted her face as if to capture its freshness. "It had rained the night before and there were mud puddles all over the place. I almost dropped the plate a couple of times, stepping around them."

Carefully, Adam tugged on her elbow, urging her to move as she spoke. Lacy went willingly enough, her eyes straight ahead now. They descended the porch steps and stepped out onto the road, Adam hanging back, but staying close enough to hear.

He didn't want anything to break her concentration.

Lacy crossed the road and he followed. "There was a mud puddle here," she pointed with her elbow, "and there. I met Lucille Marchbanks right about here." She paused in the middle of the road, eyes closed as she allowed the horrible memories to surface.

"Marchbanks?"

"Dead now," Lacy said. She moved on, not stopping until she reached the boardwalk on the other side of the road. Then she began to pause often as they walked along it. "Trudy and Horace Fimbleton passed by me, on their way to dinner with the Tidwells—the Tidwells are my neighbors." She walked a few steps, eyes half closed, then stopped again. "I was here when Allen Graves whistled by, probably on his way to the blacksmith's shop. He's a farmer—*was* a farmer south of town." Adam frowned, but kept silent. He couldn't ask a dead man questions.

"There used to be a small general store here, but it caught fire a few years back." Lacy indicated a tiny vacant lot between the blacksmith's and the telegraph office. "Ida and Kent, they built a new one there on the corner after they lost this place. That evening, they were already closed and gone for the night."

"Lacy . . ." Adam touched her elbow very lightly. He hated to risk interfering with her remarkable recall, but his curiosity was eating him alive. "How is it that you remember everything so well? Right down to the mud puddles?"

Lacy slowly turned her face to him, allowing him to see the pain in her eyes as she confessed, "I thought Sheriff Murddock was the greatest man that ever lived, and he wasn't *my* grandfather. Would *you* be able to forget?"

He shook his head, still astounded by her detailed memory. "I don't think I could have remembered *everything,* as you have."

"I've had fifteen years of dreamin' about it," she said huskily. Without another word, she started walking again, drawing abreast of the telegraph office. "Mr. Hyatt waved at me through the window and I waved back, nearly dropping the plate for the second time." She hesitated, staring at the window. "While my attention was on Mr. Hyatt, someone bumped me. I remember thinking he was rude, but all I saw of him was his back. He appeared to be in an awful hurry."

"You didn't know this person?" Adam asked as faint thunder rumbled in the distance.

"No." Lacy shook her head. "No. I didn't recognize him

at all, but then, I didn't see his face. After that, two more men came my way whom I didn't recognize. But I saw _their_ faces. They had heavy coats on, dusty coats. Everyone was dressed warmly because it was so cold."

"Blackberry winter," Adam mumbled to himself.

Lacy heard him. "Yes. Blackberry winter." She almost smiled at him. "These men looked like cowboys. Their spurs jangled when they walked and they looked like they hadn't shaved in weeks. One had a scar right in the corner of his eye—and it made him look like he was winking." Lacy gave an embarrassed shrug. "Nine year-old girls think silly thoughts like that, I guess."

"Not so silly," Adam murmured. He continued to be amazed at the vivid detail in which she described her short walk to the jailhouse on that fateful day. Amazing. "And the other man?" he coaxed.

"He was—sort of regular looking. I think his eyes were dark, and he was older than the other one. His hair was long and scraggly, unwashed." She wrinkled her nose. "He stank."

"Rusty mentioned there was a cattle drive coming through that week. He thinks that's how the fire started."

Lacy nodded. "I remember. Yes, I'm sure they were trail hands, or had something to do with cattle, because I could smell it on them." They had reached the door to the jailhouse. Lacy turned to face it, taking a deep breath. "Did you follow my instructions?"

"Yes. The lamp's out." He hesitated, concerned with the unhealthy pallor of her face. "I hung the sack of dirt in the cell, like you asked, but if you're not sure—"

"No!" She hadn't meant to shout. She shook her head and said more quietly. "No. I need it there to remind me. . . ." Her voice trailed away as her courage suddenly flagged. Oh, God, what had she done? She was reliving the nightmare all over again, as if her occasional nightmares weren't enough! But Adam needed her. . . . She squared her shoulders and clutched the plate until her knuckles whitened, then she balanced the dish in one hand and reached for the door, halting as Adam spoke. Relief rushed through her at the temporary reprieve.

"Are you certain you didn't see anyone else, Lacy?"

A moment of tense silence passed before Lacy said, "Yes. I'm certain. You're talking about the mayor, aren't you?" Adam nodded. "I didn't see the mayor." She saw the disappointment in his eyes before he masked it.

Lacy turned the knob and opened the door. A damp, musky odor invaded her nostrils and Lacy thought it smelled like old age and death, a blast of air from her past. She shivered, glad that Adam was behind her even though she knew she must ignore his presence.

Everything looked the same, or almost the same. Along with the musky smell of mildew, she smelled the tang of freshly cut wood. The new shelves, she thought, the scent momentarily distracting her. She thrust the intrusion from her mind and slowly approached the desk, her eyes searching the room. Her gaze lingered on the painting of Shadow City Adam had rehung, chilled by the realization that he had placed it in the exact same position. . . .

The shadows were there, maybe darker and more sinister than before because this time she knew what she would find—or what she was supposed to imagine she would find. She set the plate on the desk and resisted the urge to turn and assure herself that Adam was behind her. He hadn't made a sound.

The matches were in the small top drawer, where Adam had put them at her request. She took them out with hands that shook and lit the lamp. Slowly, she twisted around in front of the desk and peered into the shadows of the cell.

It was so much like before that she couldn't stop a small gasp of fear from escaping. And she wasn't really thinking when she reached around and fumbled for the lamp, finding the handle and dragging it forward. She only knew that she had to have the light to see what was in the cell, what was causing those frightening swinging shadows.

She thrust the lamp forward and screamed, her eyes glued to the garish silhouette of the harmless sack of dirt strung from the ceiling of the cell in the exact same spot where Colt Murddock had died.

When her scream died away, she swallowed hard and said, her voice a raspy whisper, "He was swinging back and forth. His face was all mottled, swelled-looking." Her voice dropped even lower as she added, "His eyes were open and it was like he was staring at me, begging me for help. But he was already dead." She turned and set the lamp on the desk, her mind grappling with the unforgettable image her words had created. Not that she had ever forgotten.

Adam reached out and touched her and she gave a startled shriek before her sanity returned. With a sob she flung herself into his waiting arms. He held her tight and murmured soothing, praising words. But he didn't say the words she really wanted—needed to hear. She wanted him to say he loved her and he would be with her the next time she awoke with Colt Murddock's sightless eyes staring into her soul.

Finally her sobs ebbed. She stirred in his arms, grabbing the cloth from the empty plate and wiping her eyes. Adam was staring at her, his blue eyes dark with concern.

"Did—did any of this help?" she asked. God, she prayed it had so that what she had done would not be in vain. Because of this recreation, the nightmares would come tonight, she knew. If only Adam could be there. He could hold her and remind her that it was just a dream, a nightmare that would fade with the morning light. She'd fall asleep in his arms, or maybe he would make love to her, blot out the awful images with his lips and his hands. . . .

"You said he was swinging," Adam mused, placing comforting kisses on her nose, her lips, and her cheeks. Licking away the last trace of tears. Lacy shivered, beginning to notice how tightly he held her against him. She'd never felt anything so wonderful before in her life. Never. And his tender administrations made her feel like a child again, a loved, cosseted child.

The rest of her felt all woman.

"Yes. He was swinging. I remember how the shadows

from his . . . body danced around the walls. That was why I picked up the lamp, to see what was causing them."

Absently, Adam rubbed his hands up and down her shoulders. "So that means he hadn't been hanging long, if he was still swinging."

Lacy's eyes widened. "I hadn't thought of that."

Adam nodded, more confident now. "Yes. This means you probably came close to bumping into whoever killed him. They must have just left before you arrived."

His deduction sent a cold chill down her spine. Oh, God, she thought, if she'd been a few moments sooner, she might have saved Sheriff Murddock!

Adam took one look at her horrified face and quickly shook his head. "No darlin'. You couldn't have done anything. They would have killed you, too." He shook her gently when her expression didn't change. "Do you hear me, Lacy? They would have killed you, and you wouldn't be here to help me now."

Lacy's eyes snapped to his, the horror slowly receding as his words sank in. "But—but I haven't helped you at all! What good does it do to know that Sheriff Murddock hadn't been dead long?"

"Damn! I don't know, but there's got to be *something,* some clue hiding among this rubble!"

Abruptly, he dropped his arms and began pacing the floor. A fierce frown drew his dark brows together as he contemplated everything she had told him up to this moment. Lacy watched him walk back and forth, thinking that he looked dangerous and vulnerable all at the same time.

Her knees began to tremble and she reached a hand out to steady herself against the desk. Reaction, she thought. She felt drained of emotion, sucked dry of spirit. Even her voice, when she spoke, lacked strength. "Can I go home now?"

Adam looked blank, then rueful. "Of course. I'll get the key and lock up." At her questioning glance, he added, "Rusty and I are supposed to go for a drink, to talk about what we're going to do. I don't want any surprises waitin' on me when I get back."

"Oh." Lacy took a deep breath, fear lancing through her.

"Please . . . be careful, Adam." For answer, he sidled up behind her, pressing into her and bending his head to nibble her neck right in front of the open door.

Right in front of God and everybody.

"Why? Would you miss me, darlin'?"

How could he joke at a time like this? she wondered, getting angry. Sharply, she said, "That's not the point. . . ."

Warm air stirred the curls at the nape of her neck as he breathed in her ear, "Forget me already? Shall we go back in and reacquaint ourselves?"

"Adam!"

He laughed, his mood changing so swiftly that Lacy could scarcely keep up. "No matter how hard you try to ignore it, it's not going to go away."

Forcing herself to move away from the tempting warmth of his body, Lacy stepped onto the boardwalk and turned to watch him lock the door. She pasted a prim expression on her face that made him laugh again—which sparked her temper. "Adam Logan, you behave yourself," she whispered, glancing around to see whether anyone was watching.

He joined her on the boardwalk and took her arm, careful of the bandage beneath her dress sleeve. With a jaunty smile and a step to match, they set off down the street. After a moment, he grinned down at her face. "You know," he began with a casualness that immediately made her suspicious. "Rusty warned me that his old shotgun still works."

Lacy tripped over her feet. Her startled eyes flew to his smiling face. "He didn't!"

"He did," Adam said, his expression smug. "If he knew about our . . . tumble in the hay—"

Lacy jerked to a stop. "You wouldn't!" Suddenly, his words registered. *Tumble in the hay?* She opened her mouth, but nothing came out. She tried again, but just as she found the appropriate words to describe what a low-down, dirty dog he was, she saw the laughter in his eyes. "Oh, you! You make me so mad sometimes I could—" she ended her frustrated spurt of words abruptly as the lamplighter called a greeting from the across the road.

Adam tipped his hat and waved. Lacy smiled and
returned the greeting to the old man, then shot Adam a look
that should have felled him on the spot. When he offered her
his arm again, she stuck her nose in the air and ignored it.

She'd taken no more than ten steps before she stopped
again. She froze with her hands holding the edge of her
dress out of the dirt. The lamplighter. . . . *The lamplighter!*

"Adam." Her voice came out hardly above a whisper.
Adam continued walking. She cleared her throat. "Adam!"

Adam halted and turned. "Hmmm?" When he saw the
expression on her face, he reached her in two long strides.
"What is it?" he demanded, reaching for his gun as he
scanned the area around them. He saw nothing out of the
ordinary, no lurking shadows at the corners of the buildings.
He turned back to face her, a question hovering on his lips.

She looked like a statue, as if she were frozen in time.

15

*T*HE LAMPLIGHTER! *T*HE words tumbled around and around inside her head. She grew dizzy with the effort it took to remember if she'd seen him that evening so long ago. The memory whispered into her mind, then danced away. She was almost certain she'd seen the lamplighter. Almost. The old man was a common sight, scurrying up and down the street in the late evening, then again in the early morning to extinguish the flames. She hardly noticed him anymore unless he called out to her.

Meeting Adam's impatient gaze, she said, "I think the lamplighter was there. His name is—"

"Noel. I know. Go on to the house, I'll be there directly," he ordered, his gaze going to the old man across the road.

Reluctantly, Lacy did as he said, glancing back once to note that Noel and Adam appeared to be in deep discussion. Maybe Noel would be able to help where she had failed, she thought hopefully.

Rusty was waiting for her on the front porch. He met her

before she could reach the steps, guiding her up the wooden planks. "Watch your step—noticed a loose board there today. I'll fix it up right good tomorrow."

Lacy was too distracted to pay much attention to his ramblings. She stepped where he instructed. "Adam's talking to Noel, Grandpa."

"Noel?" Rusty opened the door for her, his bushy eyebrows topping his forehead. "What for?"

"I think he might have been lighting the lamps when . . . when Sheriff Murddock was killed." She hadn't realized her choice of words until Rusty clapped her on the back so hard he nearly sent her sprawling into the living room.

"I knew my gal would come around! I jes' knew it. You know ol' Colt didn't kill himself."

Lacy rolled her eyes to the ceiling, admitting defeat. There was no use wasting her breath trying to explain to Rusty that she had never really thought about it one way or the other. She had been in shock, and later she had tried to block it from her mind.

"Come on, lets get some coffee going. 'Magine Adam'll want a swig when he gets here." Rusty sprinted ahead of her in the direction of the kitchen.

Frowning, Lacy followed. She took a chair at the table and watched Rusty stoke the fire beneath the coffee kettle. "Adam said something about you and him going for a drink?"

The fire door slammed shut with a bang. Rusty darted his eyes to her, then quickly away again. Lacy knew the signs. It meant he was hiding something. "Grandpa? Did you hear what I said?"

"What? Oh, that. I forgot, is all. Well." He dusted his hands on his trousers. "You'll be wantin' some coffee, won't ya?" He shook his head, muttering, "I must be losin' my memory these days."

Now Lacy was very suspicious. Rusty didn't forget anything, to her knowledge. And sometimes to her regret. "Grandpa . . ." The warning in her tone came through loud and clear.

Before Rusty could come up with a believable explanation, they heard a crash, followed by a pain-filled curse. Exchanging a startled glance, Lacy and Rusty raced to the sound and found Adam sitting on the porch steps, his right leg stretched out before him.

Beneath the light of the porch lamp, his face was a mask of pain.

"What on earth—Adam? What happened?" Lacy crouched beside him, attempting to examine the ankle he was clasping with both hands.

Rusty answered for him. "I'll tell you what happened. He fell through that damned broken board on the steps. I shouldn't have put it off. Ain't that right, Adam?"

"Yeah, that's what happened."

With Lacy and Rusty's help, Adam tried to stand. He grunted as he tried to put his weight on his ankle. Rusty grunted along with him, then announced, "Looks like you'll be stayin' the night here, Adam. Can't walk to the jailhouse on that injury. Might do more damage."

Lacy tried to keep the joy from her face, but some of it bled through in her voice. "Guess you're right, Grandpa. We'll have to take care of him tonight."

Adam grumbled, looking from one to the other. "Is this a conspiracy?" he demanded in mock anger.

Lacy blushed and quickly covered her discomfiture with a brisk manner. "You flatter yourself, Sheriff." She absolutely refused to look at his face because she knew she'd find a knowing smile on his lips.

Ha! She wasn't so certain it *wasn't* a conspiracy, but if it was, *she* had played no part in it!

Rusty went to the saloon alone, which Lacy thought was a little odd. Before he left, he helped Lacy settle Adam onto the sofa and brought in a pan of cold well water so that Adam could soak his ankle.

After he had gone, Lacy became fidgety. Ben had gone to bed, tired from a hard day's work helping Ida and Kent down at the general store, and Takola was in her room working the soft leather that Lacy had purchased for her into a new dress.

It was too early to go to bed, yet she felt nervous with Rusty gone. She hesitated in the doorway of the living room. "You're sure you don't want me to fetch Doc Martin?"

Adam shook his head, smiled, and winced. "Yes, I'm sure. Just a little sprain. Hardly any swelling at all."

Lacy toyed with the end of her braid, still undecided about what to do. Normally at this time of night, she would sit in the living room, sewing or reading. If Rusty was home, they would talk for a while. "Well . . . if you're sure."

"I'm sure." Adam smiled and patted the sofa beside him. "Come here. You're as nervous as a cat."

"Oh, I don't want to bother you—"

"Don't be ridiculous. You would bother me more if you went to bed."

"I would?" Lacy lifted a questioning brow. She clung to the doorjamb as if it were the only thing holding her upright.

"Yes. Then I'd have to sit here wondering if you sleep naked, or if you snore in your sleep."

"I do not snore, Adam Logan." She tossed her head. "And further more, I do not sleep in the raw."

Adam muffled a sound of regret, but Lacy heard it. "You couldn't leave me with my fantasy, could you?" He patted the sofa again, his eyes appealing, his grin boyish. Lacy noticed that he didn't look as if he were in pain now. "Come and talk to me."

"What—what do you want to talk about?" She swallowed and came slowly into the room. Instead of taking the place he offered, she sat in Rusty's favorite chair by the cold fireplace. He was right; she *was* being ridiculous. Wasn't this what she had wanted? Adam spending the night under her roof? There was just something about that gleam in his eye that she didn't trust.

Water sloshed in the pan as Adam adjusted his foot. She had rolled up the hem of his pants to keep them from getting wet and she averted her eyes from the disturbing sight of his muscled calf. With a smile meant to ease her nervousness, Adam said, "Tell me how Ben's doing."

Lacy pounced on the harmless topic with all the vigor of

a chicken chasing a grasshopper. "He's doing wonderfully, but you should know that. You see more of him than I do."

"Not lately." When Lacy looked alarmed, he hastened on, "No, nothing like that. He's been working a lot of odd jobs aside from the work he does for me."

"Yes, I know. Say's he's saving his money, but he won't say what he's saving for." A tender smile curved her mouth. "It's like he's a different little boy, since you came to town."

Adam brushed the compliment aside. "He just needed a little boost of confidence."

"Yes, but _you_ gave him that boost. And Takola, too." It was true, and she wasn't about to let him forget it. "Even Rusty has changed for the better."

A little silence fell. Lacy adjusted her skirts and fiddled with her apron. Adam remained relaxed, studying her with a lazy expression that made her heart pound with excitement and anticipation. It was there between them, still fresh in both their minds, she knew. She could see it in his eyes, and feel it in her heart. His next statement sent Lacy into a tailspin of emotions.

"I've changed, too, Lacy."

Hope, elation, and fear slammed into her. She was so glad that she was sitting. "How—how have you changed?" Thunder, but she sounded like a breathless schoolgirl with her first crush!

Adam seemed not to notice. He leaned his head back on the sofa and closed his eyes. "Once upon a time I was a lot like Ben. I didn't have a lick of self-confidence. Thought I was worthless." He opened one eye and looked at her, then promptly closed it again. "My stepfather didn't believe in building character; he believed in knocking it down. You see, to him, that was how you made a man out of a boy."

His tone was light, but Lacy was perceptive enough to sense an underlying pain buried deep beneath the man Adam Logan was today. A hurt little boy. Tears of sympathy burned the back of her throat but she swallowed them down. Adam wouldn't want her pity. In that way, he was a lot like herself.

Beyond the curtained window, Lacy saw a flash of

lightning. The storm was nearly upon them and Rusty was at the saloon. She soothed her worry by reminding herself that Rusty was a grown man, however irresponsible he acted sometimes. But looking at Adam, listening to him talk of the subtle torture of his childhood, she realized that even grown men needed comforting and nurturing.

She sensed Adam needed it now. "You—you mentioned that he made your mother's life a living hell. I take it she wasn't alone?" Hesitantly, she stood and walked to the couch. He still had his head thrown back, but she knew that he was aware of her approach. She sat beside him and took his hand, lacing their fingers together. Only when she realized that he would allow it did she breathe again. It was hard to forget how he'd mocked her about taking in strays and kissing their tears away. He had sounded so cynical.

But the man sitting beside her now *did* seem like a different man. Maybe he was right, and he *had* changed.

"My mother," Adam said softly. "She was the love of my life. Rudy Wagner didn't deserve her. Hell, Wagner doesn't deserve anybody." He turned his head and their gazes met, locked. Lacy held herself very still. "I never told her about the beatings the bastard gave me and I hope she never found out. She married him for *me*."

"I don't understand."

Adam's laugh was hollow sounding. "She thought I needed a father, after my own pa died."

"Oh." Lacy didn't know what to say. She could understand his mother's reasoning, but it was sad that she had picked the wrong man for the job. It took a special person to be a parent. It seemed Rudy Wagner had fallen way short of the mark, and Adam's mother had suffered as well from her unwise choice.

"He beat her as well, as I'm sure you've guessed." He lifted their entwined hands, studying the contrasting sun-tanned brown of his own against her fragile white one. "That's how I knew you had been abused. My mother had that same look in her eyes whenever my stepfather came into the room. She was scared to death of him. There were times when I plotted to kill him, but she guessed my intentions and begged me not to, because of my brothers."

A tear spilled over onto Lacy's cheek and she turned her face slightly away, not wanting Adam to see it. It was an awful story, and one that sounded very familiar. Her scars might be old, but she still remembered. Oh, how she remembered. The shame, the guilt, the fear. The freedom she had felt at the news of David's death.

Adam tugged at her chin until she was facing him again, forcing her to meet his questioning, gentle look. "Why did *you* stay?" he asked softly.

Lacy closed her eyes, the old shame swamping her. "Because I couldn't bring myself to admit failure. Because I kept thinking it was me, that I was doing something wrong. And later . . . because I was afraid he'd come after me." She drew in a shaky breath, angry at the tears slipping down her cheeks. "He told me if I ever tired to leave he'd kill me. I felt nothing but relief when he died from that snake bite. Afterward, I swore to myself that the only men in my life would be old men and little boys."

"Rusty and Ben," Adam murmured, as if to himself. "And now?" he prompted.

She kept her eyes closed, but felt him come closer as his breath wafted across her face. It was soothing, and he smelled of peppermint. He always smelled of peppermint. Ida must be stocking double the amount of peppermint sticks since Adam's arrival in town. The thought made her smile. It was a wan smile, but a smile none the less. Adam had a way of sweeping away the dark clouds.

As if to mock her dramatic thoughts, thunder rumbled and behind her closed lids, she saw a quick flash of light. She jerked her eyes open, catching Adam's tender expression. It took her breath away.

He was waiting for an answer, and she knew him well enough to know that he could wait a long time.

"Now . . . I don't know. Obviously I've broken my own rules." She managed a self-derisive laugh.

Adam's fingers tightened on her chin as if to scold her. "But you don't know if you want to continue breaking them," he guessed.

"I do, but—"

"You're afraid."

"Yes."

"Of me."

"No."

"Bullcrap."

Lacy moved out of his grasp, relieved when he let her go.

Adam wouldn't let the subject drop. With a hard edge to his voice, he asked, "What would it take to convince you I'm not like David?"

"I *know* you're not like David!" Lacy realized she'd nearly shouted. She glanced at the stairway, then glared at Adam as if it were his fault. "I told you, David's not the problem—or my problems with David are not the issue."

"Bullcrap."

"Stop saying that."

"Okay. Bullshit."

"Oh!" Lacy thought about punching him, but just managed to refrain. He brought out the beast in her, the rat! One minute he had her smiling and the next she was mad enough to spit.

He also made her say things she would normally not have the courage to say. "Why do you care? You're leaving town as soon as your business is finished."

"You could change my mind."

Lacy felt the shock of his words all the way to her toes. God, how she wanted to, if he but knew! But that would put him in further danger and she couldn't bear the thought.

"Adam, I—"

To Lacy's immense relief, the front door burst open, saving her from having to answer. Adam gave her a look that clearly promised they would resume the conversation at a later date. Of that, Lucy had no doubt. He was a stubborn man.

"Grandpa, you're all wet," Lucy said, jumping to her feet. "I'll get a towel." Feeling Adam's mocking eyes on her, she raced from the room.

It wasn't until much later, when she was snug in her own bed and on the verge of sleep, that she remembered she had completely forgotten to ask Adam about his talk with Noel.

When Lacy disappeared up the stairs, Adam addressed
Rusty, keeping his voice low. "Well? How did it go? Any of
the mayor's henchmen in the saloon?"

Rusty shook the rain from his head, grinning. "Yep. Two
of the varmints. Made sure they heard every word, too."

"And they don't know that I'm here?"

"Nope. They think you're sawin' logs at the jail."

Adam rubbed his hands together. "Good. Now all we can
do is wait and see what develops. You talk that granddaughter of yours into retiring for the night so we can stand
watch."

Rusty nodded. "And Noel? Did he remember anything?"

His expression hard, Adam said, "Yes. He saw the mayor
go into Colt's office before he died, but he's not sure of the
time. He never saw him leave."

Rusty rubbed his jaw. "Well, it had to be close to the same
time, with him lightin' the lamps and all. It was gettin' dark
when Lacy found him."

"Right."

The harsh clanging of the fire bells woke Lacy from a sweet
dream. She groaned and buried her head beneath her pillow
as she tried to recapture the image of Adam's passion-filled
eyes. In her dream, Adam had been on the verge of kissing
her.

And she had thought she'd have nightmares. . . . She
smiled a dreamy smile and snuggled into the mattress.
Wonderful dreams, instead of nightmares.

But the clanging continued, followed by shrill cries of
"Fire! Fire!"

The words finally penetrated the fog of sleep in which
Lacy fought so desperately to lose herself.

She jerked upright, panic skimming along her nerve
endings. The word *fire* spread fear in the stoutest of hearts.
Everyone helped out, no matter what time it was, or whose
building was ablaze. She was no exception. Women, chil-

dren, anyone who could haul a bucket of water was expected to answer the summons.

The last fire had been several years ago, when the small general store had gone up like a gas-soaked torch. Luckily, the building had stood alone, unlike most of the businesses in town.

Swiftly, Lacy threw back the sheet and scrambled into her clothes. She buttoned her dress as she hurried to wake Ben and Takola. When she was certain they were awake and dressing, she raced down the stairs to Rusty's room, a small bedroom adjacent to the living room.

It was empty. Spinning around, she tripped her way through the darkened living room to the sofa. Adam was gone, too. They must have already left to help put out the fire. How long had the bells been ringing before she awoke? she wondered, tugging her shoes on. And how was Adam getting around on that bad ankle? It sounded just like him, hobbling around trying to help. . . .

Ben and Takola appeared at the foot of the stairs, hastening after her as she jerked open the front door and stepped out onto the porch. The sharp smell of burning wood and tar stung her nose and eyes.

The fire was close, she saw, watching the billowing black smoke pour into the dark sky. Flames suddenly shot upwards, causing Lacy's heart to stutter to a stop.

The fire was at the jailhouse; from the position of the flames, it had begun at the rear of the building.

Adam's bedroom.

Fear lanced through her before she remembered that Adam was not there, had in fact been sleeping on her couch. She raced down the road in the direction of the fire with Ben and Takola at her side, heedless of the mud splattering her skirts from the recent rain. Other townspeople began to pour into the street, moving in the same direction. Many were still dressed in their nightclothes, caps bobbing on their heads as they ran.

Reaching the crowd, Lacy saw that two assembly lines had already formed. Buckets of water swung from hand to hand, taken from the nearest well. As they were emptied, they were then passed to the second line to be returned and refilled. A third and fourth line were forming as more willing hands arrived.

Lacy found Adam and Rusty at the head of the first line, shouting for haste. She glanced quickly at his foot, frowning when she realized he wasn't favoring it at all. Perhaps the sprain had turned out to be a minor bruising, instead. She thrust the worry from her mind and concentrated on the more important task at hand.

Thank God, there would be no casualties, she thought as she took her place at the end of the line. Ben and Takola fell in with her. Takola looked serene, as usual, but Lacy noticed that Ben's eyes were round with shock.

The bucket swung her way and Lacy grabbed it and hauled it around to the next person in line, who happened to be Dr. Martin. She hadn't noticed when she'd taken her place, so intent had she been on locating Rusty and Adam. Then she glanced over his shoulder. Her heart stopped.

Adam was disappearing through the front door of the jailhouse and straight into the fire.

Dear God, what did he think he was doing? He was insane! Without thinking, Lacy broke from the line and ran toward the jailhouse. She splashed through mud puddles and slipped her way to the door just as Adam came running back out.

He nearly slammed into her. Furious, Lacy yelled at him over the roaring of the flames and the shouts from the men. "What are you doing?" And then she saw the painting he held.

"Take this," he shouted, and disappeared back inside.

Stunned, Lacy caught the painting by the frame, feeling the heat from the scorched wood seep into her palms. Before she could gather breath to scream for him, he returned once again, carrying what looked like a photograph and a stack of papers. He thrust those into her already fully laden arms.

"Put these somewhere safe," he ordered before trotting back to the front line to resume his position.

Mumbling beneath her breath, Lacy carried the items to

the overhang in front of the blacksmith's shop and set them down before rushing back to help.

The entire population of Shadow City worked for over an hour, battling the flames as they continued to eat their way to the front of the building. The buckets of water seemed about as effective as spit on a roaring fire. Finally, Adam must have realized it was useless to try to save the jailhouse, for he began directing the water to the buildings on either side. Lacy approved of his decision, knowing that if they didn't get those buildings doused sufficiently, the fire would spread and eat them, too.

Her arms ached, so she could only imagine how Ben and the slender Takola felt by now. Soot blackened most of the faces she looked upon and she suspected her own was just as dirty. But no one cared; they were all intent on saving their town.

Morning wasn't far away before the fire ran out of fuel. The water-soaked buildings on either side of the jailhouse had suffered smoke damage and a few charred patches, but otherwise remained standing. They hadn't saved the jail-house, but they had all done the best they could.

Weary, dirty, and depressed over the loss, people began to drift homeward. Lacy had the same thoughts, gathering Ben and Takola and glancing around for the men. She found them searching among the smoldering ruins. Sighing, she turned away, deciding that they could find their own way home.

"Hey! We found somebody!"

Lacy froze. The shout had come from Rusty. Slowly, she turned back around, a feeling of dread adding to her weariness.

It seemed she was wrong about there being no casualties.

16

$\mathcal{R}$USTY AND ADAM had discovered the body in the yard a few feet from what had once been the back door to the jailhouse. The man was lying face down with his arms stretched above his head as if he had been attempting to crawl away from the inferno.

And he was wearing a gun.

Adam used a shovel to turn the body as people crowded around to get a look at the gruesome find. Lacy gripped Ben's shoulder and turned his face away from the terrible sight, gasping as she recognized the slightly burned features. Takola stood silently beside her, her small round face expressionless. She'd seen death in many ways—far more brutal than this.

Rusty peered at the body, shaking his head. "That's not the one that was at the saloon," he said for Adam's ears only.

"Looks like Brody Peters," Matt Johnson announced, stepping forward to get a better look. "He works for the mayor, don't he?" Several people nodded or murmured their agreement.

Adam and Rusty exchanged a knowing glance, and Adam knew it wouldn't take much to convince the crowd that the mayor was responsible for the fire. All the evidence they needed was lying on the ground before them. Still, Adam hesitated before he said, "Guess this means another chat with the mayor." He stared at the body through narrow, assessing eyes. Something wasn't right, he thought. If Brody had started the fire—at the mayor's order—then why was he now dead?

"You think *he's* behind this?" an astonished voice asked.

Adam searched for the speaker, his eyes finally landing on the soot-blackened face of Dr. Martin. If not for his muttonchop whiskers, Adam wouldn't have recognized him. "I'll need to find out what Peters was doing here at the time of the fire," he hedged, then added, "Can you take the body to your office and take a closer look? Just for my peace of mind. I want to make sure this man died because of the fire."

Dr. Martin looked puzzled, but he nodded, asking for volunteers to help carry the dead man to his office. Several younger boys came forward, eager to impress the sheriff with their brawn.

To the silent crowd, which consisted mainly of men because the majority of the women and children had gone home—with the exception of Lacy, Ben and Takola—Adam said, "I'll need a few extra men to go with me when I talk to the mayor." He wasn't a coward, but neither was he a fool. "Anyone who volunteers will need to bring a rifle. If you don't have one, we'll get you one." He passed a weary hand through his smoke-roughened hair as an impressive number of hands lifted, vowing their support.

"You expecting trouble, Sheriff?" Matt Johnson asked, after volunteering to go with Adam.

Adam managed a weary grin. "I always expect trouble, Matt. That way I'm never surprised. Right now I suggest everyone go home and get some rest. We'll meet here at five o'clock this evening before headin' out to the mayor's house."

The crowd dispersed, and by unspoken agreement Rusty and Adam headed down to the street in the direction of home.

Home. Adam stumbled and Rusty put out a steadying arm. He mumbled his thanks and regained his balance. He was thinking of Lacy's house as *home*. Which wasn't really surprising, considering the way she made him *feel* at home.

Along the way, Adam detoured to retrieve the items Lacy had placed on the boardwalk and away from tramping feet and smoke and fire. Someone had placed a stone on the stack of wanted posters to keep them from blowing away, Adam noticed.

"You'll have to make a new frame for that," Rusty commented, pointing at the charred and blackened frame around the painting.

Luckily, the painting itself wasn't damaged. It had buckled in a few places from the heat, but otherwise remained untouched. Adam smoothed his hand over the canvas. He'd gotten it just in the nick of time. And the photograph of Colt Murddock had been in the desk, protected from the smoke and heat, as had been the wanted posters. He shook his head, still not sure why he'd grabbed the posters. If his suspicion proved true—and everything so far verified that it was—his job would soon be over and he'd be on his way out of town to Wyoming.

Wouldn't he? The thought of leaving Shadow City didn't fill him with anticipation as it once had. In fact, he didn't like the prospect worth a damn. If Lacy had given him the slightest encouragement . . . he might have reconsidered.

But she'd hesitated, telling him all he needed to know. She couldn't trust him, or any man. Relationships could not be built without trust. Adam absently widened his stride to step across a mud puddle, his thoughts deep and grim. If Lacy was with child, then she *would* marry him, whether she wanted to or not. Maybe in time she would learn to trust him.

Love him, as he loved her.

Adam startled Rusty by laughing out loud. If his face had not been black with soot, the blush would have given him away. He kept his eyes on the road and ignored Rusty's upraised eyebrows.

He loved Lacy Ross. Damn. *He*, Adam Logan, had fallen for the stubbornest, orneriest, proudest woman in Callaway County.

Dr. Martin parted the dead man's hair and pointed to a bulging knot at the base of his skull. "Might have fell trying to get out after he started the fire. Probably panicked, then the smoke got to him." He washed his hands in a pan of hot soapy water and dried them, looking at Adam. "Or that bump could have knocked him out and he never knew what happened."

Adam continued to stare at the body, absorbing the doctor's words. "Or someone could have hit him with something," he said slowly, lifting his eyes to meet Dr. Martin's startled ones.

"But why?"

Shaking his head in frustration, Adam growled, "I don't know, Doc, I don't know. Something just doesn't feel right, but I can't figure it out."

But he would. He *had* to. "Let's gather up the others and go talk to the mayor. He's got the answers."

Dr. Martin covered the body with a blanket and followed Adam from the room.

The mayor was waiting for them. Adam tipped his hat to the housekeeper and followed her into the spacious parlor. The men fell in behind him. Rusty, Dr. Martin, Matt Johnson, Kent Middleton from the general store, and Lester Salvage were among the men Adam had brought along. There were ten of them altogether, but Adam knew that if the mayor balked at the arrest, ten men—nine carrying rifles or guns, because Dr. Martin had refused—wouldn't be nearly enough to ward off his dozen or so henchmen posted around the house.

He didn't want any of these good men getting themselves killed, so he kept his expression cool and his hand far away from the butt of his gun. He had already advised the men to act on his orders and not before.

Adam saw right away that the mayor wasn't alone. Graham Silverstone was with him, looking thin and elegant in a charcoal-gray suit with a black-and-gray pinstripe vest. His aged, sharp-nosed face was somber as he met Adam's quizzical gaze. He was the first to speak as the townsmen filed in behind Adam, forming a solid barrier at his back.

"I'm acting as the mayor's attorney, Sheriff Logan. Am I correct in assuming this is an informal questioning, and not a lynching?" The half-smile on his lips didn't reach his eyes.

Adam was surprised to see the attorney, although he probably shouldn't have been. Jamis Goodrich wasn't the type of man to just sit back and wait for someone to haul him to jail, and he'd had the entire day to pull in favors.

Not that there *was* a jail any longer. The thought brought a grim smile to Adam's mouth. He bowed at Graham Silverstone, then focused his cold eyes on the mayor. In contrast, the mayor looked smug and prosperous in his burgundy velvet jacket, but a nervous sweat beaded his forehead. His nose was swollen and bruised and he couldn't hold Adam's gaze for more than a few seconds at a time. So, Adam mused, the mayor wasn't as confident as he wanted them to believe. And he was scared.

"Found one of your henchmen at the back of the jail—what's left of it, and him." Adam spoke softly, taunting the mayor. "Guess he got too close to the fire. You wouldn't happen to know how he came to be at the jailhouse—and how he ended up dying there?"

The mayor shot Silverstone a nervous glance. Silverstone nodded encouragingly. Goodrich cleared his throat before speaking. "I've . . . I've had some trouble down at the mill and I had sent Peters to talk to you about it."

"Awful late for that, wouldn't you say?" Adam drawled. He never took his eyes from the mayor's face, not even to blink. He could only pray that the men behind him would remain silent. The mayor was doing a mighty fine job of digging his own trap.

Goodrich looked to Silverstone again and received a

second encouraging nod. It was almost comical. Adam
thought he heard a snicker from someone behind him, and
suspected Rusty was the culprit. He could hardly blame
him; if the situation weren't so serious, he would have
laughed too.

"I . . . I didn't think of it until late. Figured you'd be up
until the saloon closed."

Adam scratched his ear, feigning puzzlement. He could
almost feel the tensions radiating from behind him. "Wonder why he came around through the back way? Seems like
a lot of trouble, climbing that old splintery fence when he
could have come to the front door."

At Adam's words, the mayor looked desperate. He
opened his mouth, then quickly shut it when the distinguished attorney stepped forward. His sigh of relief could be
heard by all.

"Look, Sheriff," Silverstone began in a professional
voice, "why don't you just come to the point?"

"All right." Adam, too, had begun to tire of the game. "I
have reason to believe that Brody Peters set fire to the
jailhouse—following a direct order from Jamis Goodrich. I
also believe that Peters got caught in the fire before he could
make it out." With a mocking bow, Adam turned to the
mayor. "In light of this evidence, I'm taking you in for
further questioning."

"You can't do that," Silverstone said. "You don't have
any concrete proof of anything, Sheriff Logan. There are
laws in this country that everyone has to follow, yourself
included. Without evidence, without witnesses, you can't
take him anywhere. He told you why Peters was there and
unless you can prove that he's lying . . ."

He sounded confident, too confident. Unfortunately, Adam
suspected he was right. No matter how much he believed
that the mayor was behind the fire and that the intent had
been to roast him alive, he didn't have any proof, any
evidence save his own instincts. As for witnesses, his only
witness—Brody Peters—was dead.

Damn and damn! At the time of the fire, he and Rusty had
been watching the front of the jailhouse, never considering

that someone might sneak through the back way. Why? Why hadn't they thought of the possibility?

But Adam knew why. Because he'd been thinking about his grandfather, and how he believed *his* murderer had walked through the front door with the confident belief that no one would ever suspect him.

A fine upstanding citizen like the mayor.

Adam stared at the mayor's perspiring face. Dammit! The lamplighter had seen him, and the mayor had already proven he was capable of ruthless measures to get the results he wanted. They knew that from the way he'd set fire to Salvage's lumber mill a few months back. And finding one of his henchmen, no matter how dead he was, was too much of a coincidence after the way he and Rusty had set the stage.

Yet . . . he couldn't forget how sincere the mayor had seemed before he'd plowed his fist into his nose yesterday.

Something wasn't right, as he had told Dr. Martin. It was obvious to him that the mayor was guilty of something, lying about something—he just wasn't sure what it was.

If he could get the mayor alone, he could make him talk.

Slowly Adam looked around the room, silently counting the mean-faced men under Goodrich's hire. Five in the room, a dozen or so outside the door, and more guarding the house. He swallowed a frustrated growl. Too many. He couldn't risk taking the mayor by force, not with the untrained men he'd brought along.

Suddenly, he felt a push from behind. Rusty shouldered him aside, his expression as ominous as Adam had ever seen it. Shaking his fist at the mayor, Rusty shouted, "You might have slipped your way out of this one, Goodrich, but if anything happens to the sheriff here, we'll know who to look for." There was a chorus of vigorous agreements from Matt, Dr. Martin, and the rest. "And we'll be prepared next time. We'll get every man in Shadow City and if we have to burn you out, we'll get to you. Law or no law."

"You can't threaten my client—"

"Oh, shut up, you old fool," Rusty snapped, glaring Silverstone into silence. "I'll threaten whoever I want, and furthermore"—he made a sound of pure distrust—"if you're gonna represent slime like the mayor here, then I don't have no use for you neither."

"Yeah, me either!"

"That goes for me, too."

"And me," another shouted.

One by one, the businessmen of Shadow City added their pledges not to use Silverstone's services. Not surprisingly, Silverstone began to look less and less sure of himself. It was the first time Adam had ever seen the man anything but confident. Too bad, he thought with genuine regret, for Silverstone hadn't struck him as a dishonest man. In fact, he had liked him.

But what type of man stood beside the likes of Jamis Goodrich?

Lacy filled the coffee kettle with water and stoked the fire. Bacon sizzled in a frying pan and beans bubbled in the pot. She had a pan of cracklin' cornbread warming in the oven. Takola was setting the table and she'd sent Ben to the garden to gather a mess of green onions to have with their meal.

Rusty and Adam sat around the table, their voices steadily rising. Soon, Lacy thought with a nervous sigh, she'd have to douse them with cold water.

"I can't stay here," Adam argued. "If they're still after me, the rest of you will be in danger."

Rusty banged a fist onto the table. "And you don't have eyes in the back of your head. You can't go off by yourself, and if you insist on doing something that foolish, I'm going with you."

"No. Someone has to stay here."

At that moment Ben came through the back door, a handful of green onions clutched in his fist. He caught the tail end of the conversation and said, "I can watch 'em, Sheriff." He touched his deputy star with his finger. "I'm a deputy, ain't I?"

Lacy bit her cheek to keep from smiling, wondering how Rusty and Adam were going to get out of this one without hurting Ben's feelings. She stirred the beans and moved the bacon around in the skillet, listening intently.

Adam cleared his throat and smiled at Ben. "Of course you're a deputy, Ben. I know you can watch over Lacy and Takola, but—"

"Well, that settles it," Ben announced with sparkling eyes. "Rusty can go with you, and I'll stay and protect the womenfolk."

"Ah . . . Ben—"

"What's the matter, Sheriff? Don't you think I can do it?"

Lacy swallowed a chuckle, feeling sorry for Adam. She turned from the stove and gave Ben a small push in the direction of the back door. "Go wash those onions—and yourself. Dinner's almost ready. We'll talk about it later."

"But, Lacy, I—"

"Go." She pointed her finger at the back door and Ben made a face but obeyed. When Ben left, she stared at the discomfited faces of the two men she loved most in her life. Rusty picked at a deep groove in the table; Adam studied his bruised knuckles—courtesy of the mayor's nose.

"First of all, we don't need protecting. They're not after us, they're after you. We're perfectly capable of staying by ourselves." She fell silent, satisfied when neither man seemed inclined to argue her point. "Secondly, don't think that I've forgotten about your ankle, Adam Logan. Why did you feel you had to lie to me?" Her attempt to hide the hurt behind the lightly voiced question failed.

Adam sighed, drumming his fingers on the table. Finally, he looked up. Lacy braced herself against the powerful tenderness in his expression. "We didn't want you to worry. If you had known what we were about, you would have paced a hole in the floor. Am I right?"

Lacy couldn't lie. He was right; she would have worried herself sick thinking of Adam and Rusty out there alone, watching the jailhouse. *He knew her so well!* A rush of pleasure weakened her knees. "And the purpose of your 'injured' ankle?" she prompted.

"I needed to be here, instead of the jailhouse. How else would I have weaseled an invitation to spend the night?" A disturbing warmth had entered his eyes and Lacy moved away from the hot stove, suddenly feeling the need to step outside for a breath of cool air. The kitchen always seemed hotter with Adam in it.

There was a breathless sound to her voice as she said, "Well, I wish you two had just told me the truth. I feel like a fool, thinking you had hurt yourself and then later, seeing that you were perfectly fine . . ."

"I'm sorry, Lacy," Adam said with husky sincerity. He hadn't known she would react so deeply to the small but necessary deception.

Apparently, neither had Rusty. Reluctantly, he grumbled, "I'm sorry, too, gal. Didn't think . . . I guess."

"It was my idea," Adam confessed, his eyes darkening to the color of storm clouds. Lacy suppressed a shiver of longing as he continued, his voice deepening, his gaze caressing her. "Rusty was just going along with me."

Rusty bristled, not caring that Adam was attempting to help him. "You think you're so smart. It might have been your idea to spread it around the saloon about Lacy rememberin' everything and tellin' you about it and makin' 'em think it was something big," he paused to draw breath, "but it was *my* idea for you to fall through those steps."

Adam let out a long-suffering sigh as Ben bounded back into the kitchen. Lacy dished the food up and set it on the table while Takola poured glasses of tea from a jug that had been cooling in the well. When they were all seated, Adam said, "If I could just get to the mayor, I'd get to the bottom of this mess."

Rusty snorted, obviously still miffed over Adam's patronizing remark. He spooned a helping of beans flavored with bits of ham onto his plate. "Fat chance of that, with all them gunmen around. The mayor's sure to keep 'em close after today." He waggled his fork at Adam, his bushy brows drawn together in a frown. "And mark my words, he knows how bad you'd like to get him alone." He nodded as if pleased with his observation. "Yep. The mayor's not stupid. He's gonna make sure that don't happen."

"I should have squeezed it out of him when I had the chance—"

Lacy coughed and lifted her eyes from her plate. She raised an eyebrow and looked pointedly from Ben to Takola, both of whom were listening to the conversation with wide-eyed interest.

Adam mumbled an apology and helped himself to crisp fried bacon and a steaming square of cracklin' cornbread.

When dinner was over, Takola whisked their empty plates away and stacked them on the counter before hurrying from the room. Lacy watched her hasty exit with a frown as she poured coffee for herself and the men. It wasn't like the girl to leave before the dishes were done, she thought. After a moment, she shrugged, deciding Adam's presence was responsible for Takola's bashful actions. She could think of no other logical excuse.

Adam offered to help wash up. Rusty mumbled something about gathering a few things together and disappeared from the kitchen. Without being told, Ben gathered the scraps for Big Red and slammed out the back door.

They were suddenly alone in the hot kitchen. Lacy stood at the wash pan, absently swishing her fingers to mix the soap shavings into the warm water. She jumped when Adam pressed into her from behind, sliding his strong arms around her waist. He tugged until she fell backward with a sigh of surrender, resting her head onto his shoulder. Weak tears stung her eyes even as a tremor shook her. Memories of his flaming touch hovered at the surface of her mind, teasing her body. He felt so solid, so real. So heavenly.

"Where will you go?" she asked softly, running a soapy hand back and forth over his arm.

Adam nuzzled damp curls aside to kiss her neck, sliding his lips upward to her ear before he said, "It would be best if you didn't know, in case . . . in case they come here asking for me."

Lacy twisted her head around, drawing a sharp breath as her lips grazed his chin. The rough bristles scraped gently over her tender skin, sending thrilling shivers down her spine. She fought the strong urge to move closer to his mouth, knowing that she needed all the willpower she could muster to say what she had to say next.

"I think you should leave Shadow City. Now. Tonight." The words tumbled out in a rush, each one striking her heart a painful blow. She forced herself to go on, ignoring Adam's suddenly tense body pressed against hers. His breath no longer teased her ear and she knew he had stopped breathing. "Forget what you came for, Adam, and leave now before anyone else gets hurt."

Slowly, Adam turned her around in his arms. She didn't have to see his face to know he was angry. "Is that all you're worried about, Lacy?"

She kept her eyes on his chest. To look at him now would break her and she had to be strong, for his sake. "I'm worried about you most of all, but . . ." *God forgive me!* "Innocent people might get hurt." She lifted her hand as if to press it against his chest, but dropped it instead. "One man is dead because of your quest to find out what happened to Sheriff Murddock. Who'll be next? Rusty?" His fingers tightened on her arms and she bit her lip to still a gasp of pain. She didn't blame him for being angry, didn't care as long as it meant he would leave Shadow City.

Coldly, he said, "So, you've decided not to break your own rules. You've decided it's too risky letting someone else into your well-organized life." His voice grew harsh, making Lacy flinch. He had no idea how wrong he was, and she wasn't about to tell him. "Does this mean that what we shared was no different than what I've paid for in the past?"

Her reaction was instinctive. The sharp crack of her open palm against his face echoed around the room. Shock stilled her features as she lifted her horrified eyes to his. She had struck him again! For the second time. . . . The blood pounded through her veins at his icy, determined look. She waited for the fear to rise up and choke her, but it never came.

He held her frozen gaze with the strength of his will as he lifted her against him and turned. With a measured sweep of his arm, he rid the table of the few items remaining. Glass shattered and silverware clanked to the floor. Lacy gasped, clutching his arms to keep from falling. He hoisted her onto the table and shoved her skirts up, thrusting his lower body between her thighs. Without pause he jerked her hips against him and crushed his mouth to hers, claiming, devouring, making a statement that left her in no doubt of its meaning.

Lacy felt his passion trembling through every muscle and her body responded immediately, pressing forward. After a brief, initial struggle, she opened her mouth and let him complete the possession.

And he did. He swept his tongue inside and left no part of her untouched, unbranded. Heat flickered, flared to life, searing their souls together. Callus-roughened hands slid up her thighs, pushing the layers of her dress along in their wake.

Lacy shuddered, knowing she was lost. Adam had won. With a great effort of will, she gripped his face in her hands and jerked her mouth free. Gasping for breath, she panted, "Adam . . . Ben—Takola—"

Adam's eyes glowed with raw desire. He gave his head a little shake, then dipped his mouth to claim her lips once again. This time when he pulled away, it was Lacy who resisted. With a rough growl, he covered her breasts in both big hands. His voice was thick and as raw as the blaze in his eyes. "Kids need to see what it's like between two people who . . . care for each other. It's natural, more natural than you being alone."

Lacy didn't protest when he bent his head to nip her neck and slid his hot mouth across the brief span of tender flesh above the neckline of her dress. She quivered, tensing her legs around his hips. "This is insane . . . we can't . . . not here!"

"No," Adam agreed with a deep sigh of regret. But he didn't let her go. "We can't. But I can hold you and kiss you and show you what you'll miss if you send me away."

"I—I don't *want* to send you away," Lacy blurted, then bit her bottom lip until Adam captured it with his own teeth. She moaned in response. A warm tongue slid across the bruised lip, erasing the hurt.

Ben's matter-of-fact voice washed over Lacy like a bucket of cold well water.

"Ma and Pa used to do that. I remember."

"Ben!" Lacy shoved at her skirts, heat searing her face. Adam stayed in front of her until she had finished arranging her clothing, a half-smile playing about his lips. Lacy jerked her gaze away from the tantalizing sight of his mouth, remembering how it had felt on hers, and on her neck and other places another time. She had a sudden, aching feeling that her life would never be the same. "Ben," she croaked again, pushing at Adam and sliding ungracefully to the floor. "I was just—Adam was just—"

"Getting something out of Lacy's eye," Adam concluded casually. He smiled at Ben and to Lacy's mortification, Ben winked.

"Ben, don't you have something to do? A room to clean? Letters to study?"

"Oh," Ben said, with a grin. "You want me to leave so you and Adam can kiss again?"

"No! Ben . . ."

"I'm going, I'm going." He lifted a hand to Adam and skipped from the room.

Greatly flustered, Lacy shot Adam an accusing look. "See what you've done? Now Ben will think . . . He'll think . . ." Adam grinned. She clenched her fists and hissed, "Go to hell!" But her curse lacked the heat she had intended it to have.

With a warning in his eyes, Adam stalked her. Lacy retreated through the kitchen doorway, trying to stifle her breathless laughter, feeling happy and enormously sad at the same time. *How can we laugh and joke at a time like this?* she wondered, struggling to regain her equilibrium. The realization that they could—and *had*—brought a shocking vision of what the future could be like with Adam Logan in their lives. The bad times would be good times, and the good times would be heaven on earth.

A knock at the door had Lacy stopping in her tracks. She glanced behind her as Adam came swiftly out of the kitchen, pressing a finger to his lips. Her bubble of joy burst as he drew his gun and strode across the living room to the door. When he'd positioned himself behind the door, he motioned to Lacy.

Lacy swallowed and called, "Who is it?" She held a hand to her throat, expecting the worst. The mayor, his henchmen. A horned devil with a spiky tail, here to taunt her for thinking—even for a brief moment—that she could hope for happiness.

Anything but Graham Silverstone's cultured voice.

"Graham Silverstone. It's important that I speak to Sheriff Logan." He sounded urgent.

Rusty clambered down the stairs, his face tense. "Who's at the door?" he demanded, drawing his gun. He saw Adam pressed against the wall by the door and relaxed slightly.

Lacy looked at him, quirking an eyebrow, wondering why he responded so quickly to the knock at the door, when he apparently hadn't heard the sound of shattering glass. "Graham Silverstone. Should I let him in?"

Adam nodded. Rusty finished descending the stairs and followed closely behind Lacy as she strolled to the door and opened it.

At the sight of Lacy, Graham bowed, his face grave. "I have a message for Sheriff Logan. You wouldn't happen to know where he is?"

Lacy jumped as Rusty's hand landed on her shoulder. She clamped her mouth shut and let her grandfather speak, conscious of Adam behind the door.

"I might know where the sheriff's at. What's this about?" Rusty didn't sound the least bit friendly, or the least bit inclined to give away information.

The attorney apparently realized this. He drew himself up and stared at Rusty along his sharp nose. "The mayor's being held hostage," he announced, as if he were announcing the kidnapping of the president.

Rusty snickered, then broke into great guffaws of laughter. When it finally subsided, he drawled, "Is that a fact. Well, then. On second thought, I believe I done forgot where the sheriff's got himself off to."

Graham's expression remained smooth, but there was an

angry glitter in his eyes. "Maybe you'll remember when I tell you who's holding him." He paused and Lacy felt a chill tingle down her back—a premonition that had her stepping forward to grip the doorjamb.

From a great distance, she heard her own voice ask, "Who? Who is it?"

Graham held out a sheet of paper. Lacy snatched it, her hands shaking with fear. She read the message, recognized Takola's distinctive scrawl and swayed beneath a wave of dizziness. Oh, God! It was Takola's handwriting, instructing the mayor to send for Sheriff Logan.

"Your little Indian girl."

17

"I'M GOING WITH you," Lacy stated, her tone daring them to argue.

They did, simultaneously.

"No."

"Absolutely not," Adam said, stepping out from behind the door. Silverstone choked on a gasp at the sight of him. Adam didn't even grace him with a nod.

Lacy drew herself up. "Takola's probably frightened out of her wits—"

"Ha!"

Three pairs of eyes focused on Graham Silverstone as he snorted the disbelieving word. He shifted, flushing. "What I mean is—she isn't—ah, I think the mayor is the frightened one. The Indian—"

"Takola!" Lacy spat at him.

Silverstone jerked as if she'd reached out and slapped him. "Pardon me. *Takola,*" he corrected hastily, "appears to be in control of the situation." He twisted his hat in his hands. "I think we should hurry."

"I'm going," Lacy said again. Rusty and Adam appeared not to have heard her. "Grandpa, you stay with Ben." A note of desperation crept into her voice. "I've got to go to her!"

Adam took her gently by the shoulders, staring into her dark eyes, his own gaze understanding, but firm. "You've got to stay with Ben."

"You'll need me to handle her," Lacy whispered, trembling inside and out. The thought of Takola there all alone twisted her stomach into knots.

Adam's grip tightened. "I can handle Takola. You know I can."

This time, Lacy had no argument ready. Yes, Adam could handle Takola. Between Grandpa and Adam . . . "Okay. I'll stay, but please, please be careful and Adam," she drew in a fortifying breath, "don't let her do anything foolish."

"I won't." Adam smiled, then pulled her in for a quick kiss. "Lock the door after we leave and don't let anyone— *anyone*—in. Understand?"

Lacy managed a nod. Her throat felt tight, as did her chest. "I understand." She grabbed his arm as he started to turn away, feeling his muscles jump in response to her touch. "Adam? Bring her back safely."

"I will."

Rusty patted her cheek as he walked by her to the door, his gaze comforting. "We'll be back afore you know it, Lacy."

"Be careful, Grandpa," Lacy bussed his cheek and squeezed his neck before he could disentangle himself. When the door closed on them, she leaned against it and pressed her hot cheek against the cool wood. Her prayer was simple: *Please God, bring them all home safely.*

She reached up and slid the bolt home, wincing at the rusty sound it made as it slid into place.

They left on foot—since Graham had arrived that way— and made most of the journey in silence. As they climbed the circular drive through the dark, silent trees, Rusty asked, "You didn't put the girl up to this, did you?"

A ghost of a smile lifted the corners of Adam's mouth before he replied, "No. I guess she was listening to the table conversation a lot closer than we thought."

Rusty was breathing hard from the uphill trek. He noted with satisfaction that the attorney had lagged behind. "She hears ever'thin', but it's hard to remember that when she don't talk none."

"Right." Adam glanced up at the light glowing from several well-spaced lamps on the massive porch. He frowned in thought. "I wonder how she managed to sneak past those men."

As if he had conjured them up, Adam heard several warning clicks an instant before he saw the shadows looming in front of him.

The mayor's men coming to greet them, he realized, eyeing the rifles pointed in their direction. Adam tipped his hat. "Evenin'."

"Unbuckle your guns, nice and easy there," one of the shadowed figures growled.

Both men did as he asked without hesitation, letting their weapons fall to the ground. *What else can we do?* Adam thought. Yet he sensed *their* unease as well and found himself looking forward to seeing the mayor. Obviously, Takola had somehow managed to outwit a whole passel of experienced men and the mayor to boot.

Adam wisely held his smile at bay.

"Walk."

Adam and Rusty obeyed, striding ahead of the henchmen and straight into the open doorway of the big house. They were taken upstairs to the mayor's bedroom, the location of which Adam remembered well. Somewhere along the way they lost Graham Silverstone.

The door stood open. As they were pushed forward into the room, Adam quickly took stock of the three men—all facing the same direction. Slowly, his eyes followed the line of the rifles to where the mayor sat in a high-backed, velvet-lined chair by the fireplace. A tray lay upturned at his feet, its contents scattered on the carpeted floor. Adam surveyed the mess, catching the pungent aroma of boiled cabbage, and figured Takola had sneaked up on the mayor while he was eating his dinner.

Takola stood behind the chair with her back to the wall. Her slender arm curved around the mayor's neck to such a degree that Adam knew if Goodrich moved or attempted to move her arm, he would be in deep trouble. The mayor himself looked petrified, his eyes bulging as if she physically choked him. Takola held the blade of a kitchen knife against the fleshy part of the mayor's neck.

Adam stared into Takola's dark, fathomless eyes for a long moment, hoping to convey a silent message. With a barely perceptible nod, Takola indicated that she understood. Adam breathed a sigh of relief; she would not harm the mayor. In fact, he detected a definite humor in her dark eyes.

Obviously the mayor wasn't taking any chances. Adam's lips twitched. A thirteen-year-old girl no bigger than a mosquito had managed to take the town giant hostage, a man who employed no fewer than twenty bodyguards.

How had she gotten past . . . ? Adam's silent wondering ended as he saw the open window. She had climbed the trellis, of course! He turned slightly, meeting Rusty's narrow-eyed gaze and realized the older man had also figured out how Takola got in. They exchanged brief, admiring glances before Rusty took the initiative.

"Girl? You all right?" When Takola nodded, Rusty removed his hat and scratched his head, leaving a tuft of gray hair standing straight up. He clamped his hat upon it. With a shrug, he looked at each of the gunmen in turn. "Guess she wants you to leave the room, boys."

The mayor started to speak—until Takola angled forward and pressed the knife a tiny bit harder against his neck. His Adam's apple bobbed, but he gave up trying to talk. The pasty white of his face became tinted with blue.

Adam choked back a laugh. He suspected the knife wasn't sharp enough to peel a potato, but the mayor didn't know that.

One of the gunmen, a short, stocky man with a wicked scar running across his nose, stepped forward and growled, "How do you know what she wants? The little savage don't talk, does she?"

Adam caught the gleam in Takola's eye and jerked his head once in a sharp, negative gesture. "She don't have to talk. We know what she wants, and she wants you boys to leave the room." His voice dropped to a low warning drawl, "And I'm figuring you'd better do it fast or that knife's gonna slip." Almost before he finished speaking, the gunmen began backing out of the room.

Rusty kicked the door shut with his boot.

"Ease up a little, Takola, so the mayor can talk without cutting his own throat." Adam chuckled at his pun. He hooked his fingers into his belt loop and sauntered closer to the mayor, beginning to enjoy himself. Rusty followed, unable to keep a silly grin from his face.

Takola eased the pressure just enough to allow the mayor to speak, but not more. She smiled openly now, knowing the mayor couldn't see her.

Goodrich swallowed hard and his voice came out as a squeak, giving testimony to his fright. "I—What is it that you want?"

"Information. Lot's of it. The truth."

"Wha—what truth? I told you all I know . . ." Takola tensed her arm and the mayor let out a raspy squeal that sounded remarkably like Big Red.

Adam nodded and Takola obeyed, once again easing the pressure. Apparently, it was enough to convince the mayor that she understood everything being said and that she meant business. "Well? We're listening, Goodrich."

"And we ain't got all night," Rusty chortled, enjoying the show.

"You can start with the day my grandfather died."

Carefully, the mayor lifted his hand and wiped the sweat from his eyes. Takola's arm held steady. "I didn't kill him."

"But you were there." Adam tensed, his eyes narrowing on the mayor's face. "A witness saw you go into Murddock's office around the time he was found."

Goodrich darted his frightened eyes from one intent face to the other. His thick, bejeweled hands trembled where they lay in his lap. "He was already dead when I got there," the mayor said with a defeated sigh. "I swear it. All I did was search the room—and him—for the will. The body was still warm, so I must have just missed whoever killed him."

Adam jerked in reaction. He loosened his fingers from his belt and let his hands fall to his sides so that he could clench them. It was either that or choke the life out of the mayor as the pieces of the puzzle began to fall into place. If the mayor had searched Colt, then that explained why he had been swinging when Lacy found him. "Why did you want the will? What did the will have to do with you?" he demanded in a dangerously soft voice.

Silence stretched. Adam nodded at Takola.

"Wait! I'll tell you, just please . . ." He gulped, sweating hard now. "I figured . . . since Murddock was dead and he didn't have no family close by . . . that it wouldn't matter."

The words whistled from between Adam's clenched teeth as he demanded, "What wouldn't matter?"

"Me and Murddock, we were partners in the mill." When Adam's eyes narrowed to slits, he rushed on, "No one knew, that's the way he wanted it. I tried to get him to sell out when I had enough money saved up, but he wouldn't. Said he wanted to keep a hand in it."

Adam felt some of the tension ease out of him. The mayor's reluctant confession collaborated with Graham Silverstone's story. Silverstone said Cold Murddock thought it best to keep a hand in a few things for the good of the town. It was a relief to discover that his grandfather had not trusted Jamis Goodrich, either.

It also raised another question in his mind; what else had Murddock "kept a hand in"? How many other upstanding citizens in Shadow City would hate to see the resurrection of Cold Murddock's will? Silverstone indicated that Colt had told no one, not even Rusty, of his assets. *Not exactly smart of him,* was Adam's reluctant thought. Unless his grandfather had been completely confident that the will was safe.

Adam shook his head, knowing he would have to sort everything out later. Right now there were questions to ask. "Did you find the will?"

"No . . . I swear on my mother's grave, I didn't find it." The look of frustration on his face convinced Adam he was telling the truth, which immediately led Adam to another disturbing question.

"So when you found out who I was, you decided to just get rid of me?"

When the mayor looked blank, Adam frowned, reminding him, "The night you or one of your boys shot at me." *And almost got Lacy instead.*

The mayor started to shake his head, remembering the knife at his throat in the nick of time. "I told you after it happened that I didn't have nothing to do with it and I'm tellin' you again. It wasn't me or my boys."

Rusty broke his unusual silence. He grunted. "I guess you didn't send that bad boy to the jailhouse last night, either."

"No. Yes." Goodrich looked pained. "I sent him, but not to kill you."

Adam's lips curved in a sarcastic little smile. "Maybe just to persuade me to leave town? But then, you had more than one reason for that, didn't you, Goodrich? You didn't like Salvage settin' up his business, and you didn't want me snooping around and finding out about Colt owning part of the mill."

Goodrich didn't deny either accusation. "Peters wasn't supposed to set fire to the jailhouse. He was supposed to rough you up a little as a warning."

Adam's brow shot upwards. "He? You sent him alone?"

"No, he wasn't alone," the mayor surprised them by saying. "That's how I know what really happened. Glen Anderson was with Peters when the fire started, but they didn't start the fire."

"Then who did?" Adam demanded tightly. His patience was beginning to wear mighty thin.

Both Rusty and Adam tensed as they waited for the

mayor's answer. Takola looked on with a sparkle of interest in her almond-shaped eyes.

Lacy stopped her pacing long enough to glance at the clock. An hour. They had been gone an hour. Please let Takola be all right, she continued to pray. And Adam and Rusty.

Thunder, but she hated waiting almost as much as she hated not knowing!

After they left, she had settled Ben into bed for the night, despite his grumbling about it being his job to watch over her. But his protests lacked strength and he looked tired. Then she'd finished her chores in the kitchen, sweeping up the broken glass and nearly bursting into tears as she recalled the passionate scene with Adam only a short time ago. When that was done, the pacing and waiting had begun.

Now, an hour later she was still pacing. And waiting.

When she came to the end of the stairs, she glanced up, catching sight of Ben peering around his bedroom doorway for the third time. She pretended not to see him, knowing he was only doing what he thought a deputy should be doing: watching over her. She felt guilty about putting him to bed, but she was too tense to have him underfoot asking a thousand questions. Soon, his natural need for sleep would keep him in bed. She whirled and began the familiar journey across the room for a quick peek out the window.

What had Takola been thinking to attempt such a dangerous task? But Lacy knew . . . she knew. Takola was doing this for Adam. With a frustrated sigh, Lacy collapsed onto the sofa. Beside her was the pile containing Adam's things that he'd saved from the fire. The painting, the photo of Sheriff Murddock . . . but no clothes. The faint odor of charred wood hovered around the painting.

Adam would need clothes, and an extra pair of boots. Shaving utensils.

A place to sleep.

Her eyes fell upon the painting, anything to take her mind off what might be happening at the mayor's house. She ran a hand over the rough surface, noticing how it had buckled in a few places. Probably form the heat, she surmised. The canvas would have to be stretched and flattened again with something heavy, and a new frame fashioned.

She could manage the former. With a burst of restless energy, she swept the painting up and marched into the kitchen. This was something to do, something she *could* do while she waited for them to return.

Safe and sound. Yes, they would return safe and sound.

She refused to believe anything else.

Lighting the lamp in the kitchen, she put the painting on the table and quickly went to work prying the blackened frame loose. The wood came apart easily in her hands. She worked slowly and carefully, aware of how much the painting meant to Adam. He had risked his life to save it, and the photo of his grandfather.

Everything else had been lost.

Finally, she pried the last piece from the canvas and set it in the pile with the rest of the dissembled frame. There was a thin wooden backing pressed to the canvas; Lacy turned the painting over so that the backing lay face up. She didn't want to tear the painting, and it appeared to be stuck. Working patiently, she loosened the edges and slowly lifted the backing free. She set the backing against the wall, doubting that it could be reused. Nevertheless, she would let Adam decide.

Dusting her hands, she turned back to the painting, her eyes falling upon the envelopes lined up neatly from top to bottom. Four in all, they were yellowed with age; the wax seals had melted and smeared. The wax, Lacy realized as she stared in bemusement at the envelopes, had been the cause of the back sticking to the canvas.

Excitement added a noticeable tremble to her hands as she cautiously pried the first envelope from the canvas. Could one of these envelopes be the missing will Adam spoke of? she wondered, not daring to so much as breathe.

She held the first envelope up to the light and had begun to pry it open before it occurred to her that what she was doing was wrong. These were Adam's belongings. But her curiosity wouldn't allow her to put it down.

If one of the envelopes contained the will, then that meant

Adam *did* own the ranch in Wyoming. Lacy squeezed her eyes tightly shut. He'd have a home to go to, and not just a dream that had yet to materialize.

Did she want to know? And what was in the other three envelopes? What could possibly be . . . Perhaps there was a clue to what had been happening, something vital that Adam would need to know about now.

Lacy convinced herself that her reasoning was justified and proceeded to open the envelope. She read quickly, her eyes widening with each word. It was a deed to the lumber mill, she realized, and one the bottom line there were two signatures: *Jamis Goodrich* and *Colt Murddock*.

Dazed, she laid the envelope aside and pried the second one loose, working more quickly now. Excitement buzzed through her, as well as shock and fear. The implications of that first deed frightened her.

The second envelope contained the deed to the Snake River Ranch in Wyoming, located near the mouth of the Snake River—all six hundred acres of it—and she wasn't surprised to note only one signature: that of Cold Murddock. She added the deed to the first and started on the third envelope.

It was a bank deposit to the tune of fifty thousand dollars at the Shadow City bank. She lifted an eyebrow at the sum, a strange despondency seeping into her heart. If the will was here, then Adam was rich. He owned a ranch, part of an extremely profitable lumber mill, and had cash in the bank. Somehow, this made him seem further out of reach than before. What would he need with a widow, two unpredictable children, and a grouchy old man when he already had everything a man could desire?

The fourth and last envelope, as she had guessed, held Cold Murddock's last will and testament. Lacy's knees began to shake. She pulled out a chair and slowly sank into it as she scanned the contents.

She was halfway down the page when a shadow fell across her line of vision. Her heart flip-flopped in her chest. Nerve endings jumped instantly alert, tingling a warning.

Someone was standing behind her and it wasn't Ben; the

shadow was too big, too dark. She could hear him breathing, could feel his breath stirring the shorter curls at the nape of her neck. She froze as her throat closed up, locking the scream inside. Ben . . . Ben was upstairs sleeping and she didn't want to awaken him. He would charge recklessly to her rescue, and she couldn't risk his getting hurt.

How had he gotten in? And then she remembered that she had not locked the back door. She'd been too worried about the others to think of her own safety, and that of Ben's. While she was pacing, he must have slipped in, hiding and watching her. . . .

Lacy strangled on a sob.

"Well, well, well," a rough voice drawled in her ear. It was followed by a nasty, pleased-sounding chuckle as the aged paper was snatched from her suspended hand.

Lacy remembered to breathe when the light began to dim, and when she did, she drew in the distinct smell of cattle, wood smoke, and stale sweat.

An unpleasant collection of scents she remembered from a long time ago.,

On a chilly day in May during blackberry winter.

Shaking inside, but striving to appear calm on the outside, Lacy stood and faced the man. He was older, and his hair was shorter, neater, but she recognized him. The bulky overcoat she remembered was gone, of course. He wore a western-style shirt with silver tassels swinging from the pockets. Silver studs decorated the sleeves, matching the silver buttons. His jacket was wrinkled, but of good quality, as were the snakeskin boots he wore. Expensive leather pants hugged his muscular thighs, but it was his belt buckle that drew her attention, nearly hidden by the strap of his holster.

In the center of the buckle was a pair of snake's eyes, pale blue in color.

And then she remembered. Adam had worn the same emblem on his belt buckle the day she'd first met him. Something seemed vaguely familiar about the snake's eyes even then, but the memory had slipped away before she could grasp it.

Now she did. Now it made sense. Snake River Ranch.

With a calm she was miles from feeling, she said, "You must be Rudy Wagner, Adam's stepfather." *And the man who killed Colt Murddock*, she added silently, with absolute conviction. His presence in her kitchen brought the pieces of the puzzle together with crystal clarity.

He was the one behind the shooting, and most likely the one behind the burning of the jailhouse. And the fire to Silverstone's office the day of Sheriff Murddock's death. He must have been erasing evidence of the will, but apparently had been unable to discover Colt's hiding place.

But *she* had, and now Rudy Wagner was here, holding the will in his hands.

Wagner grinned, showing tobacco-stained teeth. Lacy thought he could have been handsome, if not for the signs of age and the unmistakable cruelty in his dark eyes. At some point, Adam's mother had certainly found him attractive.

"So you know who I am."

There was an underlying menace in the question that Lacy instinctively knew she should ignore. She had to play for time and reveal as little as possible until Adam returned. "Your belt buckle—the snake's eyes. Adam has one like it." She lifted one shoulder in a matter-of-fact shrug. "It wasn't hard to figure out who you were, Mr. Wagner. Adam's mentioned you several times." *Which isn't a lie*.

Wagner's smile turned ugly at the mention of Adam again. "I'll bet he has, the sneaky little bastard," he spat. "You his woman?"

Was she? And which answer would be the safest one? Rudy Wagner didn't look like a stupid man, she thought, and certainly not easily fooled. She had already admitted that Adam had mentioned him, and that implied personal interest, at the very least. Yet she feared Wagner would use the knowledge in any way he could.

Either way . . . The conclusion came after a long hesitation. "We know each other . . . very well, but he certainly doesn't live here." Her subtle probing seemed lost on Wagner. She wasn't going to find out how he had known

Adam would be here—or *should* have been here. It would help if she knew how much *he* knew.

Wagner chuckled. "He don't live at the jailhouse anymore, neither."

Lacy fought for composure, for an innocent look. She wasn't good at acting, but this was a life-and-death situation. "Oh, you've heard about the fire?" If she could convince him that she knew nothing about him or his activities, then maybe she could buy enough time to figure something out.

She needed to warn Adam and Rusty.

Of one thing she was certain: she couldn't show fear. Adam had told her enough about Rudy Wagner for her to know this. Lacy knew his kind well.

Summoning all the acting skills within her, Lacy forced herself to smile politely. "Would you like a cup of coffee, Mr. Wagner? Adam should return shortly. He went with my grandfather up to the mayor's house on business, but you're welcome to wait here for him." As if she had a choice in the matter. "I'm sure he'll be glad to see you." She moved toward the stove before he could see the lie in her eyes. Just before she turned, she caught sight of his surprised expression and felt a rush of hope. *It just might work*, she thought, trying to still her trembling.

"Reckon I could use a cup." Paper rustled; spurs jangled as he shifted.

Lacy listened to the sounds, her mind racing frantically ahead. It would be disastrous for Adam and Rusty to return, knowing nothing, yet she knew Adam would want her to detain Wagner as long as she could.

She added tinder to the wood and struck a match to it. Watching the flames flicker and catch, she said conversationally, "I've been working on this old painting of Adam's." She darted a quick glance at him. He had paused in his reading, his eyes narrowed on her. She swallowed and continued, once again focusing on the stove. "It was about the only thing he managed to save from the fire. I found those papers stuck between the backing and the canvas, but I left my darn glasses at . . . upstairs, so I can't read a

word it says." *Here goes nothing!* Straightening, she shook
the kettle to check the water level and asked with casual
curiosity, "Is it anything important?"

She heard movement, then the scraping of a chair as he
drew it away from the table. Her back stiffened. Was he
wondering why she didn't look at him? *Dear God, please let
him believe me!*

"You might say that," Wagner drawled. "Are you tryin' to
tell me Adam don't know about these papers?"

Lacy let her breath out very slowly. "No. As I said, I
thought I would surprise him by flattening the buckles out
of that painting." She laughed as if she didn't have a brain
in her head. "He's probably not interested in any old papers,
anyway." Hoping he didn't notice her shaking hands, she
retrieved the coffee tin from the shelf above the stove and
measured the beans into the hand grinder before spooning
the ground mixture into the kettle.

She waited for Wagner to respond, but all she heard was
the ominous sound of a gun being cocked, followed by a
distinct thumping noise as he placed the gun onto the table.

She could feel the terror drawing the skin tight across her
face and knew she didn't dare turn around.

"I think he might be a bit more interested than you think,
little lady. Now why don't you take a seat while that coffee's
cookin'. You look nervous."

Nervous? Oh, she was more than nervous. She was
frightened out of her wits—but not for herself; for Adam
and Rusty, because she knew what that gun was for.

Rudy Wagner planned to shoot Adam when he walked
through the door.

18

THE GAME WAS over and she had lost.

Lacy moved stiffly to the chair as Wagner gathered the documents together and slid them into the envelopes before tucking them into an inside pocket of his jacket.

Lacy stared at the gun lying on the table, considering her chances of snatching it up. At his nasty chuckle, she jumped, her eyes flying to his face.

"You could try it, but you wouldn't make it," Wagner sneered. "A little lady like you, goin' up against a man like me. Seems Adam don't take after his pa. I'd have showed you what you get for having thoughts like that."

The blood drained from Lacy's face as the meaning of his words sank in. "You're not his pa!" she hissed. Surprisingly, she felt more anger than fear. Adam was nothing like this man; it enraged her to hear Wagner make such a comparison.

Wagner studied her for a long moment longer, but Lacy refused to quake. "Looks like I've got two options—no, make that three. If you were tellin' the truth about Adam not knowing about these papers, then I could kill you and leave." His eyes narrowed. "I could do that, or I could kill that sneaky stepson of mine."

Lacy moistened her lips, determined not to show how much his options scared her. "And—and the third option?"

"I could kill both of you. That way I wouldn't be leaving any witnesses."

But what about Grandpa? she nearly asked aloud. Had he forgotten that Rusty would be returning with Adam? Oh, God, Takola! Takola would be with them too!

The sudden banging on the front door startled them both. Their eyes locked. Lacy struggled to keep all traces of fear from her expression.

"'Pears the decision has been made," he said, rising from the chair. He motioned her with a jerk of his head, scooping the gun from the table. "Go answer the door. I'll be right behind you and if you try anything, I'll shoot you, then I'll shoot whoever comes through that door."

He would. Lacy saw this certainty in the mean squint of his eyes. She rose and walked slowly into the living room, praying that Ben wouldn't come racing down the stairs. He might startle Wagner, and Wagner might shoot before thinking. The image hastened her steps. When she reached the door, Wagner nudged her in the back with the gun.

"Ask who it is."

Lacy closed her eyes and prayed as she obeyed. "Who's there?"

The banging ceased at the sound of her voice. "It's Rusty. Let me in."

"It's my grandfather . . . I told you he was with Adam."

The gun poked her again. She jumped. "Ask him where Adam is," he ordered in a whisper.

"Where's Adam, Grandfather?" Oh, dear God, please let him notice that she called him "Grandfather," and not "Grandpa," or "Rusty," as she normally did. She *never* called him "Grandfather."

There was a brief silence on the other side of the door. Lacy forced herself to keep breathing evenly. Finally

Rusty's voice came to them, sounding impatient. "Adam's still at the mayor's house. Everythin' turned out fine. You gonna let me in or am I gonna have to stand out here all night?"

Same grumpy old man, Lacy thought. Yet she wondered why he didn't mention Takola. He would know how concerned she was.

"Let him in," Wagner whispered. "And remember, one wrong move and he's dead. So are you."

Lacy unlocked the door and pulled it open.

"What's gotten into you—" Rusty broke off as he caught sight of Wagner behind Lacy. His eyes rounded. "Who's that?" he demanded.

Wagner stepped out from behind Lacy, grabbing her arm in a rough grip as he pointed the gun at Rusty. "Get in here, old man, and shut the door. I'd just as soon shoot you, so be quick about it."

When Lacy heard the soft click of a gun being cocked, she dropped her surprised eyes to the gun in Wagner's hand. She thought he'd already cocked it back in the kitchen. . . .

"You're not as smart as you used to be," Adam said, pressing the barrel of his gun against Wagner's temple.

Lacy stared at Adam in amazement, blinking her eyes to make sure she wasn't conjuring him up. No, he was there, standing behind Wagner. He had obviously sneaked in through the back door while they were distracted with Rusty at the front door. Too sure of himself, Wagner had never considered that Adam might find out he was here waiting for him.

Beyond him, she saw Ben hovering in the kitchen doorway. His excited face was flushed with pride.

Ben. Ben had discovered Wagner and slipped out to warn Adam and Rusty, Lacy realized. A thrill of pure joy thrummed through her.

It quickly vanished as Wagner said, "Put you gun down, or the old man gets it."

Lacy thought she might faint as Adam laughed. "Go ahead. I'm mighty tired of his grumbling anyway."

Wagner muttered a foul curse and dropped the gun.

* * *

Takola had been waiting on the porch for Rusty's signal. She came in now, her oval face flushed with the night's victory. To her, there had been no danger, only the need to do what must be done.

Lacy hugged the little figure tight with a mixture of pride and exasperation. Later, they would have a long talk about little Indians sneaking out to take big men hostage.

She didn't object when Adam instructed Ben to tie the prisoner to a chair Rusty had fetched from the kitchen, but when that was done, Lacy sent both Takola and Ben upstairs with stern orders to remain there.

The four adults then gathered in the living room, with Wagner in the center. The scene resembled an inquisition, which, in fact, it was. Lacy watched from her position on the sofa. Rusty stood behind her, his hands on her shoulders. The air seemed thick with expectant tension.

Adam walked slowly around Wagner. "You killed Colt Murddock, didn't you? Killed him so you could have the ranch."

"I didn't kill nobody," Wagner growled, struggling against the rope. It was a useless gesture; Ben had tied him well.

Adam's voice remained even, almost casual—but relentless. "There was a witness, Wagner, so you might as well tell me how you managed to get my grandfather to write the note, and to put that rope around his neck."

"I don't have to tell you nothin'! You're talkin' about something that happened fifteen years ago, and there ain't a judge alive that would convict me."

Adam propped his booted foot on the bottom chair rung right between Wagner's legs and leaned in close to his face. Softly, he asked, "Judge? Who said anything about a judge?" Without breaking eye contact with Wagner, he asked Rusty. "You got plenty of rope left, don't you, deputy? Enough to hang this man?"

Rusty grinned. "Yep. Plenty of rope. You're the sheriff, I'm the deputy. Won't nobody stop us."

Wagner began to show the first signs of genuine fear. "You can't do that."

"Oh? Like the deputy there said, who's to stop us? Everyone will know you set fire to the jail, and everyone will know you killed Colt Murddock." He clucked his tongue. "People will be mighty angry at you when they find out. All these years they've been believing their hero hung himself."

Wagner's face filled with blood. He looked frustrated enough to knock Adam down with his spit. "Yes!" he hissed. "Yes, I killed Murddock!" He laughed wildly. "It was easy. All I did was describe to him what I was gonna do to your ma—and you—if he didn't go along with me."

Lacy tensed at Adam's murderous expression. She started to go to him, but Rusty held her back. It shamed her to realize that her grandfather trusted Adam's temper more than she did. Biting her lip, she tried to relax against the back of the sofa, telling herself that she understood his rage. Because of Rudy Wagner's greed, Colt Murddock had given his life for his daughter and grandson.

Because of Rudy Wagner, Colt Murddock's reputation had all but shriveled and died.

Adam's voice was harsh with suppressed emotion. "And you followed me here to Shadow City?" When Wagner nodded once, Adam continued, "Because you were afraid I'd discover the truth even after all these years. So you tried to kill me that night on the road into town, and yesterday, you tired to burn me alive. You also killed Brody Peters because he saw you. But you made the mistake of letting the other man get away.

He didn't wait for Wagner to deny the charges; he already knew the truth from Glen Anderson, the man who had been with Brody Peters the night of the fire. Shoving himself away, he turned his back on Wagner to give himself time to control his deep, bitter rage. He clenched his fists and ground his teeth together. Finally, he faced Wagner, but his harsh words were for Rusty. "Get him out of my sight before I kill him with my bare hands."

The pressure on Lacy's shoulders eased, then disappeared as Rusty released her. "Where do you want me to take him? We ain't got no jail. . . ."

"To hell, for all I care." Adam sighed heavily. "See if Matt's got an empty stall. Keep him tied, and appoint someone to watch him until we can take him into St. Louis to stand trial."

Rusty nodded and began the task of untying the intricate series of knots Ben had taken great pains to create. After a considerable amount of fumbling and cursing, he freed Wagner from the chair and jerked him to his feet. Before he led him out the front door, Lacy stopped him.

"Wait—Grandpa." Lacy leaped from the sofa. She'd almost forgotten! Or had she simply wanted to forget? "He's got something that belongs to Adam, something I found in the back of the painting." Crossing to Wagner, she reached her trembling hand inside his jacket and removed the envelopes. Her eyes were shadowed, somber, as she handed them to Adam. "The will, the deed to the lumber mill, a bank deposit, and the deed to the ranch."

Adam's stunned expression should have made her feel good inside. Instead, she felt as if she had lost something more valuable than all the riches he held in his hands. She turned before he could see the pain and the tears, fled before he could guess at how thoroughly he had managed to capture her heart, only to break it into a million pieces.

She knew he would leave now. He had accomplished what he came here to do and now he was free. She wasn't enough to hold him, and her pride wouldn't allow her to beg him to stay.

Reaching her room, she shut the bedroom door and dropped across the bed, burrowing her face into the pillow to muffle the sounds of her ragged sobs.

August crawled slowly by. September arrived and temperatures began to cool, much to the relief of the townspeople preparing for the celebration.

In her bedroom, Lacy held herself still as Carrianna worked on pinning the hem of her new dress. She stroked the satin material, her eyes growing misty as she recalled the look of sheer pride on Ben's face when he presented the gift. The story had unfolded then, of how Takola had drawn him a picture of the dress in the window and made him understand that Lacy wanted the dress.

Lacy was stunned, to say the least—and suspicious. She doubted Ben could have saved enough to pay for the dress, and she suspected Adam had helped.

Adam . . .

She had known there would be an empty hole in her heart, but she hadn't reckoned it would be so large. Throwing herself into the preparations for the town's anniversary with a fury that bordered on madness helped, but there were too many long, lonely nights when all she could think of was Adam. He had said his good-byes over a month ago, promising to return after he'd taken care of business at the Snake River Ranch.

Deep in her heart she feared that she would never see Adam again. She could hardly blame him. Shadow City held nothing but bitter reminders for Adam. And now there was the responsibility of the ranch.

She wasn't the only one who suffered from the sheriff's absence. Ben moped around the house, as did Rusty. And Takola . . . Takola spent long hours drawing for Adam. Lacy knew that the Indian girl was attempting to make up for the drawings Adam had lost in the fire. The stack of papers grew steadily, in anticipation of Adam's return.

Lacy felt a very real, physical pain clench her heart. She was afraid Takola was going to be disappointed. She feared they all were.

"Lacy?" Carrianna's gentle voice brought her back to the present. "You look like you're a thousand miles away."

A wan smile curved Lacy's mouth as she looked down at Carrianna, crouched at her feet. "I was. Are you about finished?"

"Just about. Then I'll start on the waist. You've lost too much weight lately, you know, and you were thin enough as it was."

The subtle rebuke made Lacy wince. Carrianna was right. Her appetite had steadily declined since Adam had said good-bye. Nothing could tempt her, and some foods made her stomach lurch with nausea. Rusty was threatening to haul her in to see Dr. Martin if she didn't start eating more.

Carrianna sensed her friend's melancholy and suspected that she knew the cause. Worry shadowed her eyes as she tucked and pinned. "What does Rusty think about running for mayor now that Goodrich has left town? I'll bet he's excited."

"A little. He's not sure he's qualified for the position."

"Better him than Mr. Silverstone," Carrianna mumbled around the pins. "I can't believe the town council would nominate him after the way he covered for the mayor."

Lacy shrugged, earning a sharp reprimand from Carrianna. "Ooops. Sorry. I think Mr. Silverstone was blind to the mayor's faults—as much as everyone else was. He can't be blamed for not knowing."

"Well." Carrianna sounded doubtful. "Maybe you're right, and my pa would definitely agree with you. I feel sorry for Mary Ann, though. Everyone's whispering behind her back about her grandfather."

"I know *that* feeling. Remember when the mayor spread those rumors about Rusty drinking on the job?" Carrianna nodded and Lacy continued, "I knew they weren't true, but I also knew that I couldn't convince everyone, so I said nothing."

"Mary Ann's not like you," Carrianna pointed out. "You couldn't care less what other people think as long as *you* know it isn't true. Social standing is everything to Mary Ann, and she relied a lot on her grandfather's reputation."

"You're right." Lacy sighed, wishing Carrianna would finish. She was getting tired of standing in one place and the sounds from the window beckoned her.

Carrianna worked her way from the shoulder to the waist, tucking and pinning. After a moment, she froze. "Lacy?"

"Hmmm?"

"I think you might have a problem."

Something in her tone alerted Lacy. She frowned and glanced down. "What is it? I'm sure we can fix it. . . ." She met Carrianna's wide-eyed gaze. "What?"

Sitting back on her heels, Carrianna removed the pins from her mouth and spoke with obvious hesitation. "I've helped you make dresses for yourself, before, right?" Still frowning, Lacy nodded, encouraging her to continue. "I know your measurements like the back of my hand, and this doesn't make sense . . . unless . . ."

Lacy placed a hand on her left hip and glowered at Carrianna. "What doesn't make sense? Spit it out, Carrie."

"You've lost weight . . . everywhere but your waist. And you've been sick."

Lacy snapped her mouth closed, staring at her friend as if she suddenly turned into a horned toad. "Are you saying what I think you're saying? You think I'm pregnant?" Her voice rose on the last word, then quickly lowered as she continued, shock thrumming through her. "I can't be pregnant . . . can I?"

Carrianna gazed at her with deeply shadowed eyes. Color crept into her creamy complexion. "Did you . . . did you and Adam . . .?"

Instead of blushing, Lacy grew pale as she realized how long it had been since her last monthly flow. Dear God, she was going to have Adam's baby! A surge of joy seized her, almost immediately followed by terror. She grabbed Carrianna's shoulders and shook her earnestly. "You can't tell a soul, Carrie. Promise me. Promise me you won't mention this to Adam if he comes back."

"I—I promise. But Lacy, what if he doesn't come back? You'll have to go to him at the ranch."

Lacy dropped her hands as the joy she'd felt on realizing she was going to have the child she'd always wanted sank into despair. She didn't want Adam to know, because she wanted him for herself. She wanted his decision, whatever that was, to be something he would be happy with the rest of his life.

And if he decided he didn't want her in his life, then she would leave Shadow City to have the baby. She wouldn't shame Rusty, although she knew her grandfather would stand by her.

She grabbed for the bedpost as dizziness washed over her. Victoria . . . She could stay with Victoria until the baby was born, then she could come back home. No one would think to doubt her story of an orphaned baby, not after Ben and Takola.

The possibility that she would have to lie to the world about her own baby made her sick. Adam's baby.

Leaving Carrianna sitting on the floor, Lacy stumbled to the open window and fresh air. She looked to the left in the direction of town. The new jailhouse was nearly finished, and soon the town council would appoint a new sheriff, since Adam was gone and Rusty would likely be elected mayor. The streets were swarming with activity as people prepared for the upcoming celebration tomorrow. Although it was a yearly event, Lacy sensed an eagerness in the air that had not always been there, not since the death of Colt Murddock.

She knew why. The townspeople knew the truth now, and the shadow that had hung over the celebration of the town's birth for fifteen years was gone. Their hero did not die a coward's death, but died in the name of sacrifice and love. A dedication to Colt Murddock was planned, and a monument would be fashioned in his honor.

Adam would be proud, she thought, leaning her head against the windowpane. Behind her, she heard the rustling of Carrianna's skirts as she got to her feet. She needed time alone to think about things, but she didn't want to hurt her friend's feelings.

Carrianna seemed to read Lacy's mind. "If you'll take that dress off, I can start the alterations." Her voice was gentle, sympathetic. It brought tears to Lacy's eyes, tears that her friend couldn't see. "If you don't mind, I'll take it home and work on it so that I can be there if Pa needs me."

Lacy moved away from the open window and began to take the dress off. She felt scared and euphoric, a combination that sizzled her nerves and made her stomach lurch in protest.

Adam had promised Ben he would return in time for the celebration. Tomorrow she would know if he told the truth.

Tomorrow she would know her future.

The day of the celebration was bright and beautiful, with clear, almost painfully blue skies. It was noon, and people began to drift toward the center of the park to gather at the hastily built platform. There, the results of the election would be announced.

Lacy felt like a princess in the lavender dress. Carrianna had loaned her a lacy black parasol, and Takola had made her a beautiful beaded purse to hang from her wrist. As she approached the crowd gathered around the platform with Takola at her side, she smiled and waved at Ben, who manned a booth that served cold apple cider. Rusty stood a short distance from the booth, surrounded by his supporters, clean-shaven and dressed in a light-blue suit with a white satin vest. Lacy thought he looked very handsome.

The only thing missing from this perfect day was Adam Logan.

Lacy smiled and nodded until she thought her face would crack from the strain. She didn't feel happy, couldn't share in the exuberance of the crowd. Her gaze continue to wander among the press of people wearing their Sunday best, looking for Adam. The longer she looked, the lower her spirits sank.

A tap on her shoulder brought her whirling around, her heart leaping into her throat. When she focused on Lester Salvage's worried face, she masked her disappointment with a bright smile. "Mr. Salvage! Where's Victoria, didn't you bring her with you? And the girls . . ."

"She's havin' her baby, Miz Ross, and she sent me to get you." He twisted his hat between nervous fingers. "I know you're busy and all, but she's having a rough time of it and I didn't know if the doc here would, well . . ." he trailed off into frustrated silence.

Lacy didn't hesitate. She grabbed Takola's hand and signaled to Rusty, who promptly left the small crowd of people and came to her. "Grandpa, Victoria's having her baby and she wants me. Keep an eye on Ben and good luck with the election." She bussed his check and followed Lester's stocky figure to the waiting wagon before he could respond. Along the way, she spotted Dr. Martin sampling jellies at a display booth. She detoured with Takola in hand.

"Dr. Martin! Victoria Salvage is in labor. I'm going, but she may need your help."

"Send for me, if you need me," Dr. Martin said, popping a biscuit filled with jelly into his mouth. He swallowed. "You've helped with birthing before?" Lacy nodded, opening her mouth to explain to him the extent of her knowledge, but Dr. Martin cut her off with soothing words. "You'll do just fine, Mrs. Ross, and she will probably be more comfortable with you."

Lacy closed her mouth and headed for the waiting wagon, relieved to know that Dr. Martin would come if needed. Once in the wagon seat, Lester slapped the reins over the two horses and they took off at a mad gallop. Lacy and Takola gripped the seat and exchanged a grin.

They reached the homestead in half the time it had taken her and Adam that unforgettable day. Jesse and Tory raced out to meet them, their little faces pinched with worry. Without a word being spoken, Takola understood what to do. She would keep the girls occupied while Lester and Lacy looked after Victoria.

They found Victoria in obvious pain. She was stretched out on the bed, a piece of thick leather clenched between her teeth. Sweat poured from her face. When she caught sight of Lacy, she managed a grimace that hardly resembled the smile she intended.

"Big baby," she panted, stiffening as another pain gripped her tiny frame. Lacy rushed to her side and offered her hand, which Victoria immediately took and squeezed until Lacy felt like screaming herself.

Gallantly, Victoria kept the scream locked inside as the pain crested, then subsided. Between pants of breath, she said, "Must push on my stomach, help me."

Lacy froze, her eyes wide and fearful. She had participated in several births after the death of the old doctor, before Dr. Martin had arrived, but they had never involved anything that sounded so dangerous. Holding the woman's hand was the extent of her experience. As she hesitated, thinking they should send for Dr. Martin, Victoria placed her hand on her hard stomach right above the navel.

"Push here!" the determined Indian woman nearly shouted.

Lacy pushed, biting her lip as Victoria strained and twisted on the bed. Lester was positioned to catch the baby; with a mighty heave, Victoria expelled the infant into his hands. Lacy's face was chalky white. Victoria laughed as Lester held the baby in the air, grinning proudly.

"It's a boy, just like you said, Vickie. A big boy."

"I knew it," Victoria said, collapsing against the pillows.

Silently, Lacy slid to the floor in a dead faint.

Lacy breathed in—and choked as she inhaled a lungful of ammonia. She struggled upright, pushing at the hand torturing her with that awful smell. Her stomach rolled ominously, and for a tense moment she thought she would be sick. She held herself still until the nausea passed, keeping her eyes tightly closed.

"Don't bring that near me again," she ordered, in a grumpy voice she hardly recognized.

"Should I expect this when we have *our* first baby?"

Lacy's eyes snapped open. She blinked rapidly, convinced that she was hallucinating. Adam's face blurred, then came into sharp focus. Several emotions glimmered in his eyes: concern, love, and that familiar hungry look she recognized instantly.

And then his words sank in. He'd said something about a baby . . . *their* baby. How did he know, when she had only discovered it herself yesterday? Slowly, Lacy sat up. She looked around, bewildered to find herself on a small bed in an unfamiliar room. Beyond Adam, Takola, Jesse, Tory, and Lester hovered in the doorway.

"I must have fainted," she murmured, her stunned gaze going once again to Adam's beloved face. She searched his features with a hunger that matched his own. God, how she had missed him. To her amazement, tears welled and began to tumble down her cheeks. She tried to blink them away, but they just kept coming. "I don't know what's wrong with me. Victoria—"

"Is fine, and so is little Lester." Lester ducked his head and smiled. "She insisted on naming him after me."

Adam cupped Lacy's shoulders and helped her sit upright. "Are you all right, now, darlin'?"

His low, husky voice spread weakness throughout her body. She hoped she wasn't expected to stand anytime soon. She glanced from one face to the other, then slowly brought her gaze back to Adam. His hair was a little longer, his face darker, but otherwise he was the same man who possessed her heart. "What—what are you doing here?" she whispered, surprised to find she could talk at all. Her throat felt saturated with still yet more tears waiting to be shed.

Adam smiled—a slow, lazy smile. His hands on her shoulders tightened, then brought her forward as he kissed her tears away. He mumbled against her mouth, "I was looking for you, and Rusty told me I would find you here. I couldn't wait, so here I am."

He couldn't wait. She repeated the words in her mind, licking her lips and tasting the salt from her tears. When she glanced at the doorway again, she was startled to discover it empty. She was alone with Adam. How many times had she imagined this moment since he'd left? A thousand? A million?

But still he hadn't said the words she ached to hear. "Why did you come back?" Their mouths were less than an inch apart, their breath mingling. She quivered, anticipating the feel of that bold, sensuous mouth claiming hers. She felt his smile.

"Because," he said, nuzzling the corners of her mouth until she thought she would go mad, "I promised Ben. And . . . I missed you. I can't live without you." And then he kissed her, proving his words true.

Long moments later they drew apart to fill their lungs with much-needed air. Lacy was as pliable as soft butter in a warm room. Beneath her palm, his heart beat strong and steady, and she closed her eyes against the painful pleasure of it. When Adam moved his hands up to cup her face, she looked at him and caught her breath at his serious, almost frightened expression.

"Will you marry me, Lacy Lynn Ross?"

Adam—doubtful? It was a new experience for Lacy.

With a tenderness that threatened to consume her, she said, "Yes. I'll marry you, and I'll go wherever you want me to go." She smiled at his huge sigh of relief.

"I've been offered the job as sheriff." He matched her smile.

"Oh? And what did you say?" Lacy held her breath, telling herself it didn't matter. She would gladly follow him anywhere.

"I said yes." Adam kissed her nose, then tenderly traced her lips with his fingers.

Lacy trembled with happiness, afraid to believe that this moment was really happening. Boldly, she flicked her tongue over the tip of his questing finger. He growled low in his throat, a warning that rushed down to her toes. "What about your ranch?" she inquired softly.

"My brothers are perfectly capable of handling the ranch," Adam said, exploring the shape of her ear. His eyes were hooded, his mouth taut with desire.

"Adam . . . how did you know about the baby?"

Adam met her liquid gaze, his brows drawing together in puzzled frown. "Rusty told me."

"Rusty?" Lacy gaped. "*Rusty* told you about the baby?"

"Yes. I went to the park first, and he told me you were here, helping Victoria with the baby."

Lacy slumped in his arms, chuckling. When he continued to stare at her in bewilderment, she relented, "I thought you were talking about *our* baby."

It was Adam's turn to freeze. His gaze stilled on her flushed face. When Lacy cocked an eyebrow at him, a look of wonder dawned in his eyes. "You mean—that is—*we're* going to have a baby?"

A wide smile spread across her mouth. She hadn't been sure how he would react, but his obvious elation was beyond her wildest dreams. "Yes. *We're* going to have a baby, too."

She was crushed in his arms for an eternity, and when she finally had to loosen the embrace to breathe, she saw that Adam's eyes were overly bright.

"You're beautiful," he whispered.

"So are you," Lacy countered, then laughed at his chagrined expression.

"That dress looks sumptuous on you, but I think you should take it off before it gets wrinkled." He rose as he spoke, kicking the door shut and latching it. When he turned back to her, Lacy's eyes widened to the extreme.

"Adam?"

"Hmmm?" He began unbuttoning his shirt, his face a mask of innocence.

"Did you forget where we are?"

"Of course not, darlin'."

She trembled as he peeled his shirt off, baring his glorious chest to her avid gaze. "Do you think they'll mind?"

He smiled. "Do you think they don't already know?" he countered huskily. "I happen to know that Takola took the girls for a walk, and Lester is with Victoria."

"But . . ." Lacy bit her lip in confusion. "But how did you know?"

His smile widened. "Because that's what I *told* them to do."

"Oh. In that case . . ." Lacy held out her arms to him, her eyes glowing with desire and a happiness that surpassed any she had ever known before. "I love you," she whispered.

"And I love you," Adam said, striding into her waiting arms.

Epilogue

$\mathscr{B}$EN SAT AT the bottom of the stairs with his chin in his hand, watching the two men pacing back and forth across the living-room floor.

Adam passed Rusty, walked to the end of the room, then pivoted. He reached into his shirt pocket for the fifth time, removing the tiny silver star.

Rusty finished his lap and returned, growling at Adam as he gazed at the star. "Told you it might be a girl, you stubborn ass. She can't wear no star!"

"Just in case, old man. Just in case." Adam began walking again, tense as a bowstring. What was taking so long? Victoria had assured him everything was going fine, but he'd be damned if he'd wait much longer before going to see for himself.

He brushed Rusty's shoulder and considered slugging him just as he caught sight of Takola descending the stairs. He froze. Ben cocked his head around and Rusty came to stand beside Adam.

"Well, girl?" Rusty demanded, when it appeared Adam couldn't find his tongue.

Suddenly, to the amazement of the three watching, Takola's mouth moved and sound emerged. Her voice was light and melodious as she said, "Girl. Lacy fine." And then she smiled.

Adam broke loose from his paralysis and took the stairs two at a time. Ben was right behind him, and Rusty came behind Ben at a spritely pace.

They all crowded into Lacy's room, but it was Adam who was brave enough to approach the bed. He crouched beside it, leaning his elbows on the mattress.

Lacy lay against the pillows, her face flushed from her recent exertions. Damp hair clung to her cheeks and sweat beaded on her upper lip.

Adam thought she was the most beautiful woman he'd ever seen.

Hesitantly, his gaze dropped to the bundle she held in the crook of her arm.

"Takola told us it was a girl," he said in a hushed voice filled with fatherly awe.

Lacy tilted her face up to look at him, a question in her eyes. "She did? She *told* you?"

Adam smiled and brushed his finger across the golden hair on top of the tiny head. The baby seemed to sense his presence; she squirmed and yawned. Adam's eyes widened at the sight of his daughter's tiny mouth. He continued to stare in amazement at this tiny human being he and Lacy had created together.

Belatedly, he remembered Lacy's question. "Yes, she told us. She also said you were fine?" He turned it into a question, pulling his gaze from the baby to look at his wife. *His woman*.

"Yes, I'm fine." She sighed, her eyes taking on a dreamy look. "Tired, happy, and fine. Thank you, Adam Logan."

"Thank *you*, Lacy Lynn Logan, for this beautiful daughter." Adam stroked Lacy's cheek with a loving hand. "Susannah, then?" If it had been a boy, they were going to name it Colt, and Susannah if it was a girl, after his mother.

Lacy nodded, rubbing her face against the coarse hair on his arm. She closed her eyes in contentment. "Susannah, and the next one will be Colt."

Suddenly, Adam was pushed aside. Rusty glowered at him. "It's my turn, you sappy goat. I want to look at my great-granddaughter."

"And *I* want to look at my new sister," Ben announced, shouldering his way between the two men.

Susannah opened her blue eyes and blinked, then shook her fist in the air as if she were admonishing her admirers for fighting.

Ben's jaw fell to his chest. His eyes grew round as he pointed and exclaimed, "She's just like Grandpa!"

Laughter echoed around the room. Adam looked at Lacy and their eyes met, held. Simultaneously, they mouthed the words, "I love you."

ROMANCE FROM THE HEART OF AMERICA
Homespun Romance

__A CHERISHED REWARD	0-515-11897-4/$5.99
by Rachelle Nelson	
__TUMBLEWEED HEART	0-515-11944-X/$5.99
by Tess Farraday	
__TOWN SOCIAL	0-515-11971-7/$5.99
by Trana Mae Simmons	
__LADY'S CHOICE	0-515-11959-8/$5.99
by Karen Lockwood	
__HOME TO STAY	0-515-11986-5/$5.99
by Linda Shertzer	
__MEG'S GARDEN	0-515-12004-9/$5.99
by Teresa Warfield	
__COUNTY FAIR	0-515-12021-9/$5.99
by Ginny Aiken	
__HEARTBOUND	0-515-12034-0/$5.99
by Rachelle Nelson	
__COURTING KATE	0-515-12048-0/$5.99
by Mary Lou Rich	
__SPRING DREAMS	0-515-12068-5/$5.99
by Lydia Browne	
__TENNESSE WALTZ	0-515-12135-5/$5.99
by Trana Mae Simmons	
__FARM GIRL	0-515-12106-1/$5.99
by Linda Shertzer	
__SWEET CHARITY	0-515-12134-7/$5.99
by Rachel Wilson	
__BLACKBERRY WINTER	0-515-12146-0/$5.99
by Sherrie Eddington (9/97)	

Time Passages

_LOST YESTERDAY
Jenny Lykins
0-515-12013-8/$5.99

Marin Alexander has given up on romance. But when she awakens from a car accident 120 years before her time, she must get used to a different society and a new life—and the fact that she is falling in love...

_A DANCE THROUGH TIME
Lynn Kurland
0-515-11927-X/$5.99

A romance writer falls asleep in Gramercy Park, and wakes up in 14th century Scotland—in the arms of the man of her dreams...

_REMEMBER LOVE
Susan Plunkett
0-515-11980-6/$5.99

A bolt of lightning transports the soul of a scientist to 1866 Alaska, where she is married to a maddeningly arrogant and irresistibly seductive man...

_THIS TIME TOGETHER
Susan Leslie Liepitz
0-515-11981-4/$5.99

An entertainment lawyer dreams of a simpler life—and finds herself in an 1890s cabin, with a handsome mountain man...

_SILVER TOMORROWS
Susan Plunkett
0-515-12047-2/$5.99

Colorado, 1996. A wealthy socialite, Emily Fergeson never felt like she fit in. But when an earthquake thrust her back in time, she knew she'd landed right where she belonged...

_ECHOES OF TOMORROW
Jenny Lykins
0-515-12079-0/$5.99

A woman follows her true love 150 years into the past—and has to win his love all over again...

VISIT THE PUTNAM BERKLEY BOOKSTORE CAFÉ ON THE INTERNET:
http://www.berkley.com

Payable in U.S. funds. No cash accepted. Postage & handling: $1.75 for one book, 75¢ for each additional. Maximum postage $5.50. Prices, postage and handling charges may change without notice. Visa, Amex, MasterCard call 1-800-788-6262, ext. 1, or fax 1-201-933-2316; refer to ad # 680

Or, check above books   Bill my: ☐ Visa   ☐ MasterCard   ☐ Amex _____ (expires)
and send this order form to:
The Berkley Publishing Group   Card#_____

P.O. Box 12289, Dept. B   Daytime Phone #_____   ($10 minimum)
Newark, NJ 07101-5289   Signature_____

Please allow 4-6 weeks for delivery.   Or enclosed is my: ☐ check   ☐ money order
Foreign and Canadian delivery 8-12 weeks.

Ship to:

Name_____	Book Total	$_____
Address_____	Applicable Sales Tax (NY, NJ, PA, CA, GST Can.)	$_____
City_____	Postage & Handling	$_____
State/ZIP_____	Total Amount Due	$_____

Bill to: Name_____

Address_____City_____
State/ZIP_____